his seventh volume of S. T. Joshi's acclaimed *Black Wings* series features an international cast of contributors who use the work of H. P. Lovecraft as a springboard for powerful and thought-provoking tales that probe the terrors and uncertainties of life in the twenty-first century.

Lovecraft was a devotee of science, but he recognised that science's role in human life is ambiguous. In this volume, Katherine Kerestman, Steve Rasnic Tem, and Donald Tyson probe the sense of human insignificance that science brings in its wake. Lovecraft knew that realism of setting fostered his signature contribution of cosmicism. Stories by Donald R. Burleson, Nancy Kilpatrick, Geoffrey Reiter, and Aditya Dwarkesh take us from the frozen realm of Antarctica to the sweltering heat of Calcutta; from ancient New England to the remote stretches of Pennsylvania. Tales by David Hambling and Mark Howard Jones tease out weirdness even in the familiar locales of Great Britain.

BLACK WINGS VII

NEW TALES OF LOVECRAFTIAN HORROR

BLACK WINGS VII

NEW TALES OF LOVECRAFTIAN HORROR

Edited by S. T. Joshi

First DIP Edition

ISBN: 978-1-78636-988-8

2 4 6 8 10 9 7 5 3 1

Black Wings VII was typeset using fonts from the HPLHS Prop Fonts Collection (http://www.cthulhulives.org).

Design & Layout by Michael Smith

Printed and bound in England by T. J. Books

PS Publishing Ltd
Grosvenor House
1 New Road
Hornsea, HU18 1PG
England

editor@pspublishing.co.uk
www.pspublishing.co.uk

ONTENTS

NTRODUCTION

S. T. Joshi

S. T. Joshi is the author of The Weird Tale *(1990),* I Am
Providence: The Life and Times of H. P. Lovecraft *(2010),*
Unutterable Horror: A History of Supernatural Fiction
*(2012), and other volumes. Among his anthologies of
classic and contemporary weird fiction are* American
Supernatural Tales *(2007),* Searchers After Horror *(2014),*
A Mountain Walked *(2014),* Nightmare's Realm *(2017),*
and the previous six volumes of the Black Wings *series
(2010–17). He is the editor of* Penumbra, *the* Lovecraft
Annual, *and* Spectral Realms.

HE ADJECTIVE "LOVECRAFTIAN" IS NOWADAYS
applied so widely and indiscriminately that we are in
danger of losing an understanding of its proper focus and param-
eters. This phenomenon is itself a tribute to the spectacular
popularity that Lovecraft's work has achieved over the past half-
century—a popularity that extends not only to the worldwide
dissemination of his writings in more than thirty languages but
also to adaptations for film, television, comic books, role-playing
games, video games, and even merchandising. But one needs
more than slimy tentacles or bug-eyed monsters to warrant the
designation "Lovecraftian," and it might be well to remind
ourselves of what the essence of Lovecraft's theory and practice of
weird fiction actually consists of.

The central pillar of Lovecraft's aesthetic theory is cosmicism—a depiction of the nearly infinite gulfs of space and time and the derisively insignificant place human beings occupy in those realms. As he states in "The Silver Key," "the blind cosmos grinds aimlessly on from nothing to something and from something back to nothing again, neither heeding nor knowing the wishes or existence of the minds that flicker for a second now and then in the darkness." This conception grew out of Lovecraft's atheism (there is no god to save us from our own meaninglessness) and fascination with science, especially that of astronomy. In this volume, such diverse tales as Steve Rasnic Tem's "The Things We Do Not See" and Katherine Kerestman's "Global Warming" suggest the cosmic while at the same time focusing on the human characters who dimly perceive their own insignificance. Donald Tyson's "The Amber Toad" effects a union of weirdness and science fiction in very much the manner that Lovecraft did in such tales as "The Whisperer in Darkness" and "The Shadow out of Time."

For Lovecraft, the expression of cosmicism is facilitated by a meticulous realism, especially that of setting. His own writing vividly re-creates both the history and topography of New England as well as other locales he had never visited—not least of them the Antarctica of *At the Mountains of Madness*, the setting for Nancy Kilpatrick's haunting "Deception Island." Donald R. Burleson draws upon his long years in New England for "The Pit of G'narrh," while other tales take us farther afield: remote rural areas of Pennsylvania (Geoffrey Reiter's "The Lime Kiln"), very similar to the Massachusetts setting of "The Colour out of Space"; and most exotically of all, the Calcutta of Aditya Dwarkesh's "Who Killed Augustus Bourbaki?" Even seemingly familiar regions in Great Britain (as in David Hambling's "Father Thames" and Mark Howard Jones's "A Very Old Song") prove far more disturbing than they appear on the surface.

Dwarkesh's story highlights another key component of Lovecraftian fiction: the use of the scholarly narrator or protagonist. Lovecraft himself regarded intellectual and aesthetic activity as the pinnacle of human achievement, even though he well knew its psychological dangers. Early in his career he wrote, "To the scientist there is the joy in pursuing truth which nearly counteracts the depressing revelations of truth." In this volume, we find such pursuits leading to unthinkable horrors in Mark Samuels's "An Elemental Infestation," John Shirley's "And the Devil Hath Power," and Steven Woodworth's "Er Lasst Sich Nicht Lesen."

In Lovecraft's fiction, human cults devoted to the "gods" of the Cthulhu Mythos play a central role. It may well be (as Lovecraft suggests in "The Call of Cthulhu") that these cults are seriously in error as to the nature of the entities they worship; but nonetheless, they constitute a baleful counter-culture on the underside of normal civilisation. In this volume, Darrell Schweitzer's "Can We Keep Him?," Mark Howard Jones's "A Very Old Song," and others revivify the motif of the ancient cult stretching back centuries or millennia.

Several tales in this book reflect Lovecraft's fascination with the notion of abnormal longevity. The wonders and terrors of living beyond the bounds of normal human life were, in his work, embodied most vividly in the figure of Joseph Curwen in *The Case of Charles Dexter Ward*, and Jonathan Thomas performs a clever riff on this character in "How Curwen Got His Hundred Years." Another kind of extended life is found in the hybrid Deep Ones of "The Shadow over Innsmouth," and Ann K. Schwader draws upon this tale (as many other leading writers of contemporary weird fiction have done) in "Open Adoption."

The "forbidden book" theme, embodied in Lovecraft's tales by the redoubtable *Necronomicon* of the mad Arab Abdul Alhazred, became something of an in-joke even in Lovecraft's own day, as several of his colleagues created imaginary books of occult lore in their own stories. But the motif has serious ramifications, in that these tomes feature the very knowledge that will make us aware of our fleeting tenure on this earth; and it is this element that

Ramsey Campbell utilises in "The Resonances," as he draws not only on Lovecraft's tales but his own previous work to create a narrative that fuses metaphysical and psychological terror.

This book is, I trust, one of many recent works that display the continuing vitality of neo-Lovecraftian writing in our day. Critics and scholars have presented a compelling portrait of Lovecraft as a writer whose philosophical vision led him to create an entire cosmogony of "gods" and monsters that embody his profound awareness of the fragility of a human race lost in the vortices of space and time. Contemporary writers have learned that it takes more to be "Lovecraftian" than merely tossing in a familiar name or reusing one of Lovecraft's own plots; it requires a deep understanding of what lies beneath the superficial flamboyance of his tales, reaching to the central core of fear and dread that his transcendent craftsmanship engendered. We are lucky that a small cadre of gifted writers can echo his vision while at the same time expressing their own ideas in tales scarcely less skilful than his.

—S. T. Joshi

BLACK WINGS VII

NEW TALES OF LOVECRAFTIAN HORROR

THE RESONANCES

Ramsey Campbell

Ramsey Campbell was born in Liverpool in 1946 and now lives in Wallasey. The Oxford Companion to English Literature *describes him as "Britain's most respected living horror writer," and the* Washington Post *sums up his work as "one of the monumental accomplishments of modern popular fiction." He has received the Grand Master Award of the World Horror Convention, the Lifetime Achievement Award of the Horror Writers Association, the Living Legend Award of the International Horror Guild and the World Fantasy Lifetime Achievement Award. In 2015 he was made an Honorary Fellow of Liverpool John Moores University for outstanding services to literature. PS Publishing have brought out two volumes of* Phantasmagorical Stories, *a sixty-year retrospective of his short fiction, and a companion collection,* The Village Killings and Other Novellas. *His latest novel is* The Lonely Lands *from Flame Tree Press, which has also recently published his Brichester Mythos trilogy.*

As STUART REACHED BRICHESTER CATHEDRAL A confusion of noises came to meet him—a dogged stony trudge accompanied by a rumble suggestive of the dragging of a tail and a repeated squeal like the complaint of joints in need of oil. If he hadn't been some years too old for fairy tales he might have fancied one of the gargoyles had gone for a wander. He pushed the door next to the massive portal wide and stepped back

3

as the wheelbarrow heaped with rubble lumbered forth, wielded by a workman with goggles dangling along with a facemask around his stubby neck. "Got yourself a job there, son," he said.

Murmurs of visitors massed beneath the vaulted ceiling of the cathedral, above the nave Stuart had learned today was Norman. The aisle led to an enormous distant window like a rainbow shattered into fragments and reassembled to depict highlights from the Bible. His research let Stuart recognise that the limestone vines decorating the walls were Perpendicular. A muffled clink of tools on stone drew his attention to the transverse aisle, where he saw Samantha in the pew closest to the lady chapel.

A plasterboard partition shut off the chapel while the renovation was in progress. The metallic hammering put Stuart in mind of miners in a cave. Samantha glanced away from an architectural diagram on the laptop she'd propped beside a hymnal. "Oh, it's you," she said.

Stuart could have felt he'd blundered into the court of the princess her delicate face reminded him of—deep dark eyes, slim nose, full pink lips—while the rest of her made him feel awkward in a different although increasingly familiar way. He meant to murmur, but it emerged as a mumble. "I've found out some things for you."

The corners of her lips turned up. "Just for me?"

"For my project as well. We can share."

"Tell me then, Stuart."

Her use of the name seemed to soften his innards. His friends—his other friends, he hoped he could begin to think—made him sound like the wrong sort of dish. "I can show you," he said.

He produced his phone as the empty wheelbarrow trundled up the nave. He was bringing up the first shot he'd taken in the archives when the workman leaned over the ledge of the pew. "Can't you kids even do without your games in church?"

Samantha's stare did without an expression. "We aren't playing any games."

"We've been asked to look into the restoration of the chapel."

"Keeping an eye on us lowlifes, are you? Doing what your teacher told you to, more like. You'd be more use seeing to the doors for us."

"That's not what I'm for and she isn't either."

"Down, boy. I wasn't going for your girlfriend. You may look big to her but you don't look big to me."

"Can you start behaving like gentlemen," Samantha said. "You aren't impressing anyone."

"Keep telling yourself that, sweetheart," the workman said, wheeling the barrow to the door in the temporary partition. Embarrassed by the reference to a girlfriend and demeaned by her rebuke, Stuart stayed mute until she said "Aren't you showing me?"

"It says the frescoes were meant to be special."

"Let me look for myself."

Her soft cool hand touched his as she took the phone, and he thought too late of keeping hold of it to retain her touch. At least he could lean close to her while she scrolled through the information. The site now known as Cathedral Mount was a place of worship long before the eleventh-century cathedral had been built there. The frescoes in the lady chapel were hailed as uncommonly beautiful by everyone who had viewed them before the walls had been covered by new stone, now in the process of removal. "Too much for the men in charge to cope with," Samantha declared. "They won't get their way any more." The frescoes had been designed to sanctify the site, and she tapped the sentence with a slim pink fingernail. "What does that mean, Stuart?"

"Make it more sacred, you know, like churches are supposed to be. Like that man tried to make out we were spoiling."

"I don't need a translation. I'm asking if you found out any more."

"Not yet."

"Find out for me tomorrow, can you? I'll be here. Just let me copy all this first." As Samantha paired the mobile with her laptop, Stuart hoped she was making more of a connection with him. "Thanks for backing me up," she said.

Perhaps she meant his research had confirmed her views, but he let himself think she might have reassessed his confrontation with the workman. As he made his way through the extensive antique churchyard he glanced back to check the man hadn't followed him. The massive pallid building glimmered in the late October dusk, and for a moment he thought the fellow had sneaked past him as a preamble to an ambush, but the crouching figure must have been a toppled monument he couldn't even locate.

His parents were at their computers in the workroom, justifying clients' tax accounts. "You were a long time at your archive," his father said.

"I went to the cathedral as well. I'm helping someone with their project."

"Is she nice?" Stuart's mother seemed to think this didn't need an answer. "What's her name?"

"Samantha. She's doing the architecture part."

"She'll be in your class, then."

"She's in my one at school."

"Not just that kind," his father said. "You're as good as any of them or you wouldn't be there."

Stuart thought this was easy to believe if you weren't at the school, where many of his classmates didn't bother hiding how they regarded him as an intruder hardly worth their tolerance. He couldn't let his parents know when they worked so hard to pay for his education. They were convinced his brain required that kind, a notion that often left him wishing he were stupid. If his intelligence won Samantha over, perhaps it was some use after all.

Next day he used the archive as soon as it was open to the public. Several tables in the long high room enclosed by gloomy oak were occupied by researchers who glanced at him as if he weren't a member of their club. The librarians brought him items—local histories, parish records, monastic reminiscences, ecclesiastical chronicles—that the archive computer suggested to him. The documents didn't tell him much that Samantha might want to learn, and he had to remind himself he wasn't there just on her behalf.

Some of the stone used to build the cathedral had been quarried from a cave, a process that had razed the cave to the ground at the summit of the hill the cathedral stood on. Apparently this had been a stage in the process of sanctification. As far as Stuart could decipher from the mediaeval language, one monk said the frescoes in the lady chapel were designed to counteract the grotesque forms carved on the corbels of the cathedral. Though Stuart hadn't noticed them, some of those were so misshapen that there had been proposals to destroy them, but presumably preservationists had won the day. Why had the frescoes been covered up? Samantha would want to know, but hours of research failed to enlighten him. As the afternoon grew dark he learned that the original site on the hill had been known as the Cave of the Voice. Following up this lead would have to wait, otherwise he might miss Samantha at the cathedral.

The plasterboard partition had been removed from the lady chapel, and there was no sign of any workmen. His surge of relief dwindled as he saw Samantha had company. Opening the restored chapel had changed the acoustic of the cathedral, which meant his multiplying echoes drew attention to him as he made for the pew by the chapel. As Samantha turned to him, so did her companion, a boy of about his age but bulkier, with a broad flattish face that looked ready to lose interest in the newcomer. "What have you brought me today, Stuart?" Samantha said.

He sidled past the other boy so as to sit beside her. "The frescoes were supposed to make up for the carvings round the outside," he said.

"What do you mean by that?" The boy's question sounded accusing, and so did "Make up for them."

"That's what some monk said. Don't blame me."

"I'm not too impressed with your helper, Sam."

"Stuart's in my class."

"I doubt it."

"Heath." Stuart hoped this was a rebuke, but she was introducing her friend. "Stuart," she added.

"And may we hear what you think of our chapel?"

"Why's it yours?"

As soon as the retort was out Stuart wished he'd been less childish—he was fourteen, for god's sake. "We worship here," Heath said.

"Well, I'm studying it like her."

"We look forward to being graced with your insights."

Stuart took this for sarcasm until he realised Heath was gazing at him, which sent him to the chapel. The exposed frescoes looked freshly painted: Mary surrounded by cherubim in the manger, kneeling at the foot of a radiant crucifixion, elevated heavenwards by angels winged with sunbursts ... "Nobody ought to have covered them up," he told Samantha. "I can't see why anybody would."

"The likes of some of us were responsible." Before Stuart could react Heath said "I must say you don't seem to have much to offer."

"So what are you doing for her?"

"Use whatever imagination you've got," Heath said and finished staring at him. "I'll leave you to your academic conference, Sam. Just phone when you're ready for me."

As Heath's retreat added echoes to the acoustic clutter Stuart said "That's all I could find today about the chapel, Sam."

"Don't call me that, thank you. You've still got the rest of the week."

Stuart was halfway to the exit, feeling resentfully dismissed, when his echoes distracted him. They sounded as if someone was blundering along the left-hand side aisle, barely able to walk, if indeed they weren't proceeding on all lopsided fours. He peered around the pillar behind which the noises appeared to have lodged, and the nearest stained-glass window merged with its vague vista to produce a furtive movement, an illusion that vanished at once.

At home questions were waiting for him. "Successful day?" his father wanted to hear.

Stuart did his best to think so. "Pretty good."

His mother was impatient to learn "How's your Samantha?"

"I helped her a bit."

"So long as it's mutual. Don't let yourself be exploited."

"We hope she knows how privileged she is," his father said.

Surely the more Stuart found that she could use, the more she should appreciate it and him, but when he reached the archive in the morning he found he was uncertain what to look for. As he passed the counter he saw that the chronicle he'd struggled to decipher had yet to be returned to the stacks. "Can I have that book again?" he said.

"Please request it by the standard method." The librarian, a stooped man who might have chosen his suit to tone with the grey of his hair, gave the volume a weary blink. "I shall hold it while you do," he said. "May we know the aim of your research?"

"I'm finding out about the cathedral."

"Perhaps there is hope for your generation after all."

Stuart used the nearest terminal to order the book, then had to wait for the librarian to read the screen behind the counter and direct an assistant to bring the massive tome to Stuart's table. The flimsy plastic gloves provided to protect the book felt like an extra hindrance, as if the mediaeval language weren't enough of one. By late morning the spiky script and antiquated spellings and bygone words were conspiring to give him a headache. He was close to the end, and so was the afternoon, when he encountered a sentence that puzzled him so much he took the volume to the counter. "Do you know what that's supposed to say?"

The librarian winced as Stuart's finger almost touched the page. "What do you take it to mean?"

"They put an extra wall in the Mary chapel to, what it looks as if it's saying is they wanted to suppress the echo of the cave."

"I believe that is an accurate interpretation."

"But there wasn't a cave any more. They'd knocked it down to build the cathedral."

"Perhaps by echo the writer meant a similarity, and I'm sure the builders must have been concerned with the acoustics."

While Stuart found this unsatisfactory, the reference reminded him to look up the Cave of the Voice. The computer listed a single citation, and he requested the book—*We Pass from View* by Roland Franklyn. His head was gaining only a further ache from the mediaeval text when the librarian came over. "Why have you asked for Franklyn?"

"The computer says it's got something in about the cave."

"I doubt there would be any information you could use."

"Can I see anyway?"

The librarian rested a ponderous gaze on him before saying "Do you propose to visit us tomorrow?"

"If there's stuff for me to look at."

"I shall consider the matter and give you my decision then."

The rest of the chronicle failed to assuage Stuart's frustration. He was tempted to stay out of the cathedral even though it was on his way home, but he ought to keep Samantha informed. As he hurried along the nave his thin entangled echoes scuttled down the side aisle, so that he could have fancied they were scurrying ahead to dislodge Heath from the pew. "Here's your assistant," Heath said.

Stuart strove to ignore him while saying "I may find out some important stuff tomorrow."

"Hardly worth coming to us if that's the extent of your contribution."

"Let me know if you do," Samantha said.

Stuart was about to take his leave when he heard sounds beyond a pillar. They seemed oddly reminiscent of the echoes he'd previously caused, and so clumsy that he stopped short of imagining how whoever was there might look. As he made his way along the nave he thought he glimpsed them dodging out of sight around the pillar. Were they so ashamed of their appearance that they would rather not be seen? For some reason he preferred this to thinking they were about to show themselves, and he refrained from glancing back once he passed the pillar.

At home his mother said "Much progress today?"

"They're getting me a special book."

"We hope all this trouble isn't only for your friend," his father said.

Stuart wanted it to help Samantha as much as him. He felt he'd been as useless today as Heath wanted him to think he was. In the chill October morning his ectoplasmic whitish breaths kept him company while he waited for the library to let him in. The librarian met him with a look that reserved any welcome. "What do you youngsters believe in these days?" he said.

Stuart sensed his answer might determine whether he was granted access to the book he'd requested. "I haven't decided yet," he risked admitting.

"I shouldn't think you'd have much time for the likes of Franklyn when you're involved with the cathedral." This sounded like the preamble to a refusal, and Stuart was about to protest that researching the cathedral didn't require faith when the librarian said "Find a seat and I'll have your request brought to you."

His assistant gave the book and Stuart a censorious blink as she planted the item in front of him. Once it must have been a brighter blue, but more than half a century had faded the library binding and flaked away most of the gilt from the details embossed on the thin spine. The interior looked self-published and read that way as well. Its mystical meandering seemed hardly worth struggling to understand. Stuart was close to abandoning the effort when a phrase snagged his attention, and he returned to the start of the paragraph.

The secret nature of some regions of the earth creates confluences of the occult and of presences not of this world. Primal practices have lingered there, and ancient powers draw down their like, attracting companions from the infinite and raising hidden dwellers from below. Thus Starfall

11

Water is home to its slumbering denizen, while Goatswood is named
for the dread avatar it harbours. The remnants of a primeval breed are
penned beneath Clotton, and the vaults under Temphill provide ingress
for feasters on unnatural sustenance. The cottages of Warrendown
disguise a covert habitation, and the depths of the forest beyond
Goodmanswood body forth their awful dweller, but Youtheven awaits
an inhuman birth. In mediaeval times and previous eras Brichester
boasted the Cave of the Voice, a hilltop cavern that conferred safety on
the venerable rite to summon an aspect of Daoloth. The site was
commandeered by Christians, who destroyed the cave in their campaign
to extirpate the rival belief. Erecting their own edifice proved
inadequate, since echoes of the ousted ritual lingered in the cathedral—
"sounds no sacred place should admit," as one cleric complained. In a
bid to quell these reverberations that even the most pious activity was
wont to rouse, the walls of a chapel were hastily clad in additional
stone. . .

Somebody was reading over Stuart's shoulder—a middle-aged
woman with tightly folded arms, above which her badge identified
her as the city librarian. "That should be on restricted issue," she
said and strode to the counter. Did she mean to have the book
taken from him? He set about photographing all the unread pages
as fast as he could. She and the archivist disappeared into the
stacks, and by the time they emerged Stuart had finished his task.
Wary of betraying what he'd done, he returned the book to the
counter and spent the rest of the day researching the official
history of the cathedral.

As he stepped into the nave he had the absurd idea that his
echoes had been waiting for him to release them. The Franklyn
book must have suggested the notion. When he made for the pew
where Samantha and his rival were seated close together, the
ungainly mass of sounds preceded him. They dodged behind pillar
after pillar like an intruder—like a prowler that would have had
to be proceeding on all fours to stay so unseen. He couldn't tell
where the noises settled as he sidled to take his place beside
Samantha. "Have you got what you wanted?" she said.

"I don't know if it's what you'll want."

"We'll be the judge of that," Heath said.

Stuart did his best to mime not having heard the comment as he showed Samantha the first page he'd photographed. *The secret nature of some regions of the earth creates confluences of the occult and of presences not of this world* . . . He kept hold of the phone rather than risk letting Heath touch it, and Samantha didn't either. "See," he said once she'd had time to read the paragraph, "they weren't getting at women after all."

As a noise lodged in the side aisle—a restless scrabbling like a belated echo of his approach—Heath said "What do you mean by bringing Sam this trash?"

"I thought she'd want to see."

"If you've any sense at all you'll be making yourself scarce."

"I'll be doing what Samantha says, not you."

"Can you hear how pathetic you sound? You tell him, Sam."

"She doesn't like people calling her that."

"I'm not people, little man. Tell him."

Stuart wanted to believe she hesitated on his behalf before saying "Heath's right. I can't use this."

"Now you've been told, so you can take yourself off. Don't come back unless you're bringing something with a bit of meat on it. Maybe that means just don't come back."

When Samantha turned her eyes to the window beyond the altar rather than speak, Stuart felt she'd mutely agreed with his rival. He shoved the phone in his pocket and stalked away, bearing his hot face topped with a renewed headache, which confused him into fancying he'd left his echoes behind. The impression made him glance back to see the nearest window and its blurred twilit vista producing the illusion that a figure had reared up beyond a pillar before dropping into a lopsided crouch. The glimpse aggravated his headache as he stumbled out of the cathedral.

The ache hadn't dwindled much by the time he arrived home. "Productive day?" his mother said.

"Can you not keep asking me stuff like that?"

"Don't take that tone with your mother," his father said.

"I hope we haven't let a grump into our house. Whatever the problem is, you know you can always talk to us."

"I don't want to talk."

"Then you'd better leave it somewhere else," his father said.

Stuart went to bed feeling the world had turned against him. He didn't want to read any more of the pages he'd photographed—just one had helped Heath set Samantha against him. He might have left them unexamined if the morning hadn't stranded him at the end of a queue of requests from the archive. While he waited for the books he'd requisitioned he gave in to consulting his phone. Suppose he'd snapped material that could win Samantha over once again?

Perhaps Plato glimpsed the truth and coded it within his dialogue about the shadows and the cave, to be deciphered by the enlightened. The rite of Daoloth calls for words none dare speak directly and a visitation even the initiated can scarcely bear to look upon, and so some syllables of the conjuration were pronounced only by the echoes of the chanting of the faithful. The summonings conferred power upon the cave, which supplied the leaders of the cult with creatures to send against their enemies. These sendings parodied their masters' form, monstrously distorted by embodying their echoes from the cavernous depths. When eventually the echoes gathered their unnatural substance, even their progenitors could tolerate only the sight of their shadows. Some familiars proving less controllable than their summoners had wished, they turned upon their creators, which helped bring about the downfall of the cult. The stone that formed the cave was incorporated into the cathedral, where the shapes of the corbels acknowledge their origin. Time itself contains echoes, so that the past may resonate into the present, distorted by the centuries . . .

A librarian planted a stack of ecclesiastical histories on Stuart's table, but Stuart read on until the sentences degenerated into mysticism too abstruse for him to grasp. Should he show Samantha the paragraph? She'd declared no actual aversion to its predecessor, after all. If he visited the cathedral earlier than usual, perhaps he would find her on her own, and he skimmed the histories at speed.

The cathedral was unusually deserted. Samantha was alone in the pew closest to the lady chapel, and Stuart was about to head for the nave when he was halted by the fancy that his echoes had begun without him. Someone out of sight must have produced the eager scrawny clatter. As he made for Samantha, the windows kept playing their optical trick that made a figure seem to dodge from pillar to pillar. Had the paragraph he'd read conjured it up— just in his mind, of course? Samantha didn't look at him until he resumed the place Heath had ousted him from. "What is it this time?" she said.

"Just thinking, just because they put the new wall up because of what I showed you doesn't mean they weren't doing it against women too. They could have put it somewhere else but they did it there."

"It took you long enough to see."

Perhaps he shouldn't have let this prompt him to blurt "Have you seen anything?"

She saved her essay on the laptop before giving him a tilted blink. "Any of what?"

"Anything that shouldn't be in here, or you could have heard."

"Don't try and scare me, Stuart." As he hoped her protest had betrayed a hint of enjoyment she said "Why would there be anything like that?"

"There's more of the book I showed you some of."

He held the phone for her to read and willed her to join her hand to his, but she said "Let me have a proper look."

Apparently this entailed handing her the phone. He was waiting for her reaction to the paragraph when he heard a surreptitious approach behind them. He twisted around to see Heath edging into the pew, having kept most of his footsteps to himself. "Trying to frighten people now, are we?" Heath said. "That's low even by your standards."

"Looks as if you wanted to, creeping round like that."

"No, I was listening to all your bilge. Are you going to move over?" When the demand failed to shift Stuart, Heath blustered past him to sit on the far side of Samantha. He leaned towards Stuart's phone and then took it from her. "Lord God almighty," he said loud enough for his echo to name the technology, "what's this rubbish now?"

"Just more of the same, Heath. It means nothing to me."

"That's mine." Stuart felt even more painfully childish for saying "Give it back."

"What sort of wretch would want that?" Heath looked ready to fling the phone into the flagstoned aisle, a threat that made Stuart's stomach clench. Stuart thrust out a hand he realised too late was bare inches from Samantha's breasts, and Heath slammed the phone onto his palm. "Take it off and yourself as well," he said.

Stuart was anxious not to let them suspect how his bruised hand was throbbing. As he retreated down the nave, his increasingly unrecognisable echoes seemed determined not to follow him. A memorial statue beyond a window interacted with the stained glass to let him imagine he'd glimpsed something like a face, which sent him a twisted complicit grin before it dodged behind a pillar. He was crossing the churchyard when he found he couldn't locate the memorial. Where he thought the statue ought to be was an extensive patch of turf.

His mother met him in the hall. He was bracing himself for today's version of her question when she said "We've a treat for you, Stuart. We'll be going to the concert to celebrate the restoration."

"Maybe we'll meet your Samantha." His father saw the need to add "If you want us to."

That night Stuart didn't sleep much. He kept waking to persuade himself he must have seen a stained-glass figure in the cathedral—an outline filled in by the view beyond the window and lent movement by his own progress. At least the cathedral would be crowded at the concert. He spent Saturday writing his essay for the project but omitted any reference to Franklyn's stupid book, which he wished he'd never read. All too soon it was time to head for the cathedral.

Floodlights surrounded the churchyard to announce the restoration of the chapel. The paths and the verges were crowded with shadows cast by visitors, although some must belong to memorials. The murmurs of the queue closed around Stuart before multiplying as he followed his parents into the cathedral. He was hoping to locate Samantha without alerting them, if she was even there, but as they passed the transverse aisle she caught sight of him. She was in her usual place, flanked by Heath and a couple Stuart deduced were her parents. His own saw the token wave she sent him, and once they were installed in a pew his mother murmured "Was that who we think?"

"Sam."

"Is that what you call her? So long as she likes you to. Was that her brother with her?"

"No."

"Oh, I see." At first his mother seemed almost as linguistically reduced as him. "Maybe you still have a chance," she said, "if she lets you call her that."

"May the best chap win," his father said, which just made Stuart feel in need of more support, although he refrained from thinking what kind. Echoes flocked into the cathedral as the last of the audience found seats. The building sounded more cavernous than ever, enlarged by echoes that seemed to extend into the outer dark. Stuart had resigned himself to the concert—he didn't know much about Beethoven except that the music came from the past—until he grew aware of some of the words of the choir.

"Kyrie . . ." This didn't sound as much like a girl's name as he'd assumed, but it was the next section that began to nag at his mind. "Gloria in excelsis deo . . ." The final syllable loitered in his head, and surely that was why it seemed to linger beneath the roof, enduring as no other echo had. Didn't it mean God? Perhaps the choir was prolonging the syllable as another stage in sanctifying the cathedral, and Stuart tried not to hear it as the first part of a word, but he couldn't fend off the notion that the choir wasn't saying which god. "Can I see the programme?" he muttered.

"Certainly you may."

The booklet his mother passed him translated the mass. "Glory to God in the highest ..." Why should he wish these were the words the choir was singing? "Domine Deus..." The second word seemed not just to lodge under the roof but to merge with the earlier version, taking on its shape. Soon the choir repeated it, and again, followed by "Agnus Dei." The variations on the word were subsumed into the mass of sound that Stuart heard refusing to dissipate overhead, where he could have imagined some presence was catching the words in an immense web. He felt compelled to search the libretto, hoping not to find any oncoming repetitions or variants of the word. No, here came "gloria Dei," and after an enormous intricate Amen a silence preceded "Credo in unum Deum." Surely this was sufficiently unambiguous, at any rate in English, but the last word amalgamated with its relatives up in the dark. Could nobody hear how these echoes were massing? Was the conductor with his wand too intent on his task? "Deum de Deo ... Deum verum de Deo ..." The twin reiterations swelled in the hovering darkness, and Stuart did his best to think they signified no more than the composer intended. Why did he need to feel uneasy? The choir wasn't about to sing the name he was nervous of hearing, and it couldn't come from anywhere else. He scanned the rest of the libretto to be certain, and then he almost crumpled the programme in dismay, except that he mustn't let his parents see anything was wrong when he wouldn't be able to explain. He could only gaze at the page and watch the syllables advancing inexorably towards him. "... qui locutus ..." The first sound of the second word rose to dally in the dark, and Stuart heard an unfinished name awaiting completion. Surely the missing syllable was too thoroughly embedded in another word to be separated. It was more a sound than a syllable, but apprehension overtook him as the choir raised the word high. ". . . catholicam . . . " At once he heard the darkness seize the rest of the name.

Perhaps this and the dread he felt were symptoms of his lack of sleep. Perhaps the floodlights and the illumination inside the cathedral didn't flicker for an instant, but he could have thought the whole of reality did. Above all, surely he didn't glimpse a shape like a face conceived by some unimaginable consciousness, a face as vast as the roof and propped up by all the pillars of the cathedral—didn't glimpse the abundance of mouths it was using to imitate the choir as though mocking their supplication, or the multitude of eyes that gaped wherever the mouths left room in the pallid gelatinous mass. Stuart ducked his head so as not to see, only to realise how his neighbours took his gesture for devoutness. The echo of a recomposed name seemed to cling to the dark while the choir sang about the church, and he didn't dare to look up until he could no longer hear even the merest trace. "Dominus Deus . . . " "Agnus Dei . . . " These roused no unusual response, and when he risked a timid glance, only the roof was above him. Perhaps for the moment some presence was placated, having regained its territory. If Stuart's glimpse had been true in any sense, what else must be? Surely he needn't be anxious for Samantha.

She and her companions preceded him out of the cathedral. As they strolled four abreast down the path through the churchyard he was almost sure a shadow paced them. Whatever was dodging from monument to monument, he would rather leave it undefined, as in one unpleasant sense it appeared to be. He dawdled out of nervousness until a surge of concern sent him after Samantha at not much less than a run. "Are we in a race now?" his father protested. "What's the prize?"

Stuart slowed before he reached the gates. Samantha and her family were taking one road, Heath another. "Not her," Stuart whispered.

He meant to be inaudible except to the lanky gibbous shape he fancied he saw at the railings between two floodlights, where it

19

slithered through a gap no wider than his arm. "If that's what you decided," his mother distracted him by responding. "There'll be other girls and I'm sure they'll be nicer."

Stuart didn't answer, and could hardly breathe while he listened for another sound. Before long his mother cried "Good heavens, what was that?"

He relaxed as far as he could. Despite how high the truncated shriek had been, the voice was unquestionably male. "I'm sure the police will deal with it," his father said. "Best not to look."

He was trying to protect his family, Stuart saw, and hoped he wouldn't need to do the same. They were almost home when he caught sight of movement behind a streetlamp near their house. It was just a shadow, but this was less than reassuring, since it was larger than any object the pole of the lamp could conceal. Stuart did his utmost not to make out the outrageously malformed shape as it dodged into an alley to merge with the dark. He came as close to praying as he ever had while he fled towards the house in the hope that it would provide him with a refuge, keep him safe. He might have believed he'd seen just a shadow, since his parents hadn't seemed to notice it, if it hadn't been for the sound the shadow left him—a whisper like a wind through tattered bones and a promise to return.

Er Lasst Sich Nicht Lesen

Stephen Woodworth

Stephen Woodworth is the author of the Violet Series *of paranormal thrillers, including the* New York Times *bestsellers* Through Violet Eyes *and* With Red Hands, *as well as the Gothic horror novel* Fraulein Frankenstein. *His work has also appeared in such publications as* Fantasy & Science Fiction, Weird Tales, *and* Year's Best Fantasy. *His collection of horror short fiction,* A Carnival of Chimeras, *is available from Hippocampus Press.*

It was well said of a certain German book that "er lasst sich nicht lesen"—it does not permit itself to be read. There are some secrets which do not permit themselves to be told. Men die nightly in their beds, wringing the hands of ghostly confessors, and looking them piteously in the eyes—die with despair of heart and convulsion of throat, on account of the hideousness of mysteries which will not suffer themselves to be revealed.

—Edgar Allan Poe, "The Man of the Crowd"

"FANCY A BIT OF LIGHT READING?"

Alyssa Mathers had thrown open the door of Gordon Tallis's office and stood with her thigh cocked against the doorframe, her South London working-class accent lilting flirtatiously as she spoke. She wore a nice short frock that showed plenty of her fancy lace tights. No white lab coat—she wasn't that kind of scientist.

Tallis, a blinking, pouch-faced mole of a man, looked up from his tedious work, a new translation of an Ionic verse fragment by the obscure Greek poet Anacreon. He welcomed the distraction from the attractive Black woman, who was younger than his eldest daughter. "You've got something, then?"

She grinned and beckoned. "Come see for yourself."

Tallis put his tweed jacket back on, buttoned his collar, and tightened his tie, then waddled in her wake as she strode out of the History Department and across the Queen Mary University campus to the Physics wing. His heart quickened, and not simply because he was horribly out of shape. If Mathers had succeeded, Gordon was quite possibly on the verge of the greatest discovery of his career—a career that desperately needed some distinction.

Alyssa led him into a rather small, unassuming room. They seated themselves at a workbench supporting a desktop computer and flat-screen monitor. Nearby rested a table upon which lay a single sheet of vellum, so ragged and mold-spotted that one could barely distinguish the cramped calligraphy of the faded Latin that crammed the page. On a metal cart lay the other pages of the ancient text from which it came, a tome that Alyssa had carefully disassembled for examination and restoration.

Above the table hung a lighting fixture with an array of bulbs designed to shine illumination in frequencies ranging from the visible spectrum to the ultraviolet. A camera mounted on the table's edge transmitted a close-up of the manuscript page, currently under ordinary white light, to the monitor in front of them. Alyssa handed Tallis a pair of polarized protective goggles to put on over his bifocals.

"As I said . . . light reading." With her own goggles on, she indicated the parchment. "There's the reading. And here's the light."

She tapped a couple of keys on the computer's keyboard, and the illumination in the room darkened to the purple fluorescence of a blacklight. The coloring of the image of the parchment onscreen also shifted toward violet, heightening the contrast and leaving the dark Latin characters in stark relief against the lavender background of the vellum.

"This is the light most readily absorbed by the ink of the prayer book text. But if I change the light a bit to correspond with the color of the remaining older ink on the page"—she hit another key, and the lighting brightened to blue—"we get a better look at the writing beneath the later text."

In the close-up onscreen, the Latin text, though still visible, faded to translucence, revealing other writing beneath it that had previously been too faint and too obscured.

"Now I take the previous scan and digitally remove the overwritten Latin text altogether, enhance what remains"—she typed a command and hit Enter—"*et voilà!*"

A title in capital Greek letters leapt forward on the screen in phosphorescent indigo script:

ΟΠΤΑΣΙΑ

Tallis's face lit up. He gazed at the word as though its letters were veined with gold.

"Eureka," he said.

The legendary ΟΠΤΑΣΙΑ.

The title's anglicized transliteration was *Optasia*, the ancient Greek word for a "vision" or spiritual reverie. Yet it also had the added connotation of the word's second meaning, an "apparition"—a manifestation or embodiment of the immaterial and spectral—which only enhanced the mystical, quasi-religious reputation of the work.

The *Optasia* was the magnum opus of the forgotten natural philosopher Theophanus of Corinth in the fourth century B.C.E. Nearly all his tracts had perished over the centuries—in the burning of the Library of Alexandria; in the neglect, ignorance, and suppression of the Dark Ages—and what little was known of the man and his thinking had been perpetuated through the testimony of his pupils and their acolytes.

A single surviving page from a medieval copy of one of his early works, discovered in Istanbul by a German collector in 1921, gave a tantalizing glimpse of the philosopher's forgotten genius. The drawings on the parchment depicted, in minute and startlingly accurate detail, microscopic organisms such as amoebae and paramecia that ought to have been invisible to the naked eye. Given the lack of glass optics in ancient Greece, some scholars believed that Theophanus must have invented a precursor to the water-droplet microscope first described by Stephen Gray in 1696.

His final manuscript was reputed to be his masterwork. No one knew the precise contents of the *Optasia*, but whatever its revelations, the effort of producing the book drove Theophanus mad.

Not unlike his successor Archimedes, who ran naked through his native Syracuse shouting "Eureka!" after he discovered the physical principle of water displacement while climbing into his bath, Theophanus shambled nude one day into the streets of Corinth in an ecstasy of enlightenment. He had not bathed, however; indeed, he was dirty and stinking, filth pressed into every crevice of his wrinkled skin, his scraggly gray hair and overgrown, unkempt beard festooned with twigs and dead leaves. And he did not shout "Eureka"—I have found it—but rather "Gégrapha."

I have written it.

With his skeletal arms, Theophanus clutched a dozen papyrus scrolls to his sunken chest as if cradling an infant. His ribs stood out like the beams in the hull of a rotted ship, and it was obvious that he'd barely eaten during the weeks since he'd retreated into the nearby forest. Yet his eyes gleamed with the manic rapture of discovery.

His most devoted student, Philemon, comforted the old man in his final hours. Historians assumed this disciple had preserved the scrolls of the *Optasia* when Theophanus expired from exposure and starvation. Philemon himself soon died by his own hand, his forearms slit along the vein. Some scholars concluded that the pupil had also been Theophanus' lover and was driven to suicide by grief.

The acolyte must have bequeathed his master's final manuscripts to one of his own trusted apostles, however, for the *Optasia* survived long enough to be transcribed onto goatskin parchment and compiled into a board-bound book sometime in the ninth century C.E. The tome had ended up in the library of Dr. John Dee, the celebrated Elizabethan scientist and mystic. Its subsequent whereabouts were a matter of speculation, and many academics presumed the work lost for the ages.

Then, a few months ago, an unnamed seller had consigned a medieval prayer book to Sotheby's for auction. In the process of vetting the manuscript for sale, the auctioneer's document experts noted that it was a palimpsest—a manuscript that has been effaced and overwritten with new text. Some frugal monk in the twelfth century C.E. had evidently deemed the original work redundant, unworthy, or sinful, and had laboriously washed, scraped, and dried each goatskin sheet in order to cleanse it for a holier scripture. Barely legible traces of the original print remained, however, and based upon some of the illustrations the document experts could make out, they believed it might contain the writings of Theophanus and perhaps the notorious *Optasia* itself. Such a find could increase the sales price for the manuscript a thousandfold, so Sotheby's contacted Gordon Tallis, one of London's preeminent classical scholars and translators, to determine the book's true contents prior to its sale, and he, in turn, had recruited Alyssa Mathers for help in recovering the original text.

But the manuscript proved more maddening than enlightening.

"What's this rubbish?" Tallis exclaimed as she brought up another page on the computer monitor.

"You tell me," Alyssa retorted. "You're the translator. I've done my job just making the gibberish legible."

After only a couple of pages in Greek, the text had abruptly shifted to a bewildering cipher of bizarre symbols that vaguely resembled the characters of both Greek and Hebrew yet made no sense in either language.

Tallis shook his head. "Can't make heads or tails of it. Print it out, and let's move on till we get to an illustration. Picture's worth a thousand words, so I hear."

They scanned a few more pages, and Tallis fretted that the book might be nothing more than a rather obscure herbal compendium. Like the infamous Voynich manuscript, which also featured an indecipherable, unknown language, the *Optasia* depicted a variety of exotic flora. Not being a botanist, Tallis didn't recognize any of the fern-like plants.

But he did recognize the trilobite, and that changed everything.

Each spine, antenna, and segment of the creature—a prehistoric, oval-shaped arthropod resembling a large pill bug—had been rendered with the precision of fine engraving.

"Might be good with some drawn butter," Alyssa commented dryly, not appreciating the drawing's significance.

Tallis tingled with excitement. Had Theophanus somehow stumbled upon a fossil of the ancient creature? If so, he might have claim to be history's first paleontologist.

"Now we're getting somewhere," Tallis mused. "Put up the next one."

Alyssa sighed. Changing pages took her nearly twenty minutes due both to the delicacy of the parchment and the necessity of scanning and digitally removing the overlapping Latin text.

The uncovered illustration was an incredibly fine drawing of what looked like a species of crinoid, albeit a version of the many-armed marine animal with which Tallis was not familiar. The creature's segmented stalk resembled a sinuous column of vertebrae, leading up to feathery arms like palm fronds. Lines extended out from each portion of the animal to what must have been anatomical labels written in those incomprehensible characters. Tallis could not conceive where Theophanus had obtained the specimen, how he'd managed to depict it in such minute detail, or why he'd devoted so much attention to such an obscure animal.

The next picture only perplexed him further, for it was another crinoid, like the first but more advanced. Its stalk had thickened, and the tendrils that once anchored its base to a rock had evidently become ambulatory, allowing the thing a crude form of locomotion. Its arms, too, had become prehensile appendages that, in Theophanus' depiction, coiled around small prey such as fish and birds, suggesting this crinoid was much larger than any currently in existence.

Tallis compared the illustrations and confirmed his supposition that the labels on the diagrams consisted of identical sequences of symbols, indicating that the same words applied to the corresponding features of both crinoids' anatomy. Theophanus clearly intended to draw parallels between the similar species.

Alyssa put the third illustration in the sequence on the monitor. "Oka . . . the old Greek's clearly gone batty with this one."

It, too, depicted a sort of crinoid, but even more fantastical than its predecessors. Its stalk had thickened further into an oblong sausage shape as thick as a tree's trunk, and it had sprouted some form of sensory apparatus at its star-shaped crown—Tallis hesitated to think of them as eyes. What really vaulted the image out of the realm of the scientific and into the mythological were its snaking appendages, which now held, not small animals, but rather a mallet and chisel. Theophanus had portrayed the monstrosity as a sculptor chipping away at some Elgin Marble-type bas-relief.

"It's like a bloody cartoon character," Alyssa snickered. "Squishy the Squid does Michelangelo's *David!*"

Her jocularity irritated Tallis, in part because he knew the public at large would smirk at the drawings the same way. Had Theophanus simply been insane, sketching monsters from his diseased fancy? But what about the trilobite? He didn't dream that up. If only Tallis could interpret that blasted text and find out what the old Greek was thinking . . .

"That's enough for now." Tallis scooped up the scattered printouts. "I've got to work on this."

A few nights later Tallis slouched in his office, poring over copies of the latest *Optasia* pages in exhausted frustration. He was the last faculty member still on campus—indeed, the only person left aside from the security and janitorial staff. Gordon had stayed so late for so many nights that his wife Penelope had started asking him, half-seriously, if he were sleeping with "that Mathers girl."

He wasn't. Instead, he was having an affair with the *Optasia,* and it had deteriorated into an abusive relationship.

Tallis already had more than enough evidence to inform Sotheby's that the palimpsest contained the authentic work of Theophanus, but he'd forestalled revealing that fact to them for fear they might yank the manuscript away and sell it before he could view the entire codex. Instead, he told the auction house the book's contents looked "promising" but that he would need to study it more closely to ensure it was the genuine article.

Far from making things clearer, though, further examination only baffled him.

Tallis took off his bifocals to rub his face, then glowered at the bearded, blank-eyed bust of Plato he kept on his desk.

"What're you looking at, mate?" He swept his glasses over the avalanche of papers on his blotter. "I'd like to see *you* make sense of this lot."

In his mind Plato quipped, *It's all Greek to me!*

Except that was the problem—it *wasn't* all Greek. It was that damnable, nonsensical non-language whose script taunted him with a latent, nagging familiarity.

Tallis had entered the strange letters into an online search engine and learned where he'd seen them before: in John Dee's "Angelical" language, which subsequent writers had dubbed "Enochian" because Dee claimed that the biblical patriarch Enoch had been the last human being to speak the celestial tongue. Tallis recalled that, in addition to owning the aforementioned Voynich manuscript, Dee had once possessed a copy of the *Optasia*, and now Tallis wondered if the mystic had, in fact, appropriated the invented language from Theophanus.

Using Dee's Enochian alphabet as a guide, Tallis made several sallies at decoding Theophanus' writing without success. He assumed that the enciphered words must still be Greek but quickly abandoned the idea: the syntax, letter frequency, and word repetition appeared completely alien from any classical language, as far as he could see. Dee must have simply copied the symbols of the *Optasia* to create his own apocryphal alphabet, which left open the questions of how Theophanus had invented such a language and why he'd chosen to record his greatest discoveries in words no other human could understand.

Tallis did hold one clue to the enigma. Right at the point where Theophanus abandoned his native tongue for the queer glossolalia he'd concocted, he apparently repeated his final sentence in Greek in the new language, thereby providing an identical text in two translations for comparison. It wasn't exactly the Rosetta Stone that Tallis needed, but it was something.

The meaning of one of the characters seemed clear enough. Theophanus had devised a kind of stick figure enclosed in an oblong outline, like so:

In his *Monas Hieroglyphica*, John Dee explicated the glyph as combining symbols of the moon, the sun, the elements, and fire, in effect encompassing the entirety of Nature. But in the one sentence of the *Optasia* that Theophanus translated from the Greek into his idiosyncratic cipher, the sigil occupied the place where the author had previously used the Greek word βασιλεύς (basileus), meaning "king" or "monarch." Indeed, one could see how the sigil could represent a regal figure: the semicircle on its head a crown; a single, all-seeing eye in the middle of its brow, like that of Polyphemus; the crosspiece of its arms outspread with authority; the lower half of its body either robed or, perhaps, seated on a low throne.

Moreover, Tallis noted that the oval around the figure resembled an Egyptian cartouche, the chiseled enclosure around a group of hieroglyphs that indicated a proper noun. It was the only symbol in the *Optasia* distinguished by such a signifier. Given that Theophanus was writing about species that ostensibly predated human beings, Tallis could only guess as to whom—or to what—the proper name referred. The fragment of Greek text only referred to a "King over all Beasts on the Earth or among the Stars."

"Theophanus rex," Tallis chuckled, shaking his head. Surveying the pages of unintelligible babble spread out in front of him, he switched off his desk lamp and finally went home.

The next pages of the *Optasia* showed that the *Basileus* glyph was no joke, however. As Tallis continued his work during the next few days, he found that the glyph reappeared at the end of the sequence of the crinoid drawings and each subsequent series, as if a form of punctuation—the period at the end of a sentence.

The next series of illustrations tracked a progression similar to that of the crinoid creatures. The drawings began with a believable image of a fish, albeit one with a Devonian, primeval fearsomeness dating to a geologic era about which Theophanus could not possibly have known. The second sketch displayed an amphibious creature of similar aspect, but which crawled about on shore with fore and hind limbs. In the third image, a grotesque, piscine hybrid being shambled upright on two scaly legs.

A heavy vertical line bordered the final drawing, followed by the *Basileus* insignia, which ended the sequence.

Other examples followed, each depicting the development of

some freakish new life form only to end with the inevitable sign of the mysterious monarch.

"The bloke was off his nut. I mean, what the bloody hell is that?" Alyssa pointed to the sketch onscreen of a gelatinous black mass that seemed to be a cancerous amoeba bloated to the size of Leviathan. With its elastic pseudopodia, it stacked enormous stone blocks to construct a titanic temple.

"I have no idea," Tallis replied absently. "No idea at all."

Except he *did* have an idea—one too incredible for him to acknowledge. Had Theophanus somehow intuited the principle of evolution more than two millennia before Charles Darwin? If so, how could he have derived his hypothesis from the descent of fantastical creatures that never existed? And why did each evolutionary chain end with the *Basileus* sigil?

"All right—cue up the next one."

Alyssa picked at the Indian food in front of her. They'd worked so late that she'd ordered takeaway for their dinner. "You're kidding me, right? Haven't we done enough for one day?"

When she saw he wasn't kidding, she dutifully set up the next sheet of the *Optasia*.

"Ugh! I think this one's put me off me curry." She recoiled from the onscreen image and left the room, abandoning what remained of her vegetable korma.

Even Tallis felt a bit queasy gazing at the picture. Whereas the previous drawings were relatively flattish like early frescoes, in this one Theophanus had vainly striven to endow the creature with three—and possibly more—dimensions.

The thing did not have a fixed shape, instead consisting of a dizzying confluence of sinuous, overlapping curves and bizarre, contradictory angles that flickered and shifted as the observer's brain struggled to interpret its false perspective. It reminded Tallis of M. C. Escher's optical illusions, alternately drawing you into its imaginary depths, then reaching out to entrap you in its web of impossible geometry. He could not conceive how the scribe who copied the *Optasia* had managed to replicate such a chaotic riot of overlapping lines, which leapt from the screen like a net thrown over the viewer.

Unlike the previous illustrations, Theophanus did not provide pointers and labels distinguishing the component parts of this unfathomable being. Yet one could make out an orb that might be an eye near its center, and its nether end trailed an indeterminate number of sinuous appendages that appeared to bifurcate and waver as one stared at them.

Only one symbol at the top of the page named the figure below: the glyph of *Basileus*.

Gazing at the image gave Tallis a headache.

He printed out a copy of the page but turned off the monitor as he did so. Disorientation, like the directionless confusion of zero gravity, had made him ill, and when he glanced down at his half-eaten chicken vindaloo, he found he'd lost his appetite.

That night he had a dream.

No, not a dream . . . a *vision*.

He found himself on a tor that overlooked a vast, glassy lake. Hanging low above the jagged silhouettes of the mountains on the opposite shore were two setting suns, one red as the heart of a forge, the other sapphire blue.

Several yards ahead of him, at the very edge of the precipice, stood a figure with its back to him. It wore royal raiment, and even in the scarlet and azure light Tallis could see that both the crown and robe were gleaming gold. Long white hair hung in tangles over the monarch's shoulders.

The strange intersection of red and blue hues gave the scene the exaggerated dimensionality of an old 3-D movie, and two unnaturally elongated shadows stretched out behind the tall monarch to form a dark V on the ground behind the figure. Tallis felt the same vertiginous queasiness he had looking at the drawing of *Basileus,* as though he were falling in every direction at once.

For no reason he could name, he did not want to attract the

figure's attention—did not want to risk that it might turn toward him—but with the inexorable compulsion of dreams he advanced toward it. As he drew closer, he saw that the hem of the robe and cape were rent and frayed into shreds, as if from battle. With each gust of wind the strips coiled and writhed like tendrils, producing the illusion that the figure was supported not by legs but by these octopoid appendages. Brittle leaves and fragments of black twig laced its white locks, and Tallis briefly fancied that here he would see Theophanus himself, crowned as the philosopher-king he deserved to be.

But when the monarch at last craned its head to peer at him, Tallis saw that, beneath its golden crown, the figure's entire face, from brow to chin, was nothing more than a single oval eye. Like a polished mask, the bulging orb glistened with liquid opalescence, its incandescent, kaleidoscopic iris dilating, opening the maw of its obsidian pupil to engulf Tallis in its gaze . . .

He cried out, flailing in bed, his outflung arm nearly hitting his startled wife in the nose.

Penny sat up and switched on her nightstand lamp. "Good Lord, Gordon! What is it?"

Panting, he blinked at the dim but comforting environs of their bedroom, at his wife's concerned expression. "Nothing, luv. Just a night-terror."

Sympathetic a moment before, her sharp-angled face pinched with reproach. "Serves you right, stuffing your head with that rot." Penelope had little use for Theophanus. "You aren't careful, you'll go as balmy as the mad Greek himself."

And she turned out the light.

Tallis didn't sleep well the rest of that night and remained groggy and irritable the following morning.

At the university, Alyssa greeted him with puckish insolence. "Have a bit too much at the pub?"

He grumbled. "No, but I might tonight."

Perhaps due to his dream—his *vision*—of the previous night, Tallis ordered Alyssa to change the sheet of parchment on the table before turning on the computer monitor. He didn't want to see that nauseating lattice of lines in the *Basileus* drawing again.

After donning his goggles, he gulped coffee from a paper cup and frowned at the next page from the *Optasia* that Alyssa placed onscreen.

The short hairs on his neck stood up.

There could be no question now that Theophanus had foreshadowed Darwin. The drawing showed what was undeniably a small hominid akin to *Australopithecus africanus*, with a chimp-like visage and a squatting posture that nearly left it crawling on all fours with its long arms. The following illustration resembled a Neanderthal, its countenance still of simian appearance but denuded of hair, its posture nearly erect.

"There's some kind of row going on outside," Alyssa said, her voice as distant to Tallis as if she called from across a canyon. "I hear people shouting."

"Put up the next one," he commanded. "Now."

She did so hastily, glancing toward the muffled ruckus beyond the examination room's closed door.

As Tallis had anticipated, the last drawing in this series depicted a modern man, nude but carrying a spear, as if he were a young Greek warrior. A dark vertical line slashed the page to the right of the human male. Unlike the previous instances, however, the *Basileus* glyph was not present on the other side of the line.

The sigil's absence did not reassure Tallis. A dreadful comprehension rose in his mind.

Popular belief portrayed gods as vain entities who crave the attention and adulation of the beings beneath them in the hierarchy of sentience. Perhaps, Tallis thought, it was merely *human* vanity for us insignificant mites to think ourselves worthy of the condescension of a being that transcended space and time, to imagine that such a deity would even desire our notice, much less our worship.

Indeed, such an overlord might view evolving intelligences as more of a nuisance—and possibly even a threat—to its unchallenged dominion over the universe. It would jealously guard the monopoly of secrets known only to its omniscience, chief among these being the fact of its own existence. Perhaps it would even cut off the ascent of any evolving species that dared to probe the realm of *Basilieus,* the absolute "King over all Beasts on the Earth or among the Stars."

Was that what happened to the crinoid creatures and the other obliterated sentient species that preceded humankind? Had they run afoul of *Basilieus?*

Tallis stared at the vertical line to the right of the human figure onscreen, and suddenly it resembled a large computer cursor, waiting to type the final character that would conclude the story of *Homo sapiens sapiens.*

"Did you feel that? I think there's been an explosion or something."

The book. The Monarch had diabolically inspired poor, mad Theophanus to create a sort of warning gauge of the progress of human intelligence. If humanity ever understood the codex well enough to learn of the transdimensional *Basileus,* the King would halt the evolution of humans as it had those of their predecessors.

And if it could speak to the mind of a meager human like Theophanus, perhaps it could also *listen* to the mind of a pathetic man like Gordon Tallis.

With crushing regret, he glanced from the computer monitor to the small side table where the remaining sheets of the palimpsest lay. It wasn't fair: he hadn't looked at even half the book. Yet he'd already seen too much.

"*Gordon!* We need to *leave.*"

It's too late, he thought. *And there's nowhere to go.*

Still, he let Alyssa yank him by the arm out of the small examination room. Staff and students clotted the corridor, most scrambling to reach the stairwell, while others panic-clustered around the doors of the nearest lift that could take them downstairs. A low rumble as of thunder made the building shudder, and people gasped as they peered out the nearest windows toward the high-rise skyline of the City of London. It was just as Gordon Tallis had feared.

Optasia.

He'd already received the Vision.

And now they would all see the Apparition.

It rose on the horizon, its black mass ballooning in the distance like the detonation of a hydrogen bomb. With the speed and fury of a pyroclastic cloud, it shrieked toward them, pushing a wall of air before it that shattered the windows with its sonic boom. Before the blast blew him and the others back against the wall in a shower of shards, Tallis caught only a glimpse of the being that had come to end his upstart race.

Theophanus' pathetic drawing could not begin to capture the cataclysmic majesty of *Basileus* itself. Seeing it was like tumbling into the yawning, senseless abysm of interdimensional space.

The opaque wraith overspread the heavens, blotting out both sun and sky, and it seemed both oppressively close and unimaginably distant at the same time. It wore not a crown, but a corona—a luminous, scintillating event horizon that arced around the black hole of its leading edge. At its tail, it trailed globular streamers of iridescent ectoplasm that varied in number and overlapped and intersected with one another in contradictory and confounding ways, the only visible traces of its limbs in this plane of existence. In the heart of the creature's blackness, a single searchlight of an eye blared a beam of unforgiving, unendurable intensity. It looked at Tallis, and he combusted as if an ant caught in the focus of sunlight from a magnifying glass.

And there, in his and humanity's last moment, all he could think of was the remaining unread pages of Theophanus' *Optasia*, wondering what subsequent species, if any, would ever be permitted to learn the secrets they contained.

HOW CURWEN GOT HIS HUNDRED YEARS

Jonathan Thomas

Jonathan Thomas, albeit a Rhode Island lifer, is often floored by the magnitude of local history he doesn't know. From bus windows he'd seen signs for Frenchtown Road, but only learned Frenchtown was real when Kristin, a bookseller friend, gave him an 1879 booklet on French settlements in colonial-era Rhode Island. His story is a Lovecraftian take on what happened to the ill-starred settlement. Thomas's newest book is Avenging Angela and Other Uncanny Encounters *(Hippocampus Press, 2021).*

"The sight of this strange, pallid man, hardly middle-aged in aspect yet certainly not less than a full century old, seeking at last to emerge from a cloud of fright and detestation too vague to pin down or analyse, was at once a pathetic, a dramatic, and a contemptible thing."
　　—H. P. Lovecraft, *The Case of Charles Dexter Ward*

I. Ayrault

MR. AYRAULT'S TRIBULATIONS, CULMINATING IN the outrages of July 23, 1700, had acutely worsened after his countryman Jean-François Charrière came knocking at his Frenchtown farmhouse. Ayrault's family was among the most eminent of Huguenot refugees to purchase acreage in the so-called Narragansett Country. But no sooner were rocky fields and thicketed forest transformed into homesteads and a church than shameless riffraff from East Greenwich contested their rightful ownership of the land. Rogues' Island indeed, as the colony's myriad detractors dubbed Rhode Island!

Here, though, was this diffident stranger Charrière, seeking entrée to a community whose less stalwart members had already removed to Boston or New York. He bore a purported letter of introduction from another Huguenot, a Captain Marchant of Newport, a native, like Charrière, of Bayonne, and likewise obliged to uproot himself for his beliefs.

Were Charrière not on the doorstep in the degraded light of dusk, he mightn't have seemed as underfed, as ashen, as unprepossessing. What's more, the doctor was acquainted with Marchant, of whom Charrière spoke as a contemporary, despite looking three decades his and Ayrault's junior. Yet the eyes had in them the leaden fullness of age, and a bad foot gave him an elder's limp, offset by a cane with ornate silver head, over which he always clamped a concealing hand.

Rules of hospitality bade the doctor provide Charrière a pallet by the hearth, a seat at the table, till his worthiness to join the settlement was decided. And Charrière repaid Ayrault's welcome by regaling his host family with anecdotes about the marvels and peoples in places he'd sojourned—Paris, Egypt, India. What listener would not be spellbound? A guardedness informed his reminiscing, though, as if spilling the wrong details might convert innocent travelogue into a confession of sins. Nor did he describe his business, or experiences, in any exotic climes.

Ayrault's shrewd wife Frances traded glances with him conveying she too was wary of these omissions, whereas their grown but callow son Daniel hung on every word as if mapping out future odysseys. When husband and wife separately quizzed Charrière on why he'd dwelt in foreign parts and why he'd left, his equivocations had the practiced ring of a play-actor's lines. Some few learned references to surgery and disease hinted at a physician's training. But he was so taciturn about any such career as to seed concerns over disgrace or incompetence.

And frankly, in this sparsely peopled colony, the doctor didn't relish professional rivals of whatever stripe. Not to say his qualms about Charrière weren't sincere! Pierre cherished his position as the virtual rock of Frenchtown, its welfare his especial duty. Thus the verdict for Charrière was set in stone with Marchant's reply to the doctor's messenger: the captain knew nobody by that name, and whether the newcomer's familiarity with Bayonne was genuine or no, an impostor and forger he was.

An unsmiling Dr. Ayrault begged a word with Charrière his fourth morning on the premises. Frances and Daniel were off tending to chores. Seated face-to-face across the dining table, Ayrault asked how recently Charrière had seen Captain Marchant. "Oh, not since winter," claimed Charrière. "He'll be in mid-ocean now, as he was due to sail once the weather broke."

"Those plans fell through, unfortunately," Ayrault stated simply, but as his unspoken import sank in, Charrière's composure crumbled into a frown of self-doubt and entrapment. It dissolved into ill-masked desperation as Ayrault elaborated, "Regrettably you cannot be invited to remain. Our toehold here is precarious, and we cannot weaken it by sheltering adventurers of questionable integrity. My reputation would be in pieces were that to happen."

Appeals to Ayrault as a fellow Frenchman accomplished nothing. "Whatever good the world can have of me, any redemption I can earn, are contingent on retiring anonymous among my countrymen," he implored.

"No, quality will out," the doctor insisted, "and in you is ample proof your kinfolk were not of Bayonne's better families."

"Is this not the New World?" Charrière countered. "Are we not here to shed obsolete burdens of prejudice and snobbery? Does not our common enemy the wilderness bind us in egality?"

The doctor was immovable, though, all the more as the dismay erupting across Charrière's features made Ayrault turn in apprehension as if a devil leered over his shoulder. Charrière behaved unlike any righteous victim of religious persecution; he rather fit the mold of a fugitive. As for why and from whom this criminal ran, what was that to Ayrault? He steeled himself to rebuff pleas more pathetic from Charrière, who in a heartbeat lapsed into a dead calm, as if loath to waste another word on a lost cause.

He rose and flatly declared, "Since we've nothing more to discuss, I'll grab my things and go." Tearier supplications would have been less bothersome than Charrière's muted exit. Had he but feigned victimhood to curry sympathy? Did he now begin to husband energies for a more serpentine, ungentle scheme? The doctor should have joined Frances and David out laboring in field and pasture; instead, he gulped drams of costly brandy that diluted none of his foreboding.

II. Charrière

Charrière slept poorly in Providence. It wasn't the ruckus of drunken midnight carousing downstairs in Whipple's Inn. To be snubbed by that buffoon Ayrault over his very pedigree was galling, especially as his life hinged on accessing a singular kind of sanctuary. Cravings for retribution spoiled his rest, as did indecision about resorting to more diffuse French havens in Boston or New York. In his charmless room he'd installed an exhaustive gamut of safeguards, statuettes of beastly-headed gods on windowsills and bedstead, amulets around door hinges and his neck, charcoal hieroglyphs on floorboards.

But these measures had their gaping limitations, for he'd scarcely nodded off one witching hour when an elegant young intruder stood coughing for attention at his bedside. Charrière's eyes snapped open, though the absence of surprise in them implied he was used to unsought midnight visitants. The caller introduced himself as Joseph Curwen, late of Salem. Charrière sat up in bed and invited him to pull up the chair in the corner.

"Whipple's gossipy niece who empties the chamberpots has been prattling about your décor," Curwen reported, "and I must say she didn't fib. On my own travels I became versed in the utility of knickknacks such as yours, and they prompt me to ask why you're here and whether we can't be of value to one another."

"All these knickknacks, as you style them, are intended to deflect the glare of one whose enmity I earned in Egypt, or have you quite surmised that?" Unlike that self-righteous prig Ayrault, this prowler, this potential ally, deserved the thumbnail biography his eyes tacitly requested, to wit, Charrière's boyhood discovery of a heathen cult in Bayonne's catacomb ruins, apprenticeship to its hideously aged archpriesthood in Egypt, his impudent pilferage of a "fillip" guaranteeing priestly deathlessness, his flight from Egypt's vengeful beast-god whose potency had been tapped in brewing the "fillip."

Curwen, in contrast, termed himself with New England terseness an alchemist, forgoing personal details. And what could Curwen do for his voluble colleague? Charrière frowned gloomily. For monstrous god to sniff him out would mean his death unless he were undetectable within the scent of numerous countrymen. But a mealy-mouthed Dr. Ayrault had ousted him like a wolf from the Frenchtown fold. Could Curwen arrange some redress, encompassing Ayrault's comeuppance, though without involving overmuch hexcraft as would attract divine scrutiny?

Curwen smiled wryly. Yes, a Salem crony who'd cultivated Rogue Island connections would deploy only the lightest magic touch to unbar Charrière's gateway to Frenchtown. In payment, Curwen demanded no greedy amount of the "fillip."

In Charrière's grasp, via some second-nature legerdemain, was a stoppered faience vial, and on his face a smile mirroring Curwen's. "This amount, sipped frugally, should buy you a good hundred years," he prescribed, "long before which you'll become inured to the swilly taste. Will you be content with that much lifespan?"

"No," Curwen drawled, "but in that little span I bank on blazing an alternate path to immortality that won't risk enraging a murderous god." Unlike lesser barterers, neither party tried softening skullduggery's inherent tensions with small talk. They agreed on a date by which Curwen's agent should get results, the vial changed hands, and then the atmosphere changed as well. The room's draftiness transformed into a breathy ebb-and-flow of moist, warm air, heavy with a marsh's or mucky riverbank's fetor. Just as tangible to Charrière was a lowering mood of doom, more cloying with every inhalation.

Curwen's wary expression implied he understood this rueful turn of events so familiar to Charrière. His shudder imparted he also endured head-to-toe the pins-and-needles of a spiteful god's abrasive surveillance. Charrière launched into a rapid-fire series of slashing, spidery signs as if for dear life, inserting harsh syllables into his dumbshow once the air grudgingly began to thin and sweeten. A sullen, shaken Curwen, when his power of speech revived, grumbled a curt goodnight and took his quicksilver leave.

For someone to react with anything but cowering awe on their first brush with ferocious Sobek, he had to be formidable indeed! Charrière, meanwhile, had to own that perhaps his sleight-of-hand in producing the vial of fillip had amounted to an incautious bit of magic after all.

III. Ayrault

"Your ill-treatment by Hutchinson and his villains was felonious, barbarous, atrocious," John Fones declaimed. "Who'd dispute that? But when you go before the commissioners tomorrow, you'll need be at your most well-ordered and succinct to plead your case successfully. It's a conundrum why Tillinghast and the rest have been unmoved by the unvarnished facts. If I weren't a son of reason I'd credit they were enchanted to act like such deaf, uncaring logs." His chair scraped as he angled it to catch more warmth from the hearth.

Between him and Ayrault, an object on a rickety stool glinted in the waning firelight: it was the jagged bottom half of an amber, short-stemmed wineglass. "By the way, Pierre, why accord this useless debris its place of honor?"

"During the mêlée it came to grief. I keep it lest my fervor for justice cool. It was the sole possession I rescued when fleeing Angers, and it was in my family two hundred years."

Frances spared Fones the effort of framing a sympathetic reply by bringing him and Ayrault flagons of warm ale she'd been spicing in the pantry. Her smile at the deputy had a tremble in it, and in her eyes was a flinching disquiet. "Would you throw a few more sticks on the fire, *ma chère?*" the doctor requested. "Always nippy here on August mornings!"

Upon her exit, Ayrault confided, "After everything that's befallen, best keep her busy, afford her scant chance to brood."

"And respecting what befell, please rehearse your testimony," Fones urged, "if only to humor my fretful old soul."

Ayrault's became the pained visage of one whose fingertip harbored a sliver too deep for tweezing out. "To portray loutish trespass in full, I would first have the record show how those who defiled my home have engaged for years in harassment, vandalizing my fences in murkiest night and even broad day, entailing losses of my cattle, pigs ravaging my crops."

"But this deposition concerns the incident of twenty-third July, does it not? I'd advise against testing the court's patience."

"The court's patience? When mine has surpassed that of Job while they lie around like dumb logs, as you say?" Ayrault threw up his hands in frustration at myopic hinterland justice, and grabbed for the ale he'd set beside his defiled glassware. "As to the twenty-third, then, night was well advanced and we were all abed, when Daniel, whose ears aren't dulled with age like mine, awoke to a commotion outside. He swears to hearing that varlet

William Weaver exhort, 'We ran off the damned Indians. These simpering foreigners will be easier, if anything!'"

"My pardon, Pierre, but best omit that," Fones interrupted, "lest the judges construe it as hearsay, for it's nothing you heard, and something your drowsy son may have dreamed."

Peevish Ayrault spat into the fire and resumed, "Everyone was wide awake, I can assure you, when some dozen brigands banged on the door and broke the lock when we couldn't don clothes and let them in soon enough. Raucous and besotted they crowded into the parlor, toppling the furniture and our meager belongings, deliberately methought. At their forefront, so close their fumy breath was dizzying, were two East Greenwich bullies, Samuel Davis and Abner Spencer. From harrowing experience with Papist mobs, though, I sought among the hindmost for the soberest, keenest onlooker, and there was the leader, Edward Hutchinson, leering gleefully at his prowess as instigator."

Ayrault downed three swallows of ale before relating, "Davis and Spencer browbeat me to attend a court in session at Pardon Tillinghast's house across the river. While I protested the lateness of the hour and the irregularity of their summons, I stole glances at Hutchinson, who carried a cubit's length of golden cord. In it his fingers tied some cunning knot after knot, all on their own; I never saw him look at what they were doing. Whenever he pulled each knot tight, the noise and agitation of the mob worsened a degree. Thus I cottoned how his leer was of an ungodly character, as he wielded influence through grossest deviltry."

"Pierre, I pray you, is this not a complaint of assault and trespassing?" Fones cut in. "Let's adhere to that without detouring into witchcraft! You'll confuse the court and weaken your case, for as you can fathom, spectral evidence has been in disfavor ever since that frenzy in Salem."

Ayrault regarded Fones as if newly unsure whose side he was on, and continued, "These ruffians insisted they had a warrant to compel my cooperation, and indeed Davis had some paper stuffed in his waistcoat pocket. But he refused to show it, and when I demanded to read it before venturing out in the dead of night, he threatened force if I didn't come peaceably. Incensed at seeing me belabored so, my wife, of like infirm state as myself, pushed between them and me, pleading they desist."

Ayrault's tone grew willfully emphatic, as if he'd resolved to talk right over any interference with his next assertions. "I beheld Hutchinson at just the instant he sharply pulled the ends of his cord, gritting his teeth, and next I knew, the mob had answered my wife's tears and cries by cuffing her about the shoulders and shoving her to the floor. It fell to my son Daniel to aid her, because those villains then laid hands on me and strong-armed me into the night."

He paid scant mind as Fones advised her bruises would suffice to mark how Frances had been abused. Again, nagged the deputy, black magic can play no gainful role in cogent testimony.

Ayrault, unperturbed, forged on, "The mob propelled me at such breakneck pace I hailed it as miraculous we poled across the river in skiffs, instead of wading in and drenching me, else I'd be shivering on my deathbed now. No one greeted us at Pardon Tillinghast's, a veritable manor in these hardscrabble precincts, as we packed into the grand front room, its yawning hearth ablaze."

Ayrault's vehement swig dribbled ale over his chin. Fones refrained from bidding him daub it off, as the doctor was proceeding in full spate, "I noted the rabble were here of milder temper, breaking or upending none of their superior's belongings. And Hutchinson no longer skulked among them, inciting violence. But where did he lavish his attention? That mystery beset me scarce a minute, for more of his toughs stormed in manhandling Daniel, groggy and weak-kneed, his clothing gashed and soiled. He told me afterward they'd pulled him away from my stricken Frances, and doubtless induced by Hutchinson's cord, pummeled him to the floor and dragged him by the feet out to the river."

"'Struth, Pierre, you and yours are lucky to be alive!" Fones exclaimed.

Not one to waste words dignifying the obvious, Ayrault professed, "Hutchinson hadn't rejoined his bewitched underlings, nor had to in order to make his brutal point: any opposition of mine to the bullies of East Greenwich would merit harsh punishment, with much harsher for my blameless family. Like an actor obeying stage directions, the clerk John Heath materialized, to mumble from a writ as real as Davis's warrant. It charged me, my wife, and son with rioting and intending the good folk in this court, signed hereunto as witnesses, bodily harm."

"At such brazen perjury you must have wished them bodily harm!" Fones remarked.

"Worse was nigh! With his next breath, Heath accused me of dealing dishonorably with a forlorn countryman of mine, surnamed Charrière, to whom I offered solace and support, only to cast him penniless, without warning, into the wilderness. I was much taken aback at Charrière's encroachment on my affairs again, the more at Heath's inclusion of inhospitality among my legal infractions. I was in no shape to conjecture at Charrière's involvement with the campaign against me, yet had the presence of mind to act the ignorant foreigner. I stammered they couldn't fairly try me, a Frenchman with poor English, without an interpreter."

"Hah! Your English is better than mine," Fones observed.

"Happily, my ploy worked, mayhap because Hutchinson's golden cord couldn't bind them as fast from afar. At this late juncture your colleague Sam Bennett, heretofore of honest repute, emerged from some hind chamber to vouch for me. They had his pledge I'd return on the morrow at a more seasonable hour, and grateful to him as I was, I was surprised we'd met at midnight in that company of scoundrels. Daniel and I were both drawn to a gleam of reflected hearth light below Sam's collar; I had the wherewithal to comment how rare it was for someone of his modest station to afford golden frippery. He replied he surely couldn't."

Fones stared floorward, frowning at the direction this discourse was evidently going. Undaunted, Ayrault plowed on, "He acted unaware of his fine necklace, and I spoke no more of it on descrying its crude pendant. A wax poppet, the size of a thumb and with a loop of gold around its throat, blended with the brown of his vest, and broadly resembled him in scarecrow outline. It had hair the gray of his own embedded in its pate, and a needle through its ears. Why then converse more, for his neckwear tokened he was under as much witchy influence as Hutchinson's gang?"

With herculean forbearance Fones held his tongue at Ayrault's ongoing drivel, "In any case, Sam begged our pardon and retired to his backroom with the dispatch of a fish on a hook. From within I overheard some murmured snatches, 'That will be all . . . Forget you were ever . . . Come again when . . .' The timbre, the accent were Charrière's, and thus I gathered he and Hutchinson were in cahoots, birds of a feather. Their game I've not divined, though trust me, we'll be the wiser before court adjourns tomorrow."

"Pierre," sighed Fones, "I regret you put me in the position of devil's advocate. You're on the docket for tomorrow all right, but as for that hearing on the twenty-fourth July, I was never informed of it, it's in no official records."

"Peace, John, I'm coming to that," said Ayrault. "You're right, no court convened the twenty-fourth, and my enemies hope to brand me a liar or loon by denying they ever told me otherwise. Toward that noon I crossed the river, and none save Sam was behind Tillinghast's door. He displayed confusion when I reminded him of his pledge and asked where the interpreter was. He shook his head the more bewildered when I japed, 'What? Is not even Charrière available to translate English?' The poppet I'd glimpsed yesterday due to Charrière's carelessness or hubris was better hid this time."

"Leaving poppets aside," argued Fones, "if Charrière was plotting revenge behind the scenes, why did he not strike on the twenty-fourth while his iron was hottest, and you in disarray? Why wait till now when you've marshaled your fortitude?"

"No wizard myself, I have to second-guess he postponed his designs pending more propitious days, or nights when the stars were right." Ayrault swished his ale's dregs around, scrunched his hawkish nose at them as if they'd be as palatable as any critique Fones was about to mount.

Fones gingerly lowered his own empty tankard to the floor beside his feet. "Please, Pierre, we stray into the realm of special pleading. I won't fault the commissioners for balking if you trot out a foreign wizard bent on your downfall and then make excuses for his timid or inept inaction. As it is, you're on shaky ground alluding to this Charrière at all, to whom no one save your wife and son will bear witness. And how could you disprove they weren't coerced into humoring you, that Charrière's not a figment or invention?"

From the pantry Frances's restrained sobs were barely audible above the crackling of the fireplace. The quaver in Ayrault's shout betrayed his inward anguish, *"Mon petit chou,* two more tankards, if you will!"

"No, thank you, Pierre!" Fones exclaimed loud enough for Frances to hear, then imparted softly, as he heaved free of his chair, "I'll be at Tillinghast's tomorrow, but not to coach you, so let me stress in parting, your affidavit will sit better if you skip over Charrière entirely. Earth-hunger and sheer roguishness, for which our colony is rightly infamous, account for your rough handling. Please, don't muddy the legal waters with witchcraft, which you might also blame for the lack of outcry at this scandal. I'll see myself out. Solace poor Frances!"

Why indeed, brooded Ayrault, didn't everyone deplore his family's mistreatment as scandalous? Not illogical for Fones to counsel expunging Charrière from his statement! Yet the deputy's offhanded dismissal of Charrière's relevance, his very reality, was disappointing. How to be absolutely certain Fones wore no wax poppet beneath his shirt? And what profit in further brooding? Ayrault snatched up Fones's tankard en route to heeding his advice about comforting Frances. Yet Fones was wrong, presuming she was tearful over lingering memories of July. Rather, she was woefully unreconciled to a "souvenir" of Captain Marchant's, usurping pride of place on a pantry shelf, whereby Ayrault would even the score with villainous Hutchinson and Charrière. The skulking Bayonnais wasn't the only one to sojourn in Egypt and remoter provinces!

IV. Charrière

Why not bask in contentment at his summer's triumphs? The morning sun on Charrière's cheeks felt like a blessing from on high, out on the front doorsill of his Frenchtown cottage—to whomever it had once belonged, he'd nary a clue. The god he still dared not name aloud was, by rights, more quiescent now: the Nile flood had crested; the occasion of the god's ancient festival was months ago, when Sirius rode the dawn horizon and the god was at his most ravenous and savage. And ironically, that gadfly Ayrault contributed to the protective scent of Frenchmen amid which Charrière's blended in, lending him a measure of serenity, of impunity, unattainable for decades.

Would that Ayrault's scraggy visage had stiffened with the look it had after the commissioners indulged his lamentations, and without ado found him guilty on an outstanding charge of rioting brought by East Greenwich gentry. They also denounced his cruelty in consigning to the forest a friendless, trusting guest. But that guest Charrière interceded on behalf of undeserving Ayrault, who could avoid gaol, fines, and disgrace on condition Charrière had his consent to occupy one of Frenchtown's abandoned farmsteads. Ayrault glowered around as if suspecting more than he let on about sorcery's role in this snap verdict; keeping that to himself was wise. Or was he merely disgusted at another typical miscarriage of Rogue Island justice?

And ever since, the bitter fogy hadn't subjected Charrière to a single peep. Out of character, yes, but why borrow worry when it was so satisfying to take victory at face value? What joy, too, adding insult to injury, compounding reasons for Ayrault to fume impotently. In playing at "fitting in" among the planters, he "improved" his property by loosing several pigs upon it. They had their run of fields reverting to saplings and brush; any escapees through tumbledown fence he never lifted a finger to recapture, root as they would in Frenchtown gardens, Mme Ayrault's included.

More boldly, Charrière unpacked his surgeon's satchel, aiming for a livelihood in rivalry with Ayrault. A borderline unnatural tolerance marked the old quack's response to this effrontery, although Charrière's irregular practices comprised much that Ayrault could decry to the authorities. Of course, with every cure, and everyone was cured, Charrière's partisans increased, whatever anyone thought about the laying on of amulets or paganish chanting. And these were often but secondarily effective, because the coup-de-grâce against every hurt and illness was a droplet of the invaluable "fillip." Too bad no dose could be tiny or sweetened enough that patients didn't gag! Was variolation the answer?

Meanwhile, he had abundant time and privacy to pursue distilling the most longevity out of his precious fillip. To brew more was impossible, and conserve it stringently as he could, its amount was finite, its depletion inevitable. The vicissitudes of flight from Egypt to India to Quebec to Arkham had reduced his initial cistern's worth to a paltry three-quarters of a firkin. He craved immortality; any lesser span of centuries, any existence briefer than the god's who hated him, would seem ephemeral, a mocking cheat, when it came to an end. Again, did variolation hold promise?

Clopping hooves, groaning wheels, and a shrill command to whoa bestirred him. On the road out front, some crony of Hutchinson's, seated on a pile of sheaves, was shouting from his haywain, on business too urgent to waste time dismounting. What, Edward had taken a turn for the worse? The driver's ill-harnessed trepidation stamped him as guilty of understatement.

Charrière gestured for patience, fetched his satchel from indoors. The timorous driver scooted aside to make room on the sheaves. *Foutre,* but was Charrière in for a breakneck ride all the way to East Greenwich? His rump was already sore between stony road and bouncy wagon.

Two days ago Edward's mild symptoms had indicated a touch of the grippe, nothing worse. Bed rest and an asafetida pouch should have done the trick; no point ransacking his kit for curatives more arcane. Today, though? Charrière alighted grimacing from the boneshaker wain, regarding Edward's home with a pang of foreboding. Even more than his own cottage, it presented a ruinous front as if it had fared badly in King Philip's War, but add to that a crop of crumpled rags, stained a bilious yellow, on the earthen walkway, apparently flung out the door.

The crony stayed put as Charrière followed the muddle of untouchable rags inside. One breath over the threshold left no doubt why Edward was alone with his disease. Any stink of asafetida was utterly swamped by a miasma like a mule kick, like moldy cheese steeping in a tub of viscous offal. How could anything reek worse than his swill-scented fillip? And more baffling, the stink wasn't altogether unfamiliar. "Whosoever god did this to me, accursed be your head!" wheezed bleary-eyed Hutchinson on realizing Charrière was in his bedroom.

Ordinarily a physician of Charrière's experience set no great store by delirious outbursts. After that greeting, however, Charrière had to conquer reluctance before peeling back the winter quilt up to Hutchinson's chin in balmy September. The charnel stench redoubled, and Edward glowered accusingly when Charrière signed for silence to concentrate on examining him. Each acute finding brought a long-submerged word nearer remembrance: the belly's lopsided swelling beneath taut nightshirt; the paradox of red-faced fever and shivery chills; on exposed limbs, motley ulcers broad as deer hooves, crusty black, bloody red, oozing the yellow pus suffusing multiple rags around the bed. Worst were the pulpy radishes of cankers blocking his nose, propping apart his lips.

"Kala-azar," Charrière heard himself mutter.

"What?" Edward croaked. "Is that more of your abracadabra? Leave off! A fat lot of good that's done me!"

Charrière shuddered inwardly. Every gurgling, malformed syllable must have been torture; nor did the mortification of flesh end there. "Edward, stop scratching! You'll just gouge out more wounds!" Hutchinson sneered and hoarded rasping breaths for another bout of invective. Charrière, though, was deaf to everything save overwhelming stupefaction. Decades ago, on wrangling a post as surgeon in French India, he'd confronted this gruesome malady all too often. It was exclusive to the tropics, so what the hell was it doing thousands of miles from its spawning grounds?

The sole salvation for those soldiers and natives he'd arbitrarily favored had been an exorbitant three drops of irreplaceable fillip. Boorish Hutchinson wouldn't have figured among his lucky elect overseas, but curing Curwen's boon comrade was politick, as was mending anyone whose hideous demise might reflect disastrously on his unorthodox methods. From Hutchinson's scarlet brow sprang a like rumination, "Damn you, Frenchman, you fix me or I'll fix you! Did I bewitch some poor bastard in Salem to hang in my stead, did I go to ground in this shithole, just to die of something I caught from your bungling?"

To protest his innocence would have made no headway against raving hatred; it would have rung hollow at that, for magic must have played some sub-rosa role in the anomaly of kala-azar here. "Ayrault's an ass," growled Hutchinson, "but nothing he did ever put a man in a state like mine! Why don't I call him in for a second opinion, see what becomes of you when he goes squawking up and down the colony about me?" Phlegmy cackles subsided into ragged coughing.

"Rest easy, it won't come to that," Charrière bluffed, already grubbing through his satchel for three single-drop vials of fillip.

He winced to picture combative patient spitting out putrid-tasting dosage, roaring he'd been poisoned, throwing punches around. But wait, hadn't Charrière been wishing for a golden opportunity to experiment with variolation, deliver fillip directly into the bloodstream? Suddenly Hutchinson's gaping lesions were a godsend: he'd probably lash out at the scraping or pricking that customarily deposited physick under the skin. If Edward simply held still ten seconds, though, painless treatment would penetrate his bloody sores, relief should commence immediately.

Charrière trained his eyes on Hutchinson's. "I'm going to cure you with the same potion Curwen so ardently besought of me. This won't hurt." The Frenchman uncorked three phials in rapid succession, poured into three separate wounds the fillip in its suspension of quicksilver that ensured no atom of it lingered on the glass.

"Bugger me, you did say three true words!" blustered Hutchinson. He sat up and breathed without hoarseness or crackling. The fillip always instilled exhilaration; alas, any cosmetic impact on his grisly kala-azar wouldn't show for days. Yet what miracle was underway? What beyond variolation could explain the cankers deflating, the ulcers drying, shrinking like a gob of spit on a hot skillet, skin reknitting with a gauzy translucence, a leathern firmness?

Charrière's amazement soured into distress, though, as new flesh browned, hardened, demarcated into square scales, some with thorny outgrowths. Even as he recognized crocodile hide where the ravages of kala-azar had healed, Edward was bellowing petulantly, "Any potion good enough for that goose Curwen is fucking well fine for me!" And so seamlessly that Charrière initially missed it, Hutchinson was railing in the reedy, sibilant speech of the ancient Egyptian priesthood and their pitiless reptilian god.

The reality was an eye-watering slap. In remaking Hutchinson, divine virulence had drastically upstaged variolation. Charrière had been hustled away from the insulating scent of Frenchtown without donning protective talismans, and he'd been too liberal with the odoriferous fillip. He'd practically lit a beacon fire for Sobek to locate him, and lent Hutchinson as a vessel of retribution. Damn him for a careless fumbler! When was Sobek not gluttonous, vindictive, vigilant like the crocodile? Oh, for a sacrificial black bull, as the scrolls ordained, to stave off almighty ire!

Headlong terror sent Charrière dashing outside, and by sheerest luck did his sightline rake, and hands clutch, his cane and satchel. He had minuscule faith in the chanting and sleight-of-hand he turned and performed to cloud supernal vision. Too little, too late! But no diabolically possessed Hutchinson crashed rampaging out the door; instead, a bawling mêlée raged back and forth within the house. Edward patently wasn't going to suffer his body's foreign usurpation gladly. Almighty Sobek hadn't reckoned on Yankee cussedness! Despite the unabated danger, Charrière smiled bleakly as furniture smashed, crockery shattered, tirade switched haphazardly between languages. Ere long, the cottage indoors would be an uglier shambles than its façade.

It was incumbent on him to make the most of this reprieve. Whoever won the tussle to pilot Edward's brawn would not be cordially disposed toward Charrière. Nor had he a future anymore in Frenchtown, now that Sobek had gotten his scent; as well, the blame he'd surely garner for Hutchinson's outbreak of crocodile skin would write finis to his medical career. But first things first, which entailed decamping at speed. The haywain's driver was still seated on the sheaves, gawking petrified toward the house, Adam's apple bobbing convulsively with each noisy spasm of violence.

Charrière had nothing to lose by brazenly resorting to magic. He wrenched a wooden button off his shirt-cuff. It would do nicely. "You, come down from there!" he shouted at the lackey, who obeyed while ogling him as abjectly as he did the house. "What good are you, sitting on hay like a craven dunce? Take this!" Charrière pressed the button into his victim's trembling, sweaty palm. The Frenchman's silver-headed cane and piercing eyes projected a wordless glamour—like that with which Hutchinson evaded the noose in Salem—to impose on hapless bumpkin a guise visible only to whichever contender won Edward's battered body.

A smidgen more spellcraft, and Charrière's dupe couldn't dream of moving a muscle. In contrast, Charrière raced to the wagon, seized its reins, and barreled off for all the tired nag was worth. He'd have to have driven a furlong farther, and then some, to be out of earshot when Hutchinson's door slammed open with hinge-rending force, and a feral devil raged, "Charrière!" The genuine Charrière had yet to decide whether god or mortal exercised that voice, when shrieks and the musket-fire snapping of bones spooked the horse into a snorting gallop.

V. Ayrault

Hutchinson's summary exodus, and Charrière's into the bargain, was months ago. No vandalism, no harassment, had befallen the Ayrault household since. To what then should the doctor attribute day-and-night funk, the lens of gloom between the world and him that made every hour twilight? Some spiritual burden oppressed his dearly earned heartsease, but neither guilt nor regret could have been responsible. He owed no amends for defending hearth and loved ones as he deemed best. His ally Captain Marchant, worldlier, more hardnosed, set the example to emulate. "What's done is done," he'd gamely counselled; bluff demeanor bespoke a keenness to look adamantly forward.

Why, Marchant had suggested the ploy, and provided the instrument, for "fighting occult fire with like fire." And amenable as he was to abetting Ayrault in the unhallowed arts, purely as surest means to empower goodness, Marchant did name one condition Ayrault had to swear on his soul to fulfill. To atone for dabbling in diablerie, the doctor had to join the captain in subscribing to establish an Anglican church in Marchant's

Newport. Marchant further recommended Ayrault transplant his household to the flourishing seaside haven: however valiantly Ayrault championed Frenchtown, its days were inexorably numbered.

The crafty captain had a knack for getting his way! By dint of plain parsimony, he'd welcome the Ayraults as neighbors sooner or later. If the doctor were oath-bound to invest in a church, he couldn't very well reside too far away to attend it. Ayrault's sights roamed the mantelshelf and lingered, as they often still did, on the fractured wineglass, fit only to contain heinous memories from last summer. Yes, on reflection, a change of scene, miles of separation from this ill-starred settlement, might dispel the melancholy to which Marchant seemed immune.

Frances had been in more buoyant spirits once the captain reclaimed his unholy Pacific "souvenir." Marchant had termed it a "kundela stick," though it was actually a man's thighbone, and closet it cleverly as he could, Frances always cringed in its vicinity. It exuded unease. One end tapered to a rapier point; a faint tracery of spirals, wavy lines, and curlicues decorated its age-worn length; a hell-racked face was carved into the ball at its blunt end, with mother-of-pearl discs for eyes and a tragic Greek mask's mouth, albeit with protruding tongue.

Remarkably, one afternoon's tutorial in the privacy of his barn, and Ayrault emerged duly versed in how to rid the colony of Hutchinson's bullying and Charrière's deceit. Marchant's manner, despite the risk of perdition, was as matter-of-fact as if teaching Ayrault to shoe a mule or string a lute. The exact character and measure of Hutchinson's downfall went undiscussed. Henceforth patience was Ayrault's biggest challenge, given the worse toll on familial nerves every day the kundela bided among them.

Putting Daniel in charge of the farm's daily rounds, the doctor was up each sunrise riding into Wickford, shaping up as a busy if modest entrepôt, a deal more convenient to West Bay trade than Newport. Hutchinson was said to frequent the town, to collect and dispatch missives and parcels, compassing addresses in

Providence, New York, and obscurer realms. Ayrault, as pretext for his visits, vouchsafed he sought to expand his practice, inspecting properties whereon to hang his shingle, treating swabs and dock hands gratis as goodwill gestures.

But he was always mindful to pick up word or glimpse of boats and coaches bearing mail, hazarding on such occasions to intercept Hutchinson. And gossip had it, Hutchinson was ever surly and intimidating, a slovenly ruffian on whom nobody squandered pleasantries. Thus the element of surprise was squarely on Ayrault's side when he espied Hutchinson debarking from a sloop, a package wrapped in oilcloth under his arm. To be hail-fellowed was clearly the last thing he expected, least of all by Ayrault. He wasn't so disoriented, though, as to defer what he'd begun: pressing a forefinger against one nostril, ejecting snot out the other in a maneuver styled "mouchoir anglais" back in Angers.

Such extraordinary luck! "Monsieur Hutchinson!" fawned Ayrault in his stagiest accent. "How do you do? Should we not let bygones be bygones?" Hutchinson tendered no comment apart from arrogant smirk. Ayrault, undeterred, gushed, "Do me the honor, if you please, to borrow my handkerchief, for amity's sake. I too catch summer colds!"

Hutchinson snatched away the peace-offering, with a lustier smirk in lieu of thanks. He voided his nostrils to the accompaniment of a thunderous, splattery, protracted honk. *Mon dieu,* did those sinuses hoard a gallon of snot? Hutchinson vigorously mopped under his nose before tossing Ayrault the fouled linen, venting a grunt as laden with contempt as was the fabric with mucus. He swaggered past his "bygone," sneering the while, during which seconds smiling Ayrault continued pretending nothing vulgar had transpired.

Once Hutchinson had swaggered away, Ayrault, with clinical dispassion, wadded the handkerchief into a drawstring bag from his waistcoat pocket. A warlock unblinkered by Hutchinson's hubris would have been charier of anyone, even a prig like the doctor, obtaining his bodily fluids. But whatever came to afflict

Hutchinson, he'd never, the doctor wagered, put two and two together, nor recall any one instance of rudely blowing his nose. Ayrault, mission accomplished, never set foot in Wickford again.

On the morrow's first light, for he'd been warned to act within twenty-four hours, Ayrault climbed a hillock in his back pasture. It was the highest elevation on the farm, with the most unobstructed prospect toward East Greenwich and Hutchinson. With that professional sangfroid essential for lancing boils, amputating gangrenous limbs, and countenancing yesterday's churlish display, he wound the abominable handkerchief tightly around the kundela's shaft, like a bandage or winding sheet. He was lancing a boil in colonial society, wasn't he? Or amputating a corrupted limb of the body politic?

Mayhap he was, figuratively, performing surgery, though using Marchant's "souvenir" put him at profoundest odds with his Hippocratic Oath. While picturing Hutchinson, he stabbed the air over and over with the thighbone as with a poignard, till he'd recited all the hocus-pocus the captain had rehearsed with him. Then he transferred his concentration into heaping malice on Hutchinson's mental image; he drew and drew a circle in the space before him with the tip of the bone, as if cutting a hole in ice with an awl.

In its own time, the bone jerked sharply, like the recoil of a pistol. Did his eyes trick him, or did tiny glints shoot northward within the width of the circle outlined by the kundela point? For the few seconds they were discernible, their aspects were of gnats or flies, not to say they weren't, if anything, dust motes in a breeze, lit by sidelong rays of the new-risen sun. The crazed visage etched into the thighbone's knobby end, Ayrault now fancied, had a sphinxlike, taunting aura, as if it knew every answer, but refused to tell.

Mystifying above all, he didn't despise Hutchinson any more. His animus must have gone with the fleeting glints, as if a door latch stuck fast within him had popped open and let it out. Good riddance then, why cleave to it, especially once Fones reported

Hutchinson's house standing derelict come October? Better still, Ayrault was able to return Marchant's "souvenir" the sooner because Charrière too had absconded within a fortnight of Ayrault wielding the kundela. What was that English adage about a gift horse?

Ayrault was lighter on his feet, an airiness leavened his mood, but the same inner door from which tension and pressure had flown soon let new apprehension in to roost. And try his best to trivialize his darkling outlook, it only intensified, making for constant unrest, as if man-eating beast behind dense foliage were watching him.

Frances and Daniel had been stealing sidewise glances as if a baleful stalker preyed on their nerves as well. They broached nothing about misgivings so vagrant, and Ayrault was glad: what reassurances of his would not ring hollow, when he couldn't say his family wasn't beset by repercussions of his amateur wizardry? Nor was his the sole homestead affected, going by the several neighbors who'd decamped on short notice, although Yankee harassment had desisted. Nobody confided why they were going, unless a motive was implicit in the shifty eyes and skittishness like those of wife and son.

Galling irony, if his gamble with magic to save the settlement had backfired into decimating it. But that being so, it were rankest folly for him to ignore how the wind blew. He initiated an orderly, deliberate evacuation to Newport, which accelerated into more of a rout after Jean Tourgée fetched him to the riverbank bounding that countryman's pasture. Ayrault's regal black bull had been missing two days, and he'd entreated the neighborhood to watch for it. Tourgée reckoned he'd found the bull but couldn't be dead certain, and in the event, neither could Ayrault, though which other could it be?

Bloated bovine carcass half-impeded the springtime freshet, beheaded as by a prodigious snaggletooth saw. Cauldron-sized chunks were also riven from belly and shoulder. Both men were versed in telltale wounds from losing stock to wolves and bears,

59

but at this stupendous carnage, Tourgée confessed bewilderment. Ayrault held his tongue, for while he'd no inkling of the predator's form, only a plumb imbecile wouldn't have suspected that bête noire besieging his peace of mind. What sign writ larger did he need of a bloodthirsty fiend circling ever closer, more malevolently, to him and his?

With Tourgée he made arrangements to haul away the remains, entertained no further speculation on the attacker's species, nodded at Tourgée's wishful thinking that the beast had eaten its fill and gone its way. "Amen to that," said Ayrault in farewell.

The slain bull he set before his conscience as evidence the powers he'd unforeseeably riled were centered on depredations against him. Otherwise he'd carry crushing remorse for leaving Frenchtown in the dark, abandoning his people to the mercies of a killer beyond their ken, likely impervious to their weaponry. Yet he dared not broadcast what he'd gathered about that killer, how Ayrault in transacting magic seemed to have redirected the hatred of whatever had haunted Charrière. No matter if Ayrault had transgressed *pro bono publico;* for practicing witchcraft he'd be hanged, and to pile Pelion on the Ossa of his guilt, his name and his family would languish evermore in disgrace, ruined.

The Ayraults quit Frenchtown with as little fanfare as Charrière and Hutchinson had pulled up their stakes. And as Charrière and Hutchinson must also have gambled, unholy nemesis was unwilling or unable to trail its quarry as many miles from its established haunts as, say, Newport. Marchant never spoke to Ayrault about deploying his "souvenir"; the Anglican church, with Ayrault and Marchant its most generous patrons, first tolled its bell in 1702.

VI. Curwen

Joseph Curwen grinned like a plump granary cat to recall Charrière's accusation of driving too hard a bargain. As if the

Bayonnais and those other clowns in the Narragansett Country hadn't blundered all on their own into their dismal straits! Had Charrière not triggered a situation to exploit, he wouldn't have been out twice as much of his priceless fillip, and withal, he was getting off easy. However adept Charrière bethought himself, he'd flouted the cardinal rule of necromancy, conjuring an entity he wasn't competent to expel again. Sobek, was it? Those Egyptian chimeras were notoriously unpredictable. Give Curwen a cut-and-dried proposition like Yog-Sothoth, whom any mage redoubtable enough could invoke and as dependably banish.

And thanks to Charrière, Curwen had acquired another hundred years in which to become that mage. Charrière must have known what the bargain would be as soon as Curwen's mahogany door opened to him, his hat in pauperish hand. To seat Charrière in sumptuous parlor, serve him cognac and pheasant, unsnap lacquered snuffbox for him were calculated to demoralize his guest the more. It was a scathing kindness thus to flaunt Curwen's much grander success at balancing a secret alchemist's and affluent merchant's careers, emphasizing Charrière's dearth of aught to barter with except the fillip.

Thus Charrière had to ignore humiliation, beseech his host to arrange some refuge in town where he could regain his footing, eke out a mousy subsistence. Curwen, fortunately for Charrière, didn't dislike him, accounted him a kindred spirit a hundredfold more congenial than swinish Hutchinson. True, he'd somehow muddled physick and magic so imprudently that his repute as a doctor was obliterated. He'd also inflamed a grotesque god's zeal to stamp him out, and had to pray divine rancor would peter out short of the distance Charrière could afford to flee.

And since Charrière's coins took him as far as Providence, who had he there to impose on besides Curwen? Despising appeals to conscience, Curwen made him squirm through a lengthy pretense of rumination. "This town is too small for two necromancers to go about their business with impunity," he admonished, "and I'll not jeopardize my virtuous front here. But as it's a small town, to be off its beaten path would constitute no onerous journey. Bear that in mind and ponder well my proposal. From whom else in these parts should you expect an invitation?"

Charrière's meet reply to that rhetorical question was a minimal shake of his head.

"I shall dwell on my side of the hill, toward the cove and the bay, and you shall inhabit your side of the hill, toward the river, with the mire of Cat Swamp between us. I will have a sturdy cottage built for you, sheltered from the wind and idle eyes, on the slope of a ravine above a wholesome spring. You will pay me another phial of fillip, in quantity equal to the first."

Curwen rode out Charrière's *de rigueur* protests with a tranquil smile. "The rivulet flowing from the spring down to the river is too measly to attract any self-respecting crocodile," Curwen elaborated, "a trickle compared with the river skirting French-town. And you'll have your housewarming when November's cold should fend off tropic reptiles, with all winter to buttress your walls against occult trespass." Charrière, of course, could either knuckle under to Curwen's extortion, or end up indigent, a vagabond, the short-lived target of god and men.

Was it another scathing kindness meanwhile to ensure a roof over Charrière's head by defraying his bills at Whipple's Inn? Yes, for what was altruism but irrational weakness? Suddenly ill-humored, Curwen promised to send word once the cabin was habitable; thankfully, Charrière parsed in that severer tone a tacit message of dismissal. Someday Charrière's stores of Egyptian lore might enrich Curwen's research into the making of substances to reanimate the dead. Barring that, Curwen could only muster a sporting interest in whether his secluded colleague survived a week or fifty years. Hutchinson was a colleague too, after all, and Charrière's role in his reversals was still unclarified.

As for Hutchinson, he'd already stopped by last night en route to Boston harbor. His travels would be perforce nocturnal for the foreseeable future: most palpably because half his face was a blot of pebbly, greenish scales, and judging by the forearms he constantly scratched, his skin overall was splotched with tea-colored, square, tortoiseshell-hard scales, itchy as hell. Swigging from the same cognac, occupying the same chair Charrière would tomorrow, Hutchinson railed, "Something got into me and did this! If I hadn't fought it off with everything I had, I'd have been much the worse! That bungler Charrière is liable. Had I an hour to spare I'd go kill him, curse his foreign prick!"

Bungler or not, incredible that Charrière's doctoring could have resulted in Hutchinson's infestation, to look at him, by a crocodile god! Curwen declined to prolong their dialogue by alluding to Sobek, inquiring rather into Hutchinson's plans, though candidly, these went without saying: board the first Britain-bound vessel and migrate beyond, where men might wear mask or veil without incurring comment, into Asia perhaps, where he'd be the rank foreigner himself. But what point goading the bigot with this irony?

According to Simon Orne, mutual acquaintance and supernaturally well-informed rumormonger, Hutchinson's reasons for migrating weren't simply skin-deep. East Greenwich had charged him with the lurid murder of a hireling whose wagon he'd stolen. Yet even at his most hotheaded, he would not wreak carnage that gained him nothing, thus implicating Sobek amok within him as the killer and thief. Again, what perverse medicine had Charrière unpacked to provoke wrathful god into scourging Hutchinson and not him? Hutchinson, doubtless, would be unamused by the further irony in reaping disfigurement and exile for doing Charrière the great good, at Curwen's behest, of roughing up the curmudgeon Ayrault. No, the less said, the sooner Curwen ushered out a jinx like Hutchinson, the better.

What's more, the puzzling extent of magic gone awry hinted at an additional hand, one too many and too green, stirring the occult pot. Curwen had intercepted gossip flitting from one household's servants to another that a Captain Marchant had loaned an unchristian relic to beleaguered Ayrault. And who if not Ayrault's tormentor Hutchinson should be the bull's-eye of dilettante spellcasting? Egad, what was thaumaturgy coming to, when even pietistic dotards were playing at it? But enough! Any time not devoted to alchemical delvings was time wasted, and egregiously wasted on that sad straggle of dirt farms touting itself as Frenchtown—good luck to it!

VII. Wequashim

Wequashim had accused no one of lying, but now had to own he hadn't heard mere stories. Too bad! The swamps nearest Frenchtown were the best hereabouts for hunting, with the least chance of encountering hateful Yankees. Yet only a fool would tarry there after seeing what he'd seen. True, it was some hundreds of feet away, behind a screen of cattails, half-submerged in a pool, but he'd gazed hard, and gazed again. His eyes weren't gulling him.

It had scales, most like a turtle's, of a drab green in shadow, a tawny gloss in sunlight. Incredibly, it was big as a longhouse, like that animal the mean-spirited Yankees made up, the dragon, to scare their children. Its jagged-fanged snout most resembled a two-man pestle, and its reptile nature was confounded by the jughandle ears it scratched with a clawed but otherwise human hand. The vehemence with which its jaws shook apart some indistinct hunk of meat constrained him into moving no muscle, breathing in mindful silence, behind his blind of late-summer foliage.

None among the squabbling Christian creeds had anything in their faith to help make sense of this voracious giant, unlike the traditions of his upbringing. The fear and awe it excited were signs of a presence divine as it was monstrous, imbued to excess with manitou. Unriddling its name, though, demanded a sagacity beyond him. It wasn't Cautontowwit, who dwelt in the dusty underworld, or Hobbamock, who ruled the night and shunned the sunshine. Who was it, where was it from, why was it here, when would it go away? About this god or spirit he'd drawn just one conclusion: to try propitiating it with offerings would be futile, for it plainly exulted in sacrificing to itself whatever pleased it.

Had he not a warrior's iron restraint, he'd have beat a suicidally noisy retreat once his straining eyes gave shape to the divine banquet. No mistaking, slime-blackened jaws playfully tossed a human skull by its remnant hair, caught and gulped it with an exuberant crunch. Leathery snout dipped into the muck and snuffled up another disintegrating corpse; from the state of this one, Wequashim surmised the beast-god had scented a cache of forsaken casualties from the war a quarter-century ago, putrefied past telling whether they were Indian or damnable Yankee. One and the same in that man-eating maw!

Swiftly as stealth allowed, he put boggy terrain between himself and ghoulish deity. No rest for him till friends and kin knew to avoid the Frenchtown swamp for the indefinite future and, for safety's sake, every swamp in former "Narragansett Country" and the waterways connecting them. Sachem Ninigret would send runners to alert outlying families. Even "praying Indians" ought to pay heed. No one sounded such alarms casually, or did so often as once each lifetime.

On hidebound Yankees, Wequashim wouldn't waste his breath. Whoever among them he approached, sober as a clam, he'd not say half his piece before they scorned him as a "drunken Indian." Of course! Let the Christian fools fire at squirrels within that ravenous giant's hearing; how terrified they'd be when bullets couldn't kill their unmissable target as it rushed them with cavernous jaws. Frankly, he wouldn't be sorry. In like fashion had colonial soldiery devoured his people, their lands.

But did scaly god sniff out unvirtuous pride in Wequashim's own heart? He'd begun breathing freer, presuming to outrun divine purview, when from across the hundreds of yards he'd sped—a testimony to the inescapable reach of manitou—a sibilant, ground-shaking bellow overtook him, demanding, in his language, "Tell the limping thief, live a million million years, I'll be there at the end!" A limping thief? A million million years? Was this god mad on top of monstrous? It had obviously been aware of Wequashim all along, so why tread lightly anymore? "Why indeed?" he mused, a heartbeat before careening wildly, kicking up leaves, snapping twigs, like any cloddish Yankee.

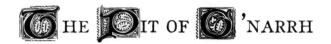

THE PIT OF Q'NARRH

Donald R. Burleson

Donald R. Burleson's fiction has appeared in Twilight Zone, Fantasy & Science Fiction, *and many other magazines, as well as in numerous anthologies including* Gothic Lovecraft, Horror for the Holidays, *and three* Black Wings *volumes. He is the author of twenty-four books, including the short story collection* Wait for the Thunder, *the essay collection* Lovecraft: An American Allegory, *the novella* The Roswell Genes, *and the non-fiction titles* UFOs and the Murder of Marilyn Monroe *and* UFO Secrecy and the Fall of J. Robert Oppenheimer. *Dr. Burleson, a mathematician who retired in 2017 after fifty years of teaching university mathematics, lives in Roswell, New Mexico, with his writer wife Mollie Burleson.*

FATE CAN BE A CRUEL AND MOCKING REMINDER that we live in a universe of cold indifference, an unsympathetic cosmos deaf and blind to the well-being of any struggling soul yearning to find solace or meaning in this madness we call life.

Had my mother and father and older sister not died in an accident when I was sixteen, necessitating, under the circumstances, new living arrangements for myself that scarcely turned out to be salubrious, I might never have seen the horrors my eyes have seen, might have had a chance to live out a life in which one looked forward with hope rather than backward with dismay, might have been able to cast my glance up to a plenitude of frosty stars on a winter's night with a sense of wonder rather than a shudder of revulsion.

After the accident, and pursuant to the offer from an uncle and aunt with whom I was barely acquainted—there being no other living family—it was determined that I should go reside with them, on the simple farm in a remote corner of western Massachusetts not terribly far from my own erstwhile home in Vermont; or not far in terms of miles anyway, however great a distance it was in other respects.

I had only rarely heard my parents speak of Uncle Lester or Aunt Mae. Lester Morgan was my mother's much older brother, yet she had been estranged from him after they grew up, finding him a distasteful memory for reasons I could never quite comprehend, at least until I came to live with him. My mother was rather more pleasantly disposed toward my aunt, feeling sorry for her, I gather, because of her having married Lester. The Morgans never traveled, and my family had never come down to see them, so my aunt and uncle were virtual strangers to me except for vague whispers now and then from my parents.

The day I arrived at the farm was quite an adjustment for me. A cab driver brought me there from Northampton, some thirty miles away to the east, the last several miles being a rocky path hardly to be called a road. The driver made haste to get me out of his vehicle, deposit my luggage on the ground, and drive away, evidently reluctant even to look at the farm.

Indeed, the place was not much to behold. It consisted of two animal corrals, a small barn flanked by some dingy outbuildings, a large well, and a farmhouse whose dilapidation was discernible even from a distance. Close around on all sides, a dense forest pressed upon the place, a stifling cloak of isolation. There were no utility lines visible of any kind. The farm was unsightly and depressing to ponder, yet even so I felt that the cab driver's displeasure was due to something more than just the farm's physical appearance. Most likely, my uncle had a reputation in town.

The Pit of G'narsh

Inside the house, these impressions only became more pronounced. My aunt greeted me with a warmth somewhat tinged with what I took to be subtle discomfort from the phlegmatic presence of my uncle, who grunted out a sort of greeting but did not rise from his chair. Soon we were seated around an old table having a simple and wordless dinner, and my new life had begun.

I was soon to learn that my adoption, from my uncle's perspective at any rate, was not motivated so much by family-related emotions, or even by my modest inheritance from my parents, as by a desire to have a farm hand capable of doing such work as the place required, which, despite its simplicity, was considerable. Uncle Lester was undergoing the common ailments of advancing age, and even the care of a few cows, pigs, and chickens was coming to be somewhat beyond his ability. My aunt did her best to bring some order to a not noticeably pristine house, and to cook the meals and wash and mend their tattered clothing, but age was encroaching upon her as well. I helped her as much as I could, but the outdoor farm tasks for the most part had devolved upon me. For me it was the end of going to school, at least in the near future, and the end of leading what might have been a normal young urban person's life.

But the strange events really started a few years after my arrival at the farm.

One evening after the chores were done, and after Uncle Lester had returned from a pickup drive to town for a few scanty supplies, including gasoline for the generator, we were all sitting around the living room for a few minutes before retiring. Aunt Mae sat knitting in a creaky rocker, my uncle reposed across the room smoking his grimy pipe, and from my own chair I cast cautious eyes about in assessment of the seedy nature of the house, not wishing to arouse any resentment in my new family by showing any of the distaste I felt. There was a musty odor about the house, despite all my poor aunt's efforts, but what arrested my attention was the large, ancient-looking, leatherbound book resting by itself on the rickety coffee table in the middle of the room. Over the years I had noticed it there many times, of course, but had never bothered to ask about it.

My uncle saw that I was looking at the book, and he gave me a not altogether friendly glance of inquiry.

I pointed at the book. "Family Bible?"

Upon my asking this, my aunt drew in an apparently involuntary gasp and busied herself all the more with her knitting, as if not wanting to be involved in whatever was about to be said. My uncle at first merely shook his head dismissively and continued emitting clouds of pipe smoke. But at length he roused himself and spoke.

"No, no, it ain't a family Bible. Nothin' ye'd know anythin' about, Russell Benson. Nothin' most anybody'd know anythin' about."

This made me wonder whether the book might be some rare and perhaps valuable volume. By now I knew that the farm provided them no extra income to speak of, and I remembered my mother once telling me, years before, that my aunt and uncle had what money they possessed due to an inheritance from a wealthy relation in Boston. I wondered if this book might have been part of that inheritance, some musty first edition whose value Uncle Lester and Aunt Mae might not wholly understand. I hazarded a question.

"Well, if it's not a Bible, what is it?"

Uncle Lester stared at me so long that I almost thought he had not understood the question, but finally he replied. "It's the Book of G'narrh."

I blinked, puzzled. "The what?"

He looked at me as if I were hopelessly ignorant. "I found it years ago at an old bookstore in New Hampshire. It's one of a kind. The Book of G'narrh."

I shook my head. "I'm sorry, Uncle Lester, but I don't know what that is."

He shook his head in turn. "There's a lot you don't know."

I nodded. "I'm sure that's true."

He refilled his pipe and put a match to the tobacco. "There's a lot the whole world don't know. About the Old Gods."

"The—?"

"The Old Gods. They was here before the earth, before the sun an' the moon an' the stars. They're just waitin' to come back." I noticed that Aunt Mae was looking uncomfortable with all this, as if she wished very much that he would not be telling me these things. She seemed to be trying to keep her eyes on her knitting.

Taking a chance on his annoyance, I said to my uncle, "Well, I'm sorry, but I never heard of them." I have never been religious, but even so, I thought I had heard of most of the gods of human tradition.

The look he gave me was a sort of sly, soundless rebuke. "Yes, you have. They're all around in the world. You've saw 'em deep in the eyes of animals, you've heard 'em in the thunder far off at night. You've saw shadows of 'em in your own dreams."

Whatever all this meant, and however ungrammatical, I thought this was uncommonly poetic for a grizzled chap like Uncle Lester. "So the Book of—?"

"G'narrh," he said, seeming to relish the name. "That's one of 'em. One of the Old Gods."

This was all beyond me. "I still don't—"

He cut me off short, rising from his chair and knocking the dottle out of his pipe. "Let's all turn in. Chores to do in the mornin'. So g'night."

A few days later, as we were all finishing breakfast, Uncle Lester turned to me and fixed me with a purposeful stare. "I think it's time for you to see the Pit." He made the word sound as if it had to be written with a capital letter.

I carried my plate and coffee cup to the sink. "The what?"

He rose and made for the door. "C'mon with me."

I followed him out into the morning air. "What about the chores?"

He pointed off to where we were headed. "We ain't goin' to be gone long. C'mon."

We walked past the outbuildings on the north side of the farm, to a spot where the woods began, thick and green and seemingly impenetrable. But he pulled aside some underbrush so that we could proceed along what appeared to be a sort of overgrown but still visible path. I had seen him head in this direction a few times before but had not thought much about it until now.

We walked for what felt like a long time, finally coming out into a sizable clearing, at the center of which a deep hole in the ground yawned before us, emitting unplaceable but decidedly unpleasant odors. Uncle Lester pointed at the chasm with what I thought was a sort of pride.

"This is the Pit of G'narrh."

There it was, that name again. I was at a loss. "Why do you call it that?"

He shook his head, smiling enigmatically. "It ain't what I call it that matters."

I stepped a little closer to the edge of the hole, almost close enough to look down into it, but was stopped by the ghastly odor. "But you said all that had to do with those—what did you call them? Old Gods."

He nodded, smiling sadly now, as if confirming something to someone simple-minded. "It does have to do with 'em. Or with one of 'em, anyhow." He paused to light his pipe. "See, a god can come close to bein' in our world if you make the conditions right."

"What do you mean?"

He puffed out a cloud of smoke which, thankfully to me, helped cloak the awful odor from the hole. "This god thrives on what you an' me would call foulness." He laughed, a bitter, mirthless sound. "What do we know 'bout what's foul and what ain't? We don't think like the gods do. The book says, 'As a foulness shall ye know them.' For more years than I can tell ye, I've been bringin' the—right things—here and dumpin' it all in the Pit."

"Right things?"

He nodded, looking more thoughtful than was his habit. "Carcasses of farm animals, stuff startin' to rot. Bags of human waste from the outhouse. Decayin' foodstuffs. Once Mae had a horrible festerin' sore on her arm, and I made her drip the stuff into the Pit. Anythin' to make it—make it right for G'narrh. And one day he'll show hisself."

I thought this was all nonsense, and my uncle could see in my face that I thought so. He snorted unhappily, looking quite disappointed with me, and turned. "Let's go back. Work to do."

Things were busy with all the tasks around the farm, and I tried not to think about what I had seen and heard. But after a few days of avoiding the urge to do so, I picked a time in the early afternoon when things were fairly well caught up and not much was happening, and without telling anyone, I made my way back along the tree-choked path to the clearing. To the Pit. Somehow I felt rather less inclined now to take it so lightly as before.

In the clearing, I hesitated before stepping up to the edge and looking down into that malodorous gaping hole in the earth. Through a buzzing cloud of flies at the bottom, I could see only a formless jumble of bones, weeds, debris, carrion, and less recognizable things, some twenty feet below. As I peered into that miasmal space, the outrageous odor suddenly hit me with full force. Pitching forward, I vomited into the hole, having to pinwheel my arms to keep from falling in. Teetering on the rim, I struggled to get my breath and my balance.

And heard something down there.

It was a sort of restless stirring, as if something were subtly shifting things around at the bottom.

Something alive.

I managed to cast only a panicky glance down the hole before fleeing back along the path, stumbling and panting, desperate to leave that charnel place behind. What had I seen? The one fleeting impression had been of—*something,* something that my mind did not want to countenance.

Back at the farm, I worked through all my chores, trying not to dwell on unhealthy things. That evening Uncle Lester, from his chair across the room, confronted me. "What's the matter with you, Russell? You've been lookin' on edge all day."

I hadn't realized my state of mind had been so obvious. "I—well, I went back to the Pit."

He eyed me narrowly. "Oh? What for?"

"I guess I was just curious to see it again."

He puffed his pipe. "And?"

I hesitated, not sure exactly what to say to him. "This time I heard something down at the bottom."

This clearly piqued his interest. "Heard somethin'? Heard what?"

I put my hands up in puzzlement. "I don't know, it was like—something rustling around down there. Kind of a dry sound, like something pushing stuff around."

Uncle Lester looked thoughtful for a long while. When he glanced up at me through the pipe smoke, I thought he had a look about the eyes that almost suggested a kind of subdued excitement over what I had told him. He gave me a nod.

"We'll be goin' back there, you and me."

We all turned in, and lying sleepless in my room, staring up into the darkness, I made myself consciously face what I had glimpsed in the Pit. The image had been vague, but it seemed to involve a twitching multitude of thin, spider-like legs.

We made our way through the woods as before, toward the clearing. It was almost as if those multitudinous boughs and branches and leaves, by retarding our steps, were conspiring to keep something hidden, some hoary secret that should never be seen. But before long we came out into the clearing and stood looking across at the Pit. Uncle Lester had brought along a large bag of some sort of unsavory miscellany from the cattle pens, possibly a mixture of feces and heaven only knew what else. Some chickens had been found dead in the coop that morning, and their remains might have been part of it.

My uncle stepped up to the rim of the Pit and emptied the noisome contents of the bag into the gaping space below, muttering some words as he did so, words that I could not make out, as they seemed to be something in another language. Something from that book, I suspected. I stayed a little behind him as he stood looking down into that strange space. I felt as if there was something I had to ask.

"Uncle Lester, why do you want to—"

He wheeled around to give me a withering look. "Don't you want to see a god?" Then he turned back toward the pit.

"Frankly," I said, "no, I don't."

Suddenly I heard the dry, whispering, somehow dreadful sounds that came up out of the hole to startle my uncle, who, wide-eyed, jerked away, turning to take a step back toward me— but a little too late.

Too late, because it was not just sound that was making its way up into the light of day.

It happened so fast that either my eyes could not follow it or my mind would not accept it, or both. A frantic fiddling of spidery legs, a huge arachnid mouth, an overall impression that was as insane as it was undeniably real—something fastened itself upon my uncle and tore him apart with an alacrity that defied belief. In a second it was over, and the gangling thing that had scrambled up out of the hole was wading through the scattered carnage of my uncle's decimated body, making its way toward me.

Later I would have no clear memory of running back along the path to the farm, though I must have done so. When I emerged from the woods and stood in the clear space around the outbuildings, I looked fearfully back at the trees, expecting to see something unthinkable come twitching out.

But nothing did. Not yet.

My hands shaking, my mind reeling, I asked myself a question: Why, why would it want to kill us? *Well, Russell,* some corner of my mind replied, *why do you step on roaches? Because they're insignificant to you.*

I ran to the farmhouse, bounding up the front steps and into the living room, where my aunt stood looking at me in wonder.

"Close and lock all the doors, shut all the windows," I told her. She looked bewildered, but complied. When the house was as secure as we could make it, and when we were ensconced once again in the living room, she turned and stared at me in panic.

"Where's Lester?"

There was nothing I could do but tell her the truth, as nearly as I understood what the truth was. "We were out at the Pit. Something came up out of it and—and got him."

The poor woman was stunned. "He's—"

I took her hand. "Yes. I'm sorry."

Tears welled up and trickled down her stricken face. She was about to speak again when a noise came from the back of the house, near the kitchen door as well as I could tell. I ran back there in time to see a confused mass of wiry, jerking legs moving over the window in the door, outside on the back porch, trying to get in. I ran back to the living room and took Aunt Mae by the hand. "Come on. We have to leave. Now!"

Some perverse impulse made me pick up the Book of G'narrh on the way out.

We reached the pickup truck before the thing on the back porch could get all the way around to where the truck was parked, but driving away with my aunt trembling and whimpering in the seat beside me, I could see its spasmodic movements back there, an apparition in the rearview mirror, groping the air for the prey that had barely escaped it.

Soon the farm was no longer in sight in the mirror. As we drove, I noticed that Aunt Mae had the Book of G'narrh on her lap. I reached over and thumped the thick leather cover with my hand. "Did you ever read this?"

My aunt shook her head vehemently. "I would never—but Lester used to read to me out of it sometimes." Her voice broke at mentioning his name. "I never wanted to hear it." But she opened the book and stared at the ancient pages, there still being enough daylight to see them. Drawing a breath, she spoke up.

"Listen to this: 'The god G'narrh, once being called into the world, will return to the realm whence he was summoned, if a human sacrifice is made.' That means—"

"But then," I interrupted, "Uncle Lester's death—I'm sorry, Aunt Mae—then my uncle's death should have vanquished the creature."

"No," my aunt replied, closing the book. "He was not a sacrifice knowingly made. The thing just took him."

"Well—" I began, but upon taking the truck around a sharp turn in the rocky road, I saw, too late, a deer run into our path. I hit it with a terrible jarring impact and, in trying to regain control, ran the truck into a large tree close beside the left edge of the road. We were stopped cold, and the truck would not start again.

I slammed the steering wheel with my fist. "Now what are we supposed to—" But that was as far as I got, because a flurry of spasmodic legs, long and spindly, thumped at the glass on all sides. The thing had caught up with us.

I turned to Aunt Mae. "We're going to have to—" I stopped speaking. Incredibly, she was opening the door. She gave me a look of tender sadness that will haunt my memory forever.

"You're young, Russ. You have your life ahead of you. It has to be me."

I reached across and grabbed at her arm, trying to stop her, but she stepped out of the truck into the road, to face the nightmare shape whose form covered the vehicle. "Take me!" was all she had time to say before it bulged upon her, its obscene legs clutching wildly, and ripped her to pieces before she could even scream. I could see through the still open passenger-side door, and immediately the creature out there seemed to raise the maggoty mass of what might have been some sort of head, churning its countless legs in the air, then simply faded away, gone—returning to its own dark, timeless domain until the next time someone should call it forth.

From the shock of what I had seen, I could barely feel my feet touching the ground as I walked several miles to the main road, where I was soon able to hitch a ride to town.

To town, but never back to a normal life.

By now I have read enough of the Book of G'narrh to understand that the Old Gods are ever-present in their own frightful way. I recall my uncle's words: we can see them deep in the eyes of animals, we can hear them in the distant grumble of thunder in the night. *G'narrh*—we can hear an echo of that name in the predatory growl of a wolf and in the tectonic murmur of an earthquake and in a thousand other places where a familiar world appears to prevail, but really does not. The Old Gods are everywhere, some of them spawned in what we cringing humans would call filth, and for me, life now can forever hold only the horror and the despair of that knowledge. When I look up at the scattered stars, I sense not beauty or intrigue, but a profoundly disheartening awareness of the soul-shattering secrets that they hide.

OPEN ADOPTION

Ann K. Schwader

Ann K. Schwader lives and writes in Colorado. Her ninth collection of dark verse, Unquiet Stars, *appeared in 2021 (Weird House Press). Her most recent fiction collection is* Dark Equinox and Other Tales of Lovecraftian Horror *(Hippocampus Press, 2015). She is also a two-time Bram Stoker Award Finalist, and received the SFPA's Grand Master award in 2018.*

"SO WHEN'S THIS FUN FEST SUPPOSED TO START, anyhow?"

Charlie barely lifts her head from the headrest. Mark has already asked her this a few times today, without paying much attention to the answer.

She glances past him. "I think it already has."

Despite late August heat, the minibus is a lively place. Tia and eleven other little girls are getting acquainted, via much seat-swapping and giggling and whispering. Though, so far, no tears or squabbles. Nobody left out. No teasing.

What's she missing?

Done with their non-conversation, her husband returns to his laptop. He's been working most of the day, despite the complications of flying between Colorado and New England with a grade-schooler.

Complications she's mostly dealt with, ever since that registered letter from New Harbors. Their third attempt. No telling what happened with the first two: Mark wasn't crazy about an open adoption to start with, though he'd finally agreed after learning that there was only one required meeting. With Tia's birth family, or some designated family member, the year Tia turned seven.

In their daughter's case, that family member was a grand-mother. Maybe great-grandmother?

Charlie frowns. Aside from the hassle of this weekend trip, it didn't seem like much to ask. New Harbors covered everything but airfare. This whole adoption process has been no worse, and certainly less expensive, than most other options.

The ones she'd researched after two rounds of in-vitro treatments failed.

Mark had been more than ready to give up. He's already got two nearly grown children with his first wife, though Charlie's never met them. His ex makes sure of that.

Stop it stop it stop it.

Charlie exhales slowly. Around her, Tia and the others go on chattering to one another—sometimes understandably, sometimes in what she's privately calling twinspeak. Don't twins sometimes develop their own private languages?

It doesn't help that Tia looks so much like the others. A dozen cousins.

Mark noticed it at the airport, but she'd put his comment down to racial bias—something a guy who owns two construction companies should get over. It was a wonder they'd passed their screening interviews. New Harbors works with a refugee community from some Pacific island so small she never even found it online. An early casualty of climate change?

Wherever Tia's family came from, though, she's *hers* now.

The thought settles some of Charlie's weekend anxieties. She wonders if she's alone in having them, though probably not. The other eleven moms—eight with husbands, three alone—also have paperwork in their laps, awaiting the Boston lawyer as she circulates around the bus.

The three on their own look apprehensive. No doubt: the letter she'd received from that same lawyer had been clear about *both* parents attending this meeting. No excuses. Also no mention of divorce or abandonment, though a short, dense paragraph explained how to submit a copy of the father's death certificate, if applicable.

No widows on this bus, she's guessing. Only women who'd wanted a child more than anything else in their lives.

More than keeping their husbands happy when that child didn't live up to expectations.

At first, Charlie hadn't noticed Mark not holding Tia much. She'd never imagined him as a hands-on dad—not with his hours—and she honestly didn't mind getting up at night. She and Tia had bonded from the first, the way she'd always imagined.

Mark had done plenty of hovering over Tia's crib, though. Hands on the top rail, he'd watch her tiny legs kick at the sunbeams filling her pink room. It took her a while to see his knuckles clenched white, or the shadows crossing his face as he turned away. And then, of course, she couldn't *not* see. The way she couldn't not see the two photos on Mark's home office desk: his athletic, collegiate, sandy blond sons grinning confidently at their future.

Tia was athletic, too. A swimmer by three. A member of their rec center's Minnow League at six, minimum age allowed—and competitive, according to her coach.

But chlorine fumes at five A.M. aren't for everybody. Certainly not for Mark, even when he had a free weekend—

"You can't start swim team until you're *ten?*" Tia's voice, high and incredulous. "That stinks!"

Her daughter is sharing a seat with another girl, whose long braid shines the exact raven black of Tia's pixie crop. The girl's mother, plump and nervous, is one of those on her own. Her eyes are fixed on the Boston lawyer heading their way.

Leaning across the aisle, Charlie motions Tia back to her own seat just in time.

And where did that *paranoia come from?*

Probably from Mark, who'd disliked the woman from the first.

Lean and sixtyish, with deeply wrinkled skin and a New England biblical name Charlie could never remember, New Harbors' legal rep punched several of his buttons. Fortunately, she'd spent most of their previous meetings speaking to her, not her husband.

Which is why Charlie's hoping that Mark never got a cheek swab kit.

Only months before they'd been approved for Tia, a small box from the Boston lawyer's office had arrived via registered mail, to her only. It held a simple DNA test kit—the kind you'd use for genealogy research, though Charlie has never been curious that way. The instructions requested return of the swabs within two weeks, using the postpaid mailer.

She'd had hers out the next morning, walking it to the neighborhood post office herself: asking Mark to mail it on his way to work just felt wrong. The confirmation note that came back only acknowledged receipt of her test. Since then, she's heard nothing.

Mark shifts uneasily beside her. "Looks like we're next."

Her hands tighten on the papers in her lap, but the Boston lawyer is taking her time. Turning away from the long braid girl's mother, she checks her clipboard before moving on to Charlie and her family.

"Denver?"

Charlie passes over their paperwork without replying. Or letting Mark notice her bright yellow test receipt, which she's certain now that he wouldn't recognize.

Thin splotched fingers riffle the pages. Vaccinations, school reports, a glowing little note from Tia's swim coach. When she reaches the yellow receipt, the Boston lawyer glances up at Charlie and nods. *Approval?*

Then the papers are whisked away, exchanged for two room keys and a folded map.

"We'll be at the hotel in fifteen minutes." The Boston lawyer's gaze slides past Mark. "You're in Number Five. Your luggage will be delivered. There's a dining room to the left of the lobby; we'll all be gathering there."

Mark starts to say something, but the older woman is already moving on.

Tia squirms out of her seat immediately, returning to her new friend. Charlie pockets both keys and unfolds the map of their seaside hotel. It's a nice little place—like a bed and breakfast, or maybe a retreat center. Not cheap, this close to Labor Day weekend.

Very much not cheap, so close to the shore. New Harbors must have more funding than most nonprofits—

"So what was her problem with our paperwork?"

Charlie forces a shrug. "I have no idea. She took it, didn't she?"

She starts collecting Tia's things from her seat, the floor, and the general vicinity, but Mark is still steaming. Shoving his laptop into his carryon, her husband glares forward at the Boston lawyer's back.

His mouth moves silently. *Bitch.*

"Doesn't matter," says Charlie, under the commotion. "She got us our child."

The hotel lobby is cool and unexpectedly quiet. Aside from a squad of teenage staffers wrangling luggage carts, there's nobody but their twelve families. Even the front desk—an imposing vintage piece—is vacant, its green glass lamp dark.

Coming in, Charlie had noticed only a few cars in the parking lot: one silver BMW—the Boston lawyer's?—the rest much older. No vacationing locals. No airport rentals.

Is there anyone else here this weekend?

It seems unlikely, but there's no time to wonder. Tia is tugging her hand, wanting the nearest bathroom five minutes ago. By the time they get back, everyone else is in the dining room. Excited little-girl voices drift out. As Tia scoots inside, Charlie spots an announcement board by the half-open door.

White pushpin letters spell out this evening's events: MOTHERS & DAUGHTERS SHORE DINNER W/

SWIMMING. FATHERS SUNSET CRUISE W/ FISHING.

Dates for Saturday and Sunday are listed, but no menus or activities. Not even TBA. Charlie stares at the dusty black material, willing it to manifest something—even those dreaded birth family meetings. But, for the first time, New Harbors lets her down.

The small dining room is set up with a speaker's stand and two refreshment tables at one end. Girls and a few mothers surround one of these, fathers have gathered at the other.

Coffee or beer? She's relieved to see steaming plastic cups—and desperately needs one herself. Heading for the ladies' table, she snags coffee and two chocolate chunk cookies before looking for her family.

Tia is sitting with the long braid girl and her mother. Mark is heading her way, clutching his coffee and a printed flyer, looking irritated.

"Tonight's forced fun." He extends the trifold sheet for the fathers' cruise. "They're taking us to the boat in an hour, and I've still got to finish my bid for that Longmont job."

He scowls at the speaker's stand. "Don't forget to take notes, assuming she says anything useful."

Before Charlie can remind him that Tia misplaced her only pen, Mark is out of earshot. She glances after him, but not for long. Her eyes still remember what she saw in him, back when she was doing web design for his second company, but her heart doesn't.

Not since she first realized how disappointed he was in their daughter.

Tia is still chattering away with the long braid girl. Spotting an empty seat at that table, Charlie heads for it—and is rewarded with a grateful smile from the girl's mother.

"Are you saving this one for somebody?"

The woman barely shakes her head. Returning the smile anyway, Charlie slides in and offers a cookie. *Chocolate: the universal painkiller.*

"Sorry to barge in, but my husband brought work along. And apparently—"

"Absolutely *no* need to explain."

The other woman dunks the cookie in the last of her own coffee. They both munch in companionable silence.

"I'm Miriam," the other finally says. "From St. Louis. Long day for you, too?"

"Charlie, from Denver. And oh yeah." Charlie glances at the speaker's stand. "Think we'll find out anything tonight?"

"God, I hope so. All the stuff we had to put in our paperwork—and what was that DNA thing about, anyhow?" Miriam hesitates. "Not that I wasn't curious. I don't know a whole lot about my biological family."

"You're adopted?"

The words are out before Charlie can stop herself, and she flushes crimson.

But Miriam nods. "You, too?"

Charlie nearly chokes on the last of her cookie. "Actually, yes." She stops short, frowning. "It sounds like you already thought I might be."

"I'd just assumed we all were." Miriam glances at the next table over. Two mothers, two daughters. No dads. "We got to comparing notes, while we were waiting for our luggage. Such weird tests—and they hadn't gotten their results back, either."

Charlie hesitates. In these past few months she's gotten good at stifling suspicions.

"That lawyer didn't mention it, when she checked our paperwork."

"Yes, but—" Miriam's frown deepens. She's not letting this go. "She wasn't too impressed with me—with us—for coming on our own, OK? But when she flipped through my papers, it was like she smiled at that yellow receipt."

Charlie's still-empty stomach twists.

"I thought I saw that, too. When she was checking ours—"

She is interrupted by the dining room door closing. Above

rising little-girl chatter, she hears the click of business heels—and an impatient grumble of male voices.

Charlie reaches to quiet Tia. Miriam tugs her daughter back into her seat as a squeal of feedback sounds from the speaker's stand.

"On behalf of New Harbors, I'd like to welcome everyone to this year's family meeting. I'm so pleased to see all these thriving young girls again!"

To Charlie's surprise, the lawyer's expression doesn't look forced. She actually seems connected with these children she's helped to place. Social work skills? Or something more?

Not for the first time, she wonders if the woman belongs to this same refugee community. Hadn't she spoken with Tia briefly as they were getting off the bus?

Yes. And it had sounded a lot like twinspeak.

"Some of you have been asking about the individual meetings with your child's relatives. We're hoping to schedule those tonight. I'll be addressing this further during the mothers and daughters shore party—"

The lawyer's phone chimes softly. She glances down.

"I've just been informed that the operators of our fathers' sunset cruise are already in the lobby, with a selection of sea-fishing gear. Unless anyone brought his own equipment, all fathers are now invited to make their choices and get some pointers."

Amid the general exodus of men, Charlie digs out her own phone and texts Mark. No response.

The Boston lawyer waits until the last father is out before continuing. In the interval, Charlie listens to the AC struggle against evening heat and humidity. A few little girls have discovered that there are no more cookies, which starts a fresh round of whining.

At last the lawyer's mike goes live again.

"I won't be keeping the rest of us much longer. It's so much nicer outside tonight, and we've got plenty of burgers and seafood for our cookout. And more cookies!"

That at least tones down the whining.

"But I did want to thank you all for coming here to reconnect with your daughters' families. This means so much. As some of you may have guessed, they are the survivors of a . . . diaspora, little-known, but very real."

Some of the women nearby start murmuring in confident tones. *Global warming. Economic inequities.*

"Your choice to mother these children has not come without sacrifice." Charlie sees Miriam stiffen in her chair. "But that sacrifice also brings rewards. The opportunities you've given these girls are amazing. And so, I hope, is the effect of their love in your lives."

Charlie nods, biting her lip. Many of the women reach to hug their daughters.

Again, the Boston lawyer waits for quiet.

"I'm sure that all of you experienced an immediate connection when you first held your daughters. Perhaps you saw this as a natural part of motherhood. And perhaps you expected the same of your girls' fathers."

A few mouths tighten in confirmation. No one is smiling.

"Unfortunately, such hopes are rarely fulfilled. The offspring of this diaspora are unlike other American children. Their talents, their temperaments—even, to some extent, their appearance—set them apart."

Her gaze sweeps the room.

"For many adoptive fathers, the challenge is too great, the distance from conventional expectations too far. Although still present in the household—"

Miriam's mouth moves silently.

"—they are absent from the vital lives of their daughters. And many of you blame yourselves for this."

In the silence that follows, the room's AC falters and fails. Mercifully, all the cookie-stuffed children are slumping toward naptime.

"Which you should not!"

The Boston lawyer watches the effect of this on her audience. None of the little girls are dozing now. Even Tia the irrepressible reaches for her mother.

Holding her close, Charlie glares at the speaker—until she notices the flash of yellow in her hand.

"You see," the Boston lawyer continues, more softly, "there's a reason why all of you bonded so strongly to your precious daughters. And I am truly sorry that New Harbors must resort to such methods"—she holds up the test receipt—"to confirm what I sensed from our first interviews."

Charlie's mood shifts to confusion. Rising exclamations all around say she's not alone.

"Each of you, to some extent, carries a trace of that same diaspora in her own genes."

The room goes quiet again. Miriam gives Charlie a small shrug. *See?*

Charlie fingers her expensively processed bob. She's spent most of her life remaking herself. From the soft honey blonde she's maintained since college to Pilates classes and flirtations with Botox, nothing about her has ever been right to begin with.

So what was she trying to erase?

"I realize this is a lot to absorb—especially without evidence. Plenty of that will be provided tonight, if you wish it. I'll have your individual results with me at the shore party."

The lawyer pauses again for a long breath.

"For now, just understand that you are more related to your daughters than you knew. And, at some level, to one another. The family gathering you came for starts tonight...sisters."

The last word seems to release their voices. Caught in a snarl of conversations, Charlie wonders how many others here grew up alone. No brothers, no sisters—and, at least in her case, no answers.

Mark has never understood how anyone could be fine with open adoption. But now, despite her misgivings, she is.

Miriam just shakes her head. "So *that's* the big secret."

She doesn't look too unhappy about it, though. And Tia and her new friend are giggling with excitement. Sisters!

"We'll be discussing this further at the shore party," the Boston lawyer finally says, as the room quiets down. "For now, please finish your refreshments. There will be changing tents and towels provided, so just pack up your swim things to bring along. We'll be departing from the lobby in half an hour—"

She checks her phone again. "—or thereabouts. There's been a slight delay."

Without further explanation, she shuts off her microphone and heads for Charlie and Miriam's table.

Oh, crap. "Is there a problem?"

"I'm afraid there is, Charlotte."

Nobody's called her *that* since she was ten. Charlie waits for the rest of it.

"We only have one bus tonight, and our cruise operators must deliver their clients to the boat before the rest of us can go anywhere. Your husband seems to be delayed."

"I can text him again."

Even as she says it, Charlie knows it's not going to fly.

"I'd really appreciate you checking on him yourself. This cruise is an important part of the weekend's activities, and all fathers are expected to participate."

Miriam is looking deeply uncomfortable. Recalling her comments earlier, Charlie stifles a flash of anger on her behalf.

How 'important' could a party boat possibly be?

"It's OK," says Miriam quickly. "I'll keep Tia with me. She and Janie—my daughter—seem to be hitting it off. We'll meet you in the lobby after you've sorted things out."

Been there, done that, her expression says. But the Boston lawyer is still waiting.

Charlie shrugs. "That should work."

Not having Tia along when she goes back to the room feels like a really good idea. After kissing her daughter on the head and telling her to behave, she heads for the door.

"I'll do what I can," she says over her shoulder. "No promises."

Charlie hesitates outside Number 5, room key in hand. It's an old-fashioned thing, like the dining room's announcement board. Heavy, too.

Or is she just weighing her options?

She can use the key, like a normal person. She can knock on the door of *her own damn room*. Or she can do what her gut keeps suggesting: let the Boston lawyer run her own interference. Turn away. There's still time for Mark to get to the lobby on his own, assuming he hasn't already. She can wait to grab their beach bag—

But she knows better. Mark is going nowhere unless she opens that door.

Charlie glances down the shadowed hallway. Then she eases forward to put one ear against painted wood. For a moment she's afraid the door's too solid—or too modern, with a metal core.

"*. . . no, I won't be back until late Sunday. No way around it. We'll just have to take a long lunch hour Monday . . .* "

Mark has never learned to modulate his phone voice, but she'd recognize that tone at a whisper. He'd sounded that way with her once, back when she was single and thought he was, too. Or at least waiting for his divorce to be finalized. Or—a few months into their relationship—separated and working on filing.

Turned out it was barely a trial separation. By the time she found out, he'd moved into her condo, taken her to Hawai'i (twice), and given her some serious jewelry. More importantly, he liked kids.

Just not the one he's got with me.

The call goes on long enough for her to start guessing: she's had a list in her head for months. Tia's swim team has been keeping her busy this summer, though. She's barely managed to update Mark's business sites, let alone drop by his office.

So it really could be anybody. Is she jealous, or just desperate?

You already know the answer.

Guilt twists in her as she listens for goodbye. When they'd first gotten together, had she really been so ignorant of his marital status? A liar is nothing without a willing believer. She'd been more than ready for a chance at family life—to say nothing of personal security, maybe even love.

She's always been realistic about that last, though apparently not enough. And not nearly so much as his ex. She's spoken to the woman exactly once, early on, when she picked up without checking Caller ID.

"He likes new things."

No tears. No shouting. A crisp, clear, utterly flat voice.

"You need to understand that. Because you're the new thing—for now."

Years later, the words still stain her mind. Tia's not here to remind her why she stayed anyhow, and the hallway's unlikely to remain empty. Charlie forces herself to focus.

"...just have a little patience, that's all. Can you do that? For us?" A long pause. *"Yes, of course I love you. It's not going to be much longer."*

The key in Charlie's hand is cold as dead dreams. Clutching it tightly, she eases away until she can risk one deep breath.

Two.

Three.

She unlocks the door and walks in.

Almost before dinner is over, all twelve little girls are back in the shallows, splashing and chattering away—mostly in that odd private language Charlie's noticed. She's reluctant to mention it to anyone else, though, for fear of sounding crazy. Or racist?

"You need more wine."

Miriam is making the rounds with a freshly opened Pinot gris, and Charlie extends her glass gratefully. If nothing else, the Boston lawyer has excellent taste. Tonight's hamburgers, hot dogs, and crab cakes with fixings were accompanied by two coolers: one with juice boxes, the other with a nice assortment of whites and rosé.

This rough shoreline is unlike any beach she's ever known, but it's pleasant enough on a late August evening. Plenty of rocks for seating near the water, with an incredible sunset just starting. Somewhere in the distance, the fathers' party boat turns slowly back toward shore.

"So what happened with your husband?" Miriam asks. "Did you get him out the door?"

Charlie nods. Sips. Keeps sipping.

Convincing Mark hadn't been hard. He was rising and pocketing his phone before she'd even closed the door.

Their eyes hadn't met. He at least suspected what she'd overheard, and she knew better than to confront him. With two college-age sons to consider, she doubted he'd offer much support for Tia once things went south. His lawyer was undoubtedly better than anyone she could scrounge up.

Because practice makes perfect.

"That bad, huh?"

Miriam's comment pulls her attention back to her glass. Charlie sets it down empty.

"I still can't figure out what the problem was with that cruise," Miriam continues. "You'd think they'd be happy having fewer dads to pay for. All three of us"—her gaze indicates the other single moms—"told New Harbors about our situation, in advance."

Charlie shrugs. "They're not into explaining. Even about those DNA results—"

"Yeah, really."

Just returned from her own one-on-one conference, another woman waves her yellow form. "Did anybody understand this? She talked about genetic markers and autosomal DNA, but all I got was that we're all slightly related."

She rolls her eyes. "Because a handful of immigrants originally from some Polynesian—I *think*—island got kicked out of New England generations ago."

Charlie glances around at the other moms. They're a pretty diverse bunch, but nobody looks Polynesian. Still, she's guessing the rest of them don't know, either. Even those who—like herself—tested higher for those very special immigrant genes.

When the Boston lawyer gets back with her own wine, maybe it's time for group Q and A—

"Hey! Janie! Get back here, sweetie!"

Miriam is on her feet, waving at her daughter as she paddles out of the shallows, long braid streaming behind her. The others are all farther from shore, too—though it's not as if they can't swim. From what Charlie's been hearing, this whole bunch were almost born knowing.

Peeling off her T-shirt, Miriam heads for the water anyway.

"Janie!"

But Janie's not stopping. Head up, stroking efficiently, she looks for all the world like a determined otter. The other girls aren't splashing around any more. They've gone quiet and alert, looking out at the waves past Janie, pointing. Listening?

Now Tia's paddling after her friend, leading the rest as they leave the safe shallows, following Janie and her shining braid. Heading for whatever they've been looking at in the water.

And still, unmistakably, listening.

"Tia!"

Charlie fumbles with the buttons on Mark's old shirt, then rips it off and runs into the ocean. All around her, women are shouting for their daughters—or for the Boston lawyer, who still hasn't shown—but she's not waiting. She's been hitting the gym these past few years, and she captained her high school swim team. Tia and the others are coming back with her, right now.

Just ahead of the swimming children, a thin mist rises over the waves.

Y'ha-nthlei . . .

It's a whisper in her mind. A vague, rippling image of massive structures deep underwater. Maybe a city. There are more words,

93

but not in any language Charlie recognizes—until she does. *Twinspeak.*

She stops swimming and treads water, glancing around. Is anyone else hearing this? Miriam and the rest of the mothers are far behind her, some struggling. Ahead, all twelve little girls paddle steadily toward the rising mist.

And there's something inside that mist now.

Something big.

Raw mother-terror starts Charlie swimming again, heading for Tia at full speed. The whisper in her mind is now a deep, full-throated female voice, still speaking that language she shouldn't understand.

O my daughters, your true home in Y'ha-nthlei awaits you . . .

Cries of surprise and delight from the little girls ahead. A few panicked yelps from the moms behind. Charlie blocks out both, focused on reaching her daughter before whatever's rising with the mist turns dangerous. Has anyone else even seen it? The party boat was out there, somewhere, just minutes ago.

". . . the dry world above has turned bitter. Defiled. No longer wholesome. No longer welcoming to our ageless blood. O my daughters, return and be known . . ."

Charlie's breath comes more easily. Her heart slows, steadying into a rhythm that drives her through the waves. She's hearing no more alarm from the rest of the mothers. When she glances back to check, though, there's a figure standing on shore, arms lifted to the sunset sky. Maybe chanting. Or praying?

Too far away to be sure, but her gut says she was right about the Boston lawyer.

And very wrong about the nature of that diaspora.

She's almost caught up with the children when the mist starts clearing—or perhaps her eyes have just gotten better at penetrating it. Talk about mixed blessings. Even with that mindvoice wrapping itself around her freaked synapses, Charlie knows she's never seen anything even remotely like what's rising from the ocean ahead. She just hopes she's not the only one seeing it.

"Tia!"

Her call triggers a chorus from the others behind her. None of their daughters are stopping, though. Not even as the apparition's head emerges fully from the waves, shaking water in all directions from its iridescent spiked crest.

Her spiked crest.

Surely nothing so aquatic should have breasts? *But mothers do.* As she catches up to the cluster of little girls, threading her way through to her own child, Charlie knows for certain that this is a mother. A mother whose outstretched arms end in webbed, scythe-clawed hands, sweeping outward in welcome and love.

A single gigantic wave from that gesture swamps the returning party boat. It starts sinking before anyone on board has a chance to take action. As the men's shouts rise on the evening wind, the apparition lifts her arms skyward. A burst of ... song? ... emerges from the wide slash of her mouth.

I should feel something.

But that voice is still wrapping her mind, calling Charlie close to her daughter and the rest of the girls. To the other women catching up now, swimming for their own daughters without a moment's hesitation.

Maybe all our lives were alike. She takes a shuddering breath and reaches for Tia. Her daughter's small, strong hand catches hers, gripping tight. She feels new delicate tissue between those fingers—

Charlie glances from her daughter to the waiting apparition.

"Sweetheart, who is she?"

Tia giggles. "You're silly, Mom. That's Grandma!"

Or possibly great-great-how-many-greats-grandmother? But the difference doesn't matter in the language she and Tia are speaking, just as it doesn't matter that Tia's grasp is pulling her underwater. Drawing in a last lungful of air, Charlie squeezes her daughter's hand and follows.

Wherever they are going, they will both be all right.

 THE LIME KILN

Geoffrey Reiter

Geoffrey Reiter is Associate Professor and Coordinator of Literature at Lancaster Bible College and Associate Editor at the website Christ and Pop Culture, where he frequently writes about weird horror and dark fantasy. As a weird fiction scholar, Reiter has published academic articles on such authors as Arthur Machen, Bram Stoker, Clark Ashton Smith, and William Hope Hodgson. His poetry and fiction have previously appeared in Spectral Realms, Star*Line, Penumbra, ParABnormal, *and* The Mythic Circle.

ESTHER GOOD ADJUSTED THE PINS ON THE THIN lace oblong of her head covering one more time before checking her phone to see if anyone had texted her, but there were no new messages. Tugging at her T-shirt, she sat down on a half-rotted oak stump and reached over her striped skirt to double-knot the laces of her sneakers, then began her pacing once again. Isaiah was only ten minutes late, but he was usually early, so her heart raced even faster than it would during a *normal* day with him.

To pass the time, she looked around her, observing more closely than she ever had the features of the forest. She heard the sharp, lyrical fluting of robins and the unhurried, unembarrassed rush of the creek deeper in—the perennial chorus of a south Lancaster spring. Her eye caught a web, diaphanous and glistening in splinters of sunlight. A spider was approaching from its perimeter toward the center, where a lone wasp lay, beating its wings. To her surprise, with a twist of its torso the wasp tore through the sticky filaments, thrusting its stinger into the spider's body, again and again and again, until the paralyzed spider folded in upon itself and became the prey.

She watched with grotesque fascination until a strange sensation pulled at her attention, a ripple through the breeze like a sharp whisper. Out of the corner of her eye she thought she saw an unnaturally violet shade, but when she turned, only the deep green of the wood met her view. The odd noise was gone, and all she could hear was a typical Susquehanna wind, and now her heart beating above it.

"Esther."

She turned with a start to the north; she hadn't expected him from that direction, for the little patch of gravel where she had parked was south of the woods. He emerged though a thick crowd of chokeberry shrubs, his favorite faded red T-shirt standing out from the green and the brown. His face bore its usual wry, lopsided smile within the thin frame of his ruddy, freshly shaved countenance. Not for the first time did she wonder what it might be like to kiss those dry, wryly smiling lips.

"Were you trying to scare me?" she asked, arms crossed, channeling her energies into a gaudily artificial scowl.

"I found it," he replied. "Through the woods that way. I'll show you in a minute."

She raised an eyebrow. "Seriously? I'm impressed, Mr. Yoder. I figured it had collapsed after all these years. Show me! We've only got a few hours before volleyball at the church."

"Yeah, sure. It's not far this way. But I wanted to show you something else first."

He fished around in the pocket of his jeans. They were tight on him—*Not their least endearing feature,* she thought—and it took him an awkward moment before he could get what he was fumbling for. At last he pulled out a pendant, shining in the sunlight that trickled through the trees into the woods, which he placed gingerly in her hand. She held it up into the morning light and saw on the end of a necklace the glinting form of a dove, sculpted from tin, its wings spread as though in embrace of the sky.

"Isaiah, where did you get this?"

He shrugged. "I made it. Mr. Zook let me use the equipment after my shifts were finished. He's not *that* bad, you know." He hesitated, looked around at the trees as if listening to them, then added, "I wanted to give you something memorable, and I figured you'd probably be okay with it, but maybe it's too much like jewelry. I don't know what your folks would think. It's not a *ring* or anything, but you don't need to wear it if you don't want, you know. It's just, I was planning for today to— Oh, crap, this is all turning out wrong."

Esther pulled a stray strand of earth-brown hair away from her hazel eyes so she could look at him. He was breathing deeply, and his usually steady arms appeared to be trembling. "Isaiah Yoder, are you asking me to marry you?"

He nodded, seemingly relieved that she had understood him. "I don't think I'm doing it very well, not like how I practiced it, but yeah. Um, Esther Good, will you marry me?"

She handed the dove pendant back to him. "Here, help me put this on." She brought her shirt collar below the line of her clavicle and, lowering her head, used her left hand to pull to one side some rebellious wisps of hair that had slipped from her bun, leaving the nape of her neck bare. With care and precision, even reverence, Isaiah fastened the necklace in place. Esther paused, caught in the moment like a bird on a breeze; then she let her hair fall back down and turned to face him. The smile burst from her mouth, inevitable as the rising sun. "Yes, I'll marry you." She almost added, "You big idiot," since that is what she'd usually say, and she knew he'd receive it in good humor. But she also knew somehow that this was a distinct time, a time for solemnity to leaven her joy.

She pulled out her phone. "Okay, we need a selfie. Just for us, no one else."

Isaiah smiled gamely and crouched beside her on the left. She stretched out a hand toward a clearing in the trees until they were both in the frame, and then took the picture. The lighting was uneven, a swath of shade dimming the right-hand side of the image, but their faces showed clear enough through.

"Now," she added, "are you going to show me what you found?"

He grinned eagerly. "Yeah, it's this way." He led her through the underbrush, for there were no trails here. They walked past posted signs reading "Private Property: No Trespassing," though she couldn't see any fences or boundary markers.

"Who owns this land?" she asked.

"Technically, I think it's the Brubakers'. Hank Brubaker, not Abram. But he's too old to do anything with it, so he's going to pass it on to the township. He wouldn't mind me being here. And it's the perfect time to check it out, before anyone from the Historical Society gets the chance to explore. We should have plenty of time before volleyball."

Here the grade of the ground sloped sharply, fading clusters of henbit and deadnettle crowding a declivity of dry dirt over an outcropping. Isaiah took Esther's hand and helped her down to the next tier. As the soles of her sneakers found purchase, she glared playfully at him, one hand on her hip while she left the other in his.

"Isaiah, do you really believe I care that much about volleyball? On a day like this?"

"I never underestimate how seriously you take your volleyball," he responded. "What would a weekend look like if Esther Good didn't get in a few kills?"

"It can wait," she insisted. "We're engaged. Let's just enjoy that. And . . ."

"And?"

"And so you found it? There's really a lime kiln?" she inquired excitedly.

"Yeah."

"And is it a double kiln?"

He nodded. "Just like you said."

Esther thought the day couldn't get better. Since she was in diapers, she had been listening to her grandfather talk about the history of the area. As a girl she would scutter off as soon as her chores were done and start digging in the back yard, convinced that a relic of her ancestors lay one more dig beneath the grass or the soil, even just an old coin or a nail—something that would connect her across the centuries to the communion of souls that had passed before her. When she was old enough, she volunteered at any local history group she could find.

And that was how she learned about the old Wolff estate. For decades, from the waning of the eighteenth century to the dawn of the nineteenth, it stood adjacent to the property of a Zimmerman clan, but unlike the Zimmermans, the Wolffs had not emigrated for religious reasons. The reclusive Wolffs were odd neighbors for the gregarious Zimmermans, and their respective houses were almost a mile apart. But in the manner of the day, they had for practical reasons constructed a shared lime kiln on the boundary-line of their properties.

As time passed the Wolff line died out quietly, while the Zimmermans abruptly and enigmatically moved eastward shortly thereafter. The land went to the Brubakers, who for almost two centuries showed no proclivity to cultivate or develop it, a striking neglect for landowners of the day—and an irresistible mystery for Esther to solve. She was a research nerd of the sort that baffled most of her peers, and Isaiah already knew that she was as comfortable in an archive as she was in a kitchen. But today, she just wanted to see the kiln.

And then, after fifteen minutes of navigating a maze of oak and shagbark hickory, they arrived. The kiln had been built into the side of another descent in the landscape, and Esther could see why it had been lost to time. Dogwood and ferns, along with encroaching soil, had crowded from view most of the two top chambers, the great pits into which the families would have dumped large blocks of the limestone from their land. She and

Isaiah clambered down the slope side until they were looking directly at the front of the edifice. From this point it became clearly visible as an artificial structure, quarried gray stones mortared tightly together to a height of some twenty feet, with twin stoke-holes four feet high and rounded like sockets at the base. It was here that, some two centuries ago, the Zimmermans and the Wolffs would have lit the lower fires that burned the limestone poured into the chambers above until it crumbled down the shaft and became quicklime: fertilizer for their crops and protection for their wood. On one side the interior of the kiln had completely filled with detritus across the years, but the other looked clear, and Esther crouched down.

"This is it," Esther said.

"This is it," affirmed Isaiah.

Esther gave a couple quick, excited claps, then ducked further until she was able to shuffle into the open stoke-hole.

It was in that moment, as she crossed the threshold of the little portal, that everything around her shifted. A noise like a scream resounded within her temples, a scream with no voice yet agonized and seemingly without end. Her body felt as if it were suddenly caught in a strong current, though she knew she wasn't moving. But she was being immersed in *something*, in a turbulent flow of images, sensations, memories, carrying her and spinning her, not across acres but through centuries—perhaps even eons. She floundered, her limbs thrashing at the walls of the kiln, until her hand caught the steady hand of her own Isaiah, who pulled her out of the stoke-hole. Only then did she realize that she too had been screaming.

Isaiah, kneeling, held her close to his chest, stroking the hair outside her veil, as he never had done before. "Esther," he gasped uneasily, "what happened?"

She swallowed, trying to remind her lungs how to breathe again; and though it broke one of the rules they had set themselves, she let Isaiah keep holding her. Her eyes roamed the terrain, the spring's glorious eruption of growing green, and the brilliant blue sky beyond. And there before her, the cold gray frame of that hateful kiln.

"I—I know it now," she whispered, her words just barely audible above the wind and the buzz of woodland life. "The Wolffs, the Zimmermans—I know what happened here."

She was shaking, as though a January chill had caught her, but she gently removed herself from Isaiah's tender hold. Then she crawled back toward the kiln entrance. Isaiah stayed close by but didn't move to restrain her. She reached her hands into the stoke-hole, running them through recent dirt and older layers of fallen quicklime, feeling it beneath her fingernails as she dug, and there seemed a burning on her skin, though the ground was cool and dry. At last she stopped, pulling both her hands out. She held up her right hand so that she and Isaiah could see clearly: between her thumb and forefinger, still caked in a matrix of soil, was a human molar.

"She's here," Esther said. "She still here, after all these years. And so is *it*."

Isaiah's attention turned from the tooth to Esther's face, and she looked back into his eyes, blue as the sky. "What are you talking about?" he asked softly.

She gingerly placed the tooth on the ground beside the kiln, then took his face in her hands. "I love you, Isaiah," she declared, as she had so often before, but she had never uttered the words with true urgency, with the thought that these words were sacred and cosmic. "You know me. You know who I am. Can you trust me?"

"I mean, sure, yeah. But what are you . . . ?" Then peering at her, at the resolve that now glowed like a nimbus from her round face, he said simply, "I love you, Esther, and I trust you."

She nodded, rising to her feet. She held out a hand and helped him stand beside her. "Thank you," she sighed. "I promise I'll explain it to you while we walk."

"Where are we going?"

"To the Wolff house."

"Why are we going there? We just got here," he began, but Esther was already moving. He scrambled up the slope into which the kiln had been built, trying to keep up with her. Soon they had ascended back to the ledge upon which they had stood together just a few minutes earlier. She forged out in a different direction, westward through pathless oak and hickory and crowding shrubs.

"Jerusha Zimmerman," Esther said once they were passing through more level land. "She was seventeen, living with her family on the homestead here, two hundred years ago."

"You never told me about her."

"I didn't know," Esther replied. "No one knew. I learned just now, down there in the lime kiln." She didn't stop but turned to Isaiah beside her as they walked. "When I stepped in there, it all poured in on me. She shared with me her memories, her experiences, her desires. For a moment I knew everything she had known."

"You met—what, her ghost?"

Esther drew in a breath nervously. "I didn't want to say the word because . . . because I was afraid if I did, you'd think I was crazy."

Isaiah reached out and took her hand, and they paused their trek. Once more she peered at him with iridescent eyes, lips parted as if she would say more. She searched for mockery or incredulity, for a caustic grin fluttering at the corners of his mouth. But his slightly angular features and his wide, clear eyes were firm.

"Esther, you're about the smartest—and the wisest—person I know. You're a step ahead of me every day. I'm just a welder from Providence Township. I meant it—I trust you." He turned back toward the wood and resumed walking. "So let's get going, and you tell me about Jerusha Zimmerman."

Jerusha Zimmerman, hair pouring like maple syrup, snuck away from the house as sunset neared, looking for Julian. She knew his father would be out at town, and she sighed in relief to think of it, her breath clouding into the cold early evening. Gregor Wolff frightened her, with his wild wide brown eyes and billowing, tumultuous white beard. When she saw him outside, he so often seemed to be scanning the land, sunken in an abstruse gloom; when he was in the house, she sometimes heard him muttering syllables in some tongue that was not English or German or Dutch.

How unlike Gregor was his son, willowy Julian, shining hair like an alchemy of blent gold and silver, free of word and mien, relentlessly curious. Jerusha knew that her father mistrusted the Wolffs; though he joined funds with them years ago for the building of the kiln, he did not know their faith and held in scorn any who would not work their fields with their own weather-beaten hands. Why he even tolerated them, she could not say.

Lantern in hand for the journey back, Jerusha approached the Wolff house, its two-story masonry looking almost like a castle on its hill, set against the blazing scald of the orange sun behind it. Most of the windows were dark, save a guttering sprig of luminescence in one on the first floor. She walked to the east-side entrance, casting glances about in the hope that she might not be seen by their servants. Then she opened the door, which, new-oiled, did not creak on its hinges. The little light was coming from the family's study—a vain extravagance, her father would think—into which she strode with caution and confidence.

The room seemed empty at first, no movement save the pale, frolicking flame of a candle on the desk. But Jerusha perceived more light deeper in, seemingly sourceless, and then she saw that it was emanating from the back wall. A shelf of books had been displaced—it was, she realized, a door, behind which were stairs that led down, beneath the first floor of the Wolff house and into the marrow of the hill. She had ever been wily, but never hesitant, and with care she quietly peeked down the steps and into the glowing cellar.

Here were books, ancient books with flaking, weathered spines whose musty smell of centuries wafted with the scent of candle-smoke up to her nose. On shelves they ringed the small room in a riot of brown, the brown of dry, fallow soil. A small, simple table stood in the center, its surface concealed by books and papers, and sitting at the table, his fair hair gleaming, was the man she sought.

"Julian!" she exclaimed, enthralled, for she had half feared she would see his father. She loped down the stairs as he looked up from his books, smiling, his crystal eyes hidden in the sheening glass of his spectacles.

"My darling Jerusha," he said, "have you come all this way for me?"

"Of course. What else might bring me hence?"

He closed the book he had been reading, wisping atomies of dust into the air as he did. Removing his spectacles, he seized her hand. "Then let us make the most of our time."

Esther's strides ceased abruptly, and she looked around her at the great overstory of oak and maple.

"Have you actually *been* to the Wolff house, Isaiah?" she inquired.

He shook his head. "No. Why? It seemed like you knew where it was."

"I know the land as Jerusha knew it, which was different. And I'm still trying to fit together everything she was showing me."

A movement caught their eye, and both Isaiah and Esther turned their attention northwest. Through the trees, some fifteen yards distant, they saw a strange glow well up like a pustule in the air. It came as a distension of dark purple light—not the purple of royalty or of exquisite storm-clearing sunsets but the purple of a bruise, swelling with sour and sticky infection. Then, seconds later, it burst, and the wood was clear again. Yet not quite clear, for the whole atmosphere it left behind it looked altered in some unnamable way, and they could see little deaths within its ambit—spring leaves now autumn-crisp, bark peeling like burnt skin, bees tumbling unceremoniously out of the sky, a gray-yellow warbler plummeting stiffly to the ground.

At once Esther was walking again, tugging at Isaiah's shirt as she did.

"Do you know where the house is, then?" he asked. His baffled gaze still lingered on the aftermath of the bizarre disruption, but he never failed at keeping in stride with her.

"I'm not sure, but I hope so," she answered. "We have to hurry. It's breaking free."

"Meet me at dawn at the lime kiln," Julian had said to her. Father was already feeding the animals, so Jerusha could creep out of the house without raising much concern. It was even colder than last evening, and the stars were fading as black sky washed into deep blue, with a blush of white on the eastern horizon. Lantern in hand, she carefully edged down, the frosty dirt crunching beneath her feet.

True to his word, Julian stood by the mouth of the kiln's upper chamber, where a thick vapor rose in the frigid air. He was smiling as he helped her down to his level, and the touch of his hand was warm upon her cold fingers. He lifted her chin with his other hand, lightly kissing her lips, and she could smell the bacon of his breakfast on his breath.

"Thank you for coming, my dearest," he said. "I did not know if you would."

"I fain would travel anywhere for you, Julian," she replied.

He nodded. "That is well." Licking his lips, he added, "I had not expected to see you last night. Perhaps it was fortuitous, portending great things . . . though not as I once had hoped."

She regarded him quizzically, puzzling out his cryptic words. And then, without warning, there was a tugging at her arm, and by the time she knew that Julian was pulling her, it was too late. He thrust her toward the great column of pallid smoke until she plummeted into the vertical shaft of the kiln, and all she had time to think was, How can this be? Why would he do such a thing? *Then the ghastliness of the pains took hold—the yielding of bone as her feet hit the pile of limestone fragments, the choking stench of the gases invading her lungs, the horrific mindless burning as the flame from the stoke-hole beneath her rose through her flesh. There was nothing to see, nothing to do, in those mindless minutes but flail uselessly in the agony of her blinding, senseless death.*

The Wolff house stood at the crest of a small hill when they found it. From afar it appeared as Jerusha would have seen it, but the landscape was altered. The chestnut trees had died out decades ago, leaving a vacant gap gouged out of the forest, and the grass was tall and unruly. Any trace of the track on which their carriages would have driven had long since been swallowed up by an orgy of weeds.

Esther could see Isaiah's disgust as she told him what she knew. He held her back when she spoke of Jerusha's death, a sickly pallor across his usually suntanned face.

"What happened to her . . . Is that what you felt when you went into the kiln?"

Esther looked up into his eyes and nodded.

"But I don't understand. I mean, why?"

Once again she started walking. "We have to keep moving," she insisted. "Julian and his father, they were both . . . sorcerers, I guess you'd call them. They learned some kind of magic from these old books they had. But they used it in different ways. Gregor Wolff just wanted some land to be farmed, and when he came to Pennsylvania he found this little patch that no one had claimed, and no one wanted to. And there was a reason no one wanted to."

"What kind of reason?" Isaiah asked as they began the climb toward the brow of the hill and the house. The closer they came, the more the wear of the centuries stood out in crumbling masonry and lichenous fractals.

"There was something here already," Esther replied. "Something old, something not part of our earth but that had lived here for . . . a really long time. A monster, or a force. Isaiah, I don't know what kind of word to use for it. Whatever it was, it scared people away. So Gregor did some kind of magic, and he trapped it, and then the land was safe and good for a farmer. And cheap, which is probably why Levi Zimmerman jumped in next door."

"But what about Julian?" Isaiah persisted.

As they continued further up, leaving the thickest trees behind them, Esther said, "Julian didn't just want a quiet farm as his father did. That thing—it was powerful, and he thought he could catch it and use its power. He wanted to be some kind of great man, to do whatever he wanted. But for that kind of magic, he needed . . . " She trailed off, choking back the panic that filled her as she remembered the appalling betrayal of Jerusha, which Esther had known and felt herself. ". . . a sacrifice. He needed a sacrifice."

When they reached the house, they found it boarded up, a padlock on the door, its windows occluded by planks, like obols on the eyes of the dead. But the boards had been put in place years ago, and Isaiah soon found one that was rotting at the screws. He and Esther stuck their fingers into the gap where the cheap wood had curled from moisture and time, and together they pulled. With a splintering sound the obstruction gave way, falling to the overgrown grass below. Isaiah kicked out the remaining glass, and the two crawled into the window. They set their phones to flashlight mode and walked into the Wolff house, the first people in years to breathe its oppressive air.

Esther knew others had entered it since the day Jerusha died, yet the dark interior looked surprisingly as it had then, for most of the old furniture remained. But it was an enclave of frayed shadows now, as the bright blue-white light from their phones caught scalene angles and great tapestries of cobwebs. Immense, long-concealed spiders scurried away from the light, and Esther could hear the burbling crack of their bodies being crushed beneath her shoes as she advanced. Perhaps a day ago the seething teeming of lightless life would have disgusted her, but now she had known horrors far worse than any scuttling arthropods.

Isaiah coughed from breathing in the dust, but he stifled the noise, looking hesitantly around. Esther marched forward into the study until she found the shelf on the back wall. She carefully set her phone on the filmy floor and began to tug, but it held fast.

Isaiah saw what she was doing and set his phone down beside hers. Together they pulled, yet without effect.

"Wait," Isaiah told her.

Grabbing his phone, he shone the light closely at the shelf until he found a tiny latch, concealed behind a moldering book. With a little jiggling it came free, and the shelf door swung open on its hidden hinges. Esther already had her own phone ready, and she descended the stairs into the Wolff house's cellar, Isaiah a step behind her.

Here was a wealth of arcane lore, the dark researches of millennia, now crumbling like stale bread in their rows along the walls. The work of Gregor's life, and his son's obsession, the envy of any true magician, were yielding to time and humidity and worms and bacteria—to the ineluctable procession of nature that the younger Wolff had striven so hard to conquer.

In the center of the cellar and its ring of disintegrating lore was a simple table. Lying head down at the table was a body, dressed in a rotting wine-dark tailcoat with bone buttons over a waistcoat and linen shirt. The features of the corpse were remarkably well preserved; the skin was pale as chalk, though dry and rubbery, but Esther could see no sign of putrefaction. And the face was one she now knew all too well.

"Julian Wolff," she said.

It did not end with her death—she moved from one terror into another. As Jerusha's flesh crumbled with the quicklime, her soul remained, ensnared once again by Julian's ravening, thirsting cruelty. He had woven a great web of words, casting them forth to trap the fetid power that had stalked these lands for five thousand ages. That net, when at last released, caught more than the entity toward which it had been thrown—it caught and held Jerusha too.

She was stuck, the core of her self now tangled in the tacky filaments of her lover's incantations. The elder thing thrashed against its restraints, but what could Jerusha, once a girl on the cusp of young womanhood, do against such magic? She squirmed and twitched, but the cords held fast.

And so, that which endured of Jerusha Zimmerman could do nothing but wait and exist and learn, in the dread education of the centuries. She felt impossibly small beside the vast bulk of the presence, yet her very smallness preserved her from worse harms, for the energies of the thing were all concentrated on shredding through Julian's web. Most days the magic held firm, but once in a while a predatory appendage would tear free into the world she had known. And day by day, year by year, the net grew slacker, more tattered. Two hundred years was an eye-blink in the time scale of this power, and soon, she knew, it would free itself wholly from Julian's ill-conceived work. But two hundred years to a human soul still seemed interminable, so Jerusha explored the strange boundaries of her new world and studied the beast beside which she was trapped. And all the while without ceasing she screamed, praying that someday her voice might be heard.

"Esther, what is going on?" Isaiah pleaded, putting an arm around her in the night-black circle of the cellar.

"He thought he could hold it," Esther murmured, casting her light on the dead man's horrified waxy face. "He thought his magic was strong enough to control a monster. He killed Jerusha because he thought he could control it." She laughed a hollow laugh, like the echo in a well. "And of course it didn't work. The thing reached out and destroyed him on the same day."

"Now what?" Isaiah asked.

Esther looked down at the table where Julian lay, its surface bare but for two objects. Beneath his left arm was a vellum volume, clutched in his stiff fingers. His right hand lay extended toward a small parchment, upon which were scrawled words in Latin and some other language. Esther breathed minimally to keep from inhaling the noxious dust that thickened the air, but she could feel the percussion of her heartbeats as the fear entered into her. She saw now what she needed to do.

She grabbed Julian's left hand and pulled at the fingers until they cracked, releasing the book, and then she picked up the sheet of paper to his right. Once more she was in motion, trusting Isaiah to keep pace as she ran upstairs and climbed out the window.

"Do you keep matches in your truck?" she queried.

"Yeah, I'm sure I've got some in the glove compartment," he told her.

"Good. We'll need them." She spared him a glance as she began running south toward his vehicle. "Julian used the book to summon that thing. But before that, this little note has the words Gregor Wolff used to restrain it in the first place. Gregor's magic isn't like Julian's magic; it's simpler, more like a prayer than a spell. Gregor never wanted to *use* the power; he just wanted to take this place back from something that never should have been here. So we need to use Gregor's words to get rid of the thing."

"I don't understand. Why not just do it here and now?"

Esther slowed a moment, her breath rasping from all the running she had been doing, but she kept going. "I wish it was that easy. But we have to remove Julian's trap first. And there's only one way to do that: to burn his book at the place where it all started."

"You mean the lime kiln."

"Yes."

Isaiah didn't ask again how Esther knew this, and she almost cried in gratitude that he didn't. She had always been studious, always seeking and learning for the sheer joy of immersing herself in the gift of the cosmos, and that quality sustained her now, but this knowledge was of a different order. It was both learned and instinctive, dripping into her soul like rainwater through layers of soil. She was also just as certain that the entity knew her plan; its malevolence stretched over her like the shadow of a looming cloud.

And then it was there. Like the claw of a tiger reaching through cage bars, the entity burst into the woods with them. It came once more with a purpling distension of the air and the earth, an ichorous discharge of dynamistic alienage. Behind her ears Esther heard a sound like a bellow or a laugh or an earthquake as her environment ruptured. It happened beside her, so quickly that she scarcely saw the moment it swallowed Isaiah. He was pushing her away from himself, and he had no more than a second to cry out in pain and fear as his body was subsumed within the entity's bourn.

She was perhaps three feet away, and she stumbled back from the rippling wall of negation. The emptiness that gouged her heart felt worse than any pain she had known on this day. Her Isaiah was simply gone. Isaiah, who shared his macaroni and cheese with her when her parents sent her to their Mennonite school with carrot sticks; who snuck out of metalworking class even though he loved it just to catch a glimpse of her at study hall; who smiled goofily without defending himself every time she teased him for tripping over his words. How much had gone into the making of him in his nineteen years, the building of the strong, muscular body she desired and the gentle, ardent spirit she loved? All so that he should be elided like an afterthought from the universe of things?

There was no time for Esther Good to think. She dropped the book and the paper and, touching a finger to the pendant around her neck, she ran into the inky blot beside her, hand outstretched. Inside, she felt a great cold—not the cold of a Lancaster December, but the cold of the great voids between galaxies, where stars cannot be seen. For some iota of time she knew earth as the entity knew it, as earth had been when the power first arrived from its own dimensional abysms in search of new prospect, prowling hot, shallow Cambrian seas amid spiny, scurrying *Olenellus* trilobites and voracious, undulating anomalocarids.

Esther felt herself plunging into the great gulf of deep space and deep time inside the primeval membranes of the hungering atrocity, and with it the awful inexorability of death that a falling person feels—until a little gleam of soul beckoned to her like a pole star. It was a dim flicker in that darkness, but any light is a victory, for darkness is only an absence, and in that glinting she could see just enough to reach forth into its maw and grab Isaiah, pulling him free from the frost and fire of the antinatural thing.

They stumbled into the sharded light of the sun sneaking through oak boughs, and Esther felt the refreshing itch of nettles on her palm as she tried to rise. Isaiah lay beside her, looking stiff and sickly, like Julian in his cellar, and, *Oh God,* she thought, *is it too late?* Kneeling down, she yanked him further from the bilious indigo beside them and, running her fingers through the curls of his rusty auburn hair, she kissed him in an agony of desperation. And in so doing she rejoiced, for those lips that had tripped so often over words now were warm lips through which hot breath was escaping.

His eyes opened, not gradually or flutteringly but wide with the horror of the deeps they had seen. But those eyes saw her, and their blue grew tranquil as a tide pool, and the lips smiled and said simply, "Esther."

Esther was weeping with the joy of it, but she was not still, for the entity had not vanished, was indeed transgressing close again upon their space. Isaiah coughed and rose unsteadily, but peering into the deep excrescence from which he had been rescued, he scrambled to his feet as Esther scooped up the book and the parchment, and they ran. By now her lungs were beginning to burn from the strain, yet she ran faster than ever, for she had known the pain of Jerusha's suffering and the primordial dismay of the universe's dark spaces, and now any earthly pain seemed dull and stagnant by comparison. Isaiah must have known it too, for he ran by her side, as they dodged maples and oaks and hickories, moved up and down sedimentary declivities. Her sneakers trod over moss and ferns and white clover, no doubt crushing spiders and caterpillars and wasps in their progress. Around them, more and more shafts of slimy violet light burst into the sylvan landscape.

Over a rise and through a dense line of white and amber honeysuckle, they emerged at the little gravel rectangle where

Isaiah's truck was parked. The windows were down, the doors unlocked, and he whipped the passenger side open so hard that it almost cracked at the hinges. He rifled through insurance cards and sundry tools and a flashlight until he found a small box of matches. Leaping down, he joined Esther as they reentered the forest.

The entity was never static around them. It might vanish from one patch of ground, leaving an incongruous scar of deathliness carved into the spring verdancy, then appear ten yards away in its shadowy pestilent glow. Every minute it probed the weakening of Julian's magic, pulling at the threads until they split. Soon it would reclaim this whole unhallowed ground as its own dominion.

But the lime kiln was not far, and soon they came to the stoke-hole at its base. Esther flung Julian's book into the pit of dirt and quicklime, turning to Isaiah.

"Get ready," she warned. "There's only one way to catch this thing, but I'll have to release it from Julian's spell first. Do you understand what I'm saying?"

He nodded. "We're setting it free."

"Exactly." She looked back to the ragged tome in the kiln and drew in one more breath. "Okay, Isaiah—light it."

He struck the match without hesitation, and an orange flame jumped to life at the end of the little stick. There was a grace in the smooth motion by which he brought forth that flame and set it to the book—if there was one thing Isaiah Yoder knew, it was fire. And the text burst forth with a violent red burning well beyond what its matter could have sustained, so hot that Esther and Isaiah had to leap back.

In seconds the book was gone, and the sky darkened at the flexing of the festering force in its sudden freedom. Holding Isaiah's hand, Esther read the words from Gregor's paper, not even comprehending them in full but uttering them like a plea or a petition, casting her voice into the void against the chaos that was swelling up on every side of them. As she was speaking, she could feel *it* gathering, drawing near, and she almost choked at the thought that it could swallow her before she had finished speaking. Yet something was holding the darkness at bay, a tiny spark in its midst, and as she read on, she knew it was the same light that had guided her out at Isaiah's rescue—it was Jerusha Zimmerman, her spirit at last free but remaining here in the kiln for one moment more to shield them from the frothing spite of the entity.

Esther spoke the last word, and now she heard a new scream—not the tortured cry that Jerusha had been wailing since her death but the hideous inhuman shriek of the cosmic interloper as it was bound once again. Esther could not know whether she had sent it to its home or its prison, or even if there was a difference between them. The echo of its hate shuddered in her soul, and its last outlashing hurt like a venomed sting. But the echo faded, and the hurt subsided, and she was now surrounded by trees and flowers and innocuous bugs and creatures of the great calm.

She shuffled further from the lime kiln and then lay on her back at the foot of it, breathing deep breaths, eyes closed, an inexplicable rest settling like a blanket upon her. How long she lay this way she couldn't say, but when at last she opened her eyes again she saw her Isaiah, lying beside her, and above them the night sky, brilliantly shining in through a round clearing in the canopy of the dark wood.

"Isaiah, are you here with me?" she whispered.

"Yeah, I am."

Past all the terrors she had seen on this day, Esther smiled. "I'm sorry we had to spend our engagement day like this."

Isaiah, still looking up, shrugged his shoulders against the cool earth. "I guess we'll never forget it," he chuckled. "We're just getting started. They say marriage is an adventure."

One hand to the necklace at her throat, she reached out the other and once more caught hold of Isaiah's. "I love you," she murmured, and they both laughed. Laughed—the woods rang with it. And together they looked up again, beyond the woods and into the piece-bright paling of sky and all its sparkling stars.

FATHER THAMES

David Hambling

David Hambling is a journalist and author. His fiction, starting with a collection, The Dulwich Horror and Others, *explores the Cthulhu Mythos in South London. He continues the theme in a number of novels including the popular Harry Stubbs adventures, set in the 1920s, and the epic fantasy* War of the God Queen, *and has previously contributed stories to the* Black Wings *anthologies. He lives in darkest Norwood, South London with his wife and cat.*

I do not know much about gods; but I think that the river
Is a strong brown god—sullen, untamed and intractable,
. . . the brown god is almost forgotten
By the dwellers in cities—ever, however, implacable.
                              —T. S. Eliot, "The Dry Salvages"

"He got this in London, I guess—he uster like ter buy things at the shops."
                              —H. P. Lovecraft, "The Picture in the House"

London, 1928

1

THE RUSH OF BOYS STAMPEDED FOR THE SCHOOL gates, yelling like little savages. I keep them under control in the classroom, but when the four o'clock bell goes I stand back and let the youthful energy explode harmlessly outwards.

A solitary man stood among the crowd of waiting mothers beyond the railings. Mr. Simpson was a bookkeeper at the pickle factory, an unassuming sort. I had met him and his wife on a couple of school occasions when she had done all the talking. Now he clutched his hat in both hands and tried to attract my attention above the babel as the stampede dispersed.

Simpson Junior was a middling student, clever but idle, and no more troublesome than the average eight-year-old. He was as puzzled by his father's presence as I was. I assumed it was something serious, that the mother had fallen ill and the boy would be out of school a few days. But he surprised me with a request.

"I don't suppose you could translate a little bit of Latin for me, Mr. Blake?" he asked hesitantly. "Just a word."

"I don't know if I'm up to that, Mr. Simpson," I said, forcing a smile. "But I can have a crack at it."

"I've got it here," he said, fumbling in his coat pocket for a piece of paper. I was expecting something legal or medical, two professions which like to obfuscate matters with great dollops of classical terminology. "Oh, blast."

The damp scrap of paper disintegrated in his fingers as he tried to unfold it. He squinted at the mess and showed it to me. I could not make out anything.

"It was just one word," he said, dismayed. "I think it began with an A."

"I'm afraid that's a little too cryptic for me," I said pleasantly.

"Look, would you do me a favour, please, Mr. Blake," he said. "I wouldn't ask normally, but he's moody, you know, and I promised I'd get it for him today. If you wouldn't mind walking five minutes with me, you could see the original. I'd be ever so grateful."

I might have told Simpson that my working day was far from over and I had schoolwork to mark and lessons to prepare. But he had the look of a mistreated dog that needed sympathy. I doubted whether his real problem was one of translation, though.

"Happy to oblige," I said.

"Run home quick now," he told the boy. "And tell Mother I'll follow shortly. I just have some business to attend to with Mr. Blake." The boy did not need to be told twice and sprinted off, satchel bouncing across his back.

"I am sorry about this," Simpson said, and indicated the way for us to walk. "It's for my friend Flint. I don't suppose you know Mr. Flint?"

"Does he have a boy at the school?"

"Oh, no, no," said Simpson. "I just thought you might . . . well, anyway. He has this Latin inscription, and I happened to mention there was a teacher at the boys' school who would know, and before I knew it he'd made me promise."

"It's really no trouble," I said. "Do you happen to know where the text is from?"

"It's just an inscription," he said. "But as for that—you'd have to ask him. I don't know anything."

Simpson was determined in his ignorance. It was not his place to know and he was nervous about Flint.

We turned off Elder Road and descended stairs to a basement flat, the sort with a front window that looks out into a trench in front of the house. Simpson opened the unlatched door without knocking and stood on the threshold.

"I've got someone with me," he said. "The boy's teacher, Mr. Blake. I thought—"

"Bring him in," came the order from the dingy interior.

We entered through a scullery that led into a kitchen, then through a narrow corridor into a living room. These labels are approximate because of the squalor and the lack of lighting. The place was as gloomy as a cave, and I followed Simpson's silhouette towards the pale light ahead.

"He doesn't have electric," Simpson explained as I felt my way into the living room.

"I'm not paying anyone for light," shouted Flint. "It's like asking a man to pay for the sun."

119

Simpson sat down, giving me a view of the speaker, seated at a table positioned by a long slot of a window. A row of battered kerosene lamps hung by him on the wall.

Flint's face had the leathery quality of one who spends his days outdoors, and could have been anything between thirty and sixty. His brown hair was greasy and slicked back, and he was by no means a handsome man, but there was something about him. Perhaps it might be best described by the Greek word *charisma*, a divine gift, not in the Christian sense of grace but of power. Flint had an innate authority to go with his confident manner.

"And I told the landlord if he wanted rent he could whistle for it," Flint went on, sounding a little drunk. "Sent him away with his tail between his legs. When the corporation send me bills, I use them to light my fire—or wipe my arse."

Simpson made a sound of affirmation, in case I should be in any doubt.

My eyes were adjusting. Simpson had taken a grubby armchair, and there was another by me. One wall was taken up by rickety homemade shelving.

"Sit yourself down, Blake," Flint told me. "Clear that lot off."

To call the room damp would be an understatement. Moisture hung in the air thick as mist, and there was a fetid odour of decay, overlaid with stale beer. It was too dark to see the walls properly, but I am sure they would have shown the signs of frequent flooding. This was a cellar meant for storage, not occupation, converted by some thrifty Victorian into servant's quarters.

The armchair was occupied by cleaning rags, stiff with dirt. I placed them on the floor, brushed off the seat, and took my place. The chair rocked on three legs.

"You'll have to excuse my manners," said Flint, a challenge not an apology. "I'm a bastard, you see. Wasn't brought up properly, so I've got no social graces."

I mumbled a polite response, but Flint was not interested. He handed me a piece of broken pottery, a disc four inches in diameter, seemingly the base of a pot. My fingers found something etched on one face. Holding it up to the light, I made out a word: "ARAVSJO."

"It says Aravsjo," said Flint. "Do you know what that means?"

"The Romans did not have separate letters for V and U," I said, trying not to sound like a teacher. "And the J is probably a variant I." A common mistake among the less-educated in the Roman provinces. "I believe the word is Arausio."

"Arausio? What's that?"

"It's the name of a town in Roman Gaul—the south of France. There was an important battle there in the second century B.C...I can't remember what the place is called now." As usual, I was stronger on ancient history than modern. "Most likely that was where this was made."

"Aravsjo, Arausio," he said, half to himself. "Never thought of that. Yes, that must be it."

"This is genuine Roman pottery," I said, turning it over. "How did you come by it?"

Flint's face split open in a grin, showing bad teeth, and he laughed. I noticed a white scar across his brown forehead.

"Where did I get it? Where did I get any of it?" He waved his arm at the shelving.

The shelves, just wooden planks resting on bricks, were crammed with small items of broken pottery, hundreds of them. They were arranged by colour and style: a row of Victorian bottles on one shelf, red glazed fragments on another, blue pottery on a third. There was enough to fill a museum, although it seemed to be entirely broken fragments.

Flint and Simpson were both laughing. I laughed along without knowing why.

"Flint's a mudlark," said Simpson.

"I take what the river gives," said Flint, still laughing. "That's how I make my living."

I had heard of these men, occasionally saw one or two when I was crossing Cannon Street bridge. They poked around on the foreshore of the River Thames at low tide, scavenging for whatever they could find, getting fresh pickings uncovered each day.

Other European capitals have tamed and trammeled their rivers, but the Thames still breathes freely; its daily inhalations and exhalations of sea water leave an expanse of mud on the river banks at low tide. These stir the mud daily so people like Flint could keep making fresh finds.

"He's got a licence," Simpson assured me.

Flint poured a bottle of beer into three cracked mugs. He passed one to Simpson, who took it without a word, and one to me. The mug was filthy, and I could have refused, but Flint was not one you could easily refuse. Nor did I want to give him an excuse to jeer at me for being prissy. I wiped the rim with my handkerchief, though, and let him see me doing it.

"Cheers," said Flint and we drank. "Simpson likes to come here for a drink. His wife don't let him drink at home."

Simpson smiled feebly.

"I never knew you could find so many antiquities on the Thames," I said.

"Enough to keep a man in beer," said Flint. "Whole pieces are rare, you've got to stick bits together . . . The river teases you, giving you one piece here, one piece there. I'll find the rest of Arausio, though, give me time."

"Can you really find all the pieces of an object?"

"I can," he said, the emphasis on "I," and showed me the item he had been looking at when we came in. It was a white clay pipe, from the Regency era. The stem was broken off two inches from the bowl, which was cast in the shape of a crowned head.

"Now this stem here joins with that," Flint said, attaching a narrow six-inch pipestem. "And if you can find the mouthpiece and make it whole—then that's worth something."

"Flint's a wonder for sticking things together," said Simpson.

"Invisible mending," said Flint, passing me another pipe, a complete one. "You can't see the joins, can you? I have a special recipe for the glue."

The light was not good, but there was no sign the pipe had ever been broken. It was a clever piece of work. Flint rose in my estimation.

"If you like it—it's yours!" he said. "Show that to your pupils, teacher. But mind, the stems break easy."

"Thank you—thank you very much, I shall. So you sell these . . . Who buys them?"

"People," Flint said stiffly, as though it was a trade secret. But a second later he relaxed. "Little antique shops. Collectors. University men. People who buy know others who buy, you soon find them."

"I'm impressed," I said, and I was. I had visited a couple of archaeological digs and the few fragments they had found were a pitiful show compared to the wealth of antiquities piled up around us by this rough man.

"You have to know what to look for and where to look and when," said Flint complacently. "An unskilled man like you would miss nine-tenths of it. And the timing: the river comes and goes, comes and goes, gives and it takes."

"A tidal range of twenty-three feet at London Bridge, I believe."

Hard to believe there was Roman pottery still coming to light two thousand years later, but I had heard of such finds before.

"There's an ugly side too. Drowned dogs. And dead bodies too, pale clammy things. Men like me never drown, but people who didn't respect the river, that's what happens. They sink, then they bloat, you see, and float up after a few days. Some of them don't hardly look human when they wash up. We get a few shillings for reporting them," he said with relish.

"Ugh," said Simpson, pulling a face. "I don't know how you bear it, Flint."

"I did not know they offered a bounty," I said.

"Not officially." Flint smirked. "But if they don't want bodies just to disappear again, they know they have to give us a tip. But that's not the best of it. You know what is?"

I shrugged.

"The day after a body, you always find more. That's the river's way: it takes and it gives. Sacrifice is repaid."

He leered, and I was nettled equally by the crude superstition and by his glee in profiting from the misfortune of others.

"You probably find bodies when there's some particular tidal agitation," I said. "That's probably the connection."

"Schoolteachers," said Flint, flashing anger, a lifetime of resentment in those three syllables. "What do you know except the rod?"

There was no point in telling him that I believed in modern educational principles, that I was not one of that Victorian breed—still all too common—who kept their charges in order with the strap and the cane and terrorize rather than educating. Flint's schooldays had not been happy. As the shoot is bent, so it grows. Those who are misused go on to misuse others. But I thought I might deflect his anger.

"All I know is how ignorant I am," I said mildly, nodding at the shelves of pottery. "Why, I imagine you could tell me a lot I don't know, show me remarkable things."

I had pegged Flint as an egotist, and I was not wrong about his weakness for an audience. The anger melted and Flint proudly produced a cigar box which he rattled it in front of me.

"From the river. Know what these are?"

I shook my head, and he passed me the box. Light glimmered off clear red stones, tiny as insects but exquisitely coloured.

"Treasure," said Simpson.

"Not . . . rubies?" I hazarded.

"Thames garnets," said Flint. "Aren't they beauties?"

"They are amazing," I said. I wanted to take one out of the box for a better look, but feared to provoke him. The stones were to him as other men's wives were to them: something to be shown off to others, but never touched. "Where do they come from? I mean," I amended hastily, "not where on the river, but where originally?"

"You're a schoolteacher and you don't know that," he said happily, taking the box back.

"I've no idea," I said.

"Sacrifices," he said. "People gave their jewels to the river—in olden days. People made sacrifices to the river and he rewarded his faithful."

"Well, I have learned something today," I said, thinking I must look up Thames garnets and where they really came from.

"You teach Simpson's boy," said Flint. "The sooner he leaves school and books behind for a man's job the better. I'm teaching him gleaning to make a living. You're wasting his time with trigonometry and nonsense. Let him go."

"School is compulsory now till fourteen," said Simpson, jumping in. "That's right, isn't it, Mr. Blake? It's the law now."

"What if the boy bunks off school and doesn't come back?" Flint asked me.

"I'm afraid someone from the school board will come and bring him back," I said.

"When he's fourteen he'll be free," said Simpson. "Until then my hands are tied, just like Mr. Blake says."

"You think he's too good for river work," Flint sneered at Simpson. "You want him to be a pen-pusher, tied to a desk all day."

I could see they had played out this scene before.

"Am I right in thinking these pieces are sixteenth century?" I asked, indicating tile fragments with a serpent motif.

"Early mediaeval, prob'ly thirteenth century," Flint corrected. He went on to explain how the different colours and textures of glaze showed the origin. He was off and running, and the rest of the visit was a monologue. Some of it was interesting, and he was certainly well informed. I was more than pleased, though, when Flint drained his mug and decided it was time for us to go. I held the fragile pipe in my hand; Flint did not offer to shake.

"I can't thank you enough, Mr. Blake," Simpson said when we were back on the street. "Flint doesn't show it, but he appreciated your Latin. That piece he found is something important—there aren't many he'll share beer with or give a pipe for free. He's not as bad as he seems."

"I was glad to help."

There had been no swearing, no threats, and no violence. Plenty like him held grudges against all schoolteachers which came out with drink.

"He really is a bastard, you know—illegitimate, I mean."

It was all the same to me and I said so, but Simpson wanted to get something off his chest.

"He told me about a girl who worked on the river. One night she looked into the water and saw something shiny glimmering up at her. When she tried to fetch it she fell and got swept away. They thought she'd drowned, but she washed up downriver the next day, more dead than alive."

The story sounded familiar, a modern version of a classical myth. I let Simpson complete it.

"She recovers, but the thing is—she's pregnant! She swears she's never been with a man, but her family throw her out anyway. Nine months later, our man Flint is born. Two years later and she's drunk herself to death and he's in an orphanage."

"That's very unfortunate," I said. Society is more tolerant now, though few people are as modern as they imagine.

"He's proud of it. He's a bastard, with no father but the river, he says. Nobody ever cared for him and he doesn't care for anybody."

"But you're his friend," I said. "Or are you in his debt?"

"Owe him my life."

We walked on a few steps.

"May I ask how?"

Those of us born too late for that much-glorified outburst of nationalistic mutual slaughter will spend our lives listening to war stories endlessly repeated and embellished. This one was less grandiose and self-serving than most.

"We were in camp, not at the front lines, getting ready. There were stories going around, and I started to get ideas about deserting. I saw a chance and took it, now or never, the night before we were due to be sent forward. Slipped through the fence and away over the fields. Had some idea about making my way to the coast and stowing away back home. I hadn't got a quarter of a mile before I hear feet behind me and Corporal Flint's hand on my shoulder."

"How did he find you?"

Simpson shook his head. "He persuaded me to go back with him and, would you believe it, we just walked in through the gates. He gave them some story about a special pass and they just waved us in. Should have known they didn't care about men coming in, only going out."

He was in awe of Flint's audacity.

"And that was how he saved your life," I said. Close to the front, the penalty for desertion was a firing squad. A good many men had been executed to encourage the others, and Simpson's escape was lucky.

"Our battalion was posted to a quiet sector. We were lucky, hardly saw action. I needn't have worried."

"But Flint had latched on to you," I said.

"After the war we said goodbye and I thought that was it," he said. "Never heard a word. But he showed up a few weeks ago, sniffing around, and then moved here."

"An inconvenient district for a man who makes his living on the foreshore five miles away," I said.

"What I said," said Simpson, gloomily. "But he found that empty place and moved himself in."

"And he wants your boy as his apprentice? And you're cooperating?"

"I owe him my life," said Simpson, almost whining. "And he could still go to the authorities, you know? I'd lose my job . . . what can I do?" This was nonsense, of course. The real reason was Simpson's obvious fear of the other man. He worked hard to justify himself. "The boy's happy to go with him too. Flint's got a way with kids." The bronzed, feral, beer-swilling outlaw must seem like a dashing figure to a boy whose father was a clerk. "But he's got to continue his education, of course."

"Of course."

"What can I do?" he repeated.

All Simpson needed to do was summon the nerve to tell Flint to leave him and the boy alone, but there was no use telling him that. He never would challenge Flint, and they both knew it. Flint had a talent for spotting broken things he could make use of.

2

The Conquering Hero was thick with tobacco smoke and abuzz with bellowed conversations and the clink of glasses. We had to lean our heads together in the snug like conspirators just to be heard.

"This Flint is indeed a questionable character, to say the least," said Harry Stubbs, laying out his notebook in front of him.

Stubbs was a granite slab of a man with the widest shoulders I have ever seen. His broken nose and battered features gave him an ogrish look, but his tie was straight, his collar crisp, and an immaculate bowler hat rested on the seat beside him. His polite manner belied his brutish appearance, and he was a thorough and meticulous investigator.

"As in, he associates with criminal types?" I asked, sipping my pint.

"There's no call for casting those sort of aspersions, Mr. Blake," he said. "I might remind you wherein you sit."

I never could get him to drop the "Mr." We are friends, but Stubbs does not share my views on social equality, and when he talks to me he tries to sound like an official report.

"I withdraw the suggestion," I said. I do not believe the pub was exactly a thieves' den, but in these straitened times men supplement their incomes however they can. "You mean something more specific."

"Indeed I do. You heard, I believe, the account of his birth?"

"Oh, Lord, that's pitching it a bit high, old man," I said, half-laughing. "I just wanted to know more about Flint. I didn't expect a sharp left turn into the supernatural."

Stubbs investigates insurance claims for a living, but his real interest is elsewhere. He is quick to see the uncanny in the everyday; too quick. I do not deny such things, but I know how rare they are.

"You might be interested to say what Paracelsus says about such conceptions," he said. "Seeds of sea creatures are carried about the water, and give rise to monstrous births . . . "

Like many self-taught men, Stubbs has latched on to one particular author as his lodestar, and has an undue reverse for this particular sixteenth-century alchemist. Those who are better read rarely put quite so much trust in any single authority; truth is distributed democratically, and you have to go digging for it. But Stubbs takes Paracelsus as his gospel.

"Laying aside his nativity, miraculous or otherwise—the man is mad, but is he dangerous?"

Stubbs turned over a page in his notebook with a slightly reproachful air.

"He is far from popular with others of his trade," he said. "They dislike him, I should say they fear him, but they do respect him. More than one informant told me that nobody crosses Flint. They say he carries a knife."

"He's not an outcast among them, then?"

"Far from it. He has an instinct for where to look, the way some anglers do for fish. The others follow him and go where he goes—when he allows. Also, he is laying claim to all finds of a certain type of pottery, for which he pays the finder generously. And guess what he is collecting?"

He turned over another page and looked up expectantly.

"Green glazeware from the Roman period," I said. Paid for, no doubt, in garnets. "But the idea you can find all the pieces of a broken pot after two thousand years and reassemble it—"

"Flint believes the pieces of this particular relic are fated to come to him," said Stubbs. "But do you know what Arausio means? Besides being the name of a place."

"I didn't know it had any other meaning."

"Everything has other meanings," Stubbs said, as though stating a well-known fact. "And as well as being the name of the town now known as Orange—"

"*Orange,*" I said, automatically correcting his pronunciation to the French.

"As you say, *Orange*. Arausio happens to be the name of a river god associated with that self-same locale. Of the Roman and pre-Roman era. The pot is a sacred relic."

He wrapped one immense hand around a pint glass and drained a quarter in one go.

"That would explain Flint's interest. River gods are his *idée fixe*, his obsession."

"Which of course got me wondering whether there might be some truth behind the old legends. Whether, as Machen has it, the pleasant fables might conceal some darker and more concrete reality. Could there be, I wonder, some sort of being, not currently known to science, which might be in some way co-extensive with the river. Now, this is far beyond my level of knowledge, but maybe you know something . . ."

He trailed off, looking at me hopefully. Stubbs is a wild theoriser, but unlike many others, he always knows when he is out of his depth. Few have his humility.

"This is beyond anyone's knowledge," I said. He waited for more, and I went on, to indulge him, or perhaps to show him the error of his ways. "I could speculate about some kind of diffuse, tenuous liquid entity, one that draws its life-force from hydrodynamic forces rather than sunlight or consuming organic matter. One that might coalesce at places into a semi-solid material form when it needed to manipulate matter. But such an organism would be more like pond slime or algae than an intelligent, let alone godlike, being."

"Pond slime," Stubbs said, clearly struck by the thought. "Spreading slowly over the millennia."

"'Vaster than Empires, and more slow,'" I joked.

"But isn't it so, Mr. Blake, that we ourselves evolved from something very like pond slime?"

"Only on my mother's side, old man," I joked. "Yes, we could spin a tale about some fantastic, nebulous entity, and grant it intelligence if you like, projecting psychic emanations that can be sensed by some humans"—I knew how Stubbs' mind worked— "but you're just putting a gloss on the ancient river god. You have no more actual evidence than the Celts had. Every culture dresses him up in new clothes—Dagon to Neptune to Davy Jones. Making it genus *deus*, species *flumen*, subspecies *Thamesis* does not make it any more plausible."

"Not strictly impossible, though, scientifically speaking?"

Stubbs is incorrigible. I may have seen things that people call supernatural, but I do not assume every creaking floorboard is a ghoul and every shadow a vampire.

"Strictly no." Don Quixote will always see the windmills as giants. And, I suppose, Sancho Panza will always see the giants as windmills. But the sane world is with Panza. "But the man is the problem here. Flint believes in a river god, and perhaps sees himself as its high priest, but can we keep riverine deities out of the inquiry for the time being? The man is the problem, not the Thames."

"I didn't say anything about him being a high priest," Stubbs said, and thoughtfully made a jotting on his notepad.

"Just my speculation," I said. "But what does he want with the boy? Has he ever shown an interest in boys before?"

"Not as far as I gather," Stubbs said. "But young eyes are sharp and young hands are quick, so he could be useful for mudlarking. But if I was permitted to speculate . . . "

I indicated he might continue.

"In some circles children are believed to possess superior psychic sensitivity, a talent that withers with adulthood," he said, laying his left hand open in front of him. "They are in demand for some rituals. Alternatively . . . " he laid his right hand open beside it and lowered his voice. "Human sacrifice. They used to sacrifice people to the river, I understand. An unblemished child would be a good offering. And it would fit with this high priest idea."

Stubbs' mind ran on rails like a tram. But I had different concerns.

I had asked Stubbs for help because I was worried about the boy. Simpson Junior's schoolwork had declined. He was getting into fights with other boys, which had previously been rare with him. I heard one of them taunt him with being a bed-wetter.

Simpson's homework was often incomplete or absent, and he had started leaving little doodles in the margins of the page, wavy indistinct abstract things suggestive of sea-serpents, Tritons, and kraken. He had no concentration in class, except on a few odd occasions. In History I was telling of the rebuilding of London after the Great Fire of 1666, and how Sir Christopher Wren had found a broken piece of stone in the ruins of the old cathedral.

"That piece carried a single word in Latin—'Resurgam.' What form is Resurgam?"

Hands went up. I pointed at one.

"First person singular, future tense, *resurgo*, sir."

"Correct. Meaning?"

"'I will rise again,' sir."

"Very good, Hodges."

Wren supposedly used that piece of inscribed stone to mark the center of the foundation of the new St. Paul's Cathedral. It rose, larger and grander, from the ruins of the old, and still dominates the City skyline. A whole church raised up on a single word. Simpson drank it all in; but the next lesson he was looking out the window again.

One Monday morning Simpson came in with a sticking plaster across his forehead and in such an obvious state of distraction that

I gave up directing questions to him to force him to attend. I asked him to stay in the classroom at break time.

"Now then, Simpson," I said, squatting next to him, softening my tone. "What's this all about, eh?"

He burst into tears and was incapable of explaining himself through his sobs. All he could tell me was that he had never done anything wrong and just wanted to be left alone and it was an accident.

I kept Simpson in for detention after school and sought out Mrs. Simpson when she arrived to collect him. She was a sturdy woman of hawkish aspect, but something had rattled her. She confirmed that the boy had been on the Thames foreshore with his 'Uncle Jack' the day before, and had come back with a bleeding head. He had been unusually withdrawn since.

"I don't think you should let him go with that man again," I told her levelly.

"Nor should I!" she said, with real heat.

"Good," I said. I had been prepared to explain how I suspected Flint of being a deviant, but she did not need persuading.

"But—he touched me." Anger gave way instantly to fear.

"What do you mean?"

"I gave him an earful, and he just put one finger on my nose," she said, touching her own nose. "He said I'd better keep it out of his business or he'd cut it off."

It was the casual insolence of that touch that disturbed her. Mrs. Simpson was not accustomed to meeting wills more forceful than her own. And this one had been backed with the threats of violence.

"What did your husband say?"

"Nothing, he never does," she said bitterly. "And Flint just laughed about the cut and said the boy had been baptized and he now belonged to the river. And the boy keeps going with him, even though he's afraid of him. Do you know anything about Flint?"

Her eyes were full of worry.

"Only what I've heard from the boy and your husband, Mrs. Simpson. Certainly nothing that makes me think he should be given keeping of a young boy."

She put a hand on my arm. "You're official, aren't you? Can't you do something, Mr. Blake? Please?"

Officially of course I could do nothing. Not if Flint was acting with the approval of the boy's father.

This had led me to engage Stubbs to find out more about this strange man. And Stubbs had told me everything there was to find out. The thick air of the pub was almost choking me, and the roar filled my head with chaos.

"Really, I've put you to far more trouble than I expected," I said, reaching for my pocket and getting ready to leave. "I should at least reimburse you for your time."

"I wouldn't hear of it," said Stubbs. "Following these matters is my little hobby and the insurance business is quiet. Put your wallet away."

I had expected the rebuff. But I knew also that if I had not offered, Stubbs would have been offended. Such is our social dance.

"I could at least stand you a savoury pie," I said, seeing a vendor circulating around the pub.

"Now that's an offer I can't resist." Stubbs put away his notebook and glanced over at the golden crusts with their wisps of steam. "I do admit a weakness for a fresh-baked pie."

On my way out I paid for two pies and sent the vendor in Stubbs' direction.

The evening air was blessedly fresh and cool, and it was still light. Wrapped in my thoughts, my steps took me through the gardens around the Crystal Palace. Ideas kept chasing around my head and I walked through the crowd without seeing it. Flint was an eccentric, but a powerful personality. Simpson was a weak man, under Flint's sway. Flint had done nothing illegal. The boy feared Flint, but obeyed him.

My steps halted before a fountain surmounted with a statue: a bearded, reclining god. He was a gruff, commanding figure, with THAMES inscribed on the pedestal. Other fountains had figures personifying the Ganges, the Nile, and the Amazon—the Victorians loved to divide up the world—but this one stopped me. I considered that face, the trident resting casually over his shoulder but ready at hand if he needed to strike. Not, I decided, a particularly forgiving god. His face reminded me of someone I could not recall.

A glint of metal caught my eye; the basin of the fountain was bright with copper coins. I did not recall such offerings here before. When I checked, there were none in the other fountains.

Men will worship anything as a god: a mountain, a tree, thunder . . . it means nothing. Men like Stubbs place their trust in the new god of science, not realizing that this is as much an act of faith as any other religion.

I admit I am a neurotic, and perhaps my unconscious mind had prompted me to involve Stubbs because he would validate my worries. Flint wanted to found a new religion, or resurrect an old one. He was trying to claim his first acolyte, if I let him.

There was no legal recourse, but there might be another way to stop Flint.

3

Flint's work was dictated by the tides, so it was easy to tell when he would be down by the river. One evening I sent a note to the Head explaining that I had come down with a sudden fever and would not attend the next day. He would not question it. I had taken fewer sick days than my colleagues, and Heads are wary of contagious disease.

I waited until ten in the morning, by which time Flint would certainly have found his place on the foreshore. It was a miserable wet morning, which favoured me, allowing me to shield my face behind an umbrella. The sky was the colour of slate, and by the time I arrived at Flint's flat a steady rain beat down.

At the bottom of the steps was a puddle half an inch deep. I stood in it while assaying the door and the window. My instinct was that the whole place had seemed damp and rotten, and it would not take a housebreaker's skill to force an entrance. It was gloomy, though, under the leaden skies in the steady rain, so much so that I wished I had brought a light.

I pushed the door experimentally, preparatory to a shoulder-barge. I was not too surprised to find it unlatched. I peered through and was halfway towards stepping in when I saw the whole place was flooded. The puddle outside, level with the window, was simply the water level. Steps went down from the door. Inside the dark, chilly liquid would be knee deep.

Did Flint open a stopcock somewhere when he left every morning, to create this moat to deter thieves, making an exit wearing his waders? That was absurd. I had seen that the place was prone to flooding, and on a day like this, when our old drains struggled to deal with the deluge, the lowest lying points were the first to suffer.

For a moment I thought about taking off my shoes and socks and rolling up my trousers, but on a day like this I had a perfect excuse for being wet and nobody would give me a second look. I stepped gingerly into bone-chilling water. As I guessed, it was knee deep, and I stood for a moment getting accustomed before moving into the gloom, watching ripples spread out before me.

There was a step down from the scullery into the kitchen I had not noticed on my first visit before, and another from the kitchen into the corridor which left me thigh-deep in black water. The shock of the cold was almost enough to make me turn back. But it would be even more ridiculous now to give up than to go on.

Another step down into the living room. I gulped, steeled myself, and went on, holding my hands above the surface of the dark liquid. A few floating objects bobbed in the waters ahead of me.

This was idiotic. Of all the days, I had chosen the day of the flood.

As I waded across the living room I suddenly felt I was not alone.

"Flint?" I said tentatively, but as I approached the workbench by the window there was nobody.

The water in the living room stood at exactly at the level of the workbench, so the items on it seemed to rest on the surface of the water. My eye was arrested by the form that dominated the bench.

I had expected Flint's Holy Grail to be a ceremonial bowl or dish dedicated to the river god. Instead it was a grotesque statuette that rose, incomplete, from the water, surrounded like Ozymandias by shattered fragments.

My first reaction was to giggle. Flint was madder than we thought, and had let his imagination run away with him. The statuette could not be a reconstruction but was some freak of Flint's, with shards from unrelated pots thrown together into a chimera without regard to the forms of the classical era. The Roman sculptors had their models, their stylized hippocampus and siren and triton. Flint had ignored that; his work did not resemble any of the children of Neptune in classical friezes. It looked more like some hellish creation of Hieronymus Bosch, in which a vaguely human torso rose out of a confused tangle of every sort of water creature—whelk and crayfish and eel—all wreathed with garlands of living weed.

More pieces lay about. Flint did not have the whole jigsaw, but there was enough to make the picture clear—the way he saw it at least. All that was missing was a head. Judging from the pieces on the bench, the thing would have a face more gargoyle than Monti's anthropomorphic Thames.

Seen in the abstract, as a modern artwork, the piece had undeniable boldness and power. The crudeness of execution did not blunt its force, and it captured the texture of the watery realm and seemed to sway in an invisible current. But any critic would remark the sickness in the mind that fashioned it.

If, as the cynic says, man created god in his own image, then what must Flint be like? And what kind of homage would he offer this beslimed monster?

My first impulse was to smash the statuette into smithereens.

"We must be rational, Blake," I reminded myself.

I picked up the little river god and turned to wade back the way I had come.

I cannot be exactly sure what happened next, but somehow I lost my footing. At the time it seemed to me that a hole or trap door had opened in front of me; more likely I had stepped on a loose rug or some other debris in that disordered place. I slipped right, pratfalling like a film comedian on a banana-skin.

The cold was intense, but what first bothered me was losing my glasses. I tried to hold on to them even as my head went under.

My head banged against something hard. The water was deeper than it should have been. My waving legs could not find the floor, and I felt the touch of things brushing past me underwater.

I started to panic, but with an effort I made contact with the hard surface beneath me and stood up again, only to slip over once more as though caught in a powerful current. This time I did lose my glasses and inhaled water. I am a strong swimmer and not afraid of water, but my first thought was that I was drowning.

Worse, everything seemed to be moving as though I were in a whirlpool.

I held on to the statuette. I cannot say why. I can only say that, at the time, it felt as if I was holding on to a lifejacket and that it was the only thing keeping me afloat. There is no logical reason for this. Perhaps, psychologically speaking, I was holding on to my purpose for being there.

When my face broke the surface for the second or third time everything was moving, and the floor, which ought to have been within easy each, approached and receded, so my attempt to stand up just made me spin.

The only light was from the rectangular window over the workbench, and it passed me by in a whirl. Rationally, even while I was drowning, I reasoned that this must be like the illusion that drink can give of the room spinning, which the drinker attempts to counter by rotating himself. I waved my arms, trying to catch on to something solid, but only succeeded in splashing about helplessly.

My foot caught in something and would not come loose. For some reason I thought of seaweed. I thrashed madly to get free, and in the process my head went under again.

I doubled over, feeling for whatever was wrapped around my ankle. A part of me was still completely calm and rational, while the great part was screaming that I was drowning, and a third, smaller part sat back and laughed that I could be drowning in someone's living room.

I gulped a breath before I went under again. I could no longer tell up from down, and whirled at ever greater speed.

It no longer seemed bizarre, and I had ceased panicking. That each of us is fated to die is a secret we all hold in the dark of our hearts, concealed from ourselves. Now that secret revealed itself to me, I was no longer afraid. I felt that I was now under the control of a great power, and my feeling as I gave myself up to it was one of relief.

Then something clamped hold of me and I was hoisted up clear of the water. As easily as a heron snatches a minnow, I was hauled out and found myself lifted through the air, gasping and choking, while the room flowed past me. Some lurching steps and I was back on solid ground, lying in a shallow puddle outside the house, while the rain pattered down around me.

"Mr. Blake, can you breathe?" Stubbs asked. "Are you injured?"

I tried to tell him that I was fine, but choked and coughed from the effort. Black spots swum before my eyes.

"I'm actually quite a good swimmer," I said at last.

"You recover your breath now, Mr. Blake," he said. "Lie easy."

Stubbs was doing something with a length of stout rope. It took me a minute to see that he had tied himself to the railings outside the flat like a mountaineer before wading inside, and was now untying the knots and packing the rope into a canvas bag.

"You can let go of that now," he said, gently prizing my fingers from the river god and placing it in the same bag. "We'd better get you to an hospital straight away. I'll run and get a taxi from the station."

"I'm quite all right," I said, raising myself to a sitting position and coughing again. "But I was in trouble for a minute there. Thank you, Stubbs."

"Don't mention it," he said. "Can you stand? Here, let me give you a hand."

I had to lean on Stubbs for support at first, but I persuaded him to take me, wringing wet, to my lodgings rather than the hospital. By then my head had cleared but I felt weak. I could feel my arms and legs and body covered with bruises as though I had been in a rocky maelstrom rather than just slipping over in a flooded cellar. I kept trying to tell him how embarrassingly comic it was, but Stubbs was stone-faced.

I went on to explain my plan for the statuette. He had formed a similar idea and had arrived later if better prepared.

"When we deal with Flint," I said. "We must make it clear we will only give the statuette back if he swears to leave the boy alone. Swears on Arausio, or swears by the river. Nothing else will do."

"Understood," he said.

I was planning to change out of my wet things and go with Stubbs, but I was too weak. For some reason I felt completely exhausted. I could only get Stubbs to leave by promising him I would go straight to bed. He went off with the river god and his instructions, which I knew he would follow to the letter.

I had no intention of actually going to bed, but as soon as I had stripped off and toweled myself dry I was overcome by fatigue.

The next thing I knew it was dark, and I was in bed, and my landlady was bringing me warm milk and telling me I had a fever.

4

"You're looking well, Mr. Blake," Stubbs announced, his form filling the doorway.

"Come in and take a pew," I said.

He pulled up a straight-backed chair and lowered himself carefully into it beside my sickbed.

"There's nothing too much wrong with me," I said. "Except the aftereffects of swallowing a little dirty water. Lucky it wasn't sewage, or I'd have typhoid."

It was a routine fever that had almost burned itself out after forty-eight hours, no worse than a bout of the 'flu. The worst part was that some latent Oedipal impulse had taken charge of the content of the inevitable fever dreams, replaying my accidental near-drowning as a struggle with some malevolent fluvial father-figure.

"Technically, they were the waters of the River Effra," said Stubbs, insisting as always on small points. "The old river was paved over and runs under Elder Road, but it still floods at intervals. An old tributary of the Thames."

"The Thames," I said. "Speaking of which—what has happened with Flint?"

Stubbs looked down. "I'm not sure you want to know. I don't want to put you in a difficult position, legally speaking."

"Please, Stubbs. Spill the proverbial beans."

He chewed this over. Stubbs is never hasty. He leaned back and recited his report.

"After bringing you here, I returned to Flint's residence to await his return, with the intention of commencing negotiations as discussed. However, he did not return; instead, the house was approached by Mr. Simpson. He was surprised to see me, and in a highly agitated state."

"How do you mean?"

"When he realized I had the idol he attempted to assault me with a pointed implement. To wit, a German army bayonet, which I disarmed him of, and restrained him until such time as he was less violent and more communicative."

"Good God!"

"Furthermore," Stubbs went on, unperturbed, "I observed

that the said implement, and indeed Mr. Simpson's hands, were much stained with what appeared to be, and in fact was, human blood."

I could only stare.

"Simpson had had his own discussion with Flint earlier that day. Like you and me, he had decided to act before Flint would see the boy. It seems that, as they say, the worm turned, and Simpson finally found a backbone. The discussion turned violent. Flint drew a weapon. Best you don't know the particulars of what and when and how."

"I can guess," I said.

Stubbs leaned over to look at something on my bedside table—my watch, which was still waterlogged. It would dry out in due course and run as well as ever. It had survived a few dunkings in my college days.

"Stopped at ten-twenty-five," he said.

"The time that you found me," I said. I cannot have been in the water more than five minutes.

"Rather later than that," he said, and seemed about to say something else before going on. "That was about the time Simpson decided to confront Flint."

People will always find coincidence if they look for enough of them. Stubbs obviously thought my intrusion into Flint's sanctum had something to do with Simpson's freeing himself from the man's influence. The stopped clock is a cliché of cheap supernatural fiction. "But Simpson and Flint—"

"Mr. Simpson was far from coherent," Stubbs said. "He said Flint was drowned. He was at pains to tell me that you have to keep puncturing the gut to prevent a body from bloating and rising to the surface, and he had attended to that."

"It was self-defence," I said. "The police will need to understand that. I take it they are holding him? Has he a lawyer?"

"When I say Mr. Simpson was less than coherent, I use the term advisedly," said Stubbs. "There is no body, no witnesses, and hence no known crime. I could only piece together an account because I know so much of the background to the case. Simpson's speech is . . . fragmentary." He paused as if trying to make sense of a string of ravings. "In such cases of trauma the patient does sometimes recover, but they say it's doubtful in this instance. They'll be keeping him in."

I sensed that more had happened than Stubbs had so far recounted.

"What do you mean, 'the patient'? And who is 'they'?"

"The doctors at the mental institution where I took Simpson. It seemed best. Which reminds me." He produced a paper sachet from an inside pocket. "This is a mild sedative. They recommend it for cases of severe shock, when there is trouble sleeping. A half-teaspoon in warm water."

"I've had no trouble sleeping," I lied, and involuntarily moved my legs as though to free them from weed.

"Keep it just in case." He placed the sachet on my bedside table. "No other ill effects, I trust?"

"None at all. Why should there be?"

"No reason. And that effigy—the thing Flint was reconstructing—it is back where it came from, in a hundred pieces. Father Thames can sleep on his river bed for a few centuries more."

That seemed like an unsatisfactory approach, if you accepted Stubbs' unlikely premise that the statuette had some significance. If I had believed as Stubbs did, I would have taken extreme measures to ensure the thing was destroyed utterly, beyond any possible recovery. But Stubbs is less ambitious than I. He just wants to keep the Old Gods at bay, not to defeat them. He knows his limitations.

"Good, good," I said.

"And the boy . . . " he started.

"I'll keep an eye on him. We don't know what Flint did to him, or how it may come out later. But boys are a resilient lot, generally speaking."

It occurred to me that if the boy's father was to be institutionalized the family would have no income. Stubbs assured me that a local philanthropist, a man called Renville, would undoubtedly help out, as he had done in similar cases.

"Similar cases?" I said, "This one seems rather unique."

"I suppose so," Stubbs said, disinclined to argue.

He was not his usual disputative self, being determined to treat me as an invalid, which I resented. I could be no more than polite to him, and the conversation petered out.

"I'll be getting on then," Stubbs said, taking his bowler.

"I hope I will see you for a pint in the Conquering Hero in the not-too-distant," I said. "I believe I owe you one, old man."

"I believe I will take you up on that," he said, with the trace of a smile. "Get well soon now, Mr. Blake."

After he was gone I took my hand from under the bedclothes. I had not wanted Stubbs to see the marks on my wrists, much less the larger and deeper wounds on my ankles. Those lacerations would only fuel his wild speculation about what 'really happened.' They would have convinced him that something reached out from the river to drag me under with ectoplasmic tendrils or some such nonsense.

That would be quite irrational. Not when there are other perfectly good explanations. I really cannot tolerate that kind of thinking.

I really cannot tolerate that kind of thinking at all.

At all.

I picked Herodotus from my bedside and busied myself underlining sections for my class to translate.

WHO KILLED AUGUSTUS & BOURBAKI?

Aditya Dwarkesh

Aditya Dwarkesh is an undergraduate pursuing mathematics and physics. When not doing science, he engages enthusiastically with philosophy and literature. He enjoys taking long walks on the beach and entertaining his imagination, which has an affinity towards the uncanny. He has also been an editor and regular contributor to local science communication magazines in the past.

IT TAKES COURAGE TO PUT UP A HAPPY FRONT, but even more to be able to openly acknowledge one's sadness. Only when an awareness of my great despair was *forced* upon me did I gain the courage to be miserable.

I remember well those sleepless nights after it first overwhelmed me, when I would stare at the moon with senseless desperation, unable to arrive at an understanding of what the matter was.

That was when I gave up my career in mathematics. It had been nothing more than an activity to distract me from my depression. I resolved to be no longer an escapist. As it so happened, however, mathematics wasn't done with me.

When I was fresh into the field, I had heard faint whispers of the existence of a cult in the far Eastern corners of India, the sole purpose of which was to indulge in a bizarre and esoteric variant of mathematical discourse. Of course, it is often said—only half in jest—that mathematicians in general form a cult of sorts,

145

thanks to how alien the language game they play is to natural language. However, *this* mathematical cult set itself apart by the fact that its obsession—for any cult is defined by a singular obsession it concerns itself with—happens to be a *person*.

And yet, it so happens that nobody—not even those in the innermost circles of this cult—has ever been actually able to meet Augustus Bourbaki. No more than suggestive whispers of shadows glanced at exist, and up till now, the only manner in which he communicates with the world is by the written word: publications of conjectures, of resolutions to long-standing hypotheses, and of other mathematical results with varying importance.

Another problem exacerbating the whole situation surrounding his identity was a frustratingly mundane set of bookkeeping mistakes: the dates attributed to his articles are most certainly terribly mistaken.

Take, for example, the two-part proof he produced on the validity of the Kakuro conjecture. The second article is dated to have been published in the year 2006—whereas the first article, written by the same man, has been archived by all libraries as a publication produced in the year 1926! An eighty-year gap is not impossible, perhaps, but must almost certainly be erroneous.

To begin with, I dismissed the whole affair as not worth much of my time or attention. I had never heard anyone else in academia ever referring to this whole business of the cult and the unseen mathematician it centers its discourse around, and I concluded that the whole affair was just a series of unlikely errors and misunderstandings that merely appear to have the form of a coherent picture (as they seem to do surprisingly often). The cult did not exist, and the mysterious mathematician was a clerical error.

But this changed two nights before I abandoned the pretense of joy forever, when I stepped into my institute's library with an uneasy feeling at the pit of my stomach. Where it came from, I do not know; it was a fatality, this feeling, which made me stray off into a hitherto unexplored corner of the fairly massive library.

But to call it merely unexplored does not quite do it justice. I had not even known of the *possibility* of the existence of this cranny until that night. For its structure seemed to be quite impossible to reconcile with the overall spatiality of the library: my visualization skills are not too bad, and it seemed to me that where this small opening took me was right where a wall should form a barrier to the corridor. I would probably never have found it had my foot not, by pure chance, struck against the side of the wall and found a turning appear—almost magically—where there should have been none.

I half fell into the opening and saw two bookshelves huddled together in it. It looked as if they were cowering from me.

There was a sharp clash between the visual and the olfactory experience of the opening. While the appearance of the books led me to expect the overabundant emanation of a musty smell, what I actually received was a combination of old rubber and fresh paper.

I moved closer to the shelf on the left and reached out to a text, half-expecting another surprise in its tactility; but the impressions that its surfaces imparted upon my hands were nothing out of the ordinary.

The binding was in tatters, falling apart in my hands; its title was nearly unreadable. All I could make out from its remains was *Ma—matical Pri—ples of Ze—gogy*, with the number 1816 identifying its publication year. The author—and this was a name I recognized, a mathematician of the early nineteenth century—was Axel Engset.

I had a fair idea as to what the first two words were, but the third was entirely alien to me. No branch or discipline I had ever heard of held even a vague resemblance to it.

I opened it gingerly. Half the pages promptly fell to the ground, and I jumped in a moment of fright at this sudden spike in movement in my environment.

I left the book back on the shelf, scrambling to gather all the loose sheets in whatever order I could grab them in, observing that none of the sheets had any page numbers on them.

It was then that a particular sheet happened to catch my attention, by pure chance. It was one of those academic artifacts that look more like some exotic artwork than a mathematical proof; for when I picked it up, I saw no recognizable symbols, not even any English letters, except for a single digit somewhere in the middle of this mathematical artwork—indicating a footnote—and the footnote itself, which was written in English and read thus:

"We owe the proof of the same to Augustus Bourbaki, as presented in 1806."

I stared at it. It was quite impossible, of course. Augustus Bourbaki had published the second part of his proof of the Kakuro conjecture in 2006. Two hundred years: certainly, it follows that Augustus Bourbaki could not possibly have made any contribution to mathematics in the year 1806.

But, even more impossibly, *this very text claims to have been written by Engset in the year 1816.*

I was then seized by a terrible suspicion. Carelessly shoving the sheaf onto the shelf, I picked up another book at random. The title was once again distorted beyond recognition, but I could see that it was written by Leibniz. I began flipping through the pages and opening them at random.

I came across his expressions of many now-familiar ideas, and I was just beginning to feel at ease until I once again was struck by an anomaly:

Page 74, footnote 6: *"Similar work has been advanced by Augustus Bourbaki, a few decades previously, and I here borrow partially from his results."*

A few decades previously—placing Bourbaki in the seventeenth century.

I slowly put Leibniz's treatise back in its place. I was still busy rationalizing the whole thing as some sort of hoax, but my discomfort began increasing in intensity.

It was then that I saw the small, yellowing booklet half-hidden at the top corner of the second bookshelf, quite possibly entirely untouched ever since it had first been put there by someone (or—what, some*thing*?).

The whole place had an ominous stillness—a silence so loud that I could hear my heartbeat throbbing in my own ears. Had someone else turned into the opening just about then, I would have fainted in a dead fright.

I grasped the booklet and nearly dropped it immediately. It was burning cold. Holding it with only my fingertips to minimize surface contact, I turned it around gingerly. On the first page was only an intriguing-looking emblem of sorts, a small diagram representing the concatenation of a book and a clock.

I opened it and looked through the table of contents.

Chapter I: Collected papers from Bourbaki's tenure at Calcutta University. Found in Bourbaki's Mutationes in libro. *(21st century)*

Chapter III: Bourbaki's predecessor to the Riemann hypothesis. Found in Bourbaki's Mutationes in libro. *(19th century)*

Chapter V: Selected Dialogues between Descartes and Bourbaki. Found in Bourbaki's Mutationes in libro. *(17th century)*

Chapter VIII: Augustus Bourbaki and Roger Bacon: A little-known friendship. Found in Bourbaki's Mutationes in libro. *(13th century)*

Chapter XV: Euclid's commentaries on Bourbaki's geometric ontology. Found in Bourbaki's Mutationes in libro. *(300 B.C.E.)*

I thought to myself with some amazement that this was certainly an elaborate piece of forgery, if nothing else.

How does the creator of a falsity introduce it to the world? By openly declaring its untruthfulness? But then it would cease to be untruthful. By playing along entirely? But that would mean the creator has hoodwinked his own self into believing his lies. What, then?

It was at this stage that my eye made the vile decision of glancing upwards and showing me something that could not possibly be. Where there should have been only the back of the bookshelf, I saw for a moment a mirror—and in this mirror I saw the reflection of a figure crouching silently behind me.

But the figure was my own self.

It was I, but terribly disfigured: I was naked, and my skin had everywhere an awful black color of bile, and hellishly red eyes stared out of a devilish, vulture-like face.

I screamed. My vision blurred, and in a moment the creature and the mirror disappeared. I threw the booklet back and ran out of that otherworldly corner, now reeking of filth. Fleeting footsteps approached me, and in my madness I took it to be the creature returning to do as it would with me; a wave of dizziness hit me, and the world flickered momentarily.

Of course, it was only the librarian.

The librarian had a good laugh when she saw the scare she'd given me. I did not ask her about the books I found hidden in the turning. The vision, apparition, phantom I saw behind me must, of course, have been some trick of the eye; but I was still feeling terribly anxious as I hurriedly walked back to my rented apartment.

It was bitingly cold; there was a full moon on that night. An irrational fear gripped me every time I looked up at it. I was afraid I would see upon it the face of the disfigured demon that so resembled me. Somewhere in the distance, dogs howled up at it.

I did not know it then, but my fate had already been sealed. The obsession with Bourbaki—something I myself did not know I possessed, at that stage—was to become the final straw. Something deep within me was already telling me that I must, I must, I absolutely must find out everything I could about this man. I began getting the altogether incoherent idea that he might be mathematics itself.

Two nights later, I booked a ticket to Calcutta. One never

knows what ultimate aim one's life is driving one toward until it finally blows up in one's face.

My preliminary inquires upon reaching Calcutta consisted of going to the most well-known universities of the city and asking for a mathematician by the name of Augustus Bourbaki. In spite of how unfruitful these investigations began turning out to be, the way the city presented itself to me began bolstering my confidence about it being the home of Bourbaki.

The juxtaposition of people living on the streets a stone's throw away from urban dwellings blindsided me; the aggression with which every wall seemed to be plastered with various political posters and revolutionary slogans; the mundanity of how unreservedly and freely everyone spoke.

The people in the first university I paid a visit to gave me some furtive looks and declarations that they'd never heard of the name before. Their dispositions betrayed them, but I did not bother pressing anyone. I was under the impression that the need for insistence would never arise.

Outside the gates of the university, it struck me how the roads of the city were always filled with so many people; how none of them were ever standing around idly; the noise and crowds amplified by how the vehicles running and the people crossing the roads did so in a completely arbitrary manner, with utter disregard for typical traffic guidelines. It all made me more prone to the disorientation of realizing how every other person I saw was living a life with as much depth as my own.

On the sidewalk there stood a man who didn't seem to be in his right mind. He was holding a book in his hand and loudly making some proclamations. At a glance, it appeared to be the Bible; perhaps he was preaching. There was a small crowd around him, but it was clear that they weren't interested in what he had to say. They just wanted to see the show the madman was putting up for them. The whole thing felt vulgar and base.

The weather in the city was unbearably humid, but nobody seemed to care. I went a little closer to listen to what he was saying—and froze. The title of the book didn't have the word Bible in it; I had misread the fading print. It said Bourbaki.

I pushed through the crowd. The man saw me coming and read my intentions; he fell silent and gave me a terrible, angry stare. I began feeling the crowd's eyes on me. And before I could open my mouth to ask him about the book, he was gone.

The second institute I went to, I was told sternly and without explanation to leave the premises after I asked my questions. Just outside the gates of the complex, I had a knife pulled out on me. I immediately put my hands in the air and asked the man to take what he wanted. Unfortunately, what he wanted from me seemed to be something he could not simply take in such a manner. I was asked how I had stumbled upon the name. I explained that I had found a variety of "interesting" mathematical volumes to which he had contributed back in my own university. I did not mention anything else. The man with the knife gave a sardonic laugh.

It was only after I left that I realized why his face had looked so familiar to me: he was none other than the madman on the sidewalk.

Strangely undaunted by the incident, I pressed on. I seemed to have lost any regard or value for my own life; and Bourbaki had become everything.

Nobody had seen Bourbaki; nobody had even heard of Bourbaki; and nobody knew anybody who may have seen or heard of Bourbaki. Over the course of the next week I found myself facing an entire city united in a subconscious determination to deny the existence of one man.

And yet, in the shadows of the many dingy alleyways this city hosted, I sensed the insincerity of the denials. In the strange dustiness of all the roads and buildings in this metropolis, I sensed the presence of that which I was seeking.

In my mind he had taken up the form of a cloaked, nondescript figure who would roam the city clutching an aging and yellowing book under his arms. An entity invisible in plain sight, caught in a trance-like state, abruptly and violently producing brilliant results in the subject.

And so passed the days, largely fruitless, until, in the middle of the night after my tenth day of inquiries, the door of my room rattled wildly enough in its frame to awaken me. My instinctive fear was dulled by the unexpected nature of the situation and my own mounting excitement—for I knew that something must be afoot.

It was a strikingly ordinary sort of night for something so extraordinary to happen. There was neither some raging storm, nor had some otherworldly atmosphere settled in; just the usual imperfect and rather ugly silence of the average urban city.

I opened the door recklessly and found standing on the other side of it the man who had pulled a knife on me around a week back, the madman on the sidewalk. He seemed to have taken a bit of a beating on his face, but before I could inquire, he grabbed me by my collar. It was not hard enough that I was helplessly dragged along with him as he started walking off, but hard enough nevertheless for resistance on my part to cause considerable damage to the shirt I was wearing. I briskly started walking along behind him, at least partly because it was a pretty nice shirt. Nevertheless, the violence of the act aroused some fear in me.

I expected him to say a word or to indicate some explanation, but he maintained his silence. Around ten steps in I finally asked breathlessly, "What is it?" His grip on me loosened, and I started resisting. "Who are you? What have you come for? What do you want from me?"

He stopped. We stood at the edge of the flight of descending stairs.

Then: "You asked me for Bourbaki."

A pause.

"I will give you Bourbaki."

I blinked in a show of vague astonishment—as if I was trying to remember what a Bourbaki is, as if I hadn't guessed his purpose

153

the moment I had awoken—and then nodded. My sense of healthy apprehension toward potentially dangerous situations had evaporated the moment I stepped into this city, anyway.

And so he continued leading the way; and I followed, just like that, empty-handed and in my nightclothes. There was a momentary sensation of vulnerability and nakedness that coursed through me, but before it could persist and intensify enough to make me visibly disconcerted, we burst out onto the road.

The yellow lampposts cast immutable shadows, strange deformations of the objects inducing them, illuminating the hard road soporifically. There was a taxi waiting for us. He got into the driver's seat and gestured for me to take the adjacent seat. I did so.

I decided that I was simply going to have to wait and watch. The car started up, and after some five minutes of travel along the anonymous, yellow, deserted urban roads, in spite of my best efforts to follow the car's path, I was completely lost.

Suddenly a scream pierced the sky. I awoke with a start. I had half-drifted off. The man felt me jump and gave me a dead glance that betrayed nothing.

"We're nearly there," he said.

I looked around. There was virtually nothing but empty grasslands as far as the eye could see—with the exception of one small building situated in the middle of the field, a few minutes' walk away from the main road.

He stopped the car in the middle of the road and got out. I followed suit, and we started walking toward the building.

The moment my feet left the road, an unbearable chattering assaulted my ears. The grass was whispering, and it seemed to be relaying some great secrets to me about nature. I tried paying attention.

Of course, grass can't whisper; it must have been the wind, must have been some crickets, must have been an exaggeration of the mind.

My guide continued walking, unfazed. As we approached, however, the building seemed to be getting *smaller*, rather than larger. I stopped trying to size it up. The grass had become too fearsome for me to be able to look down at my feet.

I looked up at the sky. It was a full moon. That was odd; I remembered seeing a full moon just about half a month ago.

And then, before I knew it, the building had crept upon us; we were right in front of it.

Now that I was closer to it, I could see that it had a dome-shaped structure. It wasn't very large, and could probably contain a 50-seater auditorium at the most, but it had a threatening aura disproportionate to its apparent size.

My guide opened the main door, a cold, iron slab. He gestured for me to enter. I swayed hesitantly. He grabbed my arm and tried to pull me in roughly. I took a deep breath and plunged out of the cold moonlight into the darkness behind the door. The air of the night stopped dancing upon my back, and I nearly fell down headfirst; a flight of stairs lay just inside.

The man closed the thick door. It became immediately clear that there was only one source of light: a small, white, evanescent glow coming from the bottom of this flight of stairs.

It looked distant, as if I stood at the top of an unbelievably long flight of stairs. I glanced behind to make sure the man was behind me. He wasn't. I looked at the door. Even without examining it, even in the dim light, I could tell that it was locked.

I started descending.

There was nothing to hold on to. For some reason I dared not touch the wall. It was making me feel claustrophobic. I was afraid it might animate itself and swallow me into a sea of murderous insects.

I continued descending.

The soft, white glow at the bottom was shimmering; my journey was interminable and climactic. I was in limbo; in stasis; my whole life consisted of this singular journey. Endless liminality.

I continued descending.

And then it was all over; as abruptly as the building had rushed up to me previously, the bottom of the stairs did the same. The soft light was coming from somewhere ahead.

I looked up and found myself standing at the back of a large, dimly lit auditorium.

A great many silhouettes were shuffling into seats rather haphazardly. I sensed some muted whispers among certain of the silhouettes that were grouped together; I saw also the rest of them roaming around (or standing still like me) all by themselves, exuding an aura of fear and uncertainty by the shadow of their dispositions. Finally, they too began taking their seats.

An impressive-looking figure was striding up and down the slightly more illuminated stage (which, as it turned out, had been the source of the light), shuffling through some papers he was holding. I could make out only a ruddy face and the lack of any hair upon the head belonging to it. At any rate, it seemed clear that he was going to be offering a speech of sorts—an important one, by the look of things.

Without taking my eyes off of him, I moved to the nearest empty seat and sat down. My peripheral vision told me that virtually everyone else was already seated. The speaker now looked up at his audience; there was a moment of perfect, crystalline stillness.

And then he began speaking.

"Good morning, everybody. My name is [unintelligible], and I will be answering a few questions in which some of you—no doubt esteemed mathematicians—might recently have found an obsessive interest. There is no beating around the bush in our convocations; let us arrive straight at the heart of the matter: Who is Augustus Bourbaki?

"Have we not all glimpsed upon the hand of this man extending itself across centuries after centuries, nudging and directing the course of mathematics itself with an almost insidious subtlety? It may be presumed that Bourbaki is not a man at all but an abstraction of sorts, concatenated out of the greatest mathematicians of all time. Let me make myself very clear, then:

Who Killed Augustus Bourbaki?

Augustus Bourbaki is a real person. The facts we have with us right now are too few and too vague in order for me to offer a very detailed biography, but we have reason to believe that he first stepped upon this planet in roughly the same geographical region as we are now, around three thousand years ago.

"How many of you are aware of the *I Ching*—often otherwise known as the 'Book of Changes'? An ancient Chinese divination text that almost certainly fell into the hands of Bourbaki one day. It is a book with a singular, endlessly inventive principle: it offers imprinted a fixed set of signs, alongside which is outlined a set of instructions *indispensably dependent upon the transient nature of the present*, on the basis of which the signs are to be interpreted. It is the ever-changing *now* that gives the *I Ching* its infinitely many continued meanings. And what Augustus Bourbaki did was write his own *I Ching* for the discipline of mathematics: *Mutationes in libro*. And as human society, civilization, and culture evolve, so does that which we read out of it.

"And so it was that at around three hundred B.C.E., Euclid found the predecessor who inspired his own fifth postulate; while also, nearly fifteen hundred years later, in the very same signs, Bernhard Riemann found a most curious and interesting question posed by the text. And why should we say that it was Euclid who put forth the fifth postulate? Why Riemann who proposed the hypothesis named after him? Is it not all Bourbaki? In the final analysis, was it not all found in the text? Is it not true that today we can even find the proof of Gödel's incompleteness theorems in the text? That is, of course, if we read the signs *correctly*, in the way Gödel himself did.

"And to wit, why must all this be dated back to a thousand B.C.E.? Referential inversion is what gives Bourbaki life: the proof is dated not in accordance to when it was published, but to when it was *found*. In which case, Bourbaki proved Gödel's incompleteness theorem in the year 1921, when Gödel found it in the *Mutationes in libro*. This is the key to Bourbaki's continued existence; the key to his everlasting soul. One may say that he is still with us, locked up in a cupboard behind the stage. He speaks to us from the text; perhaps, one may suspect, *he is the text.*

"But something most peculiar seems to have been happening of late; something signaling the end of an epoch. A little over a month ago the appearance of a sign almost apocalyptic in nature was reported. You see, out of necessity we maintain a hierarchy of sorts. Four men alone lock themselves up in the innermost chambers of our labyrinthine library, dedicating their whole life to poring over Bourbaki's text and uncovering the fleeting mathematical secrets lying within. The rebellion in 2002 was the first symptom of our downfall, but it is only now that the degeneration has really grabbed us by the scruff of our necks.

"The four practitioners of this highest form of art would typically follow a fixed path every day: they would fix their gaze upon a mote of dust and follow its trajectory for as long as they could, as it lay suspended in the air, wrested around by forces beyond its control. This tiny mote of dust is elevated to the supreme status of symbolizing the present in its entirety, and its trajectory, which is seen as capturing this, is traced out and used to finally read the signs presented by Bourbaki in his Book of Changes.

"The method has begun to fail. Last week, after a whole day's labor, what was reported from the Book was nothing mathematical at all but, rather, an endlessly inventive and detailed description of copulation between two grotesquely designed creatures. And there are only two ways in which such a failure can occur: either the dust mote has become corrupted as a symbol of the present, or the present itself has become treacherous. But the mote of dust is infallible, the *perfect* representation of the blindingly concrete, fleeting, and unassuming Now! In other words, one may conclude nearly *mathematically*—pardon the pun—that it is the present itself of the mathematician, captured by those four servants of the world (who labor in their dungeons even now!), that has betrayed us.

"Plainly evident is the chain of causation that can lead to this degeneracy: it is nothing but the overabundant presence of an ignorant rabble. A fool may spit his buffoonery in quite a different place and context than this one, but the universe captures all; the spit of the fool may throw a small fly ever so slightly off its trajectory, which in turn causes an unseemly flutter of dust around it, which in turn represents itself in nothing but that very mote of dust which tells us how to read Bourbaki, ultimately leading to the skewed nonsense that we see in Bourbaki nowadays. Now you may understand our initial hostility toward you: *For Bourbaki cannot sustain more corruption.*

"It is at its—*he* is at his tether's end. The identity of the book was always a stress point, a paradox far exceeding that of the Ship of Theseus in intensity, and it is finally going to make the whole thing burst at the seams. For you see, this is the final punchline, our ace-in-the-hole: *There are virtually no empirical grounds upon which one can claim that the book that lies with us right now is the same one Bourbaki once wrote.* To paraphrase a certain someone, the signs and their interpretation do not form two sides of a monster Dedekind cut in the middle of which stands man. As we change the way in which we read Bourbaki, the physical signs constituting the book change themselves in a fatally real manner.

"And when we *pull* this ocular flexibility beyond its elastic point by reading all kinds of buffoonery into it, this book will explode into itself, and mankind's greatest treasure will be lost once and for all.

"With this, it is at last time for me to arrive at the most important part of my speech, of your indoctrination—"

The microphone screamed for a moment, after which the lights ceased to illuminate the stage and a deafening silence rang out in the pitch darkness, all converging to end the impassioned speech of the man in a horribly abrupt manner.

A few moments passed in a confused silence, after which I caught an exchange of anxiety-filled whispers by some individuals on the stage. And then, with a shocking violence of movement that completely broke the drowsy incomprehension of the room, a man took to his heels and began running.

He passed right by me just before I understood what was going on. But when I caught a glimpse of him in the pseudo-darkness clutching something tightly under his arm, I knew immediately: he was trying to steal Bourbaki for himself.

A moan of desperation issued from the stage. The crowd's chattering increased to a climactic pitch, but nobody seemed to have any realization of what the situation was. Some higher power seized control of my body, and I leaped out of my chair and ran after the thief.

How does one describe the absence of temporality? Is it not a contradiction in terms to say, "For a few moments the passage of time ceased to exist"? There it is: there is no real way to express that timelessness except by condensing the set of events to a single point, to the eternal Now; for that always lies beyond temporality. Much as when an object has ended up breeding too much mass for its own spatiality, it collapses into itself to form a black hole, it was that the passage of time between my chasing the man and ultimately reaching him that was unsustainably high; it collapsed in on itself and transformed itself into a prolonged specious present.

There were the endless stairs again; he ran up them—they must have been the only way out. I chased him as hard as I could. I was gaining on him, but it wasn't enough. If the door was open, he would get away.

I tramped up the stairs, taking three at a time. In the tone and tempo of the thief's footsteps I could hear his desperation and terror getting the better of him. He nearly slipped a couple of times. My footing was sure; I gained on him some more.

But it wasn't enough. He'd nearly made it to the door. I screamed and made one final, desperate leap forward toward him; my hands missed him by a hair. He whimpered in fear, but in a few moments I heard him clasp and jiggle the door-handle.

It didn't open.

He began banging wildly against the door, but it was too late. I caught up to him and smashed his head against it; for a moment I was an animal bent on tearing my rival apart to pieces.

He immediately slumped down to the floor. Whether he fainted out of fear or because of the blow to the head, I was not sure.

Suddenly the door opened. I saw my guide standing anxiously just outside, with one hand on the door. His eyes widened at the sight of me, and he fled.

It was then that I spotted a thin, yellowing, novella-sized booklet lying beside the body of the thief, illuminated by the pure sunlight of the dawn that was streaming in through the open entrance.

My heart began beating fast; I felt as if it was about to burst out of my rib cage. I knew what the book was: that timeless, eternal masterpiece containing all the secrets of the cosmos. I had found Bourbaki.

Vaguely, as if from some faraway place, I heard footsteps approaching from below. But they were still far underground. I had time. I had lots of time.

I touched it and blacked out momentarily because of the sheer excitement and adrenaline that my find was sending through me. But it felt just like any other old book to touch, and I fell to the ground just outside, opening its pages.

The grass was all around emanating a strange smell, one that I for some reason associated with the vapor of the repulsive decaying of something once alive. I found myself on page 73 and started reading. For just one moment the text appeared to be filled with disparate symbols belonging to some foreign script; the indescribable rays of the rising sun gave it an ethereal look.

However, as I continued looking at it, I saw the signs begin linking up with one another of their own accord; and to my horror I saw that the structure it created was not any text at all but a *painting of me*—except I was terribly disfigured and naked, and my skin had everywhere the awful black color of bile, and hellishly red eyes stared out of my devilish, vulture-like face.

CAN WE KEEP HIM?

Darrell Schweitzer

A career-retrospective of Darrell Schweitzer's short fiction was published by PS Publishing in two volumes in 2020. A veritable flood of Schweitzeriana is soon to follow from various publishers in the next year or so, including a new Lovecraftian anthology, Shadows out of Time *(PS Publishing),* The Best of Weird Tales: The 1920s *(Centipede Press),* The Best of Weird Tales: 1924 *(with John Betancourt, Wildside Press), a weird poetry collection,* Dancing Before   Azathoth *(Hippocampus Press), a new story collection,* The Children of Chorazin *(Hippocampus Press), and two further volumes of author interviews (Wildside Press). He was co-editor of* Weird Tales *between 1988 and 2007.*

THAT SUMMER, WHEN I'D JUST TURNED THIRTEEN, I began to look at Zenobia Collins in a way I never had before. Yes, she was a year older than me, and my cousin, but so what? Yes, she had six toes on either foot and they were webbed, but so what? Nobody knew who her father was, but these things happen. Aunt Emily must have wandered into the woods when she shouldn't have, or sleepwalked there in a dream, which is what she always hinted at, but so what? What fascinated me about Zenobia was that she was wild. She did and said things nobody else did. For all we converse with Those of the Air or raise up the dead at our festivals, and await the coming of strange gods, the people of Chorazin (Pennsylvania, not the one Jesus curses in the

Bible, which is somewhere else) are a pretty conventional, dull lot.

Except Zenobia.

I remember that it was a particularly hot summer afternoon, and Elder Abraham (who really is a thousand years old, no question about that) was going on again with the story we'd all heard so many times before about how he once saw Charlemagne when he was a kid, and how the sacred and mysterious blood of our ancient race that flows through us all is even older than Charlemagne, and through that blood we shall all be transformed and find our places in the new world when the Earth is otherwise cleared off (yadda-yadda-yadda). I was alternately playing games with my toes on the dusty floor, or staring up at the cracked ceiling and trying to imagine that the cracks were rivers and mountains and I was looking at a map of lands far beyond our little village, and Zenobia was squirming in the row in front of me, making the bench squeak.

As soon as we escaped from that meeting house she grabbed me by the hand. We both ran well past the edge of the crowd, into the woods, and she said, "Come on, Abel! Wanna see something neat?"

Sure I did, but I had no idea what she had in mind; she could always surprise me; so I let her drag me along. She nearly pulled my arm out of the socket. She was in a jolly mood, kicking up new-fallen leaves and making quite a lot of noise, but even she grew silent when we came to the Bone Forest, which is a creepy place, even if you've grown up in Chorazin and been there during the winter festivals when the dangling bones—some of them animal, some of them not—rattle among the tree branches and turn in the wind, and some of the more prophetically minded among us are able to interpret those sounds like oracles.

This afternoon the bones merely dangled, and we walked silently, and I could feel things down in the earth, some of them our ancestors, some of them others, even the great shapes that rose out of the ground like breaching whales during some of the more extreme winter rites. Today it was just quiet. I let my toes sink into the cool mud, and the presences were there, but not stirring.

Then we came to the hollow country, and I was a little nervous. Children in particular are warned not to go there, because that's where you might meet the Other Folk, who are people whose changes were not entirely successful, or at least so different that they could no longer live among human beings. I had another cousin who became one of them, but he went away when I was four, so I didn't really know him. Nevertheless, the Other Folk are to be feared, even by us, and there were people who came back from encounters with them mutilated or insane. (Yeah, these things happen.)

Yet that was where the neat thing was, and Zenobia led me on. The hollow country is indeed hollow, where the landscape rises into jagged hills, and there are little valleys and depressions in the ground where the sun never shines and the trees are thick and mossy and you can be certain no axe has ever touched them. The forest floor is mostly bare mud and fallen needles from the evergreens, and it is quiet. It is a place where no bird sings.

We climbed down a very steep embankment, very carefully because both of us were barefoot, grabbing onto muddy roots with our hands or feet, until we came to a cave, where the way was rough for a while and then grew smooth and very cold, and that was where I first saw one of the Other Folk; and when I did I screamed and tried to run away, but Zenobia yanked me back to her and said, "Don't be afraid. You'll be okay if you stick with me."

What I saw on the path before us, in the semi-darkness a few yards in from the cave mouth, was naked and very pale. It had human hands and arms, but far too many of them, and otherwise a body like an enormous worm. The face was almost human too, the head completely bald, and when it opened its mouth it revealed fangs and hissed like a cat. Its wide nostrils flared. The eyes were black and might have been blind.

"They don't like me," Zenobia said.

"Really?" (Was that a good thing?)

"You know how Elder Abraham tells us that we will all find our own special talent as we get older? Well, mine is making them stay away from me."

Sure enough, as she led me forward, the thing backed away. I heard rustling sounds in the darkness farther back. There were more of them. Something flapped and flew over our heads.

"They can't stand the smell."

"The smell?"

"Of me." She shoved her armpit at me. I leaned to sniff. She slapped me and said, "Don't be gross!"

"But you said—"

"It's a scent. I looked up a word once. A *pheromone*. I think that's what it is. They have really good noses, like dogs. I've got this *pheromone* that they really don't like, in my sweat, in my breath, and anything I touch or breathe on or spit on, they stay away. That includes you, as long as you're with me."

"And if you don't touch?"

"Then they don't stay away."

Something in the deep inside the cave howled. Something else seemed to be singing. I wished we'd brought a flashlight, but Zenobia just groped and led me, as if she knew where she was going, every step of the way, and had been here many times before.

Then again, maybe there were things in the darkness that even she didn't want to look at.

She directed me carefully over a ledge, showing me where the handholds were, and we descended down, down, I don't know how far exactly, but it seemed like a very long way. In time the stone beneath my feet was smooth again (and frigidly cold) and at times regular enough that I think we were walking down *steps*.

Then she shocked me by actually producing a small flashlight out of her pocket, turning it on, and dropping it down a hole. I heard a scramble down there and something *caught* the light and shone it steadily up at us. My eyes were so adjusted to the darkness by then that even this dazzled me, and I drew back, but I could still see a little detail of the cave we were in. Strands of something like sopping, gooey rope covered most of the ceiling. There were indeed Other Folk up there, very spider-like, but there were others off in the distance, on the ground, as big as bears, and a little shaped like bears, albeit without any fur, and white and flabby, with enormous claws.

A web of the same ropey, gooey stuff covered most of the hole. The light shone through it.

"Hi," said Zenobia.

The voice down there was that of a man, and he sounded really scared.

"Thank God you've come back! You've got to get me out of here!"

The light flashed over my face.

"This is Abel."

"Hello," I said.

"You kids have to help me! Go tell your parents! Get the police! Get someone!"

"Can't do that just yet," Zenobia said.

"Why not? Please—"

"It's hard to explain."

"The police!"

"Ain't no police."

Behind us, the Other Folk stirred and made chirping sounds.

I broke in. "Who are you?"

"My name's Lester. Lester Nichols. I'm a reporter. *Scranton Evening Sentinel.* Look, Abel, if you help getting me out of here, you'll be a hero. I'll make you famous. It'll be a big, big story. You'll get rich. You can go on TV."

"I've seen TV," I said. "Brother Azrael has a TV in his store, and a VCR. Sometimes he shows movies to us. I've never seen anybody I knew on it."

"Jesus Christ! You don't understand, do you? I'm going to go crazy down here unless you get me out. I'm going to die!"

"Ain't no Jesus Christ here."

"I think we gotta go," said Zenobia.

That set off a frenzy of screaming and pleading and cursing. He even threw a rock at us, which came flying up and landed, rattling, somewhere behind us.

"That wasn't very nice," Zenobia said. "But I brought you this." She got an apple out of her other pocket and dropped it into the hole.

Then we left, climbing back the way we came, with the Other Folk following us close behind, but letting us pass. Once something wet and cold touched my ankle, but I kicked it away and it did not grab hold of me.

It was only when we were well along into the woods, almost to the Bone Forest, that Zenobia said, "Well, wasn't that *neat?*"

"Yeah . . . neat. How did he get there?"

"I met him in the woods. He told me all about being a reporter, how he wanted to break the big story and tell the world all about Chorazin and our ways. I don't think Elder Abraham would like that, do you?"

"No . . ."

"He actually offered me a candy bar first. I took it. Then money. Twenty bucks. Ain't much to buy around here. Anyway, I told him I would show him something neat. He was dumb enough to follow me down there, and when he first saw the Other Folk he didn't scream and run away. He said, 'This is fucking incredible,' and he tried to take their picture with a camera, but he scared them away with the flash. He even followed me into the hole. I went down first. I told him I wanted to make sure it was okay, but really because I ran my hands and feet through the dirt and I spat in it and even peed in it, so it would smell like me and the Other Folk would not go down there. Then I told him to come down. He had a little flashlight. I told him to turn it off, because the really neat thing would only appear to him if it was totally dark. What a dope. He fell for this too. He didn't even notice that I'd slipped away and was climbing out of the hole until I was almost out. Then he cursed at me and tried to climb after me, but the Other Folk let me pass and did not let him pass. They swarmed over the opening and started making that web. It comes out of their mouths."

"So you left him there?"

"Yeah. He's like a spy. I caught a spy. A really dumb spy. He carried on quite a bit for a while, but when he calmed down I told him that there really was something neat down there in that hole, and it was *him*. Now, isn't that *funny?*"

"Yeah, I guess so." (I wasn't sure about this.)

She started laughing really hard. She bent over double. Then she was dancing all around in the leaves beneath the dangling bones, and she clapped her hands and squealed in a little-girl voice, "Can we keep him? Huh? Huh? Can we?"

"Shouldn't we tell our parents, or Elder Abraham—?"

She clapped her hand over my mouth and said sternly, "Now you keep quiet about him, Abel. He's our secret, yours and mine. Don't you tell nobody else. Nobody else needs to know about this."

"Then I guess we'll have to keep him."

"Yep."

"What will happen to him?"

She shrugged. "If he tries to get away, I suppose the Other Folk will eat him. But he's okay if he stays where he is."

So for the rest of that summer and into the fall, he stayed where he was and remained, though I am sure he would not have agreed with such an evaluation, basically okay.

That first night, after Zenobia and I had returned from the Hollow Country, my mind was racing. I lay awake for hours, trying to work out the implications of what I'd seen and what Zenobia had done. This man, Lester Nichols, was an *outsider*. I'd only met one outsider before in my life. A few years back we had a teacher, who didn't last very long, though she had seemed nice, and then she went away, and nobody said much about her, although her car was left rusting in a field and the boxful of

National Geographic magazines she'd ordered for us were still in the schoolhouse, and all the kids had been through them thoroughly. Plus, Brother Azrael sometimes showed us movies. So we knew there was an outside world, which was very unlike Chorazin. It was doomed. It was transient. It would not be there once the Earth was cleared off, but that was where Lester Nichols came from, so I still felt an immense fascination for its difference and its strangeness. I thought that having a reporter from the *Scranton Evening Sentinel* right where we could talk to him anytime we wanted was, as Zenobia had put it, *really neat.*

To Zenobia, I think, he was more like a pet, something you bring home from the stream and put in your aquarium. If it's a tadpole, it swims around and eats fish food and that's fine for a while, but it's not as simple as that. When it sprouts limbs and starts to turn into a frog, you have to let it go, because frogs eat flies and there's no way you can catch enough flies to feed it. You have to learn to think of the pet as a life of its own with its own needs. You have to forget about your own gratification and let go, or else it's going to die.

But I don't think Zenobia ever got that far. To her, Lester Nichols was a toy. Besides, he was also a spy, and you don't let spies go.

Was she cruel? Yes, I think she was, particularly the time when she went to see him and told him that she'd called the police and the Marines and they were coming to rescue him.

The next time we went to see him, maybe a week later, he asked bitterly, "So what happened to the Marines?"

"Sorry," she said. "They couldn't make it. They had a war in Vietnam and all got killed."

"The fucking Vietnam War has been over for years."

Zenobia just laughed and laughed, while he screamed and cursed, and then wept. I guess he was pretty dumb. I think he had actually gotten his hopes up and thought that the Marines were coming.

Admittedly, she kept him fed, and when he said it was cold

down there, she got him a jacket from somewhere. She even went into Brother Azrael's store and stole some batteries for the new flashlight she'd given him. (His previous one must have broken or gotten lost.) But she did not let him out.

I did not oppose her in any of this. As I said, I'd started to look at Zenobia that summer in a way I'd never looked at any girl before. I was as much in her power as Lester Nichols was. I followed her around. I did what she told me to do and kept my mouth shut when she told me to. I know the other kids in the village were snickering. My parents and even Elder Abraham were aware that I was seeing an awful lot of her, but so what about that? Cousins marry cousins all the time in Chorazin. Only much later did I learn that in the outside world this wasn't considered normal. But what did the outsiders know, doomed and transient as they were? But I am well ahead of myself. We weren't exactly engaged. We were just kids.

What puzzled and bothered me was that about the time school started in the fall, Zenobia started losing interest in her toy or pet, or captive, whatever you wanted to call him. Sometimes I would have to tug on her arm and say, "Let's go talk with Lester." And sometimes I regretted it, because all she did was play another mean trick on him, but at least with me reminding her, she did keep him fed, more or less, and when the weather started getting colder she even supplied him with a pair of sweat pants.

Finally she said, in a snippy voice, "Well, if you want to go talk to him, *you* go."

"How can I, without you? The pheromones."

"I'll show you," she said, and she put her arms around me and touched me all over as if she was going to kiss me the way they do in the movies, but then she bit me gently on the neck (different sort of movie) and it felt like tiny, sharp needles going in. When she drew away I was able to see that she had two extra, tiny teeth, like rattlesnake fangs in her upper jaw, which retracted as she smiled at me, and were gone. There was blood on my neck, but I wasn't really hurt.

"Now you're a little more like me," she said.

So with some hesitation I made my way into that cave again. I was ready to bolt and run for my life at the first sign of trouble, but the Other Folk recoiled from me as they had from Zenobia. I climbed down to the edge of the hole where Mr. Nichols was and gave him a whole sack full of supplies.

Then I asked him, "Tell me about Scranton."

He said it was a big city.

"Do they have movie theaters there?"

"Yes . . . they do."

"Do they have robots and fly around in spaceships, like in *Star Wars?*"

At that he actually laughed and said, "No, that's made up. Everything in *Star Wars* is made up."

I had rather thought so, because the returning gods are in the sky. They make the stars ripple as they pass. I couldn't imagine that they'd let humans fly around much in spaceships.

Then Lester Nichols began to tell me about his life and his job, what it was like to be a reporter on a newspaper and travel all over to get stories. He also told me, with considerable sadness in his voice, about his family. He had a wife named Margaret, whom he loved. She probably thought he was dead by now. He had two kids. There was a girl, Anne, who was six, and a boy, Teddy, who was about my age.

"Does he like *Star Wars?*"

"Oh yes, very much. I am sure you two would be great friends. He'd show you his lightsaber."

"I thought you said *Star Wars* was all made up."

"It's a toy."

At this point I wasn't sure who or what was a toy, the fake lightsaber, Mr. Lester Nichols, or me. You see, Zenobia was losing interest in more than one pet at a time. I was still fixated on her. She still seemed the most beautiful girl in the world to me, six webbed toes included, but I could tell that the bond between us was weakening. She did things without me. She started hanging out with other boys. She even took up for a while with Muddy Jerry (actually his name was Jeroboam), who was four years older than her. He's the one you see around Chorazin who wears as little clothing as possible except in the winter, usually just denim cutoffs, because the way the mysterious blood that flows through us all manifested itself in him was to give him the ability to swim through the ground as if through water. So at any moment he might suddenly just drop out of sight, into the ground, on some sort of Chorazin business only Elder Abraham could understand, and when he came back up again the results were pretty messy, hence the minimal clothing and the name. Maybe Jerry could have swum all the way down to the cave and seen Lester Nichols, but he never did. Maybe he was afraid of the Other Folk. Certainly Zenobia never took him there.

I kept on going by myself, as often as I could. I slowly realized I was losing Zenobia. I was still grateful to her for the gift she had given me (including the bite on the neck) because I wanted to know more about the rest of the world and the people in it, transient though they might be, and here I had my own private source.

But even that didn't last. By midwinter Lester Nicholas said to me, "Abel, this can't go on. You know I am dying down here. If I don't get out of here, I will die very soon."

His voice sounded weak. I asked if he was sick.

He said, "What do you think?"

I thought he was heartbroken that he could not see his wife and children and they all thought he was dead. Also his hole smelled really bad, like an overflowing outhouse, which I suppose it was, because there was no place for him to go to the bathroom down there, no real drainage. I did not want to think of the man I had almost come to regard as a friend (even if he was a spy) slowly buried alive in his own shit.

"Okay, I'll get you out somehow," I said.

Think of your pet tadpole.

—.—

173

The opportunity I had for getting him out came at the Midwinter Festival. This is the most solemn of all the rites of Chorazin, when Those of the Air descend and whisper in the treetops, when the ancestors rise from their graves and speak the secrets of Azathoth. It is a busy time for Muddy Jerry, whose task it is to swim deep into the earth and lead the ancestors and others, often mounted on fantastic creatures of bare bone, up to the surface.

It is also a time when children, whose special talents have become manifest, are accepted triumphantly into the adult community. But even though I was past thirteen, I had shown nothing more than the common ability to feel things moving in the earth, so my attendance was optional. (Yes, I had some pheromones from Zenobia, but nobody else knew about that, so it didn't count.) I managed to convince my parents that I had a bad cold and when my mother took my temperature I touched the thermometer to a candle flame for an instant, with the result that they went and left me home in bed.

As soon as I was certain they were gone, and the chanting of the procession through the village had faded off into the distance, I got dressed in my warmest winter clothes, took one of my father's overcoats and an extra scarf out of the closet, and was off. There was a couple inches of snow on the ground. I ran and sometimes fell and slid. Where it was bare, the frozen mud was hard and crunchy. I had to get to the Bone Forest before the celebrants did, and through it without being caught. This I managed to do. It was a clear night with a strong wind. The bones rattled so loudly they seemed to be shouting, like a crowd raised to a pitch of excitement. Overhead, through the bare branches, I could see the stars rippling in the dark sky.

I made it to the Hollow Country, to the cave. The Other Folk crowded forward at first, but I pointed a flashlight at them, said, "Boo!" and spat, just so they were sure it was really me, pheromones and all. (I had considered that my heavier clothing might mask my smell, which would have been disastrous. It didn't.)

This time I tore away the webbing from the opening to Lester Nichols's hole. That had never been there to *keep him in.* It was there to alert the Other Folk if he tried to leave. Now that I was tearing it away, there wasn't a lot they could do about it.

I climbed down into the hole, which was still foul-smelling despite the cold. I found Lester Nichols huddled at the bottom, wrapped in a blanket. I helped him to his feet and into the winter coat, then wrapped him in the scarf I'd brought, and then the blanket.

His face was gaunt and pale, his hair and beard matted. He could barely stand. I explained to him that I had come to get him out.

He mumbled something. "I must be dreaming," he said.

There was now the question of how I was going to get him past the hordes of Other Folk. I did not actually have Zenobia's "talent." My body did not generate the pheromones or whatever they were. I'd had a dose from Zenobia's bite, which was apparently sufficient to protect me, but I wasn't sure I had enough left over, particularly in cold weather when we didn't sweat much, to take care of Lester.

I had only one chance. I had to take it. "Give me your hand," I said.

He gave it. I bit down as hard as I could. Of course I didn't have any fangs, just ordinary teeth, but I bit hard enough to taste blood.

That woke him up. He swatted me off my feet with a swipe of his hand.

"What the fuck is this? Are you some kind of cannibal? Is this a trick? If it is, I think I'll just kill you and then die, here in this shithole. I can't take it anymore."

I tried desperately, fumblingly to explain what I was doing.

At last he sighed and said, "I have to admit that after all I've seen and experienced, what you say doesn't seem any more preposterous than anything else. It might even work. I shall have to trust you."

"You can trust me."

He was very weak. I had to help him climb. I had to send him up first and get behind him and push. The moment of truth came when he reached the opening of his prison. The Other Folk were gathered there. Would they draw away, or rip his head off?

They drew away.

We kept on going. We made it all the way to the surface. Somehow he had found some inner reservoir of strength.

And who do you think we met outside, standing in the snow with her arms folded, breathing in hard, angry puffs?

It was Zenobia.

"How did you know—?" was all I could say.

"Pheromones. I can smell you wherever you go, whatever you do, now that you've got some of mine. I'm even better at it than they are." She nodded toward the cave. The Other Folk were howling in rage at the discovery that their prisoner had escaped.

"He was gonna *die*. I had to get him *out*. He was gonna be *dead*."

She didn't say anything to that. I could tell she was conflicted, angry, but pulled one way and another, until she just stood there, paralyzed, not sure what to do or say.

Nichols started to fall over backwards, into the cave. She and I both grabbed hold of him and led him by either arm, into the forest.

Once we had walked him out of the Hollow Country, through the Bone forest, into open country, you could see the lights of Chorazin farmhouses in one direction, and a dark forest and a low ridge in the other.

I pointed toward the ridge. "You have to go that way. Through the woods. Over the hills. There's a highway. Maybe you can flag down a truck."

But he only shook his head slowly and said, "I am afraid you kids haven't thought this through very well. In my condition, on a night like this, if I make for the highway I will only freeze to death long before any friendly trucker comes along. I came in that way. It's at least ten miles. I have no choice but to head into town." Then he got something out from under his coat and I saw that it was a camera, worn on a strap around his neck. "Besides which, I am still a reporter. After all I've been through, do you think I'd run away without getting the story?"

We could only helplessly follow him. He staggered toward the lights, then toward the chanting. We hid behind some rocks where we could see the circle of standing stones where the main conjurations and sacrifices take place. Just about everybody in the village was there, with Elder Abraham and Brother Azrael in their ceremonial garb, presiding.

"This is unfucking-believable," said Lester Nicholas. Then, about the time Muddy Jerry burst out of the ground in the company of a hundred or so dead people, all of them riding astride a whale-sized creature or construction made entirely of naked bone, Nichols did something really dumb.

He snapped a picture. This intimidated no one. About half the congregants, not all of them human, broke away and were upon us, screaming. I was snatched off my feet almost at once. I don't know what happened to Zenobia. I last saw Lester Nichols running toward the nearest woods with surprising energy. For half a second I thought he might actually escape. "Get away!" I shouted, though I am sure no one heard me. "Get away! Go back to your wife and kids! Get away!"

I was hauled before Elder Abraham, Brother Azrael, and my parents, all of them grim-faced but silent. No judgment was passed on me.

Of course Lester Nichols didn't get away. The miraculous thing was that somehow he actually did make it into the woods and evade pursuit temporarily, but of course he was right that he would never have made it all the way to the highway without freezing to death. But I think it was his reporter's instincts that actually finished him. They found him in the secret room in the back of Brother Azrael's store, photographing the scrolls and secret books the way a spy would do. He got the story. The story got him.

All the next day I heard him screaming, off in the distance somewhere. I think he ended up in the Bone Forest.

Elder Abraham came to see me the following evening. I was terribly afraid that I would be horribly punished too, for helping a spy, and my parents were afraid, my father silent and stoical, my mother weeping softly.

But when the Elder came into our house and sat down at our kitchen table across from me, there was no thundering doom. He merely said, "I have read the bones, and I know your future now. Some of us, though the ancient and sacred blood flows through us, shall remain entirely human in form when the new world comes upon us. You're one of those. Your task will be as a reporter. You shall go out from Chorazin when you are a bit older, get an education at some university, see the transient world and study it, then gather such scattered lore and rare volumes as may be useful to us and bring them back. Think of yourself as a scholar and explorer. It would be most undignified to refer to you as a spy."

Hearing that, I should have been happy, even overjoyed, but I felt nothing. I was dead inside.

Zenobia did not return to school. She was changing rapidly now. She wasn't beautiful anymore. Her hair was a wild mess. There was something wrong about her face. She kept to herself. Of course, in a place as small as Chorazin you couldn't help encounter her occasionally, but when I did she seldom said anything. She would just look away. I could tell that something was growing under her clothing. It might have been extra limbs. I desperately hoped it was wings, so she could rise into the sky and talk with the Voices of the Air. I could not bear the thought of her as merely one of the Other Folk, some half-spider worm-thing crawling in the mud.

Can We Keep Him?

Within a couple months she disappeared.

Perhaps it was wings, because several times before I went away to college, there'd be a scratching at my window at night, and in what I am sure was not a dream I would open that window and hear her voice from out of the dark and starry sky.

But I never actually saw her again.

THE THINGS WE DO NOT SEE

Steve Rasnic Tem

Steve Rasnic Tem, a past winner of the Bram Stoker, World Fantasy, and British Fantasy Awards, has published more than 480 short stories. Recent collections include The Night Doctor and Other Tales *(Centipede & Crossroads Press) and* Thanatrauma: Stories *(Valancourt). You can visit his home on the web at www.stevetem.com.*

ONE EVENING HE BECAME AWARE OF A GREAT SHIFT in gravitation, as if something massive had suddenly entered this world. He could not see it, but he knew it was there.

Clarity was difficult to achieve. There was so much he could not see. He wondered if he had been lonely before. Did he have friends? Did they enjoy his company? He considered whether he might have lived his life in a state of despair. He had no way of knowing, his prior existence a dream he'd forgotten.

Working all night in the print shop, Cooper compulsively checked the view from the front window: a sliver of sidewalk bathed in halogen glare, the asphalt road damp despite weeks without rain, the shambling gray figures of the dispossessed backgrounded by the stark silhouettes of the warehouses, rising above them the outlines of water tanks, transmission towers, and slender smokestacks. Beyond that he could only imagine, which all too often was an activity fraught with risk.

He heard whispering, talking, the occasional growl or moan. He could not be sure if these communications were exterior, perhaps from the abandoned parking garage next door, or interior. If he distracted himself sufficiently, they went away.

The stench was back, an oily fragrance with notes of salt and vinegar. He noticed it his first night at the *Print & Copy*, and since then it waxed and waned with no discernible pattern. Some nights he thought he'd suffocate. Even when he couldn't smell it he knew it was present, enmeshed in the fabric of the neighborhood. Sometimes he wondered if he was the only one aware of the reek. His boss never mentioned it, and Cooper was hesitant to ask.

He proofread the flyer upside-down before calling the customer to the counter. His boss once asked how he learned to read like that. But Cooper couldn't answer. As far as he knew he'd always had this useless talent, a poor trade for a lifetime erased.

"Sir, your job is ready."

The small man in the long gray coat rose unsteadily from the bench. He shuffled to the counter and glanced at the top sheet. "Very. . . nice. You were correct about the paper."

"The heavier stock holds up better on bulletin boards, utility poles, or wherever you want to put it. Take your time. Make sure everything's to your satisfaction."

While his customer examined the flyer Cooper glanced outside. A scruffy vagrant stood rubbing his forehead back and forth against the window, leaving a greasy smear. It wasn't the first time. There was a cleaning solution and cloth under the counter for such occurrences. The man's face looked distorted through the thick glass, feverish and unwell, the skin inflamed, forehead wrinkles and laugh lines receding as he appeared to de-age. Then the derelict peeled his face away, and the way it momentarily adhered to the pane, Cooper was afraid he'd leave some of it behind.

"Perfect. Simply perfect," his customer said.

Cooper focused on the task of wrapping up the flyers. "This seminar—are you the instructor?"

The fellow looked up with watery eyes. "Guide. We learn from each other. You find your own path. I can only help you launch your voyage."

"*Creating Your New Story.* I thought it was a creative writing class. But it's more than that, am I correct?"

"Oh yes. It is a journey toward self-definition, personal growth, but most of all increased connection. Loneliness has become a fundamental problem in our world. Human beings are natural story makers. Their most important story is the one they make up about themselves and their relation to others. If you are unhappy with your life, it is time for a new story."

"That idea is quite . . . appealing." Cooper gazed at the flyer the guide held in his hand. He watched as the words rearranged themselves, letters reversing, turning sideways, expanding across the sheet, some shrinking into a series of dots or nothing. Others gathered at the middle of the page, sending tendrils trawling to the paper's edge.

"Perhaps you'd like to come. I accept drop-ins. You pay at the door." The little man placed the flyer, still busy with changing typography, into Cooper's hands.

Cooper's fingers tingled as the ink appeared to enter his skin. He tried not to react, but he felt his face burn. "Thank you."

He tried to occupy himself with busywork until the next customer came in. A moist sigh issued from somewhere outside. He opened the front door a few inches and listened. He heard nothing definable, a few of the older buildings creaking and bending in the wind. Something in the distance swayed, but it was impossible to tell what it might be—a tree, surely, or a loose panel, a sign. It never paid to speculate.

Months before, Cooper found himself traveling through this district on foot. He had no idea who he was beyond the name on his ID: Stefano Cooper, with a faded photo, a birth date, and an address for an apartment which might or might not have been current, but he had a vague notion the address wasn't far away. He had a wallet full of cash but somehow knew this was the last of his funds. He needed a job. For reasons unknown to him he required a job in this neighborhood.

The area was unpromising. Sad-looking, raggedy-dressed men

and women wandered the crumbling streets and alleys. His own clothing seemed presentable. Cooper felt his face and hair. He'd recently washed and shaved, apparently in preparation for the job search.

The neighborhood was a complex of warehouses and abandoned rail spurs. Warehouses needed workers, so he searched for HELP WANTED signs on every window and door. Eventually he was drawn to the sprawling hulk of a parking garage. The entrance was fenced and adorned with warning signs, the openings in the first two levels filled with barbed wire. As he walked by, he thought he could hear movement inside, shuffling, a sigh of breath. The concrete pillars were cracked, the surfaces flaking, and yet he felt an enormous sense of, not solidity—what was it?—gravity, perhaps. It was the first time he was aware of the smell—oil, salt, vinegar—although it had a vague familiarity about it, reminiscent of aging boat docks, and birth. A row of store fronts was attached to the ground level of the garage along a cross street. All were vacant but one, the *Print & Copy*, a HELP WANTED sign in the window.

The owner was elderly, thin and tired-looking. A series of brown spots of varying sizes covered his arms and ran up his neck and the sides of his cheeks before fading into his thinning hair. They made a kind of pattern. Cooper thought of lizard skin. The man asked him several questions related to his experience. Cooper's answers felt rehearsed, but they seemed truthful. Yes, he had strong computer skills. Yes, he had experience with high-speed copies, printing, oversize laminators, trimming, pouch lamination, folding, and binding.

His new boss must have been desperate because he hired Cooper on the spot, trained him the rest of the day on procedures, and told him he was in charge until the next morning. The poor fellow seemed anxious to leave. Cooper felt no interest in stealing from his new employer, so that was at least one bit of self-knowledge: he was an honest man.

When his first customer arrived, he made himself smile and

did his work without hesitation, so perhaps he indeed had the necessary experience. He hoped his ease with the tasks the job required would trigger clues, identifying memories, but nothing came to mind.

The first time the shop phone rang Cooper stuck his hand in his pocket searching for a cell phone. He didn't have one. It seemed likely he'd owned a cell before. He'd lost it or thrown it away. He grabbed the red handset off the wall. The caller asked for prices and hours of operation, which Cooper was able to read off a sheet on the counter. But he didn't like the customer's tiny voice inside his head and couldn't wait to hang up.

The night-shift customers were generally polite, grateful to have a last-minute option for projects desperately behind, often due the next day. Inconveniently located miles from the Interstate, the shop's only appeal was that it never closed.

When his boss took over the next morning, he seemed inordinately pleased to find everything intact and more money in the till. Cooper left on foot and after many blocks noticed the houses seemed vaguely familiar, although the people he passed did not. No one spoke to him. Eventually he knew to turn into a building, walk up the stairs, and go to a door at the end of the hall. Number 14. He went into his wallet and found the key behind a small leather flap.

The two rooms were clean and nondescript. No books, no pictures, no knick-knacks, the bed made and covered with an army green blanket. Nothing to remind him of anything. A small TV beside the bed. The several changes of clothing in the closet were like what he wore now, assorted colors but within the same muted tonal range, plain cotton trousers, both short-sleeved and long-sleeved shirts, a battered pair of tennis shoes, an older pair of rubber boots. A winter jacket and scarf hung from a hook. Cooper had the perception, both despite of and because of the paucity of material possessions, that he had lived here in relative anonymity for quite a while.

He searched the apartment thoroughly for anything that might provide hints as to his personality or origins. He did so carefully, not wanting to disrupt what his previous self kept in such meticulous order. But there were no personal records or correspondence of any kind, and no cell phone.

He did find a dozen or so sheets torn from a notepad in a trash can. They'd been filled with what he assumed was his handwriting—at least the gestures seemed familiar—but overwritten repeatedly with various pencils, pens, and crayons, so none of the writing was legible. He stared at these scribblings, searching for patterns, until fatigue drove him to bed.

When he arrived the next day for his second shift, Cooper discovered a few square yards of dead insects strewn across the sidewalk in front of the print shop, moths and butterflies, a few crickets, a handful of beetles. His boss told him to get rid of them. It wasn't a big deal. Cooper swept them up and bagged them, threw them in the bin on the corner past the last empty shop.

He arrived for his shift the following day to much the same scene: a killing field of entomological carnage spreading from the front of the shop to the area around the adjoining garage. Cooper dutifully took care of the mess. As the weeks went by this proved to be a daily occurrence, and Cooper started coming in early to clean up the corpses before his shift began. He was seeing fewer and fewer live insects in the area, but he knew they were there. He could hear them distinctly buzzing as if right outside his ears.

He wanted to tell his new boss it wasn't part of his job, just as it wasn't his job to chase the homeless away from the front of the store. He might have been one of those homeless folks himself at one time. The margins of error were so narrow in life; one false move and you became a derelict wandering the streets seeking shelter and safety.

Cooper needed to keep this job. The consistency of coming to work every day made him feel alive. And his boss was too frail to take on such a chore.

But a month of dead birds, bats, and rats followed. He'd never seen so many dead in one place before. The bats had lost most of their heads, as if their tiny brains had exploded, but at least he could tell they were bats. The birds were unidentifiable as to species. Their heads had melted down the length of their bodies, and half their feathers were gone. The rats were reduced to lumps of meat and fur.

The cats and dogs came after, their hides disintegrated, faces erased, although some kept their eyes, wide open in alarm. A few other unidentifiable animals were part of the mix: a raccoon, a deer, maybe a large fox. Cleanup took Cooper hours.

He didn't know how long he could keep this up, never knowing what new dead thing would turn up next as the killings progressed up the food chain. He asked his boss what could be causing this, but the man shook his head, muttering "Death is everywhere."

Then it stopped. The problem appeared to go away.

Cooper had sufficient time to attend the first *Creating Your New Story* seminar before his shift started. It was held in a decommissioned elementary school not too far from his apartment. Although it had been repurposed as a community center, he couldn't find much evidence of use. The gym was full of shabby furniture and audio-visual equipment and the classrooms appeared hastily abandoned, with papers and books and in one classroom piles of hardened modeling clay on each desk.

A series of crudely lettered cardboard signs led him upstairs to the classroom holding the seminar. Cooper paid his ten dollars to a diminutive lady sitting by the door. Could she be the instructor's . . . the guide's mother? She didn't bother looking at him. Only a dozen or so seats were occupied. The guide dispensed with any sort of introduction. He sat at the front of the room facing them, still wearing the long gray coat, and read aloud from a paper held in front of his face.

"Our goal here is to see reality without assumptions, without interpretation, without making up a story. But if we must make up a story, because we are all story makers by nature, perhaps we can at least make it a positive one, a tale that will comfort us during these trying times. If not that, then at least something interesting, something to get the blood flowing and shake us out of our lifelong sleep." The guide moved the paper aside, looked at Cooper, and smiled slightly. Not knowing what else to do, Cooper nodded. The guide's eyes widened, as if he hadn't expected a response. He continued to read.

"True self-knowledge is a rare thing, an ephemeral moment of clarity out of a lifetime of confusion. Most of us will never experience such a moment. I wonder if it is even possible. Because our minds latch onto pain, and pain consumes us and informs our stories about ourselves. Mental health involves countering those stories of pain with more positive ones. But they are still stories, still untrustworthy narratives of the truth that is out there.

"We cannot trust our memories of who we once were. Those times, that self, are all gone now. Look around you. See what exists in your world *right now*. Trust *that*.

"We can never be sure of the things we do not see. It is difficult enough to make an accurate assessment of what is right in front of us. We cannot believe what lives in the shadows, or trust what dwells in the darkness beyond. Not until we see these things with our own eyes can we know they exist.

"The first step is emptying our minds of the old narratives, the old notions of who and what we were about. We need to let a new consciousness push aside everything that was there, and when those stories are gone we will have sufficient space for our new truth."

The lecture drifted along in a monotone, the speaker rarely making eye contact with his audience. Cooper indeed could feel the thoughts being pushed out of his head, only to be replaced with boredom. Where was the guided voyage, the learning from each other? The ideas seemed familiar, even intriguing, but delivered so poorly Cooper's attention began to wander to the other attendees.

One elderly man was so intent on the ceiling Cooper looked up to see what was so interesting. Overlapping stains made a topographical map of the graying tiles. There'd been roof problems in the past. A drop of liquid splattered the old man's glasses. So not the past. The man's body began to palsy. When the quaking subsided, Cooper noticed the crustiness on the back of the poor guy's skull, like pavement requiring repair.

Cooper was aware of that peculiar smell again. Was it leaking out of the ceiling, or from the fellow's head? He heard the distant rise and fall of conversation, but he hadn't noticed any other people in the building besides the ones in this classroom. Then, as if aware of his attention, the conversation stopped.

The two young men on either side of him appeared to be taking notes, so he assumed they were engaged with the lecture. But when he looked closely he saw they each had one of the flyers, circling specific words, adding connecting arrows and various petroglyph-like doodles. One of the men turned the sheet over and started scribbling manically, creating layer after layer of words and symbols in the same space. The flyer tore, despite the thicker stock, and soon he was etching his writings into the surface of the desk like a thoughtless schoolchild.

Many of the other attendees were asleep, heads on arms on their desktops, heads in hands and leaning precariously into the aisles. He noticed then how poorly dressed many of them were, how dirty their hands and the backs of their necks.

The sole exception was a young woman dressed primly in a white blouse, black skirt, and red sweater. She wore her light brown hair long and pulled forward, making a collar around her neck. She seemed agitated, leaning forward as if to listen, then leaning back with shoulders slumped, looking around at the others, and like Cooper trying to see what they were writing. Once she glanced back at him and he was alarmed at how pale she was, her eyes like black coals in the snow. She smiled at him self-consciously and turned back around.

They were given a thirty-minute break at the halfway point. Many went outside to smoke. Cooper, who did not smoke (had

189

he ever?), followed the young woman out to the front of the building. He was intent on leaving and going into work early, but he waited, sitting a few feet away from her on the steps. She gazed at the dark street, the lamps coming on. She rubbed and scratched the back of her hands, in one instance drawing blood.

"What do you think so far?" he asked.

She twisted her legs around and frowned. "It's not what I expected from the flyer." Then she stopped, looking as if she'd lost the thread of the conversation, or she'd heard something else and was trying to make sense of it. After an awkward length of time she blinked and began speaking again. "I don't know much about these things, but he doesn't seem very good at this."

"He's not. He's a terrible speaker. He might as well give it to us in a handout and let us leave. In any case, I'm going to go. Life's too—" He paused. "Is it too short, or is it too small? Funny, I can't remember. But it was nice meeting you." He stood up.

"Wait . . . I'll walk with you." She practically jumped to her feet. "Is that okay? I can't—I can't go back to where I'm staying. At least not yet."

He hesitated. He didn't know her, and he wondered if this was a foolish thing to do, but along with his memory he had lost his sense of what was or was not foolish. "If that's what you want to do."

As they walked in the general direction of the *Print & Copy*, he wondered if she realized they were entering a *questionable* neighborhood and if he should caution her somehow. He expected her to stop and tell him goodnight at any moment, that she should be going home now, but she never did. "I'm Cooper. Stefano Cooper . . . you can call me Stef." Had he ever gone by Stef?

"Stefano—is that Italian?"

"Could be, I guess."

"You can call me Cathy." She paused, looking down, and then didn't continue. Since this had happened before he didn't say anything, and they walked quietly together. She tugged on his sleeve, and he looked at her. The way she nodded and rose on her toes, she reminded him of an anxious child. "I think maybe I once thought I should be a Cathy. In the mirror at least, I think I look like a Cathy." They had entered the edge of the warehouse area. The prevailing architecture lost a level of refinement and visibility as they entered the darkening lanes between buildings. "Can you smell that? I thought I smelled it before, but it's stronger here."

"Then you smell it too—a little sour, and salty."

"No, more like a slaughterhouse," she said, wrinkling her nose. "Do they butcher cattle here? It smells like . . . old blood."

"Oh. One of these buildings might have been a slaughterhouse at one time. But I was thinking the ocean, and birth."

She frowned. "Well, birth can be bloody, I guess. A new life doesn't happen without pain."

There was more itinerant activity than normal, assuming all the figures moving through the shadows were the usual types he saw on these streets every day. She kept looking around and moving closer to him. Some of the figures had gathered in groups near the buildings. "We're only a couple of blocks from my work. I could ask my boss if you can stay. If you like."

"Would you? I *can't* go back there. I took ten dollars from his wallet for the seminar. By now he knows I'm gone and what I've done."

"Who is this man?"

They'd stopped beneath a streetlight. It provided a false sense of security. The brightness of the light kept them from seeing what lay beyond. The silver glare bleached her face. Her hair was thin on top, exposing regions of bare scalp.

"I have no idea who I am!" she blurted. "It's as if whoever I once was has been pushed out of my head! He found me in the park—no wallet or purse, *nothing*. Not even a watch. He said he'd take *care* of me." She made a bitter face. "Oh, he *has*. He says I don't have enough sense to be out on my own. I can't take care of myself, according to him. He's watched my every move for almost *two years!*"

Cooper didn't know what to say. He wanted to understand

more of what was going on before making his own confession. *Two years?* He pulled her hair off her neck. She had symmetrical bruises on both sides, some dark, some yellowed. "I'm sure my boss will let you stay. Then you can tell me what you want to do next." They walked further into the maze of warehouses. He liked the closeness even though it made him uncomfortable.

"What's that by the dumpster?" She was already walking toward the green container before he could stop her. She halted several feet away from the pale form lying on the pavement. He walked a few feet past her. "Sometimes people dump dead dogs and cats down here. They treat this neighborhood like the city dump. I should have warned you."

With the skin gone and the skull smashed it was difficult to identify, but it was too large to be a cat or a dog. Perhaps a large calf, but the front legs were shorter and less muscular than the back ones. He nudged the body with his foot. It moved easily, weighing almost nothing.

"What is it?" she whispered behind him.

The left eye remained. It appeared human. "Nothing. Nothing. An animal carcass, too far gone to identify. We should go." He pulled her away before she could see the other soft forms lying on the damp concrete in the shadows but a few yards away.

Something about the parking garage was different, a bit more of a general lean, more cracked and collapsed perhaps. Then he looked into those open spaces behind the barbed wire and saw people inside, hundreds of them rocking back and forth, their backs turned. He couldn't see past them. The gate blocking the entrance had been flattened, and there were other forms—he could see their legs and backs at least—milling about within. She stopped as if intending to look, but Cooper pushed her past the entrance and into the *Print & Copy*. It was foolish, but he felt safe inside this small space where he worked every day.

He was surprised to see the counter and the tables stacked high with orders waiting to be picked up. They had never been this busy before.

"You're early! Thank God for that!" Cooper didn't see his boss, then noticed a single bloodshot eye peering through the stacks on the counter. He went around the counter's edge and found the aged man slumped in his office chair, faint and shaking. Normally smartly dressed in a narrow black tie and a white shirt embroidered with his name on the pocket, his boss had stripped down to a sweaty tank-style tee. Seeing more of the man's spots reinforced Cooper's impression of *lizard,* but today they appeared liquid, as if painted on. "They've been coming in all day wanting these handouts and advertisements and pamphlets and whatevers. The oddest jobs. I told most of them to come back tonight for pickup."

"I can help." She'd come up beside him.

"Who's this? I'm not hiring."

"My friend . . . Cathy. She's . . . just visiting."

His boss waved his hand dismissively and climbed to his feet. "I don't care, really. It's your shift, whatever you want to do. I'm leaving now. If I don't show tomorrow, put the Closed sign up. I may have to take the day off."

She helped him make sure each order was in its own separate box. The old man had gotten sloppy. Some orders were just stacks of printed pages with nothing separating them. It didn't help that much of the text on these jobs were nonsense words with random illustrations of unfamiliar animals, individuals staring out of windows, and examples of odd architecture. Several of the booklets consisted of random abstract designs with no words. Cooper found the original order sheets and matched them with the jobs, printing the order number on the front of the box. She helped him move these boxes off the counter and onto the floor behind.

Now and then he paused to listen to the noises and conversation coming from the garage. At times it sounded like a variety of abstract music. He could not tell if there were instruments other than voices involved. She kept waving at her ears as if annoyed by flying insects.

As each customer came in, he had them check their order for correctness before accepting payment. As always, he proofread the jobs from a variety of angles. It made his head hurt. With each job some bit of text or image remained lodged in his thoughts and could not be removed.

By morning the disgusting odor was back, stronger than ever. He ran to the bathroom a couple of times to empty his stomach. She had already given up, collapsed in the chair with her eyes closed. He wondered if he would have to carry her or call an ambulance. He was afraid to stir her, afraid she would not open her eyes.

The final job left from the day shift was more flyers for the seminar, thousands of them in a variety of colors. Cooper couldn't imagine why they were needed, given the evening's sparse attendance.

The woman who'd taken their money at the door pulled up in a battered station wagon to pick them up. Cooper forced a smile. "He must be expecting a lot more students."

"He would never call them students," she replied, paid, and he loaded the flyers for her. She sped off without another word.

After sunrise he waited over an hour, but his boss never showed. He cautiously approached Cathy, but she was already awake and actually smiling. She helped him clean up and then he hung out the CLOSED sign.

Once outside, he felt awkward, hoping she would speak first and tell him what she wanted him to do. But she remained silent, gazing at the buildings and the streets around them. He watched as lines of people entered the warehouses through front doors, side doors, even climbing up on loading docks and pushing their way through the dingy overlapping vinyl strip curtains used to keep insects out. This had never happened before. He was anxious to leave.

They noticed the fluid in the street at the same moment: a greenish-yellowish froth leaking from inside the parking structure and flowing across the sidewalks and down the gutters and spreading into the intersection beyond. It had that awful smell, but intensified. Cooper walked out into the street, stepping over the flow, turned around, and stared up into the garage. All those ones were still there with their backs turned, but motionless, and silent.

He walked over to her and whispered. "I can't let you walk away from here alone. I can go with you, take you anywhere you want to go. A police station, or a hospital?" He should have gone to a police station when he first found himself here. The idea had never occurred to him.

"I don't know what to do," she said, avoiding eye contact. "Could I go with you to your place for a while?"

"Sure. I'm fine with that."

She looked directly at him. "But we're not going to have sex."

The statement shocked him. "I—of course not. You're perfectly safe with me." In fact, the idea had never occurred to him. In this new life of his he never thought about sex.

On their way to his apartment, they passed crowds heading in the opposite direction, toward the warehouse district and the print shop. He wondered if there was some big event he didn't know about. Certainly possible—he never paid attention to such things. He didn't even watch the news. Was it possible there was a sports arena in the area? But he'd never seen such crowds before.

It was a great mix. Many seemed in a holiday mood. Some looked as if they'd missed a few meals. He saw men and women and children in only their underwear, a dazed look about them, as if they'd come down with an unexplainable urgency and left their homes without getting dressed. Many looked confused. Many mumbled nonsense to themselves. His companion grew quite agitated. She clutched his hand and was now practically dragging him along behind her.

When they got into the apartment, she asked him to lie down with her. She looked so tired, so fragile. He was afraid she would collapse before she got to the bed. She wrapped her arms around him and lay her head on his chest. He couldn't move even if he wanted to. They both fell asleep.

He remembered how they folded themselves into each other, how nicely her hair smelled when everything else seemed so foul. How he couldn't remember her name, the fake one, or even his own. But this was a safe place away from those crowds, where he could hold on to something he could be sure of.

Cooper woke up with one hand in her hair, but his fingers went too deep, because she was far too soft.

He propped himself up on one elbow, not wanting to free his other arm from under her head. But she was too light, and the sudden motion made her float away. He heard her body land on the floor beside the bed.

He was painted with her. Most of the fluids had dried, but there was some dampness. He dragged himself over to the edge of the bed and looked down. The top of her skull had collapsed into this gritty mush. Everything else about her face appeared erased.

Hours went by, but Cooper couldn't quite catch them. He would have to clean up the mess. He threw the blanket and sheets over her and gathered what he could. She'd been right: she smelled more like slaughterhouse than ocean, and the stench was everywhere. He stripped out of his foul clothes and added them to the pile.

He showered until the water was too cold to tolerate. Still, he sprayed himself down with deodorant before slipping into fresh clothing. Even with the bedding the bag he put her in weighed almost nothing. She took up little room in the bin outside. It was already late in the day. What had he been doing?

He thought about going to work even though he suspected his workplace was gone. But he couldn't remember or imagine himself being anywhere else. He walked to the old elementary school and tried to climb the stairs. It was impassable because of all the people trying to get into the classroom. They all had their ten dollars and their flyers waving in their hands. A few shouted they'd be willing to pay much more if the old woman would only admit them.

Cooper gave up and left the building, heading back toward his apartment. He still had the vague notion he might go into work. Where else could he go?

Voices filled his head. There were many people around him, but few were talking. Now and then he stopped walking to listen. He couldn't be sure, but it seemed her voice had been added to the mix.

Crowds poured out of the buildings and filled the streets. It was like a kind of parade. Waves of people swept across yards and broke down fences, tore down bushes, and pushed over trees. Most were silent but a few tapped on shoulders and shouted questions. "Have you seen me before? I don't know who I am! Is this the way? Please tell me this is the way!" Some appeared angry. Many looked genuinely terrified.

Cooper saw one man twirl around in confusion, as if forced into a kind of dance. He fell and the people walked over him. They stepped on his skull, and it crumpled as if made of plastic. Cooper paid more attention to the ground from then on. There appeared to be bodies everywhere, their individual features disappearing as they were trampled into nothing.

He saw much of the *Print & Copy*'s recent work in evidence. Hundreds of the flyers advertising the seminar in a multitude of colors. Several people had them pressed to their faces or stuffed into their shirts. Others were eating them. Cooper found it mesmerizing the way the type flowed from flyer to flyer and hand to hand, sometimes abandoning the sheets and falling into the street where shoes and bare feet trampled them and scattered the letters around.

The tide of humanity was difficult to resist, and he knew he was being swept toward the warehouses, toward that garage where something waited to be seen into being, and awakening to the consequences Cooper realized that was the one place he did not want to be.

He turned around and had to start fighting, punching people in the face and chest, and shoving them aside. They gave him little resistance, focused as they were on what lay beyond. He made it to a less-traveled street and wasn't sure where to go, just in any direction opposite where everyone else was going. The confusion of voices was dizzying. He kept shaking his head and was relieved to discover the further he traveled the fainter they became.

He ran through a park and up a hill. The area was heavily wooded and seemed to have been avoided by the manic mob. From the top of the hill he was able to see a train station several blocks away with massive crowds pouring from the cars.

The woman at the counter was distracted, talking to herself, her mouth a confusion of tics. She printed out his ticket but did not know how to take his money.

Cooper didn't search the cars, but he appeared to be the only passenger on this outbound train.

Miles into the countryside he felt the shift, as if something massive had suddenly entered this world, or just as suddenly departed. He could not see it, so it was hard to say which. His mind was open, and he nervously awaited what might come in.

GLOBAL WARMING

Katherine Kerestman

Katherine Kerestman is the author of Creepy Cat's Macabre Travels *(WordCrafts Press, 2020), a nonfiction travel memoir to destinations associated with macabre stories in history, literature, and film, as well as numerous horrific short stories and nonfiction articles in anthologies and journals. She is a member of the Jane Austen Society of North America, Mensa, the Horror Writers Association, the H. P. Lovecraft Historical Society, and the Dracula Society. She is wild about* Dark Shadows *and* Twin Peaks *and is known to frolic in the graveyards of Salem on Halloween.*

YOU LOOK EXQUISITE—AND THAT'S GOOD advertising for me when you wear that dress and everyone asks you wheryou bought it." Amanda beamed at the petite blonde woman whowas twirling around in front of the three-way mirror, causing her full yellow skirt to float up. "I hardly feel that I am at work when I'm helping you with your shopping."

Janet regarded her friend. "Operating this darling boutique can hardly count as drudgery. In fact, my dear, you 'work' all day at what *I* do for pleasure—and at great expense, mind you. You play dress-up all day in a very large closet with a cash register."

Laughing, Amanda tossed her head, causing her lush brown ponytail to bounce. She had to acknowledge the truth. She had finally found her niche, turning her fashionista aesthetic into an asset. Janet had been her roommate in college and was now the proprietor of a bed and breakfast on the edge of town.

"I dare you to resist these fantastic new pumps." She leaned in between the calves of a mannequin in a navy bouclé dress and one in a cruise-wear red maillot to peer out the window. "Did you hear—?"

The winding wailing of sirens brought an abrupt end to their conversation. It was the emergency broadcast system—and the baritone computerized voice was intoning *THIS IS NOT A DRILL.*

"You've got to be kidding," sputtered Janet. Dropping the party dress to the floor, she pulled on her sweats and joined Amanda at the window.

The friends went outside and looked about the intersection of Main and Front Streets, which was the sum total of downtown Meriton, Connecticut—and they saw cars racing past them on the two-lane road. Halfway down the block, a woman and man were putting their children into a car. The couple slammed the doors shut, and the friends heard their tires squeal as their car made a U-turn in the center of Main Street. In the distance, they could hear other car doors banging shut and other ignitions turning. They walked to the coffee shop: it appeared to have been hastily abandoned, the blue-plate specials still on three or four of the tables, and the piped-in soft rock still playing. The drugstore was locked, its lights turned off. They tried the door of the savings and loan. It, too, was fastened tight. Despite the harsh wind that was just beginning to whistle, the laundromat door was wide open; inside the empty building, a single dryer was spinning. Business after business they found vacated. Another car door slammed, and another engine roared, somewhere out of their view behind the red-brick buildings of Meriton.

"Let's get back to the store, Janet. We had better check our phones—we must find out what is happening!"

"Honey, we'd better get out of here first—like everyone else."

When they had returned to the boutique and Amanda had

locked the front door, they hurriedly gathered their coats and purses and ran to the exit at the rear.

"Let's *go*," urged Janet, already at the door, her hand on the knob. She did not turn it, though, for she saw her friend creeping toward the stockroom. A soft, slithering rustle from that direction having attracted her attention, Amanda was tiptoeing to the door and peering into the dimly lit space—searching for motion in the shadows of the shelves and in the spaces between the boxes. Her heart was hammering against her ribs as if it were trying to break them. With a crash—from its place at the top of a pile—a box of winter fashions toppled to the floor. As she turned to see what had fallen, Amanda caught a glimpse among the cartons—a moving patch of green!

Janet, still clutching the doorknob, saw Amanda turn to leave, and she drew the door open wide. The young women sprinted across the parking lot to Amanda's blue Volkswagen.

Janet tried to open the car door and cried, "It's locked!"

Amanda felt desperately around the wallet, the coin purse, and the lipstick in her handbag—trying to find her keys. She poured the contents of the purse onto the pavement—no keys! She dropped the purse: "I must have left them on the counter."

"We have to go back for them."

"I'll go—I know where they are. Stay here—watch the door."

She hastened to the front of the store, where she could see the key ring lying on the counter, beside the cash register. As she retrieved the keys and turned, she became aware of a putrid odor—a sickly sweet, disgusting, sulfurous rotten-egg stench that was polluting her pretty dress shop!

She zigzagged a frenzied path among racks of holiday dresses and winter coats, to reach Janet, a silhouette in the doorway—but, before she had covered the winding route, the gray steel door slammed shut. She tried to open it, but it would not budge, and then . . . her stomach dropped. She felt a cold, wet, and slimy thing clutching her ankle. She looked down—a thick green rope was twining itself about her foot! She pounded the door.

"Amanda! Amanda!" Janet called to her from the other side of the door. "Is the key on your ring, honey? Is the key for the back door on your ring? Hurry!"

Fumbling, nearly dropping, her key ring, Amanda inserted a key that would not go into the keyhole, and then another that went in but would not turn. She removed the key, reinserted it, and wiggled it. The lock gave way. When the door at last was opened, Janet became aware of the scaly green rope holding her friend. She lifted the sand-filled cigarette reservoir beside the door and with both hands pummeled the tough green tube until she severed it. It oozed a sticky, malodorous orange fluid onto the concrete.

Janet pulled her friend toward the car, pried the keys from her fist, pushed her into the passenger seat, and then she sped out of the parking lot—and she kept on going, negotiating the narrow back streets that led to the highway, barely slowing down when she came to the paint-worn warehouses at the intersections, to avoid colliding with the other speeding drivers. Grim and silent, she gripped the steering wheel, oblivious to all but the road.

Wiping the drops of sweat rolling down her face and neck with a wad of tissues, Amanda directed the search engine on her cell phone to the network news. She clicked on the CBA logo and selected the "Breaking News" icon. A handsome New York TV anchor was urging his viewers not to panic. People everywhere were fleeing, he was saying. He employed bullet points to list the causes of the pandemonium: first, a horrible stench of unknown origin; second, a plague of green vine-like or snake-like wriggling things; and third, an unusually pink sunset. It was not yet known whether the green tubular entities were vegetable or animal. A list of shelters scrolled along the bottom of the screen, as he advised his viewers to stay tuned for further updates. The anchor yielded to a reporter on location in Idaho who was describing the exodus from Boise. Amanda looked up from her phone and shrieked—six or eight green tendrils were creeping up on the window from beneath the windshield wipers. They were oozing a viscous orange substance upon the glass.

Turning to see why Amanda had cried out, Janet swerved the car—barely avoiding a pedestrian on the side of the highway. Mortified, she pulled over to the shoulder, and Amanda rolled down her window and called out to the man, to ask him if he were hurt.

"Gosh, Joe, I almost sideswiped you," apologized Janet, leaning across Amanda, for she recognized their friend. "What in the world are you doing, walking along the highway?"

Joe took off his sunglasses to look at her, and he shifted the bundle he was carrying to a more secure position under his left arm. He waved his other hand: "I'm okay. You didn't come *that* close. Hey, where in the heck is everyone going in such a hurry?"

Janet put the car in park and got out. She pulled the snow brush from the luggage compartment—and bravely began knocking the slimy green tubular things from the windshield, shuddering with revulsion as they slithered beneath the hood—while Amanda handed her phone out her window to Joe so that he could see the news. The women knew him from the animal shelter where they all volunteered: Joe was a veterinarian who donated his services.

Joe shifted his wriggling bundle in his arms as he stood there, saying, "Spook, stay still, sweetheart. We'll be home in just a minute. I want to see what's happening, old girl." He looked at the mystified women in the car and explained, "Wrapped in this blanket is Spook, a very spoiled feline friend of mine." He pointed over his shoulder: "We live in a cabin in the woods over there, just off the highway. Spook, well, she just went berserk—*berserk even for her*—chasing after a green snake. So I chased after her—and I didn't catch up to her until we reached the highway. I was afraid a car would catch her before I did."

"Are you going to evacuate, Joe?" asked Amanda.

"My dear lady, given these present circumstances, that would seem to be the most appropriate course of action," he said, trying to force some levity as he worriedly studied the mass movement of vehicles. "Would you girls provide me a lift back home? I think I should lock up the cabin and gather a few necessities. I do hope this turns out to be a false alarm."

With his wriggling bundle, Joe hopped into the back seat, and Janet backed the Volkswagen up on the berm. At the top of the ramp, Joe took a short-cut through the woods to his log cabin, while Janet and Amanda contemplated the mystifying sight of so many cars speeding past them. Twenty minutes later, Joe rejoined them, driving his own blue pickup truck, with Spook safe in a carrier in the backseat, and they returned to the highway in their small caravan of two vehicles. The sky on the horizon before them was fast becoming unexplainably pink—*unearthly psychedelic patches of pink*. And the air smelled of rotten eggs! As Janet closed the car's windows, Amanda told her that she had smelled the same disgusting odor in her shop when she had gone back for the keys, and she suggested that they stop and make a plan.

Janet pulled off the freeway at the next exit, and Joe followed. They rendezvoused at an abandoned service station, where they filled their gas tanks, commandeering the portable gas cans lined up on a shelf and filling those too. Finally they refueled themselves with coffee and soda and doughnuts and then sat down on the curb to compare notes. As Joe washed down a bite of a jelly doughnut with a swig of hot black coffee, he noticed an orange and brown furry animal rooting in the dumpster; pointing to it, he whispered to his companions that he wondered what kind of animal it was, with such odd coloring. He could have sworn he had seen two tails on it.

Married for twenty-five years, Diane and Carter Harrison had each recently retired from their positions as teachers in a small New England college, and they were enjoying a long-anticipated week of backpacking among the Catskills. The weather was mild, and the fall coloring of the Hudson River Valley was magnificent;

best of all, there was not a human or a building as far as they could see—even with binoculars.

While they were removing their backpacks and unzipping their parkas, they discussed the strange fears of the Dutch explorers who had sailed up the Hudson River in the seventeenth century. Unable to understand how *anyone* could have misgivings in the midst of such beauty, Carter and Diane recalled that the colonists had looked with dread upon the Catskills. The magnificent, enigmatic mountains had inspired the tale of Rip Van Winkle, the unassuming fellow who embodies the dread we feel when we hear strange sounds during the night. In the cornucopia of the New World, *the European explorers had sensed evil.*

"You're letting your novelist's mind run amuck again, Diane," Carter chided his wife good-naturedly, putting his arm around her shoulders and giving her a squeeze. "Keep it up, dear. Tell a good enough ghost story and there will be no sleeping for us beside the fire tonight."

"All right, let's change the subject. It is high time we selected a site to build a fire and pitch our tent. It will be dark soon," she replied, unfastening her backpack and pulling from it the necessary items. "I'll gather some firewood while you erect our woodland fortress."

Diane strode purposefully into the wood while her husband unfolded the gear he had been carrying on his back during their half-day hike. Looking up at the sky over the tall pines of the forest, Carter was unnerved by its pinkness.

"Hey, honey, come here," he called to Diane, who returned with a handful of twigs to see what her husband wanted.

"I'll be darned!" she said, frowning, "What *is* that, Carter? An absolutely stunning sunset? A forest fire?"

"Somehow I doubt that fires look like pink tie-dyed fabric," Carter replied. "I simply have no idea what it is."

"Could it be a solar burst—or—or—a northern-lights kind of event?" suggested Diane. "I wouldn't be surprised if it turned out to be pollution—or even global warming: both have been in the news a lot lately. At any rate, I *must* get the kindling so we that can make a fire and roast our gourmet meal of freshly canned organic Boston baked beans. By the way, I've been toting a thermos of Riesling. Do you think that will pair well with beans, Carter?"

As the sun was sliding beneath the horizon, disappearing behind the tall pines and autumned oaks of their personal paradise, they shared their meal. It was growing cold, and the two weary nature enthusiasts were cuddling beneath a warm cover to watch the unusual sky.

"Even the sun is flamingo pink—not the usual reds and purples of most sunsets," Diane mused. "I'm cold. Let's get in the tent. Will the fire last all night?"

"I tried to build it so that it will," replied Carter. "I'm concerned, though, because the cold wind is picking up now— and Diane, *it smells just like sulfur.*" He chuckled at the thought. "We're not camping on a volcano, are we?"

"This wind is *No Joke.* Dear, let's secure the fastenings on the tent and get inside. We'll keep each other warm." Diane planted a light kiss upon her husband's cheek, and they gathered up loose items into their backpacks and pulled everything inside the small tent with them. With the whining winds pushing and pulling at the tarp—and the fabric straining against the ropes held into the ground by the little pegs that Carter had pounded with a rock— Diane and Carter fell asleep.

"Ugh!" cried Carter.

Diane bolted upright in her sleeping bag and shone the beam of the flashlight on him: a green snake was writhing on his face! With all the strength she possessed in her small fingers, Diane pried the firm, cold, and unexpectedly muscular serpent from her husband and flung it into the fire. Pink and green smoke—*which smelled of rotten eggs*—erupted. Fuchsia sparks flew in all directions!

The rising wind snuffed the flames, lifting the tent from one of its moors, and the tarp flapped crazily in the gusts. Diane told

Carter that they ought to pack their gear and return the way they had come. They had seen some caves on their way up the mountain—perhaps in one of them they might find shelter from the storm. They strapped each other into their backpacks and retreated toward the caves.

Bending low to reduce their resistance to the wind and the rain, they trod the leaf-buried trail, which was barely visible in the meager light from their flashlights. They pushed aside the overhanging and dripping branches and saw, through their rain-drenched eyelashes, a large furry animal that was *blue!* It scurried across the trail and disappeared into the brush. Diane and Carter raised their eyes and looked into each other's faces for a moment; then they put their heads down again and forged ahead. When they reached an opening in the mountain, they crawled into the low entrance of a cave. Finding it dry inside, they doffed their coats and laid them on the rocks, and then they sat upon their backpacks on the stone floor. After a brief rest, they crawled on hands and knees to explore the dank and gloomy cavity, and they discovered that the ceiling was higher further inside, allowing them to stand upright.

The storm continued to rage.

"This was not in the forecast," said Diane. "The meteorologist promised dry weather—and temperatures in the high fifties and low sixties all week."

"Our luck couldn't get much worse, honey," answered Carter with a twinkle in his eye, as he conceived an idea. "Hey, let's go spelunking. As long as we're stuck here, I mean."

So they picked up their gear and penetrated the depths of the craggy mountain, where they found much to admire—the stalactites and stalagmites and the crystal clarity of the pool of water—and they even began to think that the storm that had driven them to seek shelter might have been a good thing after all, when a bat soared past, causing them to start. As they rounded the next bend, they were nearly overcome by the overwhelming stench of sulfur.

"Look—there's another one!" shouted Diane. Carter turned to see what she was looking at and saw the tail of a green snake slipping beneath a large rock.

"Honey, let's get out of here," Carter said, "This place is getting creepy. Look—I see moonlight coming from that passage on the right. Maybe we can get out that way."

Diane and Carter crept toward the mountain aperture, through which the cold, white light was entering, and they saw that the opening was a little higher than their heads. Carter jumped up to reach the opening: on the third attempt, he was able to gain a finger hold and pull himself up and out of the cave. He lay on his stomach on the ground outside the hole and pulled Diane out by her arms. Sprawled on their backs, they gazed at the sky.

"Do you know where we are, Carter?" Diane asked.

"No."

They rose to their feet, endeavoring to get a better look. Through the spaces among the entangled tree limbs they were able to see a few stars; very high trees obscured most other views. Admitting now that they were lost, Diane and Carter walked through the shadowy wood without a plan, until they came to a path that led down from the heights of the mountain, a rough sort of road created by the clearing of the trees, which they followed until it emerged into a valley that was encircled by the high mountains. They could see some farmed land and buildings.

"Well, we wanted to get away from civilization," said Carter. "But now I'm glad to see it again. Being lost can certainly change one's perspective. What say we head to that farm and find out where we are, find out just how far we've wandered from the trail?"

Descending from the mountain, they spotted a number of quick-slithering green worms and snakes slipping in and out of the brush beside the road.

"It smells like sulfur here, too," remarked Diane. "Wherever can that smell be coming from?" They continued toward the farm.

—.—

Joe, Amanda, and Janet, their vehicles laden with provisions, prepared to move out. Joe checked under the hoods of both vehicles to make sure they were not carrying with them the curious green snakes or worms. Amanda left their IOU taped to the cash register. They had decided that it would perhaps be safer to seek shelter away from the cities and towns, and so they headed toward the wilderness of the Catskills.

Immense black clouds were swiftly moving in, darkening the surreally pink sky, as they departed the service station. As they merged onto the freeway, torrential rain began to pelt the road, creating patches of standing water, so that it was necessary to slow down to avoid hydroplaning. They attempted to find a news update on their phones, but the weather seemed to be impeding the Internet: they could not even make phone calls, and there was nothing but static on the radios in the vehicles.

"I think we should get off the freeway at the next exit and drive toward the mountains," offered Amanda. "We haven't seen any billboards advertising a business or downtown area for some time now, so this must be a rural area—and I do recall hearing of some type of nature preserve a few miles down one of these country roads."

Janet turned off the highway, and Joe followed them up the ramp. At the stop sign, he pulled his truck beside their car. Over the wind and rain Janet shouted that they wanted to head down the road to the nature preserve. Joe agreed. Their windshield wipers beat the relentless, sloshing rain as they navigated the forlorn road, passing a few darkened farmhouses and fruit stands, a boarded-up tractor dealership, and several sagging barns. Half an hour of driving past farms and orchards brought them to a dirt road, preceded by a large sign designating *EARTH'S END ARBORETUM.*

They turned their vehicles from the paved road onto the mud and gravel drive. The Volkswagen bumped and splashed through ruts and puddles, so that they were obliged to slow down and to hold onto the door frames and armrests to avoid being bounced all over. In the unlit service road, which was bereft of objects to reflect their headlights, they drove into blackness. They were feeling rather bruised and banged up, when a sudden stop caused them to pitch forward onto the dashboard—they were stuck. Joe stopped his truck and turned his high-beams onto the other vehicle. He jumped out of his door and into the downpour. Kneeling in the mud, he shone his flashlight under the car and said, "The axle's broken."

"Can we fix it?" asked Janet.

"Not now. We'll have to leave it here and all go in my truck."

They moved the contents of the disabled vehicle into the pickup, and Amanda got into the front seat with Joe and Janet into the back with Spook. Water streamed from their wet clothes, running off the seats onto the floor. In an attempt to dry them out, Joe turned on the heat, creating steam in the process and fogging the windows.

"I can't believe all this rain. So hard—and so continuous," said Amanda.

"Are we having a monsoon?" asked Joe. "Well, with climate change and all, you know, maybe we're becoming a rainforest—global warming *is* in the news every day."

"What's that ahead?" Janet asked eagerly, pointing to the right side of the road. Joe slowed down and looked in that direction.

"It's some kind of maintenance building," he said, turning his truck toward the structure. "Let's see if we can get out of the rain in there. I'll see if it's unlocked."

Getting out of the vehicle, he tried the garage door; finding that it was indeed unlocked, he hopped back into his seat and drove the truck inside. Amanda pulled the garage door shut again—and then she located a light switch and a coffee pot. There followed a communal sigh, after which Amanda set to work brewing hot coffee, while Joe attended to Spook and Janet hung their wet coats on the hangers of the coat rack.

Sitting around a desk, they dined on sandwiches brought from the gas station and downed a pot of strong brew. Joe opened a can of food for Spook and attempted to use his cell phone, and then Janet and Amanda tried theirs: still no Internet. They all agreed that they should pull blankets from the truck and try to get as comfortable as possible in the swivel chairs for a little sleep before morning, when they would be better able to reassess the situation. They were just nestling into the chairs when Spook leapt onto Amanda's lap and jumped off again, and raced beneath Joe's chair in earnest pursuit of some game.

The tired group sat up to see what she was chasing, and they saw a green rodent about the size of a hamster with a purple tail that must have been a foot long disappearing into a hole in the wall. Spook, her tail swishing back and forth with great energy, was inserting her paw into the hole, feeling around for her quarry and making the earnest mewing sound cats sing when they have their prey within reach. Alas for Spook, the green rodent was not quite within reach and she could not bring him out.

"Green worms, two-tailed orange animals, green hamsters with purple tails—what the heck is going on?" asked the veterinarian.

"Not to mention the pink sky," said Janet.

Too tired to talk and too wound up to sleep, the three pulled their blankets up and snuggled awkwardly into their chairs to try to get some rest.

When the bubble-gum-colored sun rose, the clouds had drifted away. The pink sky was clear, and the warmth of the sun was drying the soggy vegetation on the mountainside. Sitting upon a log, Diane and Carter removed peanut butter sandwiches from their backpacks. They drank water from a clear stream running down the mountain, parallel to the road they were following, and then they decided to continue walking toward the farm they had sighted from the mountain top.

Nearly two hours later, the mountain trail merged into a country road. A barn and silo, a house and other smaller buildings visible in the distance, Diane and Carter picked up their pace, eager to find someone to talk to and to regain their bearings.

"I hope they don't mind bedraggled drop-in guests," Carter said to his wife. "Ready or not, here we come!"

"I just hope they share some hot black coffee and good directions," said Diane. "Then we can find our way back to the trail and continue where we left off on our dream vacation."

Thirty minutes later Diane said, "I can read the sign now—see it there! The sign over the gate reads *Nomed Nursery*."

When they reached the perimeter fence, they found the gate open. "Maybe they'll even give us a big farm breakfast," said Carter hungrily.

A sudden commotion of barking and shuffling caught them off guard. Carter moved to protect his wife. A large black dog with curly hair and horns was growling menacingly and pacing from side to side, fixing his eyes on Diane. Carter looked around for a weapon, a stick or a rock—but there was nothing within reach, and the dog might spring at any moment.

Carter, his back to his wife to shield her, spun around. A shaggy black goat was running at them from the other direction. It too was growling and snorting—and baring its *fangs*. Carter and Diane knew this was the end for them—trapped between two vicious beasts. Diane sobbed, and Carter held his arms out to keep the monsters away from his wife in the full knowledge that they would die.

"Patience, children." The words were spoken by a black ram who was walking upright on his two hind legs. "There will be time." The horned dog and the sharp-toothed goat sat down.

"Lili, come." A slender woman approached, her body covered to the ground by her flowing black hair. She looked at the ram with her yellow eyes. "We have visitors," said the ram.

"For the sacrifice," replied Lili. Diane fainted.

The bright pink dawn barging through the windows awakened

the friends. As Joe stretched in his chair, Spook jumped from his lap and went to the dish in which Joe had fed her the night before. Amanda filled the coffee pot and turned it on; then she rummaged through the drawers of the desks and found peanut butter crackers and corn chips for their breakfast. Janet walked outside. She called to the others, "Come here."

They came to the door and gasped. An orange dew dampened the grass and was wafting up in an early morning orange fog. The air still reeked of sulfur.

"Look!" called Amanda. They looked where she pointed: there was a green snake with two tails in the grass.

"There are more over there," Joe said, pointing.

"Can we get going?" asked Janet, and the unanimous answer was yes.

After a hasty meal, they filled their gas tank from a can in the garage and returned to the rough road to the nature preserve.

"The arboretum is quite a way off the beaten path," observed Amanda.

"I think I've heard tell of some government research or something else on the QT being conducted in the area. Maybe this is the place," replied Joe. "We've already been an hour on this godforsaken path that goes by the name of road. Hold on, ladies—this is the end of the trail!"

Joe applied the brakes. Three pine trees lay across the road ahead.

"Oh, no! We either have to turn around or walk from here," said Janet. The friends decided to walk down the path to see what lay ahead, feeling they could always return to the truck. Joe rifled in the storage area of his truck and pulled out a backpack, into which he placed an indignant Spook wrapped in a warm towel. The three climbed over the fallen trees to continue their way to the arboretum. The forest was strange in the pink light, even unnatural. As they walked the muddy and rutted trail they could see green worms and snakes and rainbow-hued rodents darting among the plants of the forest floor. The forest smelled of sulfur still. They had to pick their steps with care on the road, for it was slick with mud and puddles—and treacherous with fallen branches under the cover of soggy leaves.

"Help!" Joe and Amanda heard Janet cry. They did not see her.

"Janet, Janet—where are you?" called Amanda.

"Down here. Help me, please!" was her reply. Joe and Amanda followed her voice. Amanda pulled on Joe's arm—

"Stop! Joe, stop!"she shouted. "You'll fall in!"

Joe stopped and looked down. He was standing on the edge of a deep hole. He could hear Janet calling from its depths.

"Are you okay?" he called.

"Yes—I mean, I'm not hurt. Help me get out of here!" she yelled back.

Joe lay down and reached into the hole, but he could not touch Janet's hand.

"Janet—hold on—I'm going back to the truck for some rope," he said, removing his backpack. "Amanda, watch Spook for me."

As Joe walked toward the truck, Janet called to Amanda:

"Please get me out of here! There are hundreds—no, thousands!—of snakes down here. There are millions of crabs, too—little ones and big ones. They are crawling on top of each other! Oh, God, Amanda—a big snake just killed a little snake and is carrying it away in its mouth! Oh, God—the snake is slithering—with its head up—it's carrying the little snake in its mouth! The crabs are fighting! *Get me out of this hellhole! Get me out!*"

"Try to hold on, Janet—Joe went to get some rope from the truck. He'll be right back." She continued to try to comfort her friend.

When he returned, Joe instructed Janet to tie the rope around her waist; once it was secured, she gripped the rope above her head, and Joe pulled their mud-caked friend from the abyss. Sitting on the muddy ground, endeavoring to untie the rope with trembling hands, she told her friends that she had been in a cave—that she had seen tunnels—that she didn't want to walk any more—and could they go back to the truck and try a different road, *please?*

In the truck once more, Spook was released from the backpack to cuddle in Amanda's arms, and Joe turned back the way they had come. When they came to a fork in the road, they drove the other direction—that road was waterlogged, too, but in better repair—hoping it would lead to the arboretum.

"Oh, God! Oh, NO!" cried Janet.

Joe stopped the truck. He and Amanda turned toward their friend and, following Janet's gaze, looked at the rear window, where the rain had formed the words *YOU WILL NEVER ESCAPE WHO HAVE BEHELD THE GATE OF THE GREAT UNSEEN.* Amanda, still clutching Spook to her chest, embraced Janet too. Joe erased the message with the rear windshield wipers.

"Look, girls—the sign on the right—it says *Nomed Nursery*— let's go there and see if there's someone to talk to, or at least a place to dry out and eat." And he turned down the drive indicated by the sign.

The mud-splashed blue pickup truck approached the electric gates of the nursery.

"I wonder how long this place has been closed," wondered Amanda. "Look—the trees are all black and slimy, and all the leaves are decaying on the ground."

"Do you think that sulfur smell has something to do with it?" asked Janet.

They drove past decaying crops in what was once a vegetable garden. Beetles were clambering all over the slimy black plants. Green snakes and worms were crawling through the earth. Orange mist was rising from the soil.

"Let's check out that old farmhouse ahead," said Joe. "Might be at least a dry roof. Night will be here soon."

They drove into the yard before the house, where they saw animals grazing—goats, rams, and large hairy orange pigs *with horns.*

"Maybe we don't want to get out right here," said Janet.

Amanda said, "Yes, let's see if there's a place without so many animals running loose before we get out."

Joe turned the wheel—then he applied the brake. The hairy welcome wagon had surrounded the truck, forming a circle around it. He honked the horn and yelled, "Get out of the way!" They did not move.

The goats charged the truck and punctured the tires with their horns. *Psss.* The truck sank a little closer to the ground.

A black ram raised itself on its hind legs and strode forward.

"What the hell is this?" shouted Joe.

The ram called to Lili. A slender, nude woman, with yellow eyes and ebony hair to her toes, emerged from the farmhouse. "Lili, welcome our visitors."

Lili extended her slim arms, revealing the sharp talons at the ends of her fingers. "Please follow me." She opened the door of the front seat. Spook sprang out the door and disappeared from their sight. The goats put their noses into the door and bared their fangs; they nudged Janet out of the truck. Green snakes and worms slithered on the ground all around her feet, and then the standing black ram approached her and sniffed her neck. Joe jumped out of the truck to protect her, but a pink ram head-butted him off his feet. The woman with the yellow eyes pulled Amanda from the truck. Amanda cried, "What is this? Who are you?"

The ram, walking uprightly on his hooves, came to Amanda and sniffed her mouth. Its foul, sulfurous breath made her retch. "I am Nomed . . . Demon. This is *The Nursery*. You are acquainted with my worms who toil without rest. They till the soil that Earth may yield a bountiful harvest. A harvest of Blight. *To nourish the Children*. Come."

Herded by the diabolical menagerie, the friends followed Nomed and Lili to the barn, looking everywhere for a way to escape but seeing none.

"Behold *The Children*." Nomed waved his hoofed foreleg in a sweeping circle. Numerous blue pods lay scattered about the hay-covered floor. Some were hatching—hatching red reptiles. Nomed chanted:

"The slithering serpents bring tribute
For the babes,
For the children of the Great Unseen.
From the molten bowels of Earth they come,
They bring forth sulfurous incense and flame.
From far beneath the planetary crust
From the very furnace of Earth's fiery core
From the subterranean kingdom
From the eldritch depths they prepare the way for the Great Unseen."

"There are many such nurseries. You have noticed that the temperature of the Earth has been rising. Conceited fools! It is not your carbon emissions that have wrought such great changes! The flames of the fiery pool of the abyss have been warming the planet! We have been preparing an incubator. For the little ones."

Janet screamed, one long endless wail. Joe and Amanda hugged her, and Amanda started to pray aloud. Through the open barn door, they witnessed orange lightning flashing and orange hail pounding the earth.

"Come," said Nomed, and his godless zoo nudged the three friends out another door.

They entered what had once been a pool house. "Look, Carter!" cried a woman at the far end of the building. She and a man were tied to the wall. "Help us! My husband is hurt," she cried to the three friends. The dilapidated pool was filled with dark, foul-smelling, congealing blood. The monstrous livestock pushed Amanda, Joe, and Janet to the wall at the end of the building where the couple were tethered.

"Blood. The mountains must have blood," said Lili.

Spook sank her teeth into the cursed woman's ankle. The woman kicked the cat into the gore-filled pool.

"Oh, Spook," cried Joe, tears running down his cheeks.

"The mountains must be fed," replied Nomed. "We nourish Mother Earth that she may be fruitful and bring forth unhallowed demons from her subterranean womb. Make ready the sacrifice."

The flock of hideous creatures converged upon them.

A VERY OLD SONG

Mark Howard Jones

*Mark Howard Jones was born on the twenty-sixth
anniversary of H. P. Lovecraft's death, in a south Wales
town where it once rained fish. His stories are collected
in* Songs from Spider Street *(Screaming Dreams),*
Brightest Black *(Screaming Dreams),* Dreamglass Days
(ISMs Press), and Flowers of War *(Black Shuck). He
also edited both volumes of* Cthulhu Cymraeg:
Lovecraftian Tales from Wales. *His latest collection is*
Star-Spawned: Lovecraftian Horrors and Strange Stories
(Macabre Ink).

I T HAD BEEN A BLEAK AND WINDLESS DAY AND
THE night was now still, moonlit, and quiet. Lewis
pulled the door closed behind him, making sure to lock it. Shrugging his coat closer about him, he walked away quickly from that
poisoned space.

The house was the receptacle of so many bad memories, so
much pain. Yet he knew it had to be emptied before it could be
sold. And his brother had made it very clear that he wanted no
part in that process—though he'd be more than happy to take his
share of the proceeds from the sale, no doubt.

Somewhere in the distance a cat yowled at the moon, begging
it for its cold companionship. Something in its tone made him
long for the cosy, warm interior of his car. But it had sat unused
in the garage since he'd been banned from driving three months
ago, so he began the long, cold walk across town.

When he'd shut up his photography business in order to settle his father's estate, Lewis thought it would only take a few days. It had already been a week and a half and he'd hardly scratched the surface. Just a few old books had been sold. It was as if his father had set himself the challenge of cramming as many possessions as possible into his house. He'd risen to that challenge remarkably well.

The hotel Lewis had chosen to stay in was modest but modern. It was two miles from his father's house, but there were no hotels any nearer. He simply couldn't face staying in the old house while he undertook this unpleasant task.

The needles of hot water from the shower head made him feel slightly more alive, at least, as they eased the pain in his arms from lugging heavy boxes about for most of the day.

Despite its outward elegance, the house was miserable: a mausoleum of his father's leftover life. It had been lived in, after a fashion, after his wife had died and his sons had escaped his stifling influence.

When Lewis had first arrived at the house, the loud click of the key in the lock was almost like a warning, alerting him to the dangers of stepping back into a past he'd tried his best to forget. The interior was even darker and less inviting than he'd remembered. He'd walked through the rooms, filled with abandoned furniture that had seemingly been left unused in decades, as his father's existence had retreated into smaller and smaller spaces.

Even though the house was quite large and generous, Lewis was gripped by a sense of claustrophobia. The house felt as though it was woven together out of darkness and dust. There was certainly no life left in the place.

He eyed the yellowing concert and opera posters, hung all the way up the staircase as testament to his father's lifelong obsession with music. The old man told endless tedious stories about the performances he'd attended or the famous performers he'd glimpsed briefly.

On several occasions Lewis and his brother had been forced to attend ear-splitting performances with their father. It was wise to pretend enthusiasm afterwards. For some reason he still didn't understand, their mother had been spared these ordeals.

In the bedroom he'd found a photograph frame turned face down on the bedside table. Picking it up, he saw his mother and father smiling, sunlit and happy. It was evidently taken before he and his brother had arrived.

It was a puzzle to him how such a happy relationship could deteriorate to such a degree. Maybe the arrival of children had ruined everything for their parents.

In his dream there was a door. No, two doors. Behind those doors. Something was living there. Or had lived there once. Perhaps both. There was writing on their surface. Someone was singing a strange song, a long way off. The sound stained his dream in a way he didn't understand. He felt trapped and suddenly afraid. Still, he reached out to touch the doors. And was grateful that they remained closed.

His father was behind him. "This is for you, boy." He turned at the sound of the old man's voice. There was something in his father's hands. He had no time to see what it was before he was awake again.

This is never going to end, he thought to himself as he crated up some old crockery and clothes. For the tenth time that day he cursed his brother for dumping the task entirely in his lap.

The ghosts of the house confronted him at every turn. Memories long forgotten arose out of every opened drawer and unearthed box. But he could only imagine what had happened here after he'd left at the age of sixteen.

In the roomy downstairs hall Lewis pictured his father standing in front of the mirror, straightening his tie while singing a particular song. He wondered what it was. He'd forgotten that tune for years, but now suddenly it was filling his head, insistent and unrelenting. He tried to hum it to himself, but nothing sounded right. The notes refused to come out sounding anything like the tune he recalled.

His father always fell silent before leaving home every morning to travel to the small pharmacy that he ran. It was as if the tune was only suitable for the home. No one outside was ever to hear it or was even able to appreciate it.

Neither did his father sing it at any other time of the day, as far as he could remember. What could be so special about the tune? Perhaps he was just inventing some significance for it that it never really possessed. Still, it wouldn't leave him alone.

It slowly dawned on him that the house contained almost nothing that belonged to his mother. He'd expected his father to have got rid of her clothes but, besides the odd decorative object or piece of furniture, the old man hadn't kept any reminders of her.

As a boy Lewis felt shame and disgust that he'd survived his mother's death and often wished he'd gone into the grave with her. The doctors had said it was cancer, but he and his brother knew that the old man had somehow killed her for daring to protect them from him.

He pushed the feelings aside as best he could and tried to concentrate on the mountainous task still ahead of him. But the music kept intruding on his thoughts and he realised he'd have to scratch that particular itch if he was going to achieve anything today.

An afternoon spent searching through his father's old records—and even his grandfather's antique 78s—proved fruitless. Nothing jumped out at him. He was now aware that, if he wanted to find the tune, he'd have to play each and every piece of music in turn. He decided to devote the following morning to what he knew would be an arduous task.

—.—

A Very Old Song

The minibar in his hotel room was both a curse and a blessing. The 12 Steps of Recovery hadn't been designed to deal with situations like this, he was sure. He hoped the whisky would have a reviving effect on him. His feet and his head ached equally badly and his back was beginning to complain by the time he opened the second insultingly small bottle.

He gazed into the golden liquid at the bottom of the glass, praying that the grief of the day would dissolve in the welcome burn of the alcohol.

He arrived at the house early the next day, hauling out the two large cases that contained all the vinyl and shellac discs in the house.

Lewis felt in unfamiliar territory from the moment he began playing the first record. Long-dead artistes sprang suddenly to life again as the needle sank into the groove. Voices hissed and crackled out of the past at him. There were songs from shows he'd never heard of, ballads about all sort of topics—but mainly love—and torch songs that dragged at his soul with their heavy melancholy.

The notes seemed to float up to gather just below the ceiling before falling back down onto him like a waterfall of sound. It was not an entirely pleasant sensation.

By the end of the morning he'd heard so many tenors bursting to reach the right note, so many sopranos with voices as sharp as broken glass, that his head felt like a balloon full of notes, melodies, counterpoints, and diminuendos.

But nothing had come anywhere near the tune in his head. Yet he was sure he'd heard his father sing it as a child. Sometimes the words seemed as if they were ready to drop onto his tongue like a stylus onto one of those old records. But it never happened. They always remained frustratingly just out of reach. He felt as if his father's wrinkled hands were on his shoulders, deliberately holding him back from the truth.

Defeated for the moment, he turned his attention to other

tasks. Maybe ignoring the problem would allow his mind to work away at it in the background. He hoped for a 'Eureka' moment some time later in the day.

His father's antique writing desk—one of the old man's prized possessions—seemed like a good place to start. Lewis tried the rolltop; it opened with a little encouragement. He felt relief that he wouldn't have to search around for an elusive or missing key.

There were the usual papers and bills, alongside more mementoes of his father's musical monomania. Then he spotted a pile of notebooks, stacked together at the back of the desk. Pulling them towards him, he anticipated more memories of musical moments the old man had enjoyed.

He flipped open the red leather cover of the first book and was dismayed to see the pages covered with indecipherable scribbles and inane doodles. Each of the other books contained similar nonsense. The old man had clearly lost his mind. He felt a sharp pang of guilt: he should have come home sooner. How could he have let his father descend into this?

Yet the death certificate had mentioned nothing about dementia. The cause of death had been simple heart failure. He made a mental note to speak to his father's doctor soon. Perhaps they'd be able to shed some light on why his father had filled the notebooks with such rubbish.

Then again, perhaps his father had concealed his mental decline too well for any doctor to have noticed. He stuffed one of the notebooks into his pocket, intending to examine it later.

Feeling hungry, he noticed the time and decided he'd best leave for the day. Touring the house one last time, he closed doors and turned off lights.

As he left, he glanced at the statue that stood in an alcove near the door. It was just over a foot in height and showed a woman clutching a flute of some sort. He remembered being told once it was of a Greek goddess, but he couldn't remember which one. Whoever she was, he'd never liked the expression on her face, which had always made him shiver slightly, even as a child.

A Very Old Song

Perversely, he brushed away the layer of dust so that he could see her expression more clearly. It was cold and cruel, showing true disdain for whoever or whatever she was considering. It hadn't improved one bit over his childhood memory of this distant bronze woman. He'd seen that expression once or twice in his life since—usually at the bitter end of a relationship.

He flicked the dust off his fingers and clicked the light switch off, leaving the goddess in darkness. As he opened the door and the light from a street lamp caught her face for a second, he was sure she was sneering at him. Closing the door behind him, he made up his mind that she would be the next thing he sold from his father's estate.

He woke at three in the morning with his father's song going around his head. He couldn't remember if he'd been dreaming of it or not. Whatever the truth of the matter, he obviously needed to get to the bottom of the mystery of what the music actually was.

He needed someone with a knowledge of music, which was something he lacked. Someone with "an ear." Even though they weren't very close, he decided that his brother might be able to help. Not that he'd been much help with anything else. He hadn't even turned up to their father's funeral.

His older sibling could be wearying but he'd try and keep things as brief as possible. Lewis decided to ring him the next evening. Then he turned over in bed and tried unsuccessfully to get back to sleep as the song echoed round his head.

The following day was the now familiar grind, enlivened only by the antics of a stray pigeon that had followed him into the house. It took him nearly an hour to coax the awkward avian out before he could turn to his even more irksome task.

He spent the day peeling away layers of his childhood, struggling to forget the humiliations, pushing the pain to the back of his mind. On his way out that evening, he propped a tattered toy clown on a chair near the door, carefully angling it so that it stared at the figure of the scowling goddess.

His feet ached abominably by the time he got back to the hotel. The almost antiseptic cleanliness of his room was a relief after his father's dust-laden lair. The siren song of the minibar was more or less constant now. He fought it as best he could, but he had no mast to lash himself to.

He decided that he'd best ring his brother before he had too much to drink. It would be an opportunity to drag him into all this, despite his protests. Lewis didn't see why he should suffer this alone.

The phone rang for a more than minute before his brother answered. "Hello, Josh, it's me. How are you?" His brother sounded less than happy to hear from him. He also didn't seem very interested in what progress was being made in settling their father's estate. Lewis went into the details, despite that.

"I'll be glad to find a home for that statue of the Greek goddess that's gathering dust in the alcove by the door. She's a sour-faced little witch! Gives me the shivers."

Josh chuckled slightly. "Yes, I remember her. She was one of the muses. The one who was supposed to inspire music—Euterpe. I remember Mum telling me about her."

He nodded, realising suddenly that his brother wouldn't be able to hear that. "Right," he said. "That figures. Music was more important to Dad than anything else . . . especially us!"

"Speaking of which, do you remember a tune Dad always used to sing while he was getting ready for work in the morning? It was a strange song, but it must have been catchy because I can't get it out of my head."

"Not really, no. Why are you wasting your time worrying about rubbish like that, anyway? Aren't you supposed to be selling the house? It's in a good area of town, so it should fetch an excellent price." Lewis could hear the years of accountancy training coming through in his brother's voice.

"I will . . . of course I will. But I need to get this thing out of my head. It's like an insect buzzing in my brain," he protested. He hated it when his brother forced him to defend his actions. Josh obviously felt that being the elder conveyed some sort of natural authority. But Lewis was damned if he was going to act like the runt of the litter. "Besides, as you didn't want to help in clearing the house, you'll just have to work to my timetable, won't you?"

There was silence at the other end for a few seconds. His brother wasn't rising to the bait. "All right, well, if it's that important to you, why don't you go to the library and ask the music librarian? Hopefully you can get on with something more important, after you've satisfied your curiosity."

He ignored his brother's sarcastic tone as best he could. It wasn't that difficult, as Josh had actually had a bright idea for once.

The main library was housed in a nineteenth-century architectural monstrosity covered in stone curlicues and other affectations. Lewis followed the signs and found the music library to one side of the large, cool central hall.

As he approached the desk, the librarian appeared from a back room. He was fussing with the messy edge of a coffee cup, seemingly unaware of his visitor's presence. Lewis coughed quietly and the man put the coffee cup to one side, ready to be forgotten.

"Hello," said Lewis. "I was hoping you might be able to help me? I'd like to borrow your expertise to identify a song—an old one."

The man wore a badge that said 'Stephen,' but his whitening beard and piercing grey eyes made him appear as if he deserved a much grander name. "But you don't know who it's by? Or what it's called, right?"

Lewis nodded. The man made him feel like a stupid child, whining for something indefinable. Stephen looked at him with what might have been a slight degree of pity. "All right, I like a challenge. Perhaps you can hum a few bars of it for me?"

Lewis licked his lips nervously, nodded once, and opened his mouth. A few seconds of the odd melody filled the space. The music librarian looked at him strangely before clearing his throat and shaking his head. "It sounds very . . . modern. Not my area at all. I'm afraid I can't help."

"No, no," Lewis said quickly. "It's very old. I remember it from my childhood."

"Nevertheless, I can't help you. Now, if you'll excuse me, I have a lot to do." The man glowered at him for emphasis, then turned his back and disappeared into a distant corner of the room. Lewis felt as if he had been dismissed.

On his way out, he found himself being intercepted at the door by a short woman with dark hair. She was clutching an armful of sheet music, so he assumed she was another librarian.

He stepped back as they both attempted to exit at the same time. "After you. Please." Chivalry seemed like the right thing to attempt. She smiled and stepped through, waiting for him in the tiled hallway. "Stephen was very rude to you. I didn't like that," she said. "He's normally so polite—at least, he is to me."

"Well . . ." began Lewis before being interrupted as a knot of children and their loud teacher passed in front of him. The dark-haired woman then took a step towards him. "I may be able to help you with your mystery. I'm a member of a musical group, you see. There's a place nearby where we can get coffee. We can talk there."

"But don't you have to get back to work?" he queried, glancing at the papers she was carrying.

She looked at him with a puzzled expression. "What? Oh no . . . I don't work here. These are for the musicians I mentioned."

He nodded, smiling at his mistake. "Well, in that case, please lead the way."

—.—

A Very Old Song

The café felt like an aquarium, with people crushed against the window as if trying to catch a glimpse of the curious denizens inside. "It's busy," he grumbled.

"There's a place," she said, pointing to a small table in a relatively secluded corner beside a pillar. By the time the waitress brought their coffee, Lewis had discovered that her name was Thea and that she sang soprano in a mixed choir. He'd also decided he had nothing to lose by accepting her help.

He savoured the bitter taste of the coffee on his tongue before looking into her eyes. "Can you help me? I mean, do you *think* you can?"

Thea smiled. "I'm sure we can. Our choirmaster Mr. Rubente knows *everything!* Probably every piece of music ever written." He smirked at her childish exaggeration, realising that she just wanted to reel him in. But it was worth a try.

"We're starting rehearsals next week after the summer break. Why don't you come along?" she suggested.

He nodded. "Yes, I might do that. If it'd be all right?"

She smiled at him slowly. "I'm sure it'd be more than all right. Mr. Rubente is always keen to meet new people. We don't just do the 'lollipops,' you know—we tackle more adventurous pieces. Some are very challenging, in fact. You might find it interesting."

"I'm not very musical. I can't carry a tune without dropping it," he confessed at last. "It's just this one particular piece . . . "

She nodded and reached across him to pluck another cube of sugar from the bowl. He was trying to remember if she'd already had two lumps when he noticed a small tattoo on her inner wrist. It seemed out of place on her. Perhaps she'd find such a personal question unwelcome, but his curiosity was too much for him. "What does the anchor signify?"

She turned her wrist over to look at it, as if she'd only just noticed it. "Oh, my grandfather was a sailor. It's just a little memento of Gramps really."

"My grandfather was a sailor, too," he said. "Small world."

"Good thing you can sail around it, though, eh? Or else our

grandfathers would have been shopkeepers . . . or pickpockets. Then we'd have nothing in common." She smirked at him and two previously invisible dimples appeared either side of her small mouth.

It wasn't that he found Thea odly attractive, he realised, but more that she struck him as odd but still attractive in some unusual way. Her mannerisms were slightly peculiar, but it was nothing he could put his finger on. Some of her gestures were highly exaggerated while others were a mere twitch of her limbs, as if she was in control of a body she was unused to. Several days later, however, he was delighted to find that, unclothed, she was like every other woman he'd known.

They met at her apartment, which was small but well decorated, after she'd declared his hotel "too cold" for lovemaking. He didn't think that was a complaint about the heating.

There was always music playing in her apartment, especially when they made love. Once he found a piece of music particularly intriguing and asked her about it.

"It's called 'Mysteries of the Macabre.' It's by a Hungarian composer called Ligeti. Did you like it?" She propped herself up on one elbow and cocked an eyebrow at him.

"I'm not sure . . . " He'd heard something in it that seemed familiar, but he couldn't say exactly what.

She slid out of bed and pulled on her clothes. "Well, you decide whether or not you did, while I go and make us some coffee."

Lewis got out of bed and dressed. He had to admit he was impressed by Thea's music collection. Shelf after shelf of old vinyl LPs covered almost the whole of one wall.

Her choice of audio equipment did puzzle him, however. The record turntable was housed in an anonymous wooden cabinet that looked as if it had been used by Noah for Saturday night dances on the Ark. He examined the machine, half-expecting to discover a winding handle on the side. "This is *almost* an antique," he said. "Haven't you ever thought about updating it—getting something newer?"

She walked back into the room. "I like old things. *Very* old things!" He was sure that was a comment on their age difference. He hadn't asked her how old she was, but he guessed she must be in her early to mid-thirties. Though he thought she had what people called 'an old soul.'

He took the cup and saucer from her and swallowed almost its entire contents in one gulp. "No desire to keep up with the times then?"

She stared into his eyes and touched his jawline with her metallic green fingernail, tracing a line down to his chin. "Not when 'the times' have got it all wrong, no!"

He clattered his coffee cup onto the saucer with more force than he'd intended, wincing at the discordant sound. "On that note, I've got to get back to my father's house," he said before kissing her goodbye.

The mound of boxes and bags filled with items to be discarded grew each hour. Slightly apart from it sat a much smaller pile of things to be saved. The things to sell were in a separate room.

In the large, square room off the downstairs hallway hung a small painting that held a particular attachment for him. It hung above the piano, and he took pleasure in standing on the stool and then placing one foot on the lid to reach the painting, imagining his father's fury at the action ("If you're not going to play that thing, get away from it!"). The hated thing had been an instrument of torture. Showing no musical aptitude, he'd been spared the worst of his father's obsession, but his brother had been forced to practise for hours on end. He remembered several of the ivory keys flecked with blood on the worst days.

He took the painting from the wall carefully, holding it up to the light and gazing at the dark pigment. It showed a rock-strewn landscape with a set of strange buildings gathered conspiratorially in the blue gloom near the horizon, a withered light leaking from the few windows visible. He remembered asking his mother about it, and had been told it had been handed down to her by her great-aunt, but she didn't know where the subject was. Once he'd even climbed on a chair and taken it down, to see if there was a title written on the back. But there was nothing.

When he was a boy he'd longed to enter the painting and visit the mysterious buildings. They looked as if they might be safe, if mysterious. He'd even seen a film that had a similar story once, but that hadn't ended well for the visitor to the two-dimensional realm. He placed the painting carefully on top of the pile of items he intended to rescue from the house, deciding that he wouldn't even bother asking his brother if he wanted it.

Among the other curios he'd discovered that day was a large, dark object that his mother had once told him came from 'the South Seas.' He wasn't exactly sure where that was, but it was obviously something his grandfather had brought back from one of his voyages. Its surface was smooth and it had a roughly oval shape with no openings or depressions. It was an oily green and brown colour. He had no idea if it was animal or vegetable in origin, but he thought it might be worth something, so he set it aside to sell at some point.

After the day's exertions, he sat in the chair in his hotel room as the TV struggled to hold his attention. Eventually it lost the fight and he began to think of his father once more.

Then, as if on a titanic television screen, he became aware of a landscape unfolding around him. It became clear that it was a city that was both under him and above him. The light coming from the narrow slit of sky visible was bronze, edged with a blackness at each horizon. It appeared molten, as if ready to pour agonisingly down on anyone unlucky enough to be under it. Even though the space before him was clearly enormous, he was suddenly gripped by a sense of claustrophobia.

A Very Old Song

A feeling of dread overcame him; he seemed to be buried at the centre of something. It was a place that resonated slowly with longing and fear, as if an enormous gong had been struck in some faraway building. And there were voices of a sort lost in the feeling, telling him of a place that both enticed him and repelled him equally.

The buildings around him looked as if they had been knotted together, rather than built in any way that he understood. Each structure had an abhorrent beauty that was unique. Beneath his feet was some kind of gutter, thick with an unknown fluid. Voices muttered slowly in the dim light, and he became aware of dozens of malevolent, eyeless watchers reaching for him with their minds.

He began to move forward, if only to try and escape their attention. He made progress at an enormous speed; far faster than if he were walking. This disorientation was soon swept away when he raised his eyes and saw the enormous dark building, filling the space where the ruined sky should be. It seemed to have no definite shape, reaching dark extensions to all parts of the city like an architectural cancer. The sound that wasn't a sound resonated gigantically, drawing him towards the terrifying structure. He wanted to turn away, to go anywhere except inside that dark necropolis. Once inside he knew there would be no way back. Then the hinges began to creak on the enormous doors, each bearing a baneful inscription.

Coughing as if overcome by the foul air, he became aware that he was sitting in a dusty old chair in one of the unused rooms of his father's house.

Still drowsy, he struggled to his feet. How the hell did he get here? The house was in complete darkness apart from the weak light leaking in from the street. Surely he couldn't have been sleepwalking—his hotel was miles away.

He stumbled to the wall and switched on the light. In the dismal kitchen, he cleaned a glass as best he could and filled it with water.

He tried to bring himself back to the everyday, taking several deep breaths between gulps of water. Images and feelings persisted. It was the strangest dream he could ever recall. But perhaps dream wasn't the right word, as he wasn't even certain that he'd been asleep.

He met Thea outside the café she'd mentioned on the corner of an anonymous street. They walked the short distance to the practice hall, which stood next to a very modern-looking church. The hall itself was already half-full of people.

On a table at the front was an oval object exactly like the one his grandfather was supposed to have brought back from one of his voyages. He still had no idea if it was a shell or a seed pod or something even more exotic. "What is—" he began as Thea grabbed him by the arm and dragged him away from the table.

She seemed keen to show him off to her choirmaster and pushed him into place like a mother steering a reluctant toddler. Lewis found himself facing a moderately tall man with a calm, commanding presence.

Evidently, this was the Mr. Rubente whom Thea had mentioned. He was dressed in a light grey suit with a dark blue shirt. Though his hair was grey, he seemed somehow ageless. His face was hardly lined at all, giving the impression of a child that had put on its father's clothes and a grey wig.

"This is the friend I was telling you about," said Thea, rather shyly.

"Ah, yes. Pleased to meet you. I won't shake hands if you don't mind. I understand you have a piece of music that needs identifying?" The man's voice put Lewis at ease. It reminded him of a doctor with an impeccable bedside manner who was about to impart bad news.

Lewis nodded. "Yes. I'd be very grateful if you could help."

The man raised both hands and took a step back, clearly expecting a performance. Lewis coughed and delivered a snatch of the song in his inexpert manner. There were slightly appreciative murmurs from behind him.

Mr. Rubente nodded with his eyes closed. "Yes. Yes. In fact, we'll be practising that piece this evening, if you'd care to stay and listen. Why not join us?" The man's words didn't sound anything like an invitation.

Thea grinned at him. "See, I told you, didn't I?" Lewis felt suddenly elated. At last he'd found someone with the knowledge he sought.

"We all heard our fathers sing this song," she assured him. Her fingers on the bare flesh of his arm felt suddenly like ice. He glanced around quickly at the other choristers and wasn't comforted by their curious appearance.

"Stand here. New boys always stand here," Thea giggled as she ushered him into place at the end of the back row.

"But I'm not a—" he began to protest as she pushed a music manuscript into his hands. She then took her place at the front.

On the cover of the music was a circle that somehow seemed to fold back on itself twice. He stared at it for several seconds, struggling to make sense of the optical illusion, before giving up. From what he'd read in the past he knew that some composers had experimented with different methods of notation—sometimes departing quite radically from the norm—so he put this visual conundrum in the same category. He stared at the opposite wall for a few seconds to give his eyes time to recover.

When he'd rested them, he opened the music manuscript and let out an involuntary gasp. Several people turned to look at him as he stared down at the pages of music notation, which were crammed with pictograms similar to that on the front. He was shocked to see some symbols that he recognised from one of his father's notebooks.

"I—I can't—" he began. Then Thea was at his side. "Just relax," she whispered. "It'll come. Believe me." He turned to look at her and her smile came as a relief after the madness on the page. When he turned his gaze downward again, the scrawl almost made sense. Perhaps Thea was right: maybe he shouldn't force it.

Though he felt like an impostor now that it was obvious to him how advanced the choir must be.

He thought of getting his coat, making some excuse, and leaving. But if he did that, he'd never find out what the song was. He put his mouth next to Thea's ear. "Couldn't you simply tell me what this song is called?" he whispered.

She squeezed his arm in reassurance and shook her head. "It's not that simple. I'm sorry."

Just then, Mr. Rubente called for everyone's attention with an alarming bark of command, and Lewis knew it was too late. He had to go on.

"Remember. Remember! This work...*our* work is very demanding. Never forget WHO we are and WHY we are here. The weakness that some of you showed at our last gathering caused me great personal sadness. Several members did not live up to their promise." Mr. Rubente had been staring at the first row of the choir but now turned his head and gazed straight at Lewis. "We have a new member joining us tonight. I feel confident that he will not let us down."

Lewis felt a sudden sense of panic; he caught Thea's eye and for a second the expression on her face reminded him of the cold gaze of the statue in his father's house. Some sort of sacrifice was expected of him, he suddenly understood. He felt betrayed by her—yet this was also what he'd sought all along. Uncertain whether to curse her or thank her, he quickly lowered his eyes.

Mr. Rubente crossed to the table that contained the mysterious object. Placing his hand on the dark shape, he raised the other to indicate his readiness to begin.

Those next to Lewis took a deep breath, ready to raise their voices at the choirmaster's command. He did likewise. But no command came and those around him remained silent. His lungs began to ache.

The large oval object beneath Mr. Rubente's fingers began to emit a sound. Softly at first, then louder, it sounded like the four winds filling each and every niche of an ancient cave. Lewis supposed that it must be some unfamiliar and exotic musical instrument.

He exhaled as quietly as he could to relieve the pain in his lungs. The others all continued to hold their breath. He assumed they'd all undergone some sort of special training, but it was something he couldn't match.

Then the choirmaster flung his arm out at an odd angle and the members responded with a huge exhalation. Then, just as suddenly, they all sucked air in again. He'd never witnessed anything like it before.

As the members of the choir began to sing, his gaze was caught by some movement above them. He looked up to see a mirage hovering just below the ceiling, showing a group of bodies standing in line. Each shadowy figure seemed to mirror the members of the choir exactly. Yet each had been bizarrely transformed. He felt it was an echo of something that had happened in a city very far away and long, long ago.

The music seemed to take on a kind of odd life, entirely separate from those singing it. The notes seemed to travel through five layers of colour and texture before they reached him. Only then could he join in. Within the notes, which climbed over and around each other in a familiar yet unsettling way, there was a kind of recognition.

The knowledge came to him, seeping into him through the unfathomable melodies. The song . . . *his* song . . . was just a tiny part of a vast improvisation. Barely the first few notes of a deranged composition that had stretched across the chill, lightless expanse, taking a thousand years to reach its end. Only then to begin once again. Man's poor musics paled beside the operatic obscenity of this endless song.

Those few scraps he had heard his father sing were all the human mind could hold, he realised. That minuscule sample of cold perfection had drawn him on, calling to him just as it had to his father and his grandfather and all those who had come before them. But where was he being taken?

Suddenly the music changed. He felt the pain in his throat grow as he strained to sing the profoundly alien words of this ancient song.

It was a song from a time before man was even a dark dream. A song that had once filled the vast blackness, echoing over the bones of a thousand extinct races. A song of exile and desperate exploration, filled with unbearable hunger and despair, intoned by the emissaries of the emptied centuries.

It had been born under the light of moribund stars that had burned out billions of years ago, the pain of their final fires resounding coldly in its agonised notes. Finally, he heard the torn threnodies that had reverberated down the aeons of agony and loss.

Suddenly the song became a scream as he felt himself overcome by a bright light or a desolate darkness—his mind now no longer able to distinguish between the two. The overwhelming sound became a blankness that filled his mind and scraped against the eggshell walls of his skull.

He awoke in cold, calm darkness. The sound and pain he had been immersed in were now only a memory. But one that was too close.

It took him a few seconds to realise that he was sitting with his back against a wall. The cold seeped into him through his thin clothes. Lewis didn't know if he dared to stand up in the darkness, as he had no idea where he was. Instead he snaked his fingers out along the ground on either side of him. He stretched his arms out as far as he could, but found nothing except hard stone.

Somewhere in the darkness there was a voice. He strained to hear what was being said but the words were blurred and unclear. They may have been instructions . . . or a threat.

Lewis feared that this was the black place he'd been shown. From the outside it had looked vast. He had no way of knowing where he was inside it. Even though he could feel sensations, he also feared this was death. Or a kind of death.

A Very Old Song

The voice came again, instructing or commanding. Insistent. Relentless. Once again he tried to work out where it was coming from. It sounded neither near nor far. And this time there was more than one.

It seemed to him now that the voices came from the other side of the wall. Then, in a moment of clarity, he realised that there *are* no voices in this bleak cathedral of the dreaming dead.

DECEPTION ISLAND

Nancy Kilpatrick

Award-winning author Nancy Kilpatrick is a writer and editor in the horror/dark fantasy genre. Her twenty-three novels include her current series Thrones of Blood, *recently optioned for film and television. She has just finished a science fiction/horror novel and is continuing with the final book in her series,* Imperilment of the Hybrids. *Connect with her on Facebook, Twitter, Instagram. Subscribe to her newsletter at: http://www.nancykilpatrick.com.*

"IT LOOKS LIKE A GHOST TOWN." ZEL STARED through the binoculars at the grey, rocky island to which they were headed and shivered.

"Spookiest place in Antarctica," her seventy-three-year-old Aunt Moira stated with authority. "This is where the *real* Gods live."

The two of them, plus twenty-eight other tourists, were undulating along the frigid Antarctic Ocean, ten each in three Zodiacs made of thick, black PVC. It was a bumpy ride.

They were headed toward a minor island in the South Shetlands archipelago, and this close to the water it was chillingly cold. A narrow inlet lay ahead that would take them into Port Something, named after Someone, but Zel had forgotten who— too many names on this two-week trip. Laser-intuitive Aunt Moira suddenly shouted, "Port Foster!" so that was probably it.

This was day nine of the Antarctic tour and for Zel, finally, the end was in sight.

Erik, the motor operator and tour guide on this particular Zodiac, recited a few facts from the past. Someone else whose name she missed had discovered in the navigationally hazardous bay Raven's Rock, submerged 2.5 meters below the surface. Another unknown from the past dubbed it Neptune's Bellows.

She closed her eyes for a few seconds and sent a plea to all the gods she knew about, including the ones Moira worshipped, asking for assurance that this *would* be the *very last island* they'd visit. Then, finally, she could get back to civilization and *maybe* have a crack at starting the so-called normal life she craved.

It had taken two days to get from Ushuaia, Argentina, at the southernmost tip of South America, a.k.a. *The End of the World*, to the Antarctic circle. It would take another two to get back. For Zel it had been a hellish ride through the Drake Passage on their small cruise ship where three seas converged, powerful ocean currents fighting for dominance, leaving her stomach roiling with seasickness for an entire day.

Zel, trapped in bed as the volatile oceans collided, was not appreciated by Aunt Moira, who had a history of being generally disappointed "in my *timid* niece!" Zel's fears and Moira's daring stretched to the same degree but at opposite ends of every scale.

Once Zel revived, she make the mistake of telling her aunt, "I'm really looking forward to seeing all the animals."

"Pffft!" exclaimed the indignant Moira. "While *lolling in bed* you missed a pod of Orcas and a giant tortoise. That's what happens when you give in to weakness!"

Zel felt half-guilty and half-annoyed.

Every morning on the cruise ship there was a briefing after breakfast, giving information on what was to come that day.

"Antarctica is more than 14,200,000 kilometers or 5,500,000 square miles. Of the seven continents, it is the highest, driest, coldest, windiest, and brightest, roughly the size of the United States and Mexico combined, and is almost completely covered by a layer of ice that averages more than one mile in thickness, but is nearly three miles thick in places. This ice accumulated over millions of years through snowfall. Presently, the Antarctic ice sheet contains ninety percent of the ice on Earth, and if it melted, sea levels worldwide would rise by over two hundred feet, almost sixty-one meters."

"Yadda, yadda, yadda," Moira said, unimpressed as usual.

But Zel knew something of climate change and hoped the ice down here would stay stable.

The ship's first stop was King George Island, named by the Brits long ago, now home to several international stations that researched many types of science, five countries represented on the western shore, two more on the eastern. Zel was just relieved to set foot onto solid even if snow-covered ground.

Vernadsky Station was large, icicles hanging like knives from long brown barracks-like buildings constructed on thick stilts. The mean temperature for December was 2° Celsius, but today's cold cut to the bone. In future, she'd wear a second sweatshirt under her parka.

There were always tours everywhere they travelled. Aunt Moira was addicted to them, but Zel was bored to tears. Too much info and too repetitive. Too many days of this with more to come. The hostile-to-human-life island "had been given by Britain to the Ukraine in 1947 and is run by the Russians." *And they can keep it,* she thought.

At least on this island the natives were friendly, one of the researchers a bit too much so. Grigor invited her and then hastily included her aunt to what he called "Southernmost Bar in World!"

Aunt Moira accepted on their behalf so she could dig out stories the tour guides wouldn't tell. His stories were mostly mundane, and Zel watched displeasure build on Moira's face until her aunt asked, "Yeah, and what about the murder?"

"Attempted murder," Grigor told her, "on Bellingshausen Station." He waved to the bartender for more vodka.

"Sergey, he love to read," he went on. "An engineer, so you know he is—how you say in English—um . . . "

"Boring?" Aunt Moira offered.

"*Da!* Oleg is welder, he also like to read but have unfortunate habit. He tell Sergey how books end. Sergey tell him to stop many times. Oleg did not. They argue and Sergey stab him in chest."

"Oh my goodness, did he die?" Zel asked, wondering if the vodka and this distressing topic were making her head light and her heart beat too fast.

"Of course not, he Russian! They evacuate him to Chile. He fine but decide no return."

"What about Sergey?"

"He sent back to Russia for trial."

Moira laughed and laughed, but Zel didn't think there was anything funny in that story.

Their hours at the station ended as the light dipped in the sky and a bit of snow began to fall. Moira loved the unpredictable weather, the grim stories, the harsh conditions. "If we're lucky," she said, "there will be another murder!" Zel just shook her head.

The following morning was another breakfast and then talk about where they were going that day. Moira, who believed she knew everything there was to know about the southernmost continent, was noticeably frustrated. Given the massive amount of research she did, Zel understood her aunt's annoyance.

Hearing so many details was mind-numbing, and Zel thought she'd have to be a zoologist to remember differences between the eight types of penguins, let alone their names.

"They hire such stupid people!" Aunt Moira snapped. "There's more history here than they know or care to tell. And they totally ignore the ancient *Gods!* Such disrespect. And all these ridiculous rules!"

"Well," Zel said mildly, "we do need to know some things."

"Like what?" Moira challenged.

"To wash our boots before we land, and when we depart wash them again before boarding the ship, so we don't take or bring microbes with us."

"Claptrap! Do you think this continent is isolated? There are hundreds of research stations in Antarctica. All those people traipsing back and forth, supplies sent in, work sent out. Insulting the Gods by defiling the land. You're so naive, Zel, you always have been."

They bypassed two islands further south, Brabant and then Melchior. The elderly passengers stayed on deck recording videos and snapping stills as Zel watched birds, bergs, and blue sky meeting bluer water.

She heard Aunt Moira complaining about the tour to anyone who listened. Embarrassed, Zel decided to go to the port deck and just stare at the ocean in peace for a while.

For Zel, only two things enlivened this trip to the planet's frigid southern pole: Nature, in all its icy splendor, and the delightful animals who brought life into the glacial remoteness.

Already she had seen birds of every sort: flyers (albatross); non-flyers (penguins—identified by the ship's bird and seal charts). Today she'd watched a pod of Minke whales breeching. She just caught—as the ship passed an island's rocky shelf—a small herd of walruses sunning.

The other thing that kept Zel sane was Erik, a senior crew member on the cruise ship. He'd welcomed her and Aunt Moira when they'd boarded.

At first she and Erik met accidentally, in the dining room, the lounge, at the daily Antarctica lectures. Soon their meetings became a morning routine.

Erik was pleasant enough and Zel enjoyed the company of someone in his early thirties, just a bit older than she. All the other tourists were senior citizens with spouses. Zel figured, like Moira, they were spending their retirement investments for last-gasp fun and wild adventure.

Unlike Moira, Zel didn't seek out *extreme tourism*. But it was her aunt's money that had brought them here and to so many peculiar places, so her aunt could chase down her lifelong theories about opposites repelling as much as attracting. Zel was brought along by not so much a request as a demand. Moira insisted, Zel complied, though several times a day she asked herself why she had.

"We've been everywhere," she had confided to Erik that bitterly cold afternoon on the deck as the wind whipped the strands of auburn hairs that had escaped her toque every which way. "Dog-sledded around the Arctic with an Inuit guide who fed us dried seal meat; dived the deepest and darkest parts of the Mariana Trench in a submersible; trekked the Sahara. By the way, temperatures there range from fifty Celsius to minus fourteen. We went to view one of the rare snows that stripes the sand tan and white. We've walked part of the Great Wall of China and scubaed the Great Barrier Reef. Honestly, Erik, I've been lowered inside Iceland's extinct Thrihnukagigur volcano, surrounded by the multi-colored magma chamber painted by nature. I've seen the Northern Lights across most of the northern countries on the planet, and now icebergs the size of high-rises here at the South Pole."

"What an opportunity!" he exclaimed. "You must have enjoyed those amazing places."

"Sure. They're all magical, and they're what my aunt loves. But you know, I really wish I could just visit a few popular tourist attractions from time to time. Like climb the Eiffel Tower instead of descending into the Paris catacombs—we visited three times!"

He laughed. "That seems like an easy wish to grant."

"True, but it's not what Aunt Moira wants."

"Can't you go on your own?"

Zel stared out at the endless ocean, the deepest blue-almost-black she had ever seen. "She's old. These are her last years and she needs me to go with her, and I *want* to be there for her. She was there for me."

She felt Erik staring and turned her head. "What?" she asked.

246

"You're a loving, giving person."

She laughed. "Not so much. Maybe a bit. Who knows?"

She hadn't meant to say more, but somehow with the isolation, no land in sight only white bergs, just the two of them wrapped in simpatico, Zel ended up telling him what she had told no one.

"I was fifteen when my parents died in a plane crash. Moira was my mother's sister, but they were estranged. She arrived about nine A.M. at our house and said my parents were dead and I had to come with her. It was very strange that I just went with her, but I think I was in shock.

"My mother had only mentioned her sister two or three times, and I'd never even seen a picture of Aunt Moira; I'm not sure there is one, just for the passport. What's even odder is that the plane had crashed that day about eight-thirty A.M."

She paused for a moment, the unsettling feeling coming over her again that so-many-times-intuitive Aunt Moira had known what was about to happen.

"Did you ask her about that?"

"I did, once the grief subsided enough that I could think about that and other things. She just brushed me off by saying 'I know things, that's all there is to it.'

"Anyway, it wasn't an easy transition for me, living with her. Aunt Moira has been single all her life, kind of a loner, but still she took me in, insisted on home-schooling me until I graduated high school. She told me formal education would ruin me, which is really strange because she was a university professor and taught anthropology. She retired early and we've been travelling since. Places like Egypt investigating tombs and going on digs; looking at mummified remains in the Andes; boat trips up the Amazon; avoiding rare, poisonous snakes and spiders at Cambodia's Angkor Wat; obtaining special permission to see up close the remains of Ützi in the Italian Alps, who had lived and died there five thousand three hundred years ago. It's been an incredible journey out-of-the-ordinary for me. I'm lucky, and I'm more than grateful."

"And yet," he said, "you don't sound as if it was all fun and games."

She sighed. "It hasn't been. My aunt's really eccentric, and so much of the travel has been hard work and tiring for me, especially as she ages. I have to keep a sharp eye on her. She's *very* demanding but I understand why. She's really out to validate a theory she'd developed over a lifetime that didn't get much of a positive response."

"Do you have faith in her theory?"

"I'm . . . not sure. Sometimes it makes sense to me, other times it doesn't. Sometimes it seems really creepy."

She paused. "You know, Erik, what I'd *really* like is to have some stability and permanence. A life of my own. It must be incredibly relaxing just to stay in one place for years at a time, have a home, a family, see friends, dine in favorite restaurants, watch a range of movies and *not* just documentaries. A simple life."

He smiled and she thought his face beautiful. "I think we share that desire. I've been on ships in different jobs since I was seventeen. I enjoy it, but there's nothing to go back to. No one."

The next day they rounded Anver's Island, but insta-freeze snow kept them from disembarking.

For Zel, the days passed slowly and it felt as if she'd been on this ship for months, but it was only the sixth day. When they arrived at Neko harbour, the weather was crisp and clear, perfect for exploring.

Flocks of birds swept overhead. Zel chart-identified them as Snowy Sheathbills, skuas, and maybe Dominican gulls. On one island's shore she spotted Crabeater seals, and that was exciting.

While Zel looked up and around, awed by the animals able to survive this frigid environment, Moira looked down, scowling at the ground, at the water, and at ice and snow in all its forms, searching for the-gods-knew-what.

The most spectacularly beautiful glacier Zel had ever seen took her breath away. Enormous in height and length, the elegant snow and ice wall had folded in waves formed by the winds. As sunlight bathed the white-blue to brilliance, she could not stop smiling.

Moira suddenly snarled, "Come on, damn you! Calf!"

Suddenly an eerie sound—a low groan—filled the air. The ground trembled a little and flocks of screeching birds flew up and out to sea.

They watched a large chunk of snowy ice break away from the enormous glacier, sliding down slowly as it separated, then picking up speed, leaving behind a kind of grey mist, the sound now more like a scream.

Zel wasn't the only one rattled; goosebumps rippled along her skin.

When the massive calf hit water, it forced up a huge swell that raced toward shore. The guides quickly moved the passengers further inland.

"You see!" her aunt lectured her. "When you want something to happen, good, bad, ugly, it does."

"But how did you know that—"

"You are just like your mother! Dense!"

They moved along to the nearby Paradise Harbour where cute Fur seals formed couples on the shore. Zel took a picture, respecting the distance rules: five meters from penguins; ten from seals; *never* cross in front of or try to touch *any* animal. But even as she thought this, she watched her Aunt Moira break those very rules.

One of the guides raced to Moira as her aunt approached a seal pup. The guide was furious. Moira played the *old lady card;* Zel had watched this game used often when it came in handy. As always, Moira won; she wiggled out of being confined to the ship.

Along the western shore of the Weddell Sea were rookeries of gentoo and Adelie penguins, and crowding the beaches Elephant Seals. But the best for Zel was watching the whales and dolphins playing; she found herself laughing and smiling.

Erik noticed and grinned her way.

After that, the slow-moving seniors disembarked for Argentina's Brown Research Station.

"Nobody home!" Moira announced loudly to all who listened. "This station belongs to ghosts!"

One of the tour guides tried the office door; it was locked.

Moira took over at once. "It was the rockin' nineteen-eighties—remember them? This station's doctor wanted to leave, but the government ordered him to stay over the winter. He was probably afraid of going crazy or freezing to death, with good reason!" Moira laughed, feeding her rapt audience the macabre story in ghoulish bits and pieces. "A very pretty brilliant plan hit him, inspired by the Antarctic Gods, whom he must have worshipped. He burned down the research station. Smart, huh? The government had to take him home."

The tour guide jumped in, explaining that no one had died and all were rescued. "This is the rebuilt station. It should be open. Maybe they're late this year."

"Or dead!" Moira chirped.

Zel noticed one of the other guides shaking her head.

It wasn't for the first time that she had wondered about Aunt Moira's predilection for the dark and violent. And later, Erik asked what she thought about Moira's strange outbursts.

"I don't know," Zel said. "If this was new behavior, I'd think she was losing it. But Aunt Moira has always been this way. She wants what she wants when she wants it."

Erik raised his eyebrows. "Besides proving that theory you mentioned, what does she want?"

Zel shrugged. "I guess we'll know when she finds it."

The following day was a leisurely ride up the temperate Lemaire Channel, only 11 kilometers long and at its narrowest 600 meters wide. Zel felt she could reach out and touch some of these unusual blue-tinted icebergs.

So many of the shapes were enchanting: a cathedral entrance; a giant's hat; a perfect square; a bird's head. There were bergs with multiple striations in browns and blacks and greens. The crystal-clear sky's white clouds on an azure background reflected in the calm, quiet channel. Zel felt stunned by nature's beauteous magnitude.

Moira said loudly, "There is *nothing* here worth seeing!" and stomped back to their cabin.

Zel was alone on the deck until Erik joined her. They talked a bit but mostly kept a companionable silence, enjoying this gorgeous landscape sculpted by nature.

Eventually the many hours of light changed to the very few hours of darkness, and together they watched the magical green and magenta Aurora Australis swirl and roll and flicker across the sky.

The calm and temperate Lemaire Channel led to the Gerlache Strait, which opened up to the Bransfield Strait. They were headed to the smallest island, the last island on the tour, and the only time Zel had seen Aunt Moira truly excited. She had stood on the deck beside Zel, sounding happy, using the binoculars to try to see their destination. But even from this distance it was obvious that the weather there was bad. Heavy snow shrouded details, obscuring the view.

"We're changing course to Half Moon Island," Erik said as he joined Zel and Moira at the rail. "The temperature is milder there and it's not snowing. We'll try to get you to Deception tomorrow for a pass-by if the weather cooperates. Otherwise, Half Moon will be the last island before our two-day return to Argentina."

"Not acceptable on any level!" Moira snarled, her wrinkled face livid. "I paid a lot of money, young man, and I want to land on Deception."

"I'm sorry, ma'am, but we can't control the weather."

"We'll see about that!" And she stormed off.

In the morning Zel awoke very tired and would have liked to sleep for the rest of the journey. But awareness hit and she realized her aunt wasn't in the room. She dressed in a hurry and headed starboard, stomping through centimeters-deep of crusty snow on deck that had fallen and frozen during the night.

Aunt Moira was talking with a woman. The winds were strong and Zel feared her tough-minded, physically fragile aunt or the even older woman would be blown off the deck and out to sea.

Suddenly she noticed that the ship was halfway between two islands, one being attacked by a blizzard and the other where it was not snowing. Whipping her head back and forth, she was confused. Hadn't they reached Half Moon last night?

Erik joined the three. "You have your wish!" he said to Aunt Moira. "We're leaving Half Moon and heading toward Deception after all."

Moira met this news with a *harumph*.

Zel still felt baffled. These islands were only fifty kilometers apart. How could the weather be so different?

Before she could ask Erik, Moira said to the other woman, "And they say there are no Ancient Gods!" The two women laughed, and Moira waved a hand toward the island with the clear view that they were headed toward. "Just look at that miracle!"

Or curse? Zel found herself thinking.

She was so tired of this trip. Tired of having to accompany Moira, who seemed to resent her and yet forced her to come along. Tired of her aunt's erratic behavior and cynicism and downright callousness toward other people and the environment. Tired in general of a life that seemed not her own to live. How long did an obligation last?

Before snow could completely hide Half Moon Island, Zel turned and looked through the binoculars. "There's a colony of Chinstraps," she said, "on their bellies in the snow squiggling as if they're burrowing. Some of the Weddell seals are doing the same thing!"

"Burrowing is exactly what they're doing," Erik said. "That keeps them warm and safe from the elements."

"Fleeing instead of fighting!" Aunt Moira snarled. "Stupid animals!"

Zel sighed. Moira was all about extremes, not tolerating the usual, the ordinary, the banal, the mundane. Zel knew that to her aunt, she was the most boring person in the world. It was a winner/loser game for Moira. Zel wasn't a competitor and yet was forced to play.

As the ship sailed closer to Deception Island, Erik said to Zel, "It's too bad about the sudden storm on Half Moon. You'd have loved it. That island has some of the most beautiful sites in the South Shetlands. Tall craggy rock faces where orange, yellow, and black lichen grow. Camara Station has a black tower with yellow stripes and—"

"Oh, please shut up!" Moira sniped. "Stop filling her empty head with your ridiculous trivia about towers with stripes! What a waste of breath!"

Zel felt the harsh words were a slap to both of them.

"I'm going fore!" Moira announced. "Coming?"

Before Zel could answer, Moira went one way, the other woman another.

"I'm sorry," Zel turned to Erik. "I guess she's upset."

He looked at her strangely. "It seems she's always upset, especially with you. I know I shouldn't say this, but did it ever occur to you that maybe she's just a bitter old woman?"

Zel felt shocked for a moment. "Like a witch?" She started to giggle but then clamped a hand over her mouth, turning away from Erik. "Sorry!"

Soon they boarded the Zodiacs and entered the break in what had looked from an aerial photo like a doughnut with a bite taken out. It reminded Zel of Santorini, also a volcanic island. Also an island connected with the uncanny, at least for Aunt Moira.

Suddenly Moira did the forbidden. She stood up for two seconds in the inflatable, rocking the vessel. She spread her arms wide toward Deception Island and cried into the wind, "Welcome me as I welcome you!" Whatever that meant. Zel had never seen her aunt enthused and morose at the same time.

As they entered the inlet, Zel saw on the east bay shore a couple of whiskered Fur seals frolicking and another large Chinstrap colony doing what penguins do best. She loved the look of these sweet flightless waddling birds of land and sea with the cute black strip across their white chins. Little nuclear families where the parents took turns carrying their chicks around on their feet.

Suddenly she recalled a sentence from a novel she'd read when she was thirteen, before her parents died. A philosophical detective ruminated on modern romance, comparing its deficiencies with the marvel of a male penguin placing 'a pebble at the feet of his intended.'

This Zodiac was piloted by Erik, who had just veered the craft west in the bay, which was really a caldera, formed ten thousand years ago when a volcano collapsed.

Zel glanced at Erik's profile. He was attractive in a Nordic way, with sculpted facial features, intelligent eyes, a toned bod . . . He must have sensed her scrutinizing and turned his head. He smiled, his lips wide and generous. She liked him. He must like her too, because he kept seeking her out. She wondered if he would drop a pebble at her feet.

She leaned close to him and asked, "Is it always this cold?"

"It's summer at the South Pole," he said, "or we wouldn't be here."

She knew that, of course, and unfortunately sounded sarcastic when she said, "I'd love to see winter."

"Blink and the weather changes. Maybe you'll get a taste of real cold."

Zel shivered inside her down-filled parka. She didn't want to feel anything colder than this.

Finally the six Zodiacs slid onto the rocky shore. Dark pebbles of all sizes littered sand lava-greyed from long-ago volcanic eruptions. There was little snow and ice to see but for the glaciers and low mountains that lay in the distance beyond Whaler's Bay. That much melt alone made Deception Island unique.

"Welcome to Whaler's Bay," the tour guide said. "Stay with me for the tour or you can wander alone, just don't get lost! Feel free to take a dip in the bay or get into one of the small caldera hot tubs before we head back to the ship. We will bring you towels. We meet at the Zodiacs in four hours."

A couple wandered away on their own but everyone else joined the tour, including Moira, which meant Zel did too.

"Welcome to Deception Island, seventy-nine kilometers long and fifteen kilometers wide. The highest elevation is Mount Pond, five hundred and thirty-nine meters located on the east side of the island. There are two glaciers and several volcanoes, two of which are still active—tremors are common."

"Goodie!" Moira cried loudly.

The guide talked about the island being named by a sealer. "The Deception part is this: he thought it looked like a normal island, but it's a caldera."

"The idiot had no imagination!" Moira declared. "It's a fire or ice island. *That's* the deception!"

The group followed up a semi-steep pebbly path, the guide talking about the 500,000 seals killed for the pelts, the entire population wiped out. "Nearly half a million Fur seals died, the population was annihilated."

Zel gasped, horrified.

They made their way to half-a-dozen enormous rusted tanks, used to boil whales for their oil. "At first, carcasses were cast into the bay. That stench mixing with the rotten-egg odor of sulphur from the active volcanoes must have been putrid. It's estimated that up to three million whales were killed. The good news is the scuff attracted thousands of birds that made Deception Island their home."

Zel was appalled. *Whales hunted to near extinction! Not enough good came out of that bad.*

The guide carried on about innovations in the whaling industry and the historical first airplane flights from and to the Antarctic.

Zel stared at the rusted roller used for compacting the first runway, hating that nature always paid a severe price for so-called progress.

"By 1931 the worldwide depression made oil from Antarctic whaling unprofitable."

Thank goodness! Zel thought.

"Too bad!" Moira said.

They saw a magistrate's house and a post office built by the British in the 1940s, and several workers' dormitories. It was all falling apart, weather-beaten roofs and outer walls caved in.

"I hope she gets to the good stuff soon!" Aunt Moira said as an exhale. "This is verbal scruff!"

The tour guide scowled her way, but Moira had always been immune to both criticism and censorship.

"Nineteen-sixty-seven brought two months of tremors from the northwest of the island, and then a volcano erupted. Deception Island's two research stations were evacuated and most of Whaler's Bay was washed into the sea."

Zel looked around at the remains. Ruined buildings, rusted tanks and other equipment, two lonely grave markers in the former cemetery. *What a grim place,* she thought.

"What about that empty coffin that floated back?" Moira wanted to know.

"Yes," was all the guide said, "there was one.

"In nineteen-seventy another volcanic eruption occurred. Deception Island has not been reoccupied since in winter, and only Spain and Argentina operate active stations in summer in the southeast."

Unchained from the tour, they were told to be at the Zodiacs in three and a half hours.

Zel imagined that Aunt Moira wanted a dip in the freezing bay *and* a soak in the caldera thermal waters. To her surprise, her aunt said tartly, "We're going for a walk."

Moira led Zel up a slope behind the bay's ruined buildings and massive pressure cookers. The ascent became steeper, and yet her seventy-three-year-old aunt seemed to have no problems climbing.

Zel thought that at least it was a beautiful day, a clear, cloudless cobalt sky, not exactly warm weather but not as cold as other places they'd landed. *And it's not snowing!* Almost at that thought, Zel felt wet touch her face and saw a few flakes dropping from that pretty sky.

"It looks like snow," Zel offered, thinking they'd turn back.

"Here, there's corrosion," Moira said. "An incomparable balance between attraction and repulsion."

Zel suddenly saw the surroundings as cold grey. Her body was hot and sweaty from exertion. She unzipped her parka a few inches but pulled the collar up the back of her neck.

As they traversed this rocky slope, the air chilled and yet Zel felt overheated and opened her parka halfway. Moira didn't seem to be affected by either cold air or body heat.

Zel had a toque in the parka's pocket and pulled it down to the bottom of her ears. She'd left her gloves on the ship and pushed her cold hands deep into the pockets.

A thin layer of snow covered the ground and made their footfalls slippery, causing each step to be a little slide backward. "Where are we going?" she asked. Moira did not reply.

They weren't climbing a mountain, at least not to the top. Moira was circling *around* the mountain. Zel glanced behind and saw the ship's passengers like ants wandering aimlessly through the remains of human exploitation. Two were seated in the thermal pool.

Moira seemed to be on a mission, or at least she had a goal. Zel knew she had studied maps of this island. She must know where she was going and have some specific place she wanted to reach, but Zel had no idea where or what that could be.

As they rounded the curve they'd been on, Zel took one more glance back, like a last connection to humanity. A few steps more and the bay and the people and animals were cut off from her view.

The sun had been at their backs, which made it even colder on this darker side of the mountain. They traipsed through a thicker layer of snow, but that didn't slow down Moira.

Zel glanced up. The sky had turned slate quickly. More snowflakes fell than before. "Maybe we should go back," she said, but Moira wasn't listening.

They were high enough now that Zel could see a taller mountain in the west at a distance, dark smoke erupting from the top. That had to be one of the two active volcanoes. Suddenly the ground beneath their feet trembled and she felt afraid.

You shouldn't be here! This isn't natural. Moira isn't normal. Those thoughts just came to her as if a voice in her head she'd been ignoring was calling a warning.

Moira started down the slope, which led into a narrow valley. The descent was faster than their ascent, but soon that changed and they began climbing a small mountain, really a high hill.

Now the snow fell rapidly. The stink of sulphur permeated the air. She felt another rumble beneath her feet, a bit stronger, but reminded herself that the guide said there were frequent tremors. Shivering, she zipped the parka to her chin.

Cold at other Antarctic islands had created sharp, hard air, difficult to inhale. The smell of this air had become revolting and probably poisonous. She wished she had a ski mask. Her cheeks, forehead, and nose felt frozen, and Zel worried about frostbite.

They started up the high hill, the ground rumblings more intense. Zel felt off-balance.

Snow became a blizzard. White pelted them from all directions. She called out, "Aunt Moira, we need to go back *right now!*"

Moira had gone mute. Zel couldn't physically force her to return, but she couldn't abandon her either. Panic set in and she was having problems breathing this foul air.

Suddenly they went over the top of a hill. Moira stopped just under its peak. They had reached a very long and wide ledge, at least nine by six meters.

Zel saw this for seconds before the snow blinded and the sulphur sickened her. The ground trembling was stronger and shook her so hard she cried out and automatically felt for support. Her hand caught a rock embedded in the hillside that she clung onto.

"Aunt Moira!" she screamed. "Where are you?"

Moira's voice came at her through the white obstruction. "Closer!"

Zel didn't know what she meant. Should Zel go closer? Was Moira close to where her aunt had been headed?

The storm raged, tremors rough and regular. She could hardly breathe in the foul odor.

Terror rode up her spine as she took four careful steps toward the voice.

Suddenly, shockingly, she entered an oasis. Much of the ledge had become a snowless rectangle. It wasn't snowing, yet a white curtain of blizzard surrounded the roof and four sides of this rectangular box-like space but did not enter. Grass grew beneath her feet. Amazingly, it wasn't cold.

In the center of this protected space stood Aunt Moira, arms stretched out to the west as if summoning.

"What is this?" Zel cried.

"The home of the only Gods that matter. And they've come for the offering I've brought. That's you, Zel."

Terrified, Zel's head snapped right and left quickly. The ferocious snow outside this transparent box whipped the air into swirls going in every direction.

She saw an image. A gigantic face! Twisted features that expanded and contracted, each time more horrifying. This was not anything she could identify, but something fierce, merciless, inhuman that sucked a scream from her lips.

More faces appeared in the roiling white, some similar, others not at all alike. Darkly crooked, twirling at an astounding speed that left her dizzy. These things were dangerous and savage with intent. And not from this world! She shook uncontrollably, unsure if the trembling came from tremors or from her terror.

Zel unconsciously backed up to the edge of this invisible box, but the enclosed space was now shrinking. The horrifying faces pressed hard and spread grotesquely against the translucent walls. The thought came: *They looked like otherworldly demons watching a movie!*

A tremor jerked the ground so forcefully Zel was knocked off her feet. Her head hit a rock. Her last smell was the disgusting hell-scent, her final view the monstrous creatures Moira called *Gods* closing in on their offering.

"Zel! Zel!"

She heard her name repeated and opened her eyes to a searing pain. Her head felt swollen, her vision was hazy.

"Zel! If you hear me, call out!"

She opened her mouth but no sound emerged.

"Where are you?" he asked. "Make a noise." She recognized the voice. And then Erik was over the peak of the hill and by her side.

He knelt before her, his face worried as he scanned hers. "You're okay! You are! Can you stand? We have to get back to the ship. Everyone else is onboard. It's dangerous here."

In a daze, Zel glanced around. The entire ledge was snow-covered but the blizzard was milder. There was no invisible, rectangular box. Sulphur still clotted the cold air, filling her nostrils. The earth quaked as the volcano belched out black smoke and a sound reminiscent of hissing steam. But she knew it was the sigh of monsters.

"Where's your aunt?"

Instinctively she pointed at the ground.

Erik stood and walked around looking down at the snowy ground-cover. His glance travelled over the shelf edge to sweep the surrounding area. "Did she fall?"

Zel tried to shake her head, but it hurt too much. "No," she whispered, pointing again.

"Zel, you have to stand up. We've got to get back right now."

He helped her to her feet. Arm around her waist, he tried leading her up and back over the hilltop, but she pulled away.

Zel stepped into the center of the ledge, schuffing away snow with her boot.

Like so much of the Antarctic, below snow was ice, but this ice was transparent.

"What the . . . ?" Erik said.

Aunt Moira lay embedded in the ice on her back in a coffin-sized rectangle. Her body had spasmed upward, eyes bulging, mouth wide open, as if she had screamed. Her arms went straight up, her fingers bent like claws about to grasp or attack.

The ground rocked crazily. Gases and black soot filled the air. The environment had become extremely unstable and toxic—just what Moira loved.

"Come, Zel. You can't help her now."

He held tightly to her arms and managed to pull her over the hilltop, then led her down the slope and around the mountain as quickly as she could move.

Fumaroles dotted Whaler's Bay, geyser-like steam spewing from holes in the hot, swelling land. They ran to the remaining empty Zodiac.

Once they were in the inflatable and motoring out of the caldera, Zel cupped her hands for bay water. She splashed it against her face, trying to bring herself back from what she had seen. "Did the seals and penguins escape?"

"Yes," Erik said. "We saw them take to the ocean. Their instincts tell them there's danger."

They had almost reached the cruise ship when she said, "What should I tell the others?"

"Your aunt fell and died. The volcano is erupting. Lava will cover that icy grave. Her body will never be found."

They looked at each other. "Why did you go with her?" he asked.

"Destiny."

"Yours or hers?"

261

"Both. Her name means *will of the gods*. But her Gods' will was to choose her, not me."

"Because she loved extremes?"

"Because *they* do."

AND THE DEVIL HATH POWER

John Shirley

John Shirley is the author of numerous novels, including Demons, Wetbones, Cellars, City Come A–Walkin', Bioshock: Rapture, Stormland, *and the* Eclipse *trilogy. His story collection* Black Butterflies *won the Bram Stoker Award. His new story collection is* The Feverish Stars. *His newest novel is the heroic fantasy* A Sorcerer of Atlantis *from Hippocampus Press. He is co-screenwriter of* The Crow *and has written teleplays and animation.*

WHEN ALL IS *FINALITY,* TRIPLY CONFIRMED, something remarkable begins. Finality struck thrice, like three powerful blows on a cracked gong: I met Ophelia at the *final* exhibition of the Indo-Scythian artifacts from the *final* excavation discovered in the *final* year of the life of Professor Georgi Gorgiades. I was forty-two then, and could still speak with more than pen and paper.

I had been the professor's assistant, coming right out of the Oxford School of Archaeology to join him. I worked at his side for twenty years, despite all entreaties and temptations to other, better-paying positions, because Georgi had an astonishing gift of discovery.

This is what I told the audience as I gave my eulogy, explaining my devotion, extolling his genius, before the opening of the final exhibition in Istanbul. I spoke of his untimely death, and my frustration with the authorities in Iran who claimed his murder would likely remain unsolved.

I wore a tuxedo—I have always looked good in one—and everyone was in conventional fancy dress of one kind or another, except a strange woman sitting in the front row. She gazed benignly at me, pretending she was not wildly out of place. She was perhaps in her mid-thirties, and voluptuous; her flaxen hair was piled up eccentrically on her head; but what most caught my eye was her extravagantly Gothic jet-black and blood-red gown— I had seen one like it, many years before, adorning Diamanda Galas.

Despite Ophelia's black lipstick and purple eyeshadow, her face had soft, friendly contours. She watched raptly as I showed slides of Scythian and Egyptian artifacts Professor Gorgiades had lovingly extracted from their earthen hiding places. I promised myself I would try and make this woman's acquaintance.

I had been married—once. On signing the divorce papers with me in a hotel, Meredith said, "Thus ends the catastrophe." I did not disagree. We had nothing in common except an interest in ancient history. Our taste was entirely different in everything else, from music to cinema to sex. The few women I dated after Meredith were either shallow—their attention spans damaged by the Internet and the maundering idiocy of modern life—or they were quivering balls of neurosis. I was eager to meet this woman in the Diamanda Galas stage-costume.

At the reception I made a show of chatting with the donors who supported the Turku-Greco-Scythian museum, but I furtively watched the woman in jet-black and blood-red. *Ophelia.* I knew her first name now, having been introduced for a flicker of a moment before a hefty middle-aged heiress interposed . . .

Ophelia showed no direct interest in me at the reception, spending most of her time alone examining the professor's final discoveries—the half-crumbled statuettes of obscure gods, the Indo-Scythian versions of sarcophagi, the earthenware jar containing the head of an ox; the zoomorphic lead amulets, the ice mummies with gold pendants and figured bracelets, and the faience fragments of a mural depicting still unidentified deities. But she spent most of her time perusing the museum's only real center of controversy, the professor's display of photos, charts, X-rays, and scans of the Black Sea Mechanism. Gorgiades had found it in a sealed chamber, in the deeps of a ruin outside Samsun. He had refused to let anyone but the two of us examine the actual mechanism. It was very like the famed Antikythera Mechanism, circa third century B.C.E., found in the Aegean Sea; but the Black Sea Mechanism was startlingly intact and seemed rather the inverse of the Greek device. The professor claimed it was the Antikythera device's "other half." The two mechanisms had been meant to be combined, before the tragic sinking of that ancient ship in the Aegean. Gorgiades's speculations led to scholarly scoffing: the Antikythera device was just an early analogue computer for calculating the movements of the sun and moon against the sidereal pattern . . .

After the event ended, I had to lock up—as I was the museum's director and the docents had gone home—and as I turned the lock, the click resonated with my disappointment I hadn't found a chance to talk to lovely Ophelia before the event. I told myself she'd have turned out to be married or gay or simply a disappointment.

I was locking up from inside, as I planned to begin my own study of the Black Sea Mechanism, and I turned around and yes, there she was.

"Holy fuck," I muttered. "Uh—were you in the lady's room? Allow me, uh, to let you out."

"I was indeed in the ladies' room," she said cheerfully, her eyes glittering with mischief, her full lips quirking. "I had my feet up on the seat so no one could see I was in there. I wanted to talk to you personally, and in complete private, and in this place—the most romantic place in the world to me." She waited, brimming with confidence and expectation, her eyes promising what words could not convey.

I am afraid I gaped at her for a moment; then I said the very first thing that came to my mind. "That gown—I have a video of Diamanda Galas wearing it, I mean one *like* it—"

"It's the same one, not a copy, Joshua Vasquel." Her accent was what some called mid-Atlantic, English that was neither here nor there, but she had peculiar oddments in expression. "I bought it from Diamanda some years ago, when I was twenty-one and came into my inheritance. I am her fan. I saw you in the audience at several of her concerts."

I blinked. I blinked again. "I . . . am surprised I didn't—"

"You wouldn't have noticed me then. I was a pimply frump."

"That's . . . hard to believe."

"Many things are hard to believe but strangely convincing when revealed—Gorgiades's explanation for the Black Sea Mechanism, for example. When I took archaeological engineering, I wrote a paper suggesting that the Antikythera was unfinished—that there was another mechanism to be attached. No one took me seriously—"

"Wait—where did you study?"

"As for that—the Cairo College of Archaeology! I showed the *exact* mechanical mechanisms by which the pyramids were built by the Egyptian stonemasons and engineering class—I made it crystal clear so that the 'ancient astronauts' buffoons would shut up. But of course, nothing shuts them up."

"I do so agree!" She had won my heart. "I despise the 'ancient astronauts' crowd! They are a blight on archaeology—racists, too. 'The brown people couldn't have raised the pyramids or calculated the spaces of the temples'!"

"Exactly so and indeed," she said, with that curiously antiquated wording that cropped up in her talk. "But once Professor Gorgiades did write a paper suggesting that certain ruins had hints of something . . . perhaps *extra-terrestrial*. Not in their building but in descriptions of certain gods found in hieroglyphs and cuneiform."

I was startled. "Ophelia—how did you know that? He never published that paper!"

"My father collected all kinds of arcana and—well, he paid someone to copy that document. All quite *sub rosa*. You don't have anything on the hard side to drink here, do you?"

"Well, yes." I vacillated. After all, she'd hidden herself away in here, accosted me alone—she could have simply asked to meet me afterwards and I'd have said yes. But then—so what if she was a bit eccentric? I had been feeling desperately lonely. She sparked hope in me—and she stirred my blood. "I have some in my office, if you like old Scotch whiskey . . . "

Ophelia proved to know almost as much about Scotch whiskey as about archaeology. There was not a subject in either esoteric realm that she could not ably comment upon. We sat on the leather sofa in my office, drinking whiskey, as I tried not to look at her bust or her sprawled legs, and as she did nothing to conceal these charms.

"Do you believe in visions?" she asked me suddenly.

"Not as such—but then I experimented with psilocybin and peyote in my time. Some hallucinations do seem to have meaning."

"When I saw you at Diamanda's show, I had a vision—and not as a result of drugs: I saw that I would know you later in life." She moved a little closer to me. "I saw us here—in this room and in this moment. I knew it would be vitally important to me. To us both. Life-changing!"

"Really!" But now I thought, okay, here's the other shoe dropping. She isn't just eccentric. She's schizophrenic, bipolar, something of the sort. My bad luck was running true.

Still, there were medications for such people. Perhaps I could help her. And meanwhile . . .

Then she leaned toward me and said, her voice husky, "No, I'm not a madwoman, Joshua. I'm a woman coming to completion at last—after many years of waiting."

Then she took my face in her hands and kissed me. And it was as if I were struck by an impossibly benign bolt of lightning. I felt that kiss in every cell of my body.

I could barely stop myself from ravishing her. But then she gasped into my ear, "The consummation comes . . . when . . . together . . . we touch the Black Sea Mechanism."

"What?" Dazed, I drew back. Gorgiades had made me promise that no one would see the mechanism, in person, until a certain date—a date he refused to explain. It was still seven years in the future. *"The device must be completed,"* he said. I had given my solemn word to keep the Black Sea Mechanism locked away.

She sat up on the sofa and caressed my lips with the tip of a finger, beaming at me. "It's all I ask! Just so I know I'm not a one-off for you—that you take me seriously! And anyway—I've always *dreamt* of seeing it, Joshua, and . . . "

"But I did promise him—if you'll wait a couple years. He had some obsession with—well . . . "

"With—the winter solstice seven years from now?"

Again I gaped at her. "That was not written on any document."

"It doesn't matter. If Professor Gorgiades were here—oh, I can *feel* it! He would want this!"

I looked into her eyes. I felt a carnal warmth radiating from her—and it melted my resolve.

"Very well," I said.

Like a man in a dream, I got up and led her from the office to the door marked *Museum Staff Only*. I unlocked it, and from there we went to the cleaning and preparation section of the archaeology lab. Here, past dusty relics on the tables, was another locked door.

I led her to the inner door—and then wavered. Could I do this? But I was afraid that if I didn't trust her, didn't let her through this door, I would lose her. The one woman who could understand me. And I'd regret it for the rest of my life. I took a deep breath and turned the key in the lock.

Within, the iron and crystal mechanism waited on a steel table. It was trapezoidal, about thirty-eight inches on the nearer side, thirty-five on the upper, twenty-seven to the right and left: an intricate arrangement of gold wheels and curiously imprinted disks of Anatolian steel and delicately interconnected gears; certain rods within rang like a precisely attuned bell when struck. Here and there were quartz crystals, set into its works almost like the gems in a watch. Beside it was a tray of tools: cleaning brushes, pliers, a large pincer, a very finely honed chisel, brushes. And—a multicolored xylophone for children, with a small padded hammer.

She strode to the Black Sea Mechanism, stared—and she shook her head in wonder. "It looks like something new! Is this a *model?*"

"No. We found it unusually well-preserved."

Just as I started to tell her not to, she briefly touched it. "*Unthinkably* well preserved . . . no wonder there are so many doubters . . . when they saw the photographs . . . and were refused permission to examine it in person . . ."

"Yes. The word *hoax* was used at least once. Please do not touch it again."

"And did the professor try to—to *activate* it?"

"Activate it?" Was she in earnest? "No, he—well . . ."

She turned to look at me with wide, grave eyes. "Yes?"

"Oddly enough, he brought a small xylophone in. There it is, next to the tools. A children's toy, really. He struck it up the scale, slowly, note by note, and partway, on the *la* note—there *was* a sort of . . . response. Or so we thought. Maybe it was imagination—he thought he saw something appear. He pointed it out and I—I *imagine*d I saw it too. A sort of face. It came and went. We felt a little ill then and didn't try it again. He refused to discuss it, in fact."

She nodded. "And did Gorgiades never hint at the *function* of this device?"

"At first he thought that like its counterpart, the Antikythera, it could be designed for astrology or navigation—but later he claimed that the two devices, connected, related to opening a 'metaphysical doorway.'" I shrugged. "Gorgiades believed that certain crystals locked into the mechanism resonate with particular sounds, which are then counter-resonated by these rods. But there are other sounds needed for its full functionality."

"And..." She licked her lips. "What sounds for...'full functionality'? As from a xylophone?"

"No, that's just a beginning intonation, and it needs three repetitions. Then two other sounds are needed—well, Mid-Scythian hieroglyphs found with this object suggest the final trigger requires the human throat. In fact, *two* throats—a man and woman, in sequence. But"—I laughed in mild embarrassment—"he said the sound made was something unspeakable."

"Ah...but let us just see."

She turned to the xylophone and picked up the little mallet.

I tried to stop her. "Please, Ophelia, do not—"

But she did. She struck the chime at *la*. I reached for her wrist—but she stepped aside and struck at the same bar twice more, hard.

The mechanism's crystals flashed; a gear turned, a disc shimmied, a rod spun—and a corner of the room darkened.

The corner across from me was fully illuminated by the overhead light—but abruptly it was swallowed in darkness; it wasn't *one* area of darkness, not precisely, it was a writhing turmoil of interlacing shadows. A face emerged from the darkness, a face blacker than the shadows, black as onyx and carved in flat planes, like some ancient idol; it had a high brow and thin lips and an aquiline nose, and in its deep eye sockets were orbs of sulfur yellow. Then it smiled; it seemed delighted. *"You have done very well, my dear,"* said a deep, oozing voice that slithered about the room. *"You removed Gorgiades, that vile obstruction—and after some fifty years in the Pocket of Outrage, you give me hope of release!"*

Ophelia gave a strangely archaic curtsey and then spoke in a language I did not recognize. And I heard something—I thought it was this thing's name—that I had heard mentioned by Gorgiades only once: *Nyarlathotep.*

I tried to speak—to beg Ophelia to run from here with me. But I found my mouth frozen as were my feet. I could not move.

"I hold him for you, my dear. But it's you who must persuade him . . . And then—Azathoth!"

Ophelia turned to me, her eyes alight—and she kissed me. The impossible lightning flashed through my nerves once more. My paralysis passed, but my *will* did not return to me. Not entirely. I was so overcome by the honied electricity flashing from her lips, I could not contain my sheer *craving* for her—despite the leering, hideously cheerful thing watching from the shadowed corner. A lust beyond any I'd ever felt made me rampant and afire with longing. Her mouth pressed mine, her jaws forced mine open; our tongues entwined—and then she sucked my tongue into her mouth. And with a curiously ophidian twisting motion of her head *she sank her teeth into my tongue and tore it from my mouth.*

I screamed from deep in my throat, as much from revulsion as agony. That peculiar scream—that *necessary* scream—of a man getting his tongue torn from his throat . . . it shook the room. It quivered in the crystals and twanged in the metals of the Black Sea Mechanism. The onyx face laughed, and the full figure of something resembling a man began to step out of the shadows. My tongueless scream was the required, unspeakable sound that had released the thing in the shadows.

I sank to my knees and looked up to see Ophelia grinning at me with my twitching, blood-dripping tongue still clasped like a scarlet fish in her teeth. With a titter she turned her head and spat it out and threw back her head, arching her back, howling with ecstasy—

You removed Gorgiades, that vile obstruction . . . She had killed Georgi!

I was able to move now, and in a psychotic state of rage and agony I lunged to my feet, grabbed a pincers from the tools, thrust it into her wide-open mouth, and grasped her tongue with it. I tore her tongue from her mouth—and she screamed. The second necessary scream; this one female. And the mechanism whirred and the grinning shadow ceased its grinning and Nyarlathotep wriggled and struggled—but the shadows swallowed him and then they were gone, taking him with them.

Ophelia was still wordlessly shrieking and coughing blood, as was I. She picked up the razor-sharp chisel and swung it at me. But I struck it from her grasp and gripped her throat with my hands and held on, afraid she would somehow once more summon her Lord. I spat my blood—but the pressure of my fingers prevented the escape of the blood from the root of her tongue. And she choked on her own blood.

I felt the strength go out of me, and I fell across her slumping body.

After that I remember waking to a pain at the back of my mouth so powerful I convulsed with it; I remember a choking that nearly killed me; I remember crawling, spitting blood and crawling again . . .

I found my way out of the building, and soon there were policemen and an ambulance and faces contorted with nausea.

Now I have pen to paper; I have access to the prison library, where I can write under supervision. I am determined to tell the truth, though it is unlikely to be believed. They tell me I murdered a beautiful young woman—a woman difficult to identify. She had my hand prints on her neck. I remind them of the line from *Hamlet: And the Devil hath power to assume a pleasing shape.*

In truth, I was not trying to kill her—only to keep her from making another sound that might bring back the thing of living onyx: Nyarlathotep, minion of Azathoth, who was once free to roam the world in the form of a man till he was trapped by Randolph Carter. This took place after Carter escaped from Kadath—this contretemps for Nyarlathotep, of the Pocket of Outrage, was divulged to me by Gorgiades. I had thought it was nothing but some form of urban myth.

I gave the detectives a written account, but they just shook their heads. They cannot be expected to believe me. I am writing a monograph—this is its introduction—which will explain all in detail, including scientific proofs. How Ophelia, using my scream, had triggered the available half of the mechanism; how I had shut it down with her scream. How the full mechanism, combining the Antikythera mechanism and the Black Sea Mechanism, is designed to summon evil disembodied entities and *trap* them— like Solomon's brass vessel. The Black Sea Mechanism summons; the Antikythera traps them. And in seven years, at winter solstice, the walls between worlds will become thin enough, so that Nyarlathotep—one of the dark *shadim,* as the Hebrews would have called him—will be released from the Pocket of Outrage, thanks to three *specific* finalities. The solstice alone is not enough. But if he is not stopped, he will be free long enough to summon Azathoth to Earth . . .

Worldwide catastrophe will result. Do you not see? There is but one solution: *someone* must build a new Antikythera, and attach it to the Black Sea Mechanism, and activate the combined mechanisms on that winter day. I can no longer speak aloud— nor taste!—but still, through pen, paper, and compulsion, I can call out to the world:

You have a clear choice! Believe me and live—or disbelieve and die, when the Lord of Primordial chaos consumes all and everything . . .

You have seven years. *Decide.*

THE AMBER TOAD

Donald Tyson

Donald Tyson is a Canadian who lives in Nova Scotia, Canada. He writes novels and tales that concern the occult adventures of Abdul Alhazred, the author of the Necronomicon. *The latest in the Alhazred series is the linked story collection* Return to Isle of the Dead *(Weird House, 2022). Tyson's collected horror stories were published under the title* The Skinless Face and Other Horrors *(Weird House, 2020).*

1

THE DESERT LANDSCAPE HELD A DESOLATION COLDER and deeper than anything Hal Leighton had ever imagined. Strewn boulders and red sand stretched to the horizon on all sides, broken only by rounded red hills. They had once been mountains, but countless eons had ground them down to the feeble remnants that remained. There was no trace of green, no shadow of life. A sterile orange sun hung high in the cloudless blue vault, washing out detail. In the distance, dust devils danced across the dunes.

He shivered. Not that it was cold: the ambient temperature was 19 degrees Celsius. The soulless emptiness of this nameless planet just gave him the creeps.

"Something walk over your grave?"

The air was rich in carbon dioxide and poor in oxygen, requiring members of the exploration team to wear respirators that distorted their voices. He had to turn his head to determine who had spoken.

Jill LeBrock was watching him, eyebrows arched above her brown eyes. He started to make a joke, then remembered that she was still expedition psychologist, even if she had become a friend during the long transition through the foldgate. Months cooped up in the *Aurora* had brought all seventeen members of the team close, although some relationships were healthier than others.

Walking on the coarse sand gave him a sensation of unreality. He could feel it under his boots and hear it crunch, but it seemed remote. The air left a metallic taste on his tongue that was utterly alien. He turned and looked back with a sudden pang of longing at the landing craft that had conveyed the team from the mother ship in orbit to the surface of this planet. It was the sole familiar thing on the horizon.

His heart rate began to increase. He deliberately deepened his breathing and concentrated on slowing it down. This wasn't the time for a panic attack, not with the whole team watching. It had been his own decision to volunteer for the first human mission to Kepler 62. Whatever challenges might arise, he would have to deal with them.

They climbed a low rise of sand. On the other side lay the alien city they had come to examine, an expanse of low dwellings made of reddish clay that had beehive shapes. Dust swirled between them on the fitful wind. Some distance away from the city on their left stood the gleaming stainless steel and plastic life-support habitat that robots had erected seven years ago in preparation for their arrival. It looked like a collection of toy igloos linked together with transparent plastic tubing into a cross shape. It was there they would live for the next nineteen months, until the planets of this star system realigned and the foldgate that enabled their return reopened. Seventeen human beings on a dead world almost a thousand light-years from home. He shivered again.

Several of the team went toward the habitat to verify its readiness. As systems engineer, Leighton should have gone with them, but he stayed with the larger group that descended the gentle slope toward the city. He had to see it with his own eyes. It had haunted his sleep in his tiny cabin on the *Aurora*. As they approached the planet, those dreams had gradually transformed into incoherent flashes of half-seen horrors and dangerous colors. He remembered nothing of their content, nothing except the redness of blood.

The unknown race that had built the city must have been about the same size as human beings, because the rounded doorways of their dwellings were almost high enough for humans to enter without ducking their heads. They broke up into small groups and, wandering around, investigated the structures. Leighton ran his fingertips over the surface of a closed door. It was made of some ceramic material. He tapped it with his knuckle. Thin, and hollow. Now that he looked more closely, the surface of the structure itself was not raw red clay but some kind of glaze that had a matte finish. It was as hard as the yellowish glass that filled the round window openings. He wondered how old the little buildings were, and how long they had stood empty.

Here and there where streets intersected, circular stone platforms surrounded deep desert wells that had furnished the city with water. The robots had examined them while building the habitat—they were all dry. It was the hypothesis of the team xenoarchaeologist, David Macumba, that lack of water had caused the city to be abandoned. No one knew much of anything about this alien race, not even what they looked like. Not a single image of a statue or painting had been among the data transmitted through the foldgate before it had closed. Fortunately for the team, the robots had been able to find water, but only by drilling down more than a thousand meters.

"You look relieved," Jill said.

He hesitated, wondering if he should risk confiding in her.

"I had dreams during the passage—well, nightmares, really, about what we would find here. It's silly."

"Not at all. Many of the team have reported the same thing."

"Really?" For some reason this made him feel better.

"My theory is that they are caused by the physiological stresses of foldgate transition, coupled with uncertainty about the future. I'm writing a paper on it, actually."

The leader of the team, Sven Nordström, waved for their attention.

They followed him with the others into a large structure of conjoined beehive forms that had the look of some kind of public building. The interior was lined from the floor to its multiple ceiling domes with shelves recessed into the walls. The shelves were filled with rounded ceramic cylinders of various colors. Nordström took one down and examined it. The cylinder was rose-pink and completely smooth on the outer surface.

"What do you make of this?"

He passed it around. Leighton saw that it was hollow and open at both ends.

The meteorologist, a cheerful, gray-haired woman everyone called Agee, even though her name was Myra Crabbetree, held it up to the yellow light from a window, and ran her finger along the inner surface.

"It's grooved inside."

"Is it really?" Nordström snatched it back as she was about to pass it to Harold Deeping, an energetic little rooster of a man whose job it was to maintain their hydroponics farm. The botanist glared at him. Nordström held the cylinder up to the light and peered into it at an angle. "Maybe an artefact of the manufacturing process."

While the others discussed the cylinders, Leighton wandered over to look at something that rested on a low table in the corner. He could not tell if it was a piece of furniture or a sculpture. It consisted of an upright spindle beside an oblong protrusion on a round platform a bit bigger than a dinner plate. Most of it was ceramic, but embedded in it were strips and disks of metal connected by fine lines that looked almost like wires. The metal had the yellow sheen of gold. Around the base of the spindle the surface of the plate was worn rough, as though something round had rested there.

"Give me the cylinder." He lifted it out of the hands of Victor Stossel, the microbiologist, before the bald man could protest.

He lowered the cylinder carefully over the spindle while the others gathered around. For a moment nothing happened. Then he heard a low hum. A three-dimensional projection appeared in the air above the device. It was in full color and animated. It showed two alien creatures holding a third down on its back by its arms and legs across an oblong slab of black stone. They were naked and roughly anthropoidal in appearance, with black hairless skin and long barbed tails. Their eyes were enormous black disks, their mouths beak-like structures.

A fourth creature wearing some kind of ornamented vestment of white leather that was open down the front approached the slab from the far side. It bent down and did something beneath the slab, then drew forth an object that gleamed as it lifted it high overhead.

"What is that thing?" Agee asked.

"A fetish? A religious icon of some kind?" There was no assurance in Macumba's deep voice.

"It looks like a frog," Jill said, squinting at the projection.

The creature in the robes set the object on the reclining being's chest. It immediately ceased to struggle against its captors. The priest, if that is what it was, then drew from its belt a long, broad knife and with a single efficient stroke, cut off the captive's head. Picking up the head, it turned and bowed, seeming to present it to something beyond the limit of the image.

The projection abruptly ended, eliciting cries of dismay from the watchers.

Layton lifted the cylinder off the spindle and set it back on several times. Nothing occurred.

"It may be broken, or out of power," he murmured. "God alone knows how old it is. It's a miracle it worked at all."

"Can you fix it?" Nordström demanded.

Leighton stared at the older man for a moment. "I'm an engineer, not a magician. Who knows what it uses for a power source? It doesn't even have any moving parts. But I'll try."

"Do your best," Nordström muttered. "This must be a library of some kind. It's evidence that the race that built this city was far more advanced than we had imagined."

"That slab of black stone in the projection," Agee said. "There's one like it in the Temple. I remember seeing it in videos the robots transmitted through the foldgate."

"Let's walk over there and take a look," Nordström said.

They left the library and made their way along the sandy streets toward the center of the city, where there was an open area much like a town plaza. Standing alone in the center of this space, as though shunned by the reddish beehives around it, was a low structure of massive black stones. Instead of a rounded dome, it was roofed with a single enormous slab. The low walls were vertical and, apart from a double doorway, unbroken.

"It almost looks Egyptian," Jill said in a low voice to Leighton as they approached across the square.

It had been nicknamed the Temple due to the recumbent oblong of stone that dominated the interior and vaguely resembled an altar. Alongside it there was a circular dais that appeared to be a platform for a statue of some sort, although it was empty. No statues of any kind had been found by the robots.

When they entered through the double doors, orange light illuminated the interior.

"That didn't happen when the robots searched this place," Nordström said, glancing around uneasily.

"The lighting may be keyed to body heat," Leighton told him.

"Where's it coming from?" Jill asked.

The radiance seemed to have no source, but emanated from the entire surface of the black ceiling.

Nordström walked around the altar. "In the projection the priest stood right about here."

He knelt to examine the side of the altar.

"There's something here, some kind of door or cover. I can't—
Wait, I've got it. There's something inside the opening."

He stood up slowly. Between his hands he held an object of
transparent red-gold that seemed to glow with its own inner
light.

"It's the idol the priest held," Victor Stossel said.

"What is it?" Jill asked.

"An amphibian of some kind." Macumba took it into his
hands. "Look, it has webbed feet."

"Then I was right, it's a frog."

Macumba studied the idol, turning it over before handing it
back to Nordström. "More like a kind of toad, I would say. But
definitely water-dwelling."

"There is no water on this planet," Agee pointed out. "Not on
the surface, anyway."

"There was once," Deeping said.

"Yes, but that was millions of years ago."

Gina Loeb stepped forward. She was the team geologist, a
mousy little woman with hunched shoulders who seldom spoke.
"Give it to me."

"It's heavier than it looks," Nordström said in warning before
passing her the idol. He seemed reluctant to part with it.

She turned it in her hands, examining it in minute detail.

"I think it's a kind of amber. Petrified plant resin. There's
something inside it."

Carrying it out of the Temple with the others trailing after her,
she held it up to the orange sun and pointed. "Look, some kind
of occlusion in the head."

Deeping snatched the idol from her and peered at it. The
chubby, red-cheeked face of the little botanist twisted with
excitement. He chuckled through his mask and stared at the
others.

"Do you know what this is? It's a seed, an actual seed."

—.—

2

In the dining hall at the intersection of the four wings of the habitat, the debate had raged for more than an hour. Leighton found himself growing bored with it.

"We have to cut it open to extract the seed," Deeping said.

"Impossible," Nordström told him curtly. "This is the only example of the art of the city dwellers. It's too valuable to damage."

"If we don't try to germinate it here, on the planet, we may not get another chance."

"Surely it can wait until we finish the mission."

"You don't understand. There may be unique environmental factors here essential to its growth."

"Do you really think there is any chance in the world this seed will germinate?" Agee asked. "My God, Harold, it may be more than a million years old."

"The seeds of date palms found in Egyptian tombs have germinated after thousands of years."

"Thousands, Harold, thousands—not millions," Nordström said.

"This carving may represent the deity of a lost alien race," Macumba told Deeping. "It is a precious thing. I won't let you cut it."

They were all against Deeping, but the little man was undaunted. The debate might have raged all night, had not Deeping taken up the idol to examine it and carelessly let it slip from between his hands. It shattered on the metallic tile floor like glass. He bent and picked out the seed from the amber shards.

"How could I be so clumsy?" he said.

Nordström stared at him, struck speechless with fury. The others waited in silence for his explosion. It did not come. After a while he said, "Take your damned seed. Do what you want with it, but document everything."

Deeping held up the seed between his fingers and peered at it, a satisfied little smile on his pink lips. It was a black thing about two centimeters long, with a spiky, irregular surface. In his rapture of delight he seemed to forget the presence of the others. They began to wander off, shaking their heads in disgust at what they had just witnessed. A domestic robot rolled in with a brush and a dust pan to sweep up the fragments of the shattered idol.

"It will never germinate," Macumba told Deeping before leaving the dining hall. "Not after millions of years. You must know that."

"We shall see," Deeping said.

3

"I don't think we should go in there, Hal."

Leighton looked up and down the corridor. It was early afternoon, a slack time in the habitat, and no one was in sight.

"It's a public work space. Deeping has no right to keep the door locked."

Jill LeBrock pointed to the hand-lettered sign taped to the door. It read, "DO NOT ENTER—Sensitive experiment ongoing."

"Deeping treats the biology lab like his own little kingdom. He will lose his mind if he catches us in there."

"You do what you want to do. I'm going to see what he's been hiding in there."

It was four months after the incident in the dining hall. Indignation at Deeping's apparent deliberate destruction of a priceless alien religious icon had diminished but had not gone away. The rumor was that Nordström had written him up in a report, but there had been no way to prove the dropping of the toad deliberate, so Deeping had been allowed to continue with his usual duties, one of which was the nurturing of the seed that had been inside the amber figurine. When pressed, Deeping admitted that the seed had germinated, but he categorically refused to allow anyone into the biology lab to look at it.

Nordström couldn't even get him to produce a picture of the plant.

"I'm surprised Nordström doesn't lock him away in a room. His behavior has been increasingly odd lately," Leighton said.

"How do you mean?"

"I pass him in the corridor, and he doesn't even say hello to me. It's like I'm not there. I've seen him when he thinks nobody's watching him, making these weird little gestures with his hands. He looks like some kind of giant praying mantis with the face of a demented cherub."

Jill made a sound of derision in her throat and grinned crookedly at him.

"I interview Deeping regularly, just as I do the rest of you. He may be showing signs of slight eccentricity, but his work is up to standards and he passes all the tests."

"I still say he's gone nuts. He spends hours alone in here with his precious weed, or flower, or whatever it is, talking to it. I can hear him through the door sometimes late at night."

"I thought the doors were soundproof."

"Not if you put your ear against them."

She rolled her eyes.

"I want to see what he's up to," Leighton said. "For all we know he's talking to an empty flower pot, or a stalk of celery."

"Hydroponics doesn't grow celery."

"You know what I mean. I'm going in."

She glanced nervously over her shoulder down the corridor. "Are you sure Deeping isn't in the habitat?"

"He went out on the buggy with Gina this morning to look at some fossils she found in a rock slope. They won't be back for hours."

He inserted the spare key to the bio lab he had removed from Nordström's office and opened the door. After a moment of hesitation, she followed him.

It was dark inside the room, and unusually warm. He fumbled on the wall for the light switch.

"It's like a greenhouse in here," she murmured. "Maybe he is growing something."

The lights came on with a blinding glare that Leighton quickly dimmed. They looked around. The tables were filled with measuring instruments and glassware, but there was no sign of any kind of plant.

"Maybe he's got it in one of the drawers," Jill said.

Leighton tilted his head back. His nostrils widened. "Do you smell that?"

She wrinkled her nose. "Yes. What is that stink?"

One corner of the lab was divided off with two curtains of semi-transparent plastic sheeting that hung down from sliding tracks in the ceiling. What lay behind them was blurred and indistinct. Walking over, Leighton jerked one side of the curtain open. He took an involuntary step backward.

"What the hell—"

It towered above their heads, almost brushing the ceiling panels. The broad, thick fronds that spread from its stalk were a dark green that was almost black. Along the length of the stalk grew large round pods wrapped in dark leaves. They looked like cabbages. The central stalk, as thick as Leighton's leg, extended straight up, then expanded into an orange spongy mass that was cone-shaped, with yellow sprigs like corn silk sprouting from its apex. Around its base, a series of arched root-like structures that resembled the legs of a spider descended into the bed of soil Deeping had made for it. The soil had a reddish appearance. An empty plastic pouch lay on its surface.

They stared at it in silence. Leighton noticed slight movements in the exposed root tendrils. They pulsed rhythmically.

"Is that what I think it is?" Jill asked in a small voice.

He reached down carefully and lifted the plastic pouch by its corner. Remnants of the same red liquid that stained the soil clung to its inner surface. In a white rectangle was written the name "Nordström."

"Blood. Deeping has been feeding this thing on our frozen emergency stores of whole blood."

Before embarking on their voyage through the foldgate, each member of the team had donated ten litres of red blood, which had been frozen and stored on the *Aurora*. It was presently in a freezer in the med lab.

"This has got to be against regulations. If someone gets hurt and there isn't enough of their blood type—"

"They could die," he finished for her. "Nordström has to be told about this. Keeping this plant hidden from the rest of us is bad enough, but stealing our blood—that's way over the line."

"It was necessary," Deeping said behind them, making them both jump.

The lab door was open. Leighton realized Deeping had crept in quietly while he and Jill were occupied with the plant.

"I thought you were with the survey team, looking at fossils."

"I was. We returned early—there's a storm coming."

Jill took the deflated plastic blood bag from Leighton and held it up.

"This is not acceptable. You've jeopardized team safety. How much have you stolen?"

Deeping's eyes rolled toward the plant. His round face was unnaturally smooth. Leighton suddenly realized why it looked so odd: there were no lines in it. No frown lines, no worry lines.

"It was sickening, dying," Deeping said in a reasonable tone. "Normal plant food was poison to it. I tried everything, even the artificial beef from our food stores. Then one day I cut myself on a broken beaker, and some of my blood dripped into the soil around its base. One of the suckers moved toward it and began to feed. I gave it my own blood, as much as I could spare, but it needed more. You see how large it is. Well, I couldn't let it starve, could I? This is the most important discovery of our mission. I had to care for it. I had to find another source of food."

Leighton was amazed Deeping had not exploded into one of his usual temper tantrums. Instead, he was being reasonable, a bit too reasonable.

"This won't do, Harold. Nordström will never let you keep

depleting our stores of emergency blood. Not even to keep this, this—*thing* alive." He could not keep the note of disgust from his voice. Deeping appeared not to notice.

"You think not? Well, then, let's go and ask him."

He turned and walked out of the lab. Leighton stared at Jill.

"We better go with him," she said. "He might say anything. I don't think he's stable."

"You go. I'll be along in a minute."

She hesitated, then nodded and left the lab. He turned to stare at the plant. In his heart was the same vague feeling of dread he had experienced in his disquieting dreams. He had a sense that the plant was somehow aware of his presence. He cocked his head slightly to one side, listening. Behind the hum of electrical systems and the buzz of the air conditioning fans, he heard something else, something that echoed in the memories of his nightmares.

Shrugging his shoulders, he left the lab and closed the door behind him, wondering if Nordström's fury at Deeping would prevent him from making an issue about the borrowed lab key.

4

When Leighton reached Nordström's office, Jill was talking rapidly, explaining what they had discovered in the lab. Nordström sat behind his desk, patiently listening. He had his elbows on the desk top and his fingers spread into a pyramid with their tips touching. Every now and then he cast a glance at Deeping from under steel-gray eyebrows. Deeping wore his habitual half-smile. His blue eyes and golden hair gave him the illusion of childlike innocence.

"What have you to say for yourself, Harold?" Nordström asked the biologist when Jill had talked herself out.

Deeping shrugged and spread his hands. "The plant needs blood, Sven. That's what it eats. At first I tried feeding it on blood from my own body, but as it grew in size it needed more than I could provide. What was I to do?"

"You should have come to me. We could have worked something out."

"Yes, I see that now," Deeping said in a humble tone. "What I did was rash."

"What you did was criminal," Jill said hotly. "You stole some of the emergency medical blood supply."

"Surely no harm has been done," Deeping said, looking at each of them.

"That wasn't your decision to make, Harold. Apart from your own ten liters, that blood doesn't belong to you. It belongs to the donors, who set it aside for their own personal use in the event of accidents."

"I admit it was a little forward of me," Deeping said to Nordström. "But you can see the position I was in. This plant is the most important discovery we will make on this expedition. It justifies our being here. I had to preserve it."

"You could have frozen the plant," Leighton said.

"That would kill it. We must keep it alive. At all costs, we must keep it alive."

Leighton could not help but admire his scientific passion. Deeping's eyes shone with a light that was almost fanatical.

"You've placed me in an awkward position, Harold," Nordström said quietly. "I'm not insensitive to your zeal for our mission. Even so, I must record a censure in the mission record concerning your behavior."

Jill looked at Deeping and nodded in satisfaction.

"Also, I am going to authorize you to draw upon five liters from each personal store of red blood, to be used to sustain the plant, in the event that it proves to be necessary."

"You can't do that," Jill said. "That blood is ours, for our own use."

"I'm afraid you are mistaken, Jill," Nordström said quietly. "As captain of this expedition, I have been given absolute authority to make whatever command decisions I deem necessary for the good of the mission."

They argued for several minutes, but Nordström stood firm while Deeping stood by like a cat watching a mouse, saying nothing. The smile of the little man seemed frozen in place. Finally, Jill stormed out of the office in disgust. Leighton followed more slowly, closing the office door behind him. As he was walking down the corridor, he remembered the borrowed key in his pocket and turned back the way he had come.

When he opened the office door, he found Nordström and Deeping both standing, facing each other, with their right hands raised and pressed palm to palm as the two men stared into each other's eyes. They turned to look at him without breaking their contact. Neither spoke.

"I, uh, just wanted to return this," Leighton said, holding up the key. He set it on the corner of a filing cabinet and backed out of the office.

For some reason he could not define, what he had seen stayed in his mind. He told himself that it was nothing. If Nordström and Deeping were having a homosexual relationship, it was none of his business; but the weirdness of the gesture, coupled with the lack of emotion on the faces of the two men, troubled him. Nordström's decision about the blood supply did not sit well with him, either. It was not an unreasonable compromise, in view of the importance of the alien plant to science, but it rankled him that the most personal thing possessed by the members of the team, their own blood, should not even be under their control.

That night he could not sleep. He lay tossing back and forth, listening to the windstorm outside throw sand against the habitat. Finally he got up, dressed, and made his way to the med lab. The corridors were empty due to the late hour. The walk-in freezer was not locked. He opened it and carefully counted the bags of blood that hung on racks inside. The entirety of Deeping's supply was gone. Nordström had seven bags remaining, the rest of the team eight bags, except for Leighton who counted nine bags of his own blood. Deeping had stolen blood from every member of the team.

Leighton stood for several minutes, thinking. He found an insulated box and put his blood bags into it, then piled Jill LeBrock's remaining blood on top of it. This he carried back to Section C of the habitat, where his room was. He hid the box inside the big freezer in the storage room that was used to preserve their supply of fresh-frozen green vegetables.

Exactly why he did this, Leighton could not have explained. The unease he had experienced during the transition through the foldgate had grown stronger, but still had no specific source that he could define. When he returned to bed, his dreams were a jumble of disquieting images. The ritiual sacrifice on the cylinder record. The black slab of the altar in the temple. The amber toad. The plant looming over him and moving its leaves and root tendrils. Nordström and Deeping pressing their hands together like lovers. The spherical growths along the stalk of the plant. He woke suddenly.

"Seventeen," he said to himself. "Seventeen."

He lay in bed, staring up at the light of early morning that filtered through the translucent roof of the habitat.

5

"Have you noticed how odd people are acting lately?" Jill asked in a whisper.

Leighton used his fork to toy with the food on his tray and nodded.

"This morning I saw Moralis talking to himself. He was arguing, but there was no one there to argue with. It was weird."

"Thank God. I thought it was just me, imagining things."

"No, I've been noticing it for weeks now. It seems to be getting worse."

She nodded. "Gina was in the bio lab yesterday, looking at the plant. She was just standing there, staring at it, almost as if she was listening to it."

"They all visit the lab to stare at it. Deeping leaves the door unlocked now," he said, glancing around the dining hall to see if anyone was taking an interest in their conversation. Nobody appeared to be listening. Several other people sat alone at tables, chewing with cow-like expressions on their faces, their eyes unfocused.

"Everyone's so pale," Jill murmured, leaning closer to him over the table.

"I think they've been feeding the plant on blood from their own bodies," Leighton said. "There are cuts on their arms."

Her eyes widened. "That's horrible."

"Something's going on. I'm not sure what it is, but everyone moves as if they're in a trance. It's been getting worse for weeks, even since we had that meeting with Nordström over Deeping stealing our blood supplies."

"What are we going to do?" Jill asked. "I'm frightened, Hal. We've still got over a year until the foldgate realigns and we can go home."

He leaned his head nearer to hers. "I think it's the plant," he whispered.

"How is that possible?"

"I don't know. But ever since Deeping started feeding it blood, people have been acting strange."

He had not told Jill about moving her blood bags from central storage and hiding them in the hydroponics freezer, but could it be another coincidence that she alone seemed normal?

"What are we going to do, Hal?" she repeated.

"I've made up my mind," he whispered. "I'm going to kill it."

She cast a conspiratorial glance around the dining hall. No one seemed to be listening.

"When?" she whispered.

"Tonight."

"How?"

"Poison. It's a plant, so herbicide should kill it."

"We don't have any herbicide."

"No, but I made up some from our chemical stores. We had the raw ingredients. I looked up how to make it."

"Can I help?'

"Better if you stay out of it, in case anything goes wrong."

He expected her to argue, but she remained silent.

6

The corridors of the habitat were never dark, but at night the lights were dimmed to a dull amber. Leighton did not expect to meet everyone. The entire team had a rigorous work schedule that put them in their beds early, and most of them stayed in their rooms all night. Apart from the occasional midnight flit from one room to another for sex, the corridors at night were deserted.

He walked quietly but quickly through the central dining area and into Section D, which contained hydroponics and the hydroponics lab. In his hand was a corked beaker filled with yellowish liquid. He had done his research, and had every expectation that the liquid would kill any organism that relied on photosynthesis, which evidently included the plant, since its fronds were green.

As expected, the door to the bio lab was not locked. He wondered why Deeping had gone from paranoid suspicion to blind trust. Whatever the reason, it suited his purposes. He turned on the lights. There it was, watching him. Why he felt so certain that the plant was aware of him, he could not have explained, but he was certain of it. He glanced around. The lab was empty.

The plant was even bigger than it had been when he had last looked at it. Its upper stem with its pulpy red mass brushed the ceiling five meters above his head. The spherical growths along its length were larger now, almost the size of pumpkins. They looked as if they were getting ready to open into flowers, or whatever they contained. There were seventeen of them. Seventeen. The same number as the members of the expedition. It couldn't be a coincidence.

One of the fronds of the plant nodded slightly, although there was no breeze from the air duct to move it. In the silence he heard the same faint trilling noise he had noticed the last time he had been in the bio lab, but he could not determine where it came from. It set his teeth on edge.

"Drink this, you monster," he muttered under his breath and pulled the cork from the beaker. He extended his arm toward the mass of root tendrils that spread over the box of earth Deeping had made for the plant. The foul odor of rotting flesh filled his nose and mouth and made him gag. He started to tilt the beaker, then hesitated. The thought came into his mind: Was this really a wise course of action? Wasn't he being rash? After all, this plant was unique. Every other example of it had died a million or more years ago. The seed in the amber toad might very well have been the last seed of its species.

Leighton shook his head and blinked hard to clear his vision. A dizziness swept over him, making him sway on his feet. He tightened his grip on the flask and again began to tilt it, then stopped. Try as he would, he could not make his arm obey his will. He stood there, struggling against his own body as the minutes passed and beads of sweat formed on his forehead and trickled down into his eyes.

"You can't do it, can you, Leighton?"

He turned his head toward Deeping's familiar voice and saw him standing in the doorway of the lab, along with Nordström and Macumba. Jill stood behind them, her face as impassive as theirs. In Deeping's hand was a hollow tube of some ceramic material. He pointed it casually at Leighton, who stared past him at the woman with a hurt expression.

"Why?"

"I couldn't let you make such a terrible mistake, Hal. You aren't thinking clearly yet. I had to protect you from yourself."

"Jill has been with us for several days," Nordström said, smiling slightly in a mechanical way. "She alerted me of your intentions."

"So you came to stop me."

"That wasn't necessary," Deeping said. "You stopped yourself, as we knew you would. Your own bonding is almost complete."

"I don't know what you're talking about."

"We found your blood and Jill's blood where you hid it, and fed it to the plant," Macumba explained. "You are almost one of us. That is why you couldn't use the poison."

"Give in to it, Hal," Jill said in a distant, dreaming tone. "Fighting it is futile. I know: I tried to fight, but I realize now how wrong I was."

Deeping stepped forward and gently took the flask from his hand, then went to a chemical sink and poured its contents away.

"I'm glad you're almost one of us," he said. "I would have hated to use this weapon on you." He held up the hollow ceramic tube.

"It's technology from the lost race," Nordström explained. "We're getting a wealth of precious technological information through the plant, which has a genetic memory. Science will be occupied sorting it all out for a century at least."

Leighton felt the control over his body waver for moment. He stumbled and almost collapsed. Then it was back again, steadying his legs, keeping him frozen in place.

"You came at an auspicious time," Deeping said. "The moment of my transformation. As you know, I've been feeding the plant my blood for longer than anyone else's. Soon this will happen to everyone. But I suppose you'll be last."

As he talked, he unzipped his shirt and draped it over a worktable. His bare chest was covered with fine golden hairs. He approached the plant as though approaching a holy altar and knelt before it.

There was a faint crackling sound. The leaves that wrapped around the spherical growth lowest down on the plant's stem slowly curled and unwrapped themselves. The faint trilling noise grew louder. As they opened, they revealed a human face. Leighton's stomach spasmed as he recognized Deeping's features. The eyes of the face rolled in their sockets, and from its open mouth came forth screeching sounds. He realized that it was screaming in pain.

Deeping bowed his head. "I'm ready."

Nordström took the hollow cylinder from him and stood on one side, gripped him by his shoulders. Macumba went to the other side. In his hand was a large meat cleaver from the kitchen.

"Our psychic link with the plant is strong, but for it to be completed requires a physical commitment," Jill explained at Leighton's side as he blinked cold sweat from his eyes.

Macumba raised the cleaver and brought it down on Deeping's neck. His head flew forward into the root mass of the plant along with a fountain of red blood. Deeping's body wavered but did not fall. Nordström held it upright as Macumba plucked the vegetable head growing on the plant from its stem with a twisting motion and lowered it onto Deeping's still spurting neck. Leighton saw tendrils uncoil themselves from the plant head and descend into the veins in Deeping's neck. They pulled the head firmly into place. After a few moments, blood ceased to seep from the red line that wrapped across Deeping's throat.

Nordström released him, and he climbed to his feet and stood balancing himself on unsteady legs like an infant. His rolling eyes fixed on Leighton, and his lips writhed away from his teeth into an approximation of a grin. It was horrifying in its alienness. The plant face was an almost perfect duplicate for Deeping's real face, but there was enough of a difference to make the hairs on the back of Leighton's neck bristle.

Deeping cleared his throat several times and spat out a small portion of blood. It stained his lips and chin.

"You see, Leighton," he said in a voice like dry, rustling corn. "Nothing to be afraid of."

—·—

7

Deeping picked up his former head and wrapped it in clear plastic. Its unmoving eyes seemed to stare at Leighton as Deeping cradled it under his arm. They led Leighton toward the main airlock. The other members of the team were already there, putting on heavier clothing and breathing masks. Deeping did not put a mask on his new head, but slipped one onto Leighton.

"What are you all doing?" Leighton asked.

"You are about to witness a ceremony that has not occurred for almost two million years," Nordström explained. "Consider how fortunate you are to be alive at this moment."

They filed out of the habitat and through the alien city silently, like the ghosts of the dead. Dawn was just beginning to show itself in the sky. The air was cold and still. New sand drifts lay between the buildings, the aftermath of the recent storm. Leighton realized they were headed for the low, black building that housed the slab of stone they had presumed to be an altar. The stone in his nightmares.

Leighton wondered how Deeping could breathe without a mask. The little botanist did not show any signs of distress. He stood to one side and observed the activities of the others as though silently directing them with his mind. Leighton remembered the three-dimensional moving image that had been projected from the strange machine in the building they had called a library. Had that ceremony been some kind of residual relic, still practiced by the degenerated alien race of the city, long after its true purpose had been forgotten? "You will witness that purpose unfold before you," Nordström told him. "Consider yourself blessed."

Leighton had not spoken his thoughts aloud, yet somehow Nordström had heard them.

"We are all connected, Hal," Nordström explained in a kindly tone. "We share our thoughts. Soon you will share them with us when your *tafon* matures."

The word was strange, but Leighton got a flash image of one of the cabbage-like growths on the plant. It was the one at the top.

"You see? You're already becoming one of us."

Deeping unwrapped the plastic from his old head and walked around the black stone altar once, then laid the head on it. He made a series of complex signs on the air with his right hand. The others knelt before the altar and began to chant in a strange language. Leighton realized it must be the language of the city dwellers.

Something began to move in the air above the pedestal next to the altar. The air wavered, swirled, and took on substance. At first it was no more than a patch of darkness, but it expanded and became better defined. The chanting stopped. The pedestal was covered by a mound of glistening black slime. The shape of the slime looked vaguely familiar to Leighton. He realized that it was something like the shape of the amber idol Deeping had smashed. It vaguely resembled a giant black toad. Around it slithered an elongated snake-like creature made of some cohesive black liquid. It had no eyes.

Deeping approached the pedestal with reverence, holding his old head up in his hands. He laid it gently at the base of the glistening, pulsating mass, then stepped back and knelt. The eyes in the severed head had rolled up so that now it seemed to be staring upwards, imploring heaven. The snake sliding around the shoulders of the toad-like thing darted down and coiled around the offering. It left one end of itself lying against the toad and seemed to stick to the head's face. As the chanting rose to a frenzy the serpentine black liquid drew the severed head against the body of the toad, which absorbed it.

"The god accepts our offering," Nordström shouted. "Rejoice, rejoice."

Jill and several other team members screamed in exultation.

As Deeping began to rise, the black snake darted out again and coiled around his throat. Smoke arose from his neck, and abruptly the head came free from his shoulders and was swiftly conveyed into the black mass. His body collapsed into a spurting fountain of blood.

Confusion rippled through the gathering. The hunger of the god after the passage of millions of years had not been anticipated. They milled around, uncertain of what to do. Leighton felt the psychic control over his body lift. He darted forward and snatched the hollow tube out of Nordström's lax fingers. The older man blinked and focused his attention on the engineer. He started toward Leighton with a look of murder on his gray face. Without thinking, Leighton raised the tube and pointed it. A beam shot from the end and enveloped Nordström's body. Some of the other team members stumbled against one another and shrank back.

Within seconds Nordström's body began to soften and lose its outline. A thin cry of despair issued from his throat as his arms thickened and became shorter, withdrawing themselves into his bloating torso. His legs shortened as well, until the team leader was no more than a bundle of clothing around a liquid-filled bag of skin, which split open and poured out across the black stones of the temple floor.

Leighton ran from the temple and through the deserted city with only one thought—to destroy the plant. He was not pursued, but whether from fear or the general confusion he had no way of guessing.

The long fronds of the plant quivered when he entered the bio lab. He felt the plant trying to regain control over his body but found that he was able to hold it at bay with his will, the force of which was heightened to unnatural levels by his horror.

He pointed the ceramic tube at the plant. Nothing happened. Mentally, he willed it to fire its ray. Nothing. With a curse he threw it to the floor, shattering it into small pieces. He looked around the lab for a weapon. There was no knowing how long the confusion of the group would weaken the psychic power of the plant. He felt it in his mind, striving to push away his will and regain control of his body. Crossing to a shelf of supplies, he threw them off searching for a strong acid or a poison. He was about to cast aside a two-liter plastic jug when his gaze fell upon its label: methyl alcohol.

He tore off the cap and almost fell as he hurried to throw the alcohol over the roots of the plant. It was beginning to regain its power over his limbs. His legs felt heavy, numb, as though they belonged to someone else. He tried to remember what to do next, but his mind filled with wool. Fire—that was it. Snatching up a fire starter from beside a bunsen burner on the work table, he fell against the skeletal roots of the plant and clicked it. Blue flame burst forth. Some of it got on his sleeve, but he was able to roll away and beat out the flames with his hand.

The plant howled in his mind and its fronds began to slap against the floor and the wall. As the flames flew upward, the spheres along the stem curled open, revealing the sleeping heads of the expedition. Their eyes widened in agony and they began to scream with shrill little voices that he heard as much with his mind as with his ears. The roaring flames ignited the plastic panels of the ceiling and melted them, sending down burning ropes of liquid plastic over the screaming heads.

Unconcerned for the moment with his own safety, Leighton leaned back and watched the hellish thing burn. Then he realized the flames were smaller than before. They continued to die down, as though an invisible extinguisher were being sprayed upon them. He guessed the reason with a curse. The air from the planet was pouring down through the rent in the habitat roof. It did not contain enough oxygen to support vigorous burning. The fire was going out, and the malevolent influence of the plant over his mind began to reassert itself.

In desperation, he ran from the lab and down the corridor, thinking to put as much distance between himself and the plant as possible before it retook control over him. He noticed a fire extinguisher in a recess in the corridor wall, and beside it a red axe. The axe had a spike opposite its blade. It was designed for removing debris in the event of a fire. Leighton grabbed it off its hooks and took it back to the bio lab, this time walking with purpose. Ignoring the fog the plant was trying to cast over his mind, he began to hack at the screaming heads. As the axe struck each of them, they burst like bags of blood, staining everything with red.

Macumba's head tried to curse him with its writhing lips, and Jill's cast him a hurtful look before he split it open in a shower of blood. He was drenched to the skin and his clothing stuck to him. Blood ran down from his matted hair into his eyes and mouth. This was his nightmare, the one he could never remember. He spat blood out and continued to hack like a madman at the stem of the plant, which was tough and resisted the sharp bit of the axe.

At last the plant toppled over. The highest head, which he had not been able to reach with the axe, rolled to his feet. Wiping blood from his eyes with his wrist, he blinked down at it. The head stared up at him, its eyes wide with fear. It was his face. He almost became sick, but choked back the vomit and brought the scarlet axe down upon the center of the head's nose. It split with a spray of blood. At the same instant, something exploded in Leighton's brain, and he fell into darkness.

AN ELEMENTAL INFESTATION

Mark Samuels

Mark Samuels is the author of seven short story collections The White Hands and Other Weird Tales *(2003),* Black Altars *(2003),* Glyphotech and Other Macabre Processes *(2008),* The Man Who Collected Machen *(2010),* Written in Darkness *(2014),* The Prozess Manifestations *(2017), and a "best of" volume* The Age of Decayed Futurity *(2020). He is also the author of three short novels:* The Face of Twilight *(2006),* A Pilgrim Stranger *(2017), and* Witch-Cult Abbey *(2020).*

1

AVELOCK HAD FIRST GLIMPSED THE EDGE OF Penceddo Wood from his motorcar whilst approaching the construction site of the proposed relief road. Although he had lived in the locality for six months, he had not particularly taken any notice of the woods until then. In the distance, on the plateau atop the western hillside of Thool Valley, there stretched a mile-wide swathe of yew trees with another two miles of dense woodland lurking farther back behind them. The late-afternoon winter sun was setting behind the shadowy expanse of the evergreen trees in a crimson-and-saffron riot of colour, lending the panoramic scene an otherworldly aspect. Such was the effect of the intense vision that confronted him, he momentarily forgot his sense of annoyance at having been despatched at short notice (and without being properly briefed on the latest developments) by his immediate superior at the Thool District Council Planning Department.

His thoughts turned from the sight of the wooded hill, lit up, as if ablaze, to the dull, functional interior of the musty office of Charles Beechfield OBE in the department's section for local road network development:

"Havelock," Beechfield had said, "I have to bugger off somewhere restful for at least a month, and must do so immediately. Sudden leave of absence. Under strict orders. Last day in the office. Doctor says the old ticker's playing up, if you must know. A lot of fuss about nothing if you ask me, but Mrs Beechfield's somehow got wind of it. She who must be obeyed and all that. I have to clear off at once. No choice but to dump this project in your lap. Here's the file: look through it. I've probably let the matter slide a little, but no doubt you can soon pick up the reins. Get yourself over there to the construction site tomorrow, find out what the hold-up is all about, and sort it out. There's a good chap."

Havelock had nodded at various points during Beechfield's monologue, wished his superior a swift and full recovery, and then taken the hefty, buff-coloured file to his desk, sat down, and began to leaf through the various documents contained therein.

Beechfield had let it slide all right, Havelock thought; the situation even smacked of wilful ineptitude. The whole process of constructing a local relief road to ease traffic congestion had ground to a halt, even though construction work had started two months ago. As far as Havelock could make out, only half-a-mile of the planned road had actually been laid before all manner of interminable delays had crippled the project. The nature of these delays was baffling: vague reports of inexplicable mechanical failures in heavy equipment and instances of both physical and mental breakdowns in the personnel assigned to the construction crews. It seemed that a number of local employees had flatly refused to continue to labour on the road, despite generous incentives, even preferring dismissal, and it was only by hiring workmen from London that any limited progress had been made at all. As matters now stood, no construction work had been undertaken during the last two weeks. Only a tiny fraction of Penceddo Woods had been cleared and the road terminated little more than twenty yards into its endless masses of densely packed yew trees.

Later, on the evening of the same day he had spoken with Beechfield, while unwinding at the Gryphon Tavern over a small whisky-and-soda, Havelock happened to mention his predicament to the pub's loquacious landlord during the course of their conversation.

"What, you're still going to try and build that road up through old Penceddo Wood?"

"Quite right," said Havelock. "We consulted the local populace by postal survey a year ago. There were no objections."

"And no replies at all from any sensible folk, I'm sure. Fools only learn by doing wrong, not from warnings beforehand. You ought to ask Roderick Carden, our local historian, about the woods. Shame he's not in tonight."

"What does that crank know? Are they possessed of a sinister local reputation, some sort of the usual superstitious rubbish he peddles in his books?"

"Ask him yourself," said the landlord, moving away to serve another customer and leaving the taciturn young barmaid to serve Havelock his drinks thereafter.

And so it was that, at dusk the next afternoon, Havelock found himself driving up to the construction site that was to be named, in faux-rustic-idyll fashion, "Penceddo Lane" when the road was finally completed, despite the fact that the project would cause the destruction of two straight miles of ancient woodland. The sight of those massed ranks of yew trees framed by a blazing sunset certainly gave Havelock pause for thought; but one doubts it significantly altered his feelings as to the desirability of further easing local traffic congestion. He was, after all, only an unimaginative town clerk, a minor bureaucrat with bills and rent to pay, and also one of those up-to-date individuals who are content to shrug and accede to the universal dictum that nothing and no one can be allowed to stand in the way of "progress." Even the (in his view) unsightly old village of Gallows Langley, with its shadowy cluster of Jacobean two-storey houses with their mouldering front-gabled roofs and bay windows, would eventually have to be pulled down and replaced in favour of more utilitarian red-brick developments.

He parked his vehicle alongside several others in a small clearing on the hillside that served as a makeshift car park, got out, and noted, just up ahead in the shadows, a concrete-mixer, excavator, articulated hauler, as well as various other forms of heavy machinery, all resting idle at the construction site. There was a group of half-a-dozen workmen wearing safety helmets sitting around an oil-drum fire, warming their hands in front of the flames, smoking cigarettes, and drinking steaming mugs of tea. As Havelock approached they looked up at him; one of them nudged another in the ribs, and then whispered something obscene.

"I'm from the planning department. Where can I find the foreman?" Havelock said, feeling somewhat uneasy at the suspicious expressions on the unshaven, gaunt faces, which seemed not so much menacing as menaced.

"Gaffer's over there, in that portacabin," one of them replied, pointing behind Havelock before returning his hand-rolled cigarette to his chapped lips.

Havelock turned around and moved in the direction of the site office, observing, to his right, the short stretch of road into the woods which had been completed thus far—a narrow twenty-yard long strip of tarmac that had eaten through the surrounding tunnel-like confines of the yew trees and which terminated in a huge mound of rubble and timber only half-visible in the rapidly gathering darkness.

He ascended the tiny flight of steps outside the entrance to the portacabin to find the door was unlocked and left ever-so-slightly ajar. Inside, slumped face down over a desk, was an insensible man, his head resting between a half-consumed bottle of Greenall's gin and a lit paraffin lantern giving off a warm amber glow but also exuding a thick, cloying aroma that permeated the interior cabin. There was a mass of papers scattered around the floor; mostly official correspondence and uncompleted invoices, and it seemed most of them had been trodden upon irreverently— and more than just once—by muddy boots.

Havelock picked his way through the debris and stood alongside the slumped-over foreman, listening with growing impatience to the stifled grunts and incoherent mumblings of this useless sleeptalker. It seemed that, while lost in disgusting inebriation, the man was suffering a drink-induced nightmare, one that was no doubt aggravated by guilt at his complete dereliction of duty. Having received no reaction at all to his spoken entreaties that the foreman pull himself together, Havelock roughly shook him by the shoulder until, finally, the pitiful human wreck opened his eyes and blearily awoke to some measure of consciousness.

He gazed at his surroundings—and at Havelock—with total incomprehension, and then his hand snaked across the desk to grasp the bottle of gin. He shakily poured a generous measure of the spirit into a dirty glass tumbler and tossed the contents down his throat.

"Don't you think you've already had more than enough?" Havelock said.

The foreman swore at him, slurring his words.

"Mr. Beechfield sent me," Havelock went on. "I'm an official from the planning department. I want to know what work has been going on here of late. Very little, or so it seems."

"It can't be done," the foreman said. "It doesn't matter how many machines or men you try. They all break down sooner rather than later. I tell you, it can't be done. The sounds are what's worst. It wouldn't be so bad if the woods didn't whisper to me so."

The man appeared to be on the verge of a complete nervous collapse. He was speaking gibberish.

Havelock gave up and went back outside. The brightest of the stars for that time of year were becoming visible in the vastness of the night sky, and he could just make out the familiar shape of Orion having risen far over in the distance to the southeast.

When he asked the workmen sitting around the oil drum fire what had happened to their foreman, they shrugged their shoulders, said Havelock wouldn't believe them even if they told him, that he'd think them mad, and insisted this was their final day on the job. They, too, had had enough of the place. Now that it was dark, they'd decided they were all clearing out together and never returning. He could also, they told him just for good measure, "stuff their jobs where the sun don't shine."

The following morning, while in his office, Havelock telephoned Carden the local historian and asked him whether he could shed any light on the history of Penceddo Wood. He felt absurd having to consult a well-known local crank, but if there were some record of folklore connected with the place which might account for an outbreak of collective hysteria, perhaps it might give him an insight into the best way to approach the apparently insurmountable difficulties associated with the construction of the projected "Penceddo Lane."

"Look," Carden had said to him over the telephone, "it's probably best if you come here to the cottage and see for yourself some of the research material about the woods which I've archived. Describing those photographs—for example—is no substitute for seeing them with your own two eyes."

Having only ever encountered and spoken to Carden twice previously at the Gryphon Tavern, Havelock had formed the distinct impression the man fancied himself some sort of successor to the famous so-called ghost hunter Harry Price. Havelock had a sudden vision of visiting Carden and being confronted with a ridiculous series of photographic plates of dead-eyed Victorian mediums lurking between yew trees and exuding clouds of ectoplasm from their open mouths.

"It's the 'Winton Man' photographs that I think will most interest you," said Carden, "but you need to see them for yourself. Now's as good a time as any. Come on over. I'll make us a nice pot of tea."

2

Carden lived in a former lock-keeper's cottage about half-a-mile's walk from Gallows Langley, right alongside the Grand Union Canal. The previous night's frost had lingered long in the cold sunshine of the morning and, as Havelock trudged his way along the towpath, past the dozen or so gaily coloured narrowboats moored along the waterway and the sparkling-white fields occupied by glum-looking sheep, he rather felt as if he were embarking on a fool's errand. The weird events of the previous day up at Penceddo Wood seemed fantastical and unreal; like some horrible dream he would have done better to dismiss, rather than dwell upon, after awakening.

Carden greeted him in the cottage doorway. Overweight, and in his late fifties, he was attired in a long, thick dressing-gown worn over an untucked, open-neck shirt and Oxford bags. There was a tasselled Chinaman's cap perched on his head, and red-velvet carpet slippers covered his feet. He looked as if he belonged in a circus act or else strutting onstage in the role of a professional conjurer. This bohemian garb was obviously what he chose to wear in private; whenever Havelock had seen the man previously—in public—he had been dressed conservatively in tweeds, rather as Havelock himself dressed.

"Perfect timing. Kettle's already on the boil, do come inside," said Carden.

Havelock followed him along the short hallway and was immediately struck by the series of filing cabinets and storage boxes resting up against the walls. On top of them was piled a bewildering array of musty old books on all manner of recondite subjects. There was a curiously tangy and musky smell lingering in the air, not of tobacco, but definitely of 'something else' having recently been smoked. When Carden ushered his guest into the living room, he had to make space for Havelock to sit on the armchair by removing a pile of books that already occupied its seat; volumes concerning the likes of witchcraft and black magic, each one of them written by a person named Alphonsus Winters.

Carden returned with the tea tray and set it down on the floor. He sat cross-legged on the carpet and began to pour Darjeeling from a silver teapot through a strainer into two bone-china cups. Havelock helped himself to milk and sugar.

"Do you read the books of the Reverend Winters?" Carden enquired. "Interesting old bird, though too much of a Romanist for my liking. Disappeared around here ten years ago. The area is rife with witches; notably the Degabastons, forbearers to Zebulon. But you've not heard about that before, I'm sure: they were rumoured to have—"

"I'm more interested in this 'Winton Man' you mentioned," said Havelock, cutting in. "What has he—it—this thing—to do with Penceddo Wood?"

"Of course. Let me elucidate. 'Winton Man' was a corpse from the Romano-British age that was recovered—incredibly well-preserved—in 1906 from a bog on the outer fringes of Penceddo Wood some distance farther south along Thool Valley, close to Winton Bridge."

Havelock had never heard of any peat bogs in the region, and he generally associated them with areas in the country that were farther north; up in the midlands at the very least. No peat bog had been mentioned, to his knowledge, when the construction survey for Penceddo Lane had been completed.

"Obviously the bog has shrunk during the passage of centuries," Carden continued, as if having detected Havelock's flash of scepticism, "and its extent is now probably only one-twentieth of what it once was in the first century."

"Where are these human remains currently? In some museum, I suppose?"

"Well, they were certainly displayed, being housed locally in Thool Museum. They caused quite a sensation. And then, after scarcely a week, they were—so it was claimed—stolen."

"Stolen? Stolen by whom?"

"No one was ever charged with the offence. I'll certainly tell you what I think happened, but first let me show you those photographs I mentioned over the telephone."

Carden shuffled off to another room and, after a moment or two, returned, carrying a grey folder, which he then passed to Havelock, who examined its contents.

Although there were no photographs of mediums 'posing' between trees and exuding fake ectoplasm from their mouths, the ones he saw were, it is true, genuinely horrible and extraordinary. Each one depicted, in shots taken from different angles, the naturally mummified remains of a male individual who had lived around two thousand years ago. Its flesh had been tanned into brown leather and the compression from the peat bog in which the body had rested had distorted its shape so much that the thing seemed to be half-crushed, with a body, head, and facial features that appeared to have slipped askew from the twisted skeletal structure and skull beneath the skin. The mouth was open in a fixed, yawning expression of agony. As disturbing as the sight was, however, the overall sense of horror was accentuated by the presence of masses of fungal growths sprouting from the carcass as if they had drawn sustenance from it. Although the photographs were in black-and-white, Havelock recalled having had pointed out to him on nature trails certain toxic toadstools bearing blood-red, white-dotted caps; a species of fungi that seemed to flourish only in and around the region of Thool Valley itself. The toadstools in the photographs and those he had seen with his own eyes appeared to be of the same type.

Havelock replaced the photographs in the folder.

"Human sacrifice," Carden said, "and then metempsychosis."

This last remark did not register with Havelock aside from a vague impression that it was besides the point.

"So you're saying this 'Winton Man'—stolen or not back in 1906—has returned to haunt Penceddo Wood, or something along those lines?" Havelock said.

Again, he betrayed a note of scepticism in his tone; he knew well this particular local historian's tendency to conflate local folklore with fact.

Carden shrugged his shoulders.

"I tell you the region is a nexus for all forms of psychical disturbances. The ghost story writer and inland waterways enthusiast Rupert Alderman penned a recent article in the *Illustrated London News* about a pernicious elemental infestation lurking less than a mile from here. He said that to stare for any length of time at this elemental was to invite certain insanity and spiritual suicide. The detail seems highly significant. One of our local artists, Neil Harkness, tells me he has even drawn the thing, having seen it in a mirror, in a dream. He flatly refuses to show the picture to anyone."

"Really?" Havelock replied, stifling a compulsion to chuckle.

"Tell me, what do you know about the ancient druids?"

"Not much. Only that they dress in white robes and continue to gather around Stonehenge at the summer solstice. Kindly philosophers and fortune-tellers, weren't they?"

"Stonehenge has nothing to do with them, whatever contemporary so-called druids might say; I meant the real, ancient Celtic druids. You shake your head again, I see. Well, let me advise you to put aside any false modern notions about the subject. 'Winton Man' is obviously an example of archaeological evidence supporting the claims by the likes of Pliny the Elder and Tacitus of the druids' bloodthirsty rituals of human sacrifice. You might recall that Hallowe'en has its origin in the ancient Celtic festival of Samhain. As Winters put it: 'The druids were not one homogenous Britannic grouping of high-priests and seers; each locality had its own stripe of druidry and although some were much more malefic than others, it cannot be doubted, despite the puerile objections of their latter-day imitators, that they all practised both human sacrifice and cannibalism.' Winters knew what he was talking about."

"This is doubtless very interesting but—"

Carden ignored Havelock's interjection and went on speaking, warming to his subject.

"The particular stripe of druidry which took hold in Thool Valley in pre-Christian times was especially strange. My researches hint at the fact that, as a consequence of Imperial Rome's campaign in the first century to extinguish all manifestations of druidry within its empire, the Thool druids underwent a voluntary process of mass self-sacrifice by mushroom poisoning; a process that was designed to create a final physical union with the woodlands they regarded as sacred."

"And what about 'Winton Man'?"

"If I am correct in my suppositions, then it is likely he was a Thool druid himself, but one who betrayed the cult to the Roman authorities, tried to flee, but was recaptured and forced to consume poisonous toadstools—in one form or another—and was finally thrown into the peat bog. He was also, as a punishment, and to appease the fury of the ancient gods, left permanently suspended between two worlds."

"You still haven't told me what you think finally happened to the body after it was stolen."

"I'll tell you this much: there were no signs of any break-in at the Thool Museum on that night in January 1906. The curator is on record as saying a broken window on the ground floor seemed to have been smashed from inside, and fragments of glass were discovered in only one place: outside on the half-crushed flowerbed beneath that same window. The bizarrely askew footprints totally baffled the local police constabulary. I think the call of the woods was heard and the summons was obeyed."

3

Havelock had made his excuses and left almost immediately after Carden had delivered his final, nonsensical verdict. Somehow,

Havelock imagined, the site foreman must have got wind of this ludicrous piece of local folklore and in a rapid descent into alcoholism—with accompanying hallucinations brought about by *delirium tremens*—must have passed on the tale to any workmen who had been assigned to the construction site. Although Carden had not said it explicitly, the implication of his fanciful yarn was that 'Winton Man' had returned, in corporeal form, in 1906, to lurk around inside Penceddo Woods, and was still doing so decades later. It was easy enough to see, when one was actually standing on the edge of those massed, vast ranks of yew trees, how such idle talk about cursed, whispering woods and evil spirits could spook the unsophisticated and the superstitious-by-nature.

Havelock made arrangements to have the old foreman relieved of his duties on compassionate grounds, but his subsequent medical examination resulted in his being taken into the Gallows Langley Lunatic Asylum for treatment, which institution was under the supervision of the well-respected Doctor Winterburn. However, the foreman had, it appeared, gone berserk when advised he was to be confined there, which reaction only served to further confirm the completely unbalanced nature of his drink-ravaged mental faculties and his paranoid propensity to credit entirely baseless local gossip.

A few days later Beechfield, despite being on a leave of absence for his apparent coronary problems, contacted Havelock by long-distance telephone at the planning office. Someone had obviously telegrammed him beforehand about the site foreman having been replaced, and Beechfield wanted to be informed how swiftly construction on 'Penceddo Lane' would recommence. The line was crackly and there was a slight delay on it; both men found themselves talking over each other whenever there was a momentary pause on either side in their conversation.

"You have to quash these foolish local rumours once and for all, you know," Beechfield said, "and the best way to do so is to publicly expose the whole thing as idle tittle-tattle. I want you to go along with a local reporter right into the middle of those woods and have him write a story that will show there's absolutely nothing at all to be afraid of in there. I can personally vouch for Brian Fengrove on the *Thool Gazette*. He's a sound, no-nonsense journalist; he'll do it. He owes me a favour or two. He's the one who wrote that excellent recent piece debunking the phony claptrap being talked about the ill-treatment going on up at the madhouse. Get him on the blower, explain how things stand, and tell him I put you on to him, there's a good fellow."

"Very good, sir," Havelock replied just before the line went dead.

4

Brian Fengrove was a heavy-set, bespectacled man in his late fifties with a curious physical resemblance to the well-known television personality Gilbert Harding, for whom he was often mistaken by members of the public. For many years he had worked in Fleet Street, on the *Evening News*, but had been offered the chance to become chief reporter on the *Thool Gazette* three years earlier. No doubt its new American proprietor, the strangely effeminate Zebulon de Gabiston, thought the addition of a journalist from a London daily paper to its small weekly staff would lend the local newspaper increased prestige. Fengrove himself already lived in Gallows Langley, having commuted each morning by train to London when employed at the *Evening News*, and told others he found the prospect of writing about farming and church fêtes more appealing than bank robberies and murders. He had therefore gladly accepted, so he said, the new post as a comfortable prelude to retirement. Rather than frequenting the Gryphon Tavern, he tended to frequent the Green Man Pub up on the High Street, lingering over an afternoon succession of pints of Bass, chased by glasses of port and lemon with ice, as he produced his copy for the *Gazette*.

Havelock had telephoned him as per Beechfield's instructions, and Fengrove's wife (in, it must be said, a somewhat testy fashion) informed Havelock that "her husband was, at that time of the afternoon, doubtless to be found drinking inside that awful little boozer."

The two men had met on only a few occasions and were solely on terms of nodding acquaintance, and so Fengrove evinced some surprise at noticing Havelock enter the Green Man pub, peer around its confines, and then make—with a definite sense of urgent business to discuss—his way directly to the table at which the journalist sat. The pub was the smallest and most unfriendly in the village to "non-regulars," its smoky, low-wooden-beamed interior the semi-exclusive preserve of a coterie of disparate patrons, all of whom were known to have one habit in common: that of drinking to excess—especially after hours during the weekends in secret, all-night lock-ins.

Once Havelock had explained the whole situation concerning 'Penceddo Lane,' Fengrove leant back in his chair and puffed out his cheeks.

"I'd be glad to help out old Beechfield, of course," Fengrove said, "though ghost hunting isn't really in my line."

Havelock wondered if Fengrove was about to make some excuse to avoid taking part in the proposed debunking.

"Surely you don't believe in all that supernatural rot?" he asked.

"No, I certainly don't. I imagine that's why Beechfield thought of me. Still, I'd have to take along a camera—the article will need an accompanying photograph or two. I don't much fancy tramping around those woods in the night, though. One could easily trip over an exposed root and turn one's ankle in the dark."

"I don't see why we couldn't do the whole thing in the daylight. The trees are so closely packed together, it must be quite dim in there under the branches, even at noon."

"Agreed. All right, I'm game. Care for another?"

The next morning found Havelock and Fengrove passing along

the stunted, twenty-yards beginning of 'Penceddo Lane,' crossing the wasteland of heaped rubble at its terminus, and then, at a slow, gradual pace, making their way towards the heart of the woodlands. The air was icy-cold and a harsh overnight frost still clung to the grass, leaves, needles, trunks, and branches, coating everything with a layer of crystalline whiteness. Fengrove carried a Graflex Speed Camera, one of those models that were favoured by press photographers, and would occasionally pause in order to shoot the surrounding yew trees. Havelock detected nothing particularly ominous about the woodland, despite everything he had heard concerning it and the phantasmal terrors that were said to lurk within, though he was suddenly conscious of how ancient this off-the-beaten-track region really was. He could envisage, even in his generally unimaginative mind's eye, that long-ago period, before the Romans came, when the Celtic Britons made strange

worship, not in manmade temples, but in sacred sites reared by nature itself; in groves, in caves, in hollows, and on hilltops beneath the Wolf Moon.

The two men had been tramping for over an hour, venturing ever deeper into the woods, when Fengrove rested on a fragment of a fallen tree trunk, large enough only to seat one person, set his camera down by his side, and then pulled out a hipflask from the pocket of his black greatcoat. He took a quick swig and returned it to his pocket, exhaling a great vaporous breath into the air. Above their heads, the background murmuring of the branches and their needles swaying in the wind seemed louder. He stamped his feet on the ground to try and encourage his circulation.

"I think we've come far enough," he said, "don't you? I've taken plenty of photographs. Nothing at all out of the ordinary to report. So much for ghost hunting."

Havelock nodded, feeling the physical effects of the trek himself and eager to turn back, but he then peered again through the nearby phalanx of trunks to those trees that stood immediately beyond. It could not only be his imagination; there was something genuinely curious about those shadowy yews farther on—their shapes appeared to have altered, almost as if they had been caught in the act of motion and had paused momentarily due to the sudden presence of human interlopers. A ridiculous notion, and one more pertinent to startled deer, but he nevertheless found it hard to shake off. There was something else that was curious: though it was not the usual season for them, a swathe of red-capped toadstools had sprouted around the exposed, frost-covered roots of those trees, like drops of blood splattered across white, gnarled, titan fingers.

"Thoughtless of me," Fengrove said, taking out the flask again. "Would you care for a snifter? It's early in the day, I know, but it's so bitterly cold, isn't it? There's nothing like it to keep the chill out of your bones."

Havelock took the flask with a nod of gratitude and swigged back a mouthful of the stuff. It was whisky, but it had a strange, acrid aftertaste, and it burnt his throat a little as it went down.

"Take a look at those trees over there," he said. "It might be worth getting a few shots of those. They seem to me to be very odd. Very odd indeed."

Fengrove shrugged his shoulders, looked a little sceptical at the very idea, but nevertheless got to his feet and proceeded to tramp a little farther into the distance, moving in the general direction of the trees that Havelock had indicated.

Havelock himself meant to follow him, but only once he had taken a short rest on the fragment of tree trunk that Fengrove had just vacated. Once he had sat down, however, he suddenly felt exhausted and, after a few moments, found he could not get up again. It was as if he had consumed the entire, potent contents of the hipflask in one go and not taken just one solitary mouthful.

Fengrove reappeared, smiled, looked at him with a sardonic expression, and took his picture. He turned the camera around to its reverse side, opened the back panel, and revealed that it was not loaded with a roll of film at all. Then he slung the camera by its leather strap over his shoulder, simultaneously put both hands into the two side pockets of his greatcoat, and held up two identical-looking hipflasks.

"Sorry, old fellow. I'm afraid I'll have to leave you here now," he said.

Havelock gradually slid off the fallen trunk onto the ground, with the back of his head coming to rest on its frost-coated bark. He tried to cry out, but produced only a muffled sort of grunt in the vain attempt, and it was not long before he had lost consciousness altogether. At that point, before departing himself, Fengrove dragged Havelock into the toadstool-riddled region some twenty yards farther on.

When he awoke, Havelock found his body stiff with cold; he had no sensation in his extremities and his teeth began to chatter involuntarily. In a clumsy fashion he managed to sit up, and the realisation that he had been lured deep into the woods by Fengrove on false pretences, drugged, and then left to fend for himself slowly dawned on him. Why on earth would Fengrove do such a thing? He obviously did not wish to commit murder; poison—and not merely a soporific—would surely have been employed if that were his aim. Perhaps a mistake had been made and Fengrove had simply thought Havelock already dead, dragging him farther into the interior in order to conceal his body. But what could possibly be Fengrove's motivation for such a heinous act?

Havelock realised he must have lain there in the middle of the woods for hours in that state of complete unconsciousness, for it was now dark and, through a gap in the swaying, needled branches high above his head, he saw that a multitude of stars dotted the inky-black night sky. The January full moon had also risen, the baleful, so-called Wolf Moon; its brownish-yellow disc casting half-filtered, dancing shadows on the fungi-riddled undergrowth.

The first thing to do, he thought, was to get the circulation going in his frozen legs so that he could get to his feet, retrace his steps, and make his way out of the woods. He had difficulty in pulling his right trouser leg up over his calf due to a finger-sized protuberance that kept catching on the folds. When, finally, he managed to roll up the trouser leg to his knee, he saw there was a red-capped toadstool attached to a wound in the skin of his calf. Running his fingers around it, he discovered it had not somehow become lodged there by accident, but seemed to have sprouted from within the flesh, like a noxious, parasitical growth.

The unpleasant, unwelcome memory of those photographs of 'Winton Man' suddenly came to mind.

With a grimace of disgust, he twisted at the base of the toadstool until most of it snapped off, though leaving behind a stem fragment still firmly rooted in his leg. What remained of the broken stalk oozed a viscous, blood-red liquid.

When he examined his other calf, after rolling up the left trouser leg as far as his knee, he discovered several subcutaneous lumps, as if further toadstools were in the process of sprouting inside the limb, prior to—like the one on his right leg—eventually breaking through the skin.

Havelock could, nevertheless, stand up and hobble along in a fashion. The problem now was that, though he was upright and on his feet, he had little sense of which way he should go in order to retreat back along the route he had followed with Fengrove. When he set off in one direction, it seemed to him that gaps seen in the middle distance somehow contrived to close themselves and block his path before he reached them, and he even began to suffer from the maddening sensation that he was being actively marshalled towards a particular destination.

He felt light-headed and tripped, time and time again, on the concealed obstructions in the dark, dense undergrowth. He had the distinct impression that, more than once, he glimpsed furred tentacles slithering through the shadowy vegetation around his feet. It was extremely difficult to concentrate on the task at hand, and, absurdly, despite his desperate bewilderment, he actually found himself laughing hysterically.

In the end, he was aware of having stumbled into a central hollow, one surrounded by a ring of twisted yew trees, into which clearing poured the copper-coloured radiance from the gigantic Wolf Moon overhead. Sprouting from the loamy soil underfoot was a vast mass of malformed, red-capped, and white-dotted toadstools, which also sprouted in and out of themselves, forming some kind of gigantic, cannibalistic amalgamation; an abnormal nucleus lurking at the very heart of Penceddo Woods. It was when Havelock heard the solemn whispering of the yew trees, calling on him to descend, forming what seemed to be distinct Brythonic words which he nevertheless understood, that he recalled what Carden had said previously about the ancient druids and their secret rituals of metempsychosis. And he obeyed the ancient, irresistible summons mere moments before that bubbling, festering, universe of toadstool caps in the deep hollow welcomed him and opened not only mouths with blood-stained, rotten teeth, but also opened blank, staring eyes—eyes like those found in Victorian *memento mori* photographs of the dead.

5

"The scarlet ceremony is concluded for another year," Fengrove said, speaking over the telephone on a long-distance call the next day. "You can safely return to Gallows Langley. Only de Gabiston knows about it all. That idiot Carden might try sniffing around, but he'll be dismissed as a crank. There's no evidence of foul play."

"I'll destroy all the council records personally," replied Beechfield. "It's a shame we had to use Havelock, but it's that drunken, talkative foreman who's really to blame."

The sacrifice had been accepted, and the whispering in Penceddo Wood consisted solely of the wind blowing through the vast mass of old yew trees atop the secluded western hillside of Thool Valley.

Appeased by this act of tribute, its otherworldly nucleus would remain dormant and not spread itself beyond the confines of the hollow. It still bubbled and still festered, dreaming always of those lost, far-off, days before the Imperium of the Romans. It would slumber until such time as the annual Wolf Moon again rose high in the January night-sky; and then, once more, the ancient past would reach out hungrily into the present, demanding a sacrificial homage.

Construction work on the short stretch of road that was to have been Penceddo Lane was permanently abandoned and, after only a few months, crabgrass sprang up from the cracks in the surface, overran the site, and then, by the beginning of the following January, the first small clusters of that curious species of red-capped and white-dotted toadstool rapidly began to appear.

 # WITH EYES OPENED

Ngo Binh Anh Khoa

Ngo Binh Anh Khoa is a teacher of English currently living and working in Ho Chi Minh City, Vietnam. In his free time, he enjoys reading fiction, daydreaming, and writing speculative poetry for entertainment. His poems have previously appeared in Weirdbook, Star*Line, The Audient Void, Spectral Realms, *and other venues*

I. The Eldritch Truths

How merciful Creation is
To have mankind born blind
To things that lie beyond the grasp
Of their frail mortal mind.

That mercy, though restrictive, is
The most benevolent gift,
For when that sheltering darkness fades,
Reality, too, shall shift.

Out come the Eldritch Truths behind
The Veil of sanity;
Those with eyes opened thus are damned
To depths of lunacy.

That which you seek before you lies;
Enlightened you may be,
And once transcendence is achieved,
Those horrid Truths you'll see!

II. The Prelude

Much like you, I was mortal once,
A blissfully ignorant soul,
Lured by the call of freedom of
Life on the open road.

Oh, how I miss that bygone time—
Those carefree, whimsical days—
When my eyes were by nescience cloaked;
The wide world was a maze.

I'd sell my soul to turn back time
Were it still mine to sell;
I'm but a stained existence now,
Barred from Heaven and Hell.

But I digress, so let me start
From whence it all began,
Unearthing buried memories
Of when I was a man.

When I was still a wide-eyed youth
Kindled by passion's flame
To see the glamorous world outside
The town from which I came.

Pulled by the strings of wanderlust,
I'd soon depart from home
With some essentials, papers, cash,
A camera, and a phone.

Like how a ship at sea took time
To capture Fortune's wind,
My journey took a while before
Much fortune, too, 'twould bring.

With Eyes Opened

I'd never thought that traveling would
Consume my very life,
And yet it did, and with it came
Great joys from hardships rife!

The ember stoked became a fire
That fueled my footsteps, and
That fervor to explore the world
Brought me to far-flung lands.

My feet had walked the well-worn roads
And paths so rarely trod;
My eyes had seen the well-known sights
And scenes remote and odd.

The things I'd learned and heard and done
Were all recorded for
My vlogs, from which my income came
To fund my trips and more.

And during those nomadic years
I grew an interest in
Having rare tattoos round the world
Imprinted on my skin.

Some came from shady parlors, but
Most came from ancient tribes
That I'd shed tears and blood to seek
With rumors as my guides.

Some were quite simple to persuade,
Others more dangerous;
Many a time I'd brushed with Death
Due to their fierce mistrust.

The journeys I'd embarked on were
Both long and burdensome,
And with me were three people with
My absolute faith in them.

With them, I had survived the years
With scars and ink to prove
My iron perseverance which
No obstacle could move.

Then came my latest—and my last—
Search for my mark of worth
Bestowed by one mysterious Tribe
Deep in this haunted earth.

And here is where the true tale starts,
So listen carefully,
For it's too late to turn back now,
And far too late to flee.

III. The Guide

Within this Asian jungle maze
There dwelt a cryptic Tribe
So ancient that no modern word
Could suitably describe.

To many, though, they were a myth
To scare those wandering near
The border of this lethal place,
A tale to conjure fear.

A few, though, in my network claimed
This Tribe was very real,
Who gave their sacred ink to those
That passed their harsh ordeal.

With Eyes Opened

Scarce was the information, but
One contact led me to
A website quite obscure and weird,
Whose content I'd go through.

There, symbols filled the grayish screen
In shapes of black and red,
And no translation program used
Could translate what they said.

And at the center of the site
Were empty boxes where
I'd write our names and numbers, then
Into the void we'd stare.

Time's passage was with tension charged,
The air with silence fraught
Till it was punctured by a call
That broke my wandering thought.

The voice was raspy and direct
With just a time and place;
The call came from a burner phone,
Impossible to trace.

The next day came; my friends and I
Reached that appointed spot;
Within the war 'tween thrill and dread
Our vigilant minds were caught.

Then, from the shadows midst the trees,
A figure would emerge.
At once my instinct told me, "Flee!"
But I subdued the urge.

Dark clothing hid his face and frame,
But strangely tall was he;

A white patch covered his right eye;
His left one stared at me.

He studied us awhile, and then
He signaled us to come;
And with his back to us he would,
Throughout the trip, keep mum.

We did try to record our steps
And all the turns we took;
But with the speed at which we moved,
Our cameras wildly shook.

With knowledge and experience
I marked the paths we'd passed;
But our Guide, like a panther, ran
So agilely and fast.

And soon we found ourselves besieged
By trees with no way out.
A festering fear boiled in my head;
My brain was drowned in doubt.

The searing heat and blistering air
Wore down my stamina;
I grew disoriented from
The journey, long and far.

Some hours passed, and suddenly
The Guide would speak at last.
A tongue so foreign to my ears
Was growled out, harsh and fast.

At once the jungle seemed to stir
And shift before my sight.
Distorted was the scenery;
The sky was robbed of light.

With Eyes Opened

It felt as though I had been pulled
By some invisible force;
The dark earth shook; a rumbling rang
From some unseeable source.

A maddening spell of nausea struck,
My blurry eyes were shut,
And when my wits at last returned,
Before us stood a hut.

From where that ancient thing appeared,
I did not know back then;
It stood before a towering tree
That branched out without end.

Ten hooded figures then emerged
And whispered to my Guide;
Our eyes were wide, our mouths agape,
For we had found the Tribe!

IV. The Ordeal

The figures cloaked in makeshift clothes
Like outstretched shadows stood.
And each one's eyes and face were hid
Beneath their pitch-black hood.

From where we were, we could not hear
What our Guide said to them;
Some minutes tensely passed until
That man would toward us come.

He spoke with broken syllables
As though his tongue was lead,
"Your passage has been granted. Come,"
And beckoned with his head.

We forward walked with cautious steps,
But outwardly we'd show
We meant no harm nor disrespect;
Nerve-wracking was it all.

How many times I'd done this dance,
I'd honestly lost count;
But then there was a primal fear
By which my mind was bound.

The peoples of the wild do have
An air distinct and strong,
But these ten's presence made my flesh
Feel chilly, sullied—wrong!

It felt like something else was there,
Which my eyes could not see;
It loomed amid the frozen air
And gradually crept toward me.

And as we were approaching them,
They started murmuring;
A chorus of weird syllables
Swept over everything.

"You may step forth," my Guide announced,
Which snapped my reverie;
The ten had parted to the sides
And made a path for me.

I nodded to my watchful friends,
And they'd follow my lead.
Our Guide would match our careful steps
And tell us to proceed.

The hut was rather spacious with
A minimalist touch,

With Eyes Opened

With scattered tools and utensils,
Which did not seem like much.

The symbols carved upon the walls
Were more peculiar, though,
Whose spiritual meanings I then yearned,
With all my heart, to know.

I asked about them, but our Guide
Urged us to move instead
Until we reached the backyard where
The tree loomed overhead.

We, with permission granted, then
Began our interview;
One elderly woman from the group
Was whom we'd then talk to.

Again she spoke in her strange tongue,
Which our Guide would translate:
"An ordeal you must pass to claim
Our sacred mark," he'd state.

Much more was said, but worry not,
I shall not bore your ears
With minor details that transpired
Because the climax nears.

A bed was set, on which we each
Were to in turn lie down;
And suddenly they encircled us;
Alarmed, we looked around.

The only exit had been blocked;
The Guide's voice sliced the air:
"The Elder Seed shall judge your worth
And see how well you fare."

A burst of protests thundered in
That suffocating space;
We tried to break away with force,
But they held us in place.

By no means were we frail and weak:
Throughout the years we'd spent
Traversing perilous places, but
Our knees beneath them bent.

Two figures on each side pressed me
Against the groaning ground,
And with a whisper in my ear
My whole body was bound.

I could not move or speak or blink;
My eyes were opened wide
As my friend was placed on the bed,
His head turned to the side.

His tear-glazed orbs bore into mine,
A silent, choked-up plea;
But my lips trembled, my hands froze
As I stared helplessly.

Once more the murmuring echoed in
The field behind the hut;
A wind and dust stabbed my dry eye,
But they could not be shut.

The oldest of the group then walked
Toward the gnarly tree
And with a dagger slashed the bark;
Strange was the sight I'd see.

The bark, despite appearing tough,
Would yield before that blade,

With Eyes Opened

And from the gaping wound outpoured
An ooze of coal-black shade.

The spindly lady gathered it
Unto a wood-carved bowl
And kowtowed once the wound had closed;
Her tattered hood would fall.

I felt my breath caught in my throat
When her face was unveiled;
Within the second our eyes met,
Fear had my heart impaled.

There was no color in those eyes,
Void of humanity;
Just two abyssal spheres that spread
And stared unblinkingly.

With measured steps she then approached
The bed where my friend lay,
With his head callously pressed down—
A silenced, shivering prey.

More whispers filled the thickened air
As all the figures spoke;
The landscape was enshrouded in
A purplish screen of smoke.

The woman dipped a needle in
That bowl of muddy slime;
And then a terrifying scene played out
Before me in real time.

The needle stained by that foul sap
Was brought down on his head,
And from the temple where it struck
The slime merged with blood shed.

331

It traveled downward from the wound
Till it got in his eye;
At once the spell of stillness broke
And came a wretched cry.

I watched in mounting horror as
His eye was dyed in black;
A wave of violent tremor swept
Across his thrashing back.

Heart-rending screams exploded from
His blood-stained lips, and then
That tongue—those low, accursed sounds—burst
From their lips without end.

I could not blink, I could not move,
I could not breathe nor speak;
I could but watch his torment as
He'd moan and beg and shriek.

His other eye, the normal one,
Would madly dart around;
The terror blazing that orb
Was striking and profound.

I knew not how much time had passed
Since that ordeal began,
But his whole body suddenly stopped;
Dead was the broken man.

V. The Offerings

The stillness there was shattered by
The Guide, who gravely said,
"O, may the Elder Seed accept
This Offering of the dead."

With Eyes Opened

He lifted my friend's corpse and walked
Toward the stirring tree;
And when it touched the wrinkled bark,
Gruesome was what I'd see.

The moaning tree, like quicksand, sucked
The corpse into its bark;
The chewing sounds of flesh devoured
Rang loudly in the dark.

The rumbling that I'd heard before
Grew ever louder then;
Soon, pressed down on that fatal bed
Was one more shivering friend.

Oh, have you ever been trapped in
A dream so frightfully real
Only to learn it's not a dream?
My friend, how would you feel?

Well, let's just say the screams that day
Are seared into my mind;
I hear them hoarsely pleading still;
No rest the damned may find.

Three brilliant lives with so much hope
Were snuffed out on that day;
Three valiant minds went mad with fear—
Of what? I could not say.

Then came my turn, and Death closed in
For her covetous kiss;
I stared into my captors' gaze—
Into that vile abyss.

Those eyes peaked out beneath their hoods
And bore into my soul,

Their constant, frantic murmuring flowed
And drowned my sanity whole.

Infernal was the agony!
My temple throbbed and burned!
I sobbed and begged and thrashed and wailed,
But no reprieve I earned.

The torturous heat from that cursed sap
Befouled the blood I'd shed
And ran down till it touched my eye;
Madness raged in my head!

My now infected eye went wide
When spectral shapes appeared
From out the darkening, howling air,
And then my vision cleared.

Words coined by mortal tongues cannot
Describe the things I saw,
Encompassing this twisted space
And shattering Physics' Law.

Two creatures cannot occupy
The same space, but these shades—
Clear, massive, and misshapen fiends—
Took up all empty space.

They leered with tumor-like eyeballs
And gnashed their jagged teeth;
Their sprawling tentacles wildly flailed;
How I forgot to breathe.

They floated, slithered, crawled, and limped,
And phased through all they'd touch;
Some of those things then stared at me!
Vicious was terror's clutch.

With Eyes Opened

The noises that assailed my ears
Were not just my own screams;
Their eyes! Their eyes were everywhere!
With cold and alien gleams!

My black eye tried to find a spot
Unsoiled by nightmares then;
They slowly rent my sanity,
Which naught on Earth could mend.

My muscles twitched, my body seized;
The black sap scorched my mind;
I begged for Death's embrace to come,
No saving grace I'd find.

How much time had elapsed since then?
An hour? A day? A week?
The seizure ceased; I, heaving, lay
And heard my captors speak.

The same tongue that had vexed my thoughts
Pierced through my terror, and
Those whispered words there uttered, I
Began to understand.

"A new Apostle, by Her blood,
Has his sight blessed this day,
And should he keep his pledge of faith,
Become Her Scribe he may."

When I could move my limbs once more,
A strange light caught my eye,
Which made me turn my gaze toward
That weird Tree standing nigh.

Huge knobs spread o'er its pulsing bark,
From tortured faces wrought,

Which groaned and moaned incessantly
With endless anguish fraught.

And on those shivering, spidery boughs
Were hung red, bulbous fruits,
Many of which then burst and spilled
Black sludge toward the roots.

From out each inky puddle rose
Another creeping shade,
Which, like the others, roamed about;
Ear-piercing wails they made.

The ten again, in chorus, spoke
That awful alien tongue,
Which, like a sacred mantra, washed
O'er me, and silence hung.

Those monstrous shades and trees still moved,
But no noise struck my ears—
A mercy midst the chaos that
Did not allay my fears.

VI. The Pledge

My bearings gradually returned,
But I was still on edge,
For I remembered what they'd said
About some shady pledge.

My gaze fell on the Guide and on
The patch across his face;
At once I covered up my eye
And looked around the place.

The shades were gone, the Tree appeared
Much like a normal tree,

With Eyes Opened

A mockery of the norm that masked
That ageless Entity—

First planted countless aeons past
Upon the infant Earth,
Through which a Cosmic Power may
Perform Her blasphemous birth.

The mantra flowed, and my stiff mouth
Would mimic what they said
And stumble through the alien sounds
That suddenly filled my head.

"We pray unto the Elder Seed
Wrought by the Formless Womb,
For Her protection from all that
Beyond the Clear Veil loom.

"And to Her True Incarnate to
Be born, we pledge our soul,
Through whom She shall once more descend
And claim Her sovereign role."

Those words would be my crumbling ward
'Gainst madness as time passed—
The only thing to stall the curse
That was upon me cast.

The decades came and went as I
Served this perverted Tribe
As slave and spare food like the rest
That did the sap imbibe.

The Guide before me would receive
His fated second Mark,
A ritual during which I watched
As his left eye turned dark.

And with it went the last of his
Dwindling humanity:
^Another mouthpiece to be used
By the hive-mind was he.

He thenceforth took his roots among
His mumbling peers here while
I, with my channels, snare new souls
For those Scribes to defile.

They take care of the Elder Seed
And all the Younglings born—
The failed, rejected avatars,
All mindless and forlorn.

They're crying for their Mother in
The depths of Outer Space,
Beyond the Veil imprisoning
Her dark, primeval race.

Until a True Incarnate's formed
From out the Elder Seed,
More of these Younglings shall be birthed,
And thus, the Tree must feed.

The day shall come on which the Veil
Shall fade as is foretold
When from the sunken keep ascends
The Star-Spawned Priest of old—

When all the Younglings shall become
The swords to shield Her reign
'Gainst other Powers bound to Earth
So that Her love they'll gain.

Till then, the halfling Scribes must soothe
Them with their Mother's tongue,

With Eyes Opened

Brief slumber shall befall them when
Their lullaby is sung.

But more of them means more of us,
And that's where you come in;
I've talked at length about my tale,
And now, yours shall begin.

The moment you wrote down your name
On that evil website,
You signed the pledge and sealed your fate
Unto this lethal plight.

Will you be like your friends who died
As fertilizer, or
Will you become our brethren thence,
Corrupted to the core?

Well, either way, the nightmare starts,
But will it fleeting be?
Or will it haunt your coming days
Until eternity?

The Eldritch Truths still lurk behind
The Veil of sanity;
Those with eyes opened thus are damned
To depths of lunacy.

May fate have mercy on your soul
While it's still yours to keep,
For once enlightenment's achieved,
Naught but anguish you'll reap.